Praise for *27 Letters to*

'Often funny, and moving, but always
mortality ... it reads like a message in a bottle ... easy, flowing epistolary story-telling that takes in the generations that have preceded mother and child, a central tenet being that we are the sum of all we are now as well as the ghostly past of our forebears.'

— *The Sydney Morning Herald*

'Ella's writing provokes an aching nostalgia for parties, dancing, homes and travel. Reading it I find myself nostalgic for someone else's childhood and youth. But the genius of this book is that it makes you feel like there might still be time to create this in your own life. While there's life there's hope.'

— Jessica Dettmann, author of *This Has Been Absolutely Lovely* and *How to Be Second Best*

'This is a very special book ... It's a gift to your family, but it's a gift to all of us in the ways that we can think about our own stories.'

— Jacinta Parsons, *ABC Radio Melbourne*

'Not many people write hilariously and beautifully about something really intense and life altering. [This book] takes you all the way from heartbreak to hilarity — it will be your best friend for a while.'

— Martha Beck, *New York Times* bestselling author of *The Way of Integrity*

'I've devoured every word, laughed and cried and soaked up all 188 life lessons. This is a book you'll want to read, reread and gift generously.'

Ali Hill, *Stand Out Life podcast*

'Stunning ... a truly wonderful, deeply personal and insightful read [with a] lot of joy in it as well.'

Podcasters, *The Lise & Sarah Show*

Ella Ward has worked in advertising for many years. This means she has a proclivity for profanity and needs help with punctuation. Her words have been published in places like *Frankie*, *Marie Claire* and *The Sydney Morning Herald*. Her memoir, *27 Letters to my Daughter*, was published in Australia in 2022 and the US in 2023. Ella lives in Melbourne, Australia, with her husband, child, pets and neuroses. *The Cicada House* is her first novel.

Find her at www.ellaward.com.au

The Cicada House

ELLA WARD

HarperCollins*Publishers*

HarperCollins*Publishers*
Australia • Brazil • Canada • France • Germany • Holland • India
Italy • Japan • Mexico • New Zealand • Poland • Spain • Sweden
Switzerland • United Kingdom • United States of America

HarperCollins acknowledges the Traditional Custodians
of the land upon which we live and work, and pays respect
to Elders past and present.

First published on Gadigal Country in Australia in 2025
by HarperCollins*Publishers* Australia Pty Limited
ABN 36 009 913 517
harpercollins.com.au

A catalogue record for this book is available from the National Library of Australia

ISBN 978 1 4607 6555 5 (paperback)
ISBN 978 1 4607 1732 5 (ebook)
ISBN 978 1 4607 3076 8 (audiobook)

Cover design by Christa Moffitt, Christabella Designs
Cover image by Studio Firma / stocksy.com / 5611446
Back cover image by shutterstock.com
Author photograph by Samara Clifford
Typeset in Bembo Std by Kirby Jones
Printed and bound in Australia by McPherson's Printing Group

For Tom

Chapter One

The morning of Caitlin's birthday began with breakfast cheese. She was standing in the refrigerator's glow, in her knickers, eating a hunk of pecorino. The fridge's door alarm dinged, but the cheese contained tiny flecks of truffle, so she ignored it. If Paul were home he would have yelled from the office by now, 'Caitlin! Fridge!' But he wasn't, so she ate the expensive cheese at her own pace and only closed the door when the alarm became hysterical.

When her husband was away for work, the house was hers. This meant it became a little messier, slightly noisier and considerably less filled with the things her husband bought. Like lightbulbs. And toilet paper. And breakfast cereal.

Caitlin turned from the fridge, flicked a crumb of cheese from her T-shirt and looked out to their little patch of London. It was winter. The watery light filtered itself through the small maple tree Paul had planted in their modest backyard a decade earlier. Or, paid someone else to plant. Dark stones paved a way from the kitchen door to a marble bench beneath the tree. A pigeon cooed from the stock brick wall. It should have looked idyllic. It just looked damp. Despite having nearly a lifetime of them, Caitlin just couldn't get into the spirit of a British winter. As far as she was concerned, it would be another three months until anything outside could resemble happiness. Until then, the outdoors was simply something to be withstood.

Caitlin and Paul had lived in this North London terrace for almost as long as they'd been married. It was a narrow house — dark in the winter, cool in the summer. Sometimes it felt like it had more stairs than rooms. Nevertheless, it was a calm place. The walls held oil paintings of tree-whipped landscapes, gifted from Paul's father. Lacquer-licked furniture lined the halls, care of Paul's grandparents. Caitlin hadn't contributed much to the home beyond paying half the mortgage and keeping the cheese supply up. But despite her lack of influence over the interior, she still liked spending time in it. Which was lucky, as Paul's work took him travelling at least half of every month. And this was why today she was birthday-ing alone. Soon there would be a bouquet of flowers (by way of Dubai) sitting on their front step.

After wrapping up her breakfast picnic, Caitlin went back upstairs. Wiping the shower-fog from the mirror in their little ensuite, she pulled her cheeks around with her fingers like she was moulding silly putty. Caitlin didn't pay much attention to how she looked — her face was just something she'd inherited. And as her grandmother Dot had told her once, 'You're a pretty girl: the sooner you ignore your looks, the better.'

Even so, Caitlin was heading into the office today, so she brought out her dusty makeup bag and worked through the template of four products she'd been using for twenty years. When that ritual was complete, she moved her hands through her fair hair, a bit uneasy that there wasn't more of it. She'd recently fallen into an ill-advised haircut, one shorter than she'd ever had. Paul hadn't been too sure, pulling a face as he walked in from the airport one afternoon.

'What happened?' he'd asked, like the haircut had been an attack rather than an appointment.

'I thought I'd try something different.'

'Bloody hell.' Paul had said this through a laugh. Caitlin had quietly admonished herself for ignoring her grandmother's advice.

She figured she could squeeze in a call to her grandfather before she left the house. Caitlin rang Bill once a week, on a Thursday. Her grandfather liked routine. That today was her birthday didn't occur to her and wouldn't to him.

'Eh-up.' Caitlin wondered if he picked up the phone to everyone like that, and then quickly remembered than she was the only person who called him.

'Hello, Grandad.'

She said it louder than she had last week, when he'd hung up in the middle of her sentence, grumbling about goblins on the line.

'Eh-up, Caitlin.'

Every week he spoke with a little more breath, and a little less voice. She wondered how long he'd be alive for. Eighty-nine years old. Last month she'd received a call from the care home's manager and there was a tight second before answering when she thought to herself — *Well. This is it then.*

It was in the next minute, while Mrs Chandra had outlined some changes to Bill's medication, that Caitlin realised she had not moved a muscle in the brief moment when her grandfather was dead.

'Happy birthday, pet.'

This time speaking with volume borne from surprise, Caitlin responded, 'Oh. Thank you, Grandad. Gosh. I didn't think you'd —'

But he was continuing. 'Your grandmother was waiting for this day. You're forty, you know.'

She knew, but was surprised he did.

Her grandmother had been dead for well over a decade and suddenly she worried Bill had lost his marbles in a week between calls, forgetting 'his Dot' had died.

'My Dot.' He wheezed sharply in a way Caitlin thought was a chuckle. She realised she was white-knuckling the phone so she deliberately loosened her grip and started to make the bed, to distract herself. Already this felt like the most intimate conversation she'd had with her grandfather for a long time. Maybe forever.

'She was a special lady, Caitlin.'

'She was, Grandad.'

Caitlin wondered if she was lying. Her grandmother had been a nice woman; in a cautious, precise sort of way. Dot was kind to the small Caitlin who had come to live with her grandparents at the age of five. She was kind in a way that someone is when they have no choice. But she wasn't special. Caitlin had never cast Dot in anything but an ordinary light. She winced at what a shitty person this thought made her, and her knuckles tightened around the phone again.

'You're forty, Caitlin. And my Dot left some money for you. Today's the day, pet,' he breathed slowly, speaking the words with ceremony. 'You … have an inheritance.'

'Sorry?' Her nose was screwed up over an open mouth. 'Why now? Gran's been dead for' — an embarrassingly long pause for the arithmetic — 'fifteen years?'

'You know what Dot was like, Caitlin: that woman didn't believe anyone would do one damn good thing until they were over forty.'

This time, the wheeze was definitely a laugh.

Afterwards, when Bill had told her the solicitor would have emailed overnight (where did Bill find a solicitor?), Caitlin sat on the edge of the bed. She pressed her palms flat and firm into the mattress, her brow furrowed. This was not expected. She looked up and laughed. Said, aloud, to the empty bedroom, 'Holy shit!'

She stood up. She sat down again. She picked up her phone and dialled Paul. She ended the call immediately. No. She wouldn't tell him like this. This was a fantasy come true: to be able to impart the good news of a dream-like windfall to someone else. She would need to plan this out carefully. Caitlin opened the solicitor's message on her phone and stared at the number sitting in black and white on her screen. She had never seen that many pounds in one place. And her name was on the email.

* * *

When she and Paul were falling in love, they used to spend entire afternoons lying on things together. His couch, the grass, even — one glorious weekend — a wrought-iron daybed dragged out from his parents' shed. They'd hit the mattress until it stopped producing puffs of dust, threw an old sheet over it and installed it beneath the family's beloved weeping willow. Caitlin and Paul lay down, alongside and on top of one another — like sleepy puppies. They talked. They dozed. They made up stupid jokes and shared strange dreams. One late summer's day, maybe this was after they were engaged, they spent an entire afternoon meticulously detailing what they each would do upon winning the lottery. Paul had his fingers in her hair (it was still very long then) and his mouth up against her neck.

When he spoke, his voice was muffled. 'Somewhere hot. The Caribbean. We'd buy an island and bring everyone we know and party for a month.'

'Everyone *we* know?' Her hands were under his shirt, pressed into his chest, feeling the vibrations as he talked.

'Well, everyone I know.'

They had laughed, because this was long enough ago that Caitlin's reclusiveness was still a delightful eccentricity.

Caitlin asked Paul, 'What if you win, and I don't? What if it's only *your* prize?'

She liked to ask Paul questions that could tempt him to be cruel. She dangled the opportunity like a prickled fishing lure and wondered if this, finally, was the time that he'd take the bait and break the spell.

'That's the very best scenario.'

'Paul!' she yelled with faux outrage. Faux outrage that gave her an excuse to faux hit him and to be faux angry and all in the most safe way possible.

He was laughing, a high *yuk-yuk* in the way he used to. 'No, no! Hear me out! It's the best way to win, because then *I'd* be able to tell *you*. I'd set up a treasure hunt, with rhyming clues, and …'

And?

Paul could try to be poetic but never creative. Even so Caitlin encouraged him to continue with this fantasy.

'And?'

'And, the last clue would say, "We're multi-millionaires!" and then we'd drink ludicrously expensive champagne and call our bosses dickheads on Facebook.'

Yes, this must have been just after they were engaged, when Facebook was the white-hot centre of popular culture, and Caitlin and Paul still shared made-up stories.

* * *

Melanie's was the first face to appear as Caitlin exited the work lift, her ears gently popping from the swift ascent. Leaning at her over a mug of tea, the vice president was all nostrils and pearls.

'Caitlin! You've graced us with your presence I see? We're in "Mist".'

Melanie clopped her sensible heels away from Caitlin in a morse code that said *follow me.* Caitlin didn't reply. It was 8.55 am, and she wasn't going to apologise for *not* being late. Particularly not today, when she had just come into a significant sum of money.

Caitlin had thought about not going in to work at all, but then she considered what else she was going to do and couldn't come up with anything better. She followed Melanie's heels to the big boardroom at the end of the hallway. It had a name, like all the meeting rooms on the floor. This one was called 'Mist', the one down the hall was 'Breeze', and the small room where redundancies were made was called 'Flash', but someone had scratched the top of the 'a' off so now it read — aptly — 'Flush'.

Caitlin had worked at HHB for fifteen years — long enough to remember when it was still called Hart & Hart Beverages. Long enough to have experienced four company strategies, eleven away-days and more vice presidents than Melanie would care to know.

Caitlin was good at her job. Marketing fizzy drink was the perfect role for her. She analysed marketing trends and scoped taste profiles and attended Christmas parties; she did it all without caring about the carbonated beverages she helped sell. Thanks to the American takeover last year the whole team had received idiotic title changes. Caitlin was now something called a 'regional brand development leader'. This had been bestowed without a pay rise, so she hadn't taken much notice. Paul had, though. He had brought a bottle of wine home and they'd drunk it on the couch watching a documentary on BBC Two. He did a 'cheers' and said 'congratulations' and made sure they both held eye contact before they drank. It was the perfect celebration, because like the promotion, nothing more was actually required of Caitlin.

This morning, the boardroom smelt of chemist aftershave and instant coffee. Caitlin took up her seat at the long table while various other colleagues did the same. As the team shuffled in, she noticed they were all carrying their laptops.

'Shit,' she said, and immediately coughed to cover it.

Caitlin, it seemed, was the only member of the 'Beverages — Southern Europe' team to forget that today was the quarterly Blue Sky meeting. Last quarterly meeting, everyone had been tasked with presenting their Sky High Mind Maps next time they met. How the bloody hell had three months passed, and which memo had Caitlin missed? She chewed on her thumbnail and realised she'd probably missed many memos. Mainly because they would have been from Melanie, sent with the 'High Importance' symbol: two things that ensured Caitlin ignored an email.

Trying to extricate herself from the front row, Caitlin braced a toe against the boardroom table and pushed herself and her wheeled-chair backwards, rolling with a *bump* into the wall behind her. As the enormous screen bloomed to life above them, Caitlin knew she'd have to do better than hiding in the back row. She'd have to remove herself entirely. The title spun onto the first PowerPoint slide: *HHB and BEYOND!* Someone half-clapped.

Blessedly, Caitlin's phone buzzed. She barely glanced at it before crouch-walking out of her chair. The call was only her sister-in-law, but Melanie didn't know that. Caitlin pushed open the door of the boardroom with her shoulder, the phone in her hand, while miming *sorry* to her colleagues.

'Happy birthday, darling. You're forty. How does it feel?'

Caitlin keep her voice down as she hurried back to her own office, 'Oh, you know, like yesterday. But worse.'

Jan laughed and Caitlin smiled inside; her sister-in-law knew exactly how to manage Caitlin's Eeyore-ish energy.

'Alright, birthday girl. Come around for a drink tonight? I know Paul's not back until tomorrow.'

Caitlin loved Jan. She was the closest thing to a sister that she could hope for, and as such knew Caitlin well enough to understand she would have made no other birthday plans.

'I'd love to, but I'm grabbing a drink with the team here.'

Jan would also know this was a lie. And Caitlin knew Jan would know, and together they would both be okay with this. Caitlin hated social interaction. The energy it took to be 'on' could be overwhelming. Thankfully, she had carved out a life for herself where her on switch was rarely pressed. At forty, with a job and a husband and enough money for overpriced cheese, Caitlin was delighted to be stuck at the off position. Paul used to question his wife about this. He knew that a life grown up under two grandparents did not a social butterfly make, but even years after they'd been living together, he'd still be asking her midweek, 'Any ... plans with friends?' in the same hopeful tone as mothers used to her classmates: 'Why don't you ... show Caitlin your room?'

Caitlin didn't need anyone to show her their room, and she didn't need any friends. She said as much to Paul. 'I don't need friends, I have a husband!'

There had been a brief wash of a look across his eyes that had poked something deep inside her. She'd ignored it.

'Oh, work drinks? Fun! Fair enough, darling, you enjoy. Maybe I'll see you tomorrow night.'

Melanie tapped on the glass wall of Caitlin's office, her voice muted through it. 'Hiiiya. All okay?' She raised her eyebrows and pointed a spiky fingernail at Caitlin's phone.

Caitlin matched Melanie's raised eyebrows and threw in a thumbs-up to make her response even more irritating.

'Jan, I've got to go.'

'Bye then, sweet — and, happy bloody birthday!'

Melanie hovered by the glass, but Caitlin turned her back and fiddled with her phone, feigning work. After fifteen years selling fizzy drink to Southern Europe, Caitlin had met plenty of Melanies. She could have *been* Melanie, a number of times, but, as she said every time a promotion was thrown her way, 'I'm happy keeping my nose down and sales up.'

Oh, the bosses loved that. She'd receive a gentle pay increase to reward her lack of ambition; all she had to do was ignore whichever Melanie happened to be sitting in the corner office until they moved up and out.

Her door opened and Melanie's perfume wafted in.

'Caitlin, your Mind Map presso is up next, will you be joining us?'

Caitlin looked at her phone, the solicitor's email glowing white on the screen. She turned half an ear to her boss, distracted by the fact the number had not changed, and still remained really rather large. Melanie crossed her arms and actually, literally, tapped a foot.

'Oh? Yes. Of course. Coming.' She stood up and followed the bristling woman back into the boardroom. While she may be a beneficiary, this birthday Caitlin had inherited money, not courage.

Chapter Two

The problem with waking up a newly minted heiress was you were still forty and you still had to take out the dustbins.

Stop.

Scratch that.

The problem with waking up a newly minted forty-year-old was you were still an heiress. The dustbins could wait.

That was better.

Caitlin rolled onto her back and spread-eagled across the mattress like she did every morning that she had it to herself. Their bedroom was yet another space in the house where she often felt more like a lodger than the owner. The double bed looked strangely small in the large cream-carpeted bedroom. Most things in the room were cream. It was like sleeping in a meringue, especially when the pale winter sun came through the two sash windows that overlooked the road. Caitlin had once suggested, almost absent-mindedly, that they get a bigger bed. 'Then we wouldn't spend all night touching,' she'd said.

It wasn't until she looked up from her shoelaces and caught Paul's expression that she realised she'd said something wrong.

'Well that's bloody romantic,' he'd huffed.

*

She stretched as far as her limbs could go, trying to take up as much space as she could. It felt wonderful. Her phone pinged and she curled around to read Paul's message which had made its way from another time zone.

Though we're far apart, you are in my heart — happy birthday x

'Poetic Paul', she'd called him once. She decided to not bother mentioning that he was twenty-four hours off.

Thx, see you tmw x

No-one had ever called her poetic.

Before she could unfurl even further, she heard the bin men turn onto their street, the lorry lumbering its way towards her house. *Shit.*

Five minutes later, cold and panting, Caitlin tiptoed her bare feet back up the damp front path. She used one hand to keep her T-shirt over her knickers while she fumbled with the door. Before she could escape inside, she heard the click of next door's latch.

'Didn't make it, dear?'

Mrs Maloney was also still in her nightwear, but hers had three layers and an actual collar and so managed to make Caitlin feel even more underdressed than she was.

'No. Whoops!'

Old ladies always made her speak like she was thirteen. Caitlin wondered if her bum was visible to the whole street, or just the woman peering over the bushes. Mrs Maloney pointed at the still full bins Caitlin had just failed to get to the truck.

'Paul away? It's always tricky when the man of the house isn't available to do his jobs.'

'He's back later this week.'

'Ah. You'll be pleased about that.' A pause, where Caitlin was meant to agree. Mrs Maloney persisted. 'Would you like to pop around for a nice cup of tea later?'

Caitlin admired her tenacity. This was the third time in a month that she'd had to decline an invitation from the old woman.

Recently Paul had gently scolded Caitlin when she mentioned hiding from Mrs Maloney, waiting behind the door to avoid another wide-ranging chat including: the neighbourhood cats, some cousin's dengue fever and — always — the price of biscuits. Paul had shaken his head at her without looking up from the stack of unopened bills that had arrived during his Boston trip.

'The lady's just lonely, Caitlin. And it wouldn't be so terrible to have a little company while I'm away, would it?'

Caitlin realised she was staring at Mrs Maloney's hands, one on the door, the other gripping her velour dressing gown.

'I've even got some of the good biscuits in, from M&S!' The old woman said this with her eyebrows up, in the conspiratorial way of those who like biscuits more than most. The mottled, delicate skin on the backs of her hands reminded Caitlin of her grandmother. Although Dot wouldn't have been caught dead outside in her dressing gown.

'No, thank you.'

As she closed her door on Mrs Maloney, Caitlin heard Dot's voice, 'Caitlin. "Never complain, never explain". If it's good enough for Our Majesty it's good enough for us.'

* * *

Caitlin was fourteen when she started closing doors. As a furrowed, quiet young woman, she hadn't made that many friends at school. She didn't understand how the rest of the girls in class did it so easily. They shared quips and in-jokes and sniggers about gags that hadn't even existed a day earlier. It was an ever-changing collection of social enigmas and Caitlin could never say the right thing to solve one. But now, she'd received An Invitation. It was Kerryn Bothe's fifteenth birthday. The whole class was invited to watch the Battle of the Bands, at the boys school down the road. Caitlin was both delighted to be included and terrified of what that required of her.

She brought the photocopied invitation out of her school bag after dinner and now held it tightly in her hand, watching her grandparents as they moved about the kitchen in a slow polka, washing dishes and putting away their dinner plates.

Bill, Dot and Caitlin had finished their sausage and mash and it was time to broach the folded invitation Caitlin held resting on the kitchen table. Bill opened it carefully, like it may contain ricin powder.

'It's called Battle of the Bands. Like a concert.' Caitlin's voice sounded small in that little beige kitchen.

Dot tutted. Caitlin took in a shared glance between her grandparents. It was quick and tight and in that short moment she knew what the answer would be.

'A music concert?' asked Dot.

Caitlin couldn't put her finger on the energy shift in the room. What was it exactly? They weren't angry — but it didn't feel good.

This time her grandad spoke up, shoulders set square beneath his brown house cardigan. 'No, pet. I don't think so. Not at your age.'

That was it: sad. They were sad.

Later that evening all three had sat together in the front lounge, watching Nick Berry be blandly handsome in *Heartbeat*. They drank tea and rested chocolate digestives on their knees while headlights moved past the curtains drawn tightly against the night and the road and the world where fourteen-year-olds were allowed to go to music concerts.

* * *

Caitlin's mind played this memory while she pottered about downstairs. With Paul homeward-bound, she'd begun to return the house to the way her husband required, which really just meant shifting items from one place to another. Shoes removed from the stairs, mugs taken from bookshelves, and brown bananas out of the bowl. Her mind left her grandparents and drifted around the chores, avoiding the large, money-shaped elephant in her brain. Bill hadn't been forthcoming on the phone. While she had gathered herself well enough to ask 'What?' and 'How?', she hadn't had the presence of mind to ask the questions that had since played through her head all night, and continued to today.

Where had her grandmother pulled this unexpected sum from?

Why had they held it quietly for so many years?

How exactly was she going to break this news to Paul?

And, the most important question: What were they going to do with this bloody money?

The house was back to almost-order, but it had taken up much more of her Saturday than she expected. The sun was setting in the mid-winter gloom. There was still no food in the fridge. Caitlin switched on the various lamps that made the dark rooms feel warm again and was just readying herself to venture to the supermarket when somebody knocked on the glass pane by the front door. Caitlin scolded herself for turning on the lights — *Rookie error, Caitlin.* She stood still and wondered how long Mrs Maloney was going to hover on her front step.

'Darling. I can see you.'

It was Jan. Just Jan. Her wonderful sister-in-law, who warmed the threshold as soon as Caitlin opened the door. One hand gripped the straining handle of an overpacked bag of groceries. The other brandished a wine bottle, upside-down, like a Viking holding a joint of meat. Caitlin spied muesli and for some reason missed Paul.

'Oh wow. Thank you. Come in.'

Jan entered and kissed Caitlin on the cheek. She was freezing. Her sister-in-law only lived on the next street, and so even on the sharpest winter days she insisted on walking. Which was one of the reasons her cheeks were always glowing. Jan had, as her wife referred to it, a 'country complexion'. Caitlin followed her down the hall because Jan was already marching to the kitchen and unloading the bag, each item placed with purpose and punctuated by a booming voice.

'I was doing The Shop. Again. Bloody hell my children insist on eating constantly. They eat and eat and they simply will not stop. Caitlin, it's more than one woman can take. Let alone two. My poor wife. She's beside herself. "Marigold," I told her, "you were the one who wanted these damn *progeny*."'

Jan stopped. Looked at Caitlin with her eyes wider than before.

'Shit. Oh, darling. Sorry.'

Caitlin reached for the bottle.

'It's okay. I told you. We're okay.' She gestured for Jan to continue, 'And this always helps. Please, tell me more about what arseholes my nephews are.'

'Okay. But I am sorry. We did enough cycles of IVF; there's no excuse to forget the stuff I shouldn't say. I remember Marigold's mother said once, after a failed round, "Maybe this is a sign you should foster cats." *Cats*, Caitlin. That woman.'

Jan shook her head and Caitlin was quietly relieved Paul wasn't here to see his sister complain. He was definitely more broken about ending their fertility treatment than she was. He'd cried on and off for a week. It was awful. Caitlin felt squirmy at the memory.

'Honestly, it's fine. Paul and I don't even talk about it anymore. It's been two years. Fertility treatment was just a really expensive hobby.' She flinched at her own flippancy and hoped Jan wouldn't repeat that particular gem back to her brother. 'We've actually been saving for a lovely holiday instead,' said Caitlin, and then immediately blushed.

In Jan's flurry of an entrance Caitlin had forgotten about the inheritance. At the mention of their childless holiday, it came back to her immediately. Jan didn't seem to notice her red cheeks.

The patter of conversation and wine and cheese was more cheering than any birthday gift Caitlin could have received. Jan had exhausted all of her complaints about her boys (mainly the eating), her job (people in finance had no EQ, apparently) and even her wife (too perfect, always). Jan did that — turned her love on like a firehose, so powerful it was impossible to stay dry and, sometimes, impossible to stay upright. And as much as Caitlin preferred not to seek other people out, being drenched by Jan's adoration did feel … not terrible. Or maybe that was the wine. The bottle was empty now. Caitlin fossicked around the drinks cupboard looking for something that was appropriate for 5.30 on a Saturday evening. She used the fact that Jan couldn't see her face as an excuse to speak up.

'I had some news yesterday.'

There was Campari and gin, and a dusty bottle at the back that looked like a nineteenth-century tincture. She stood up, grabbed one of the mandarins that had rolled from Jan's bag of goodies and began to make some mangled form of negroni.

Jan was still and quiet. It was unusual for her to have news at all let alone want to share it.

Why was Caitlin nervous? This was good practice. She'd have to get much better than this before she announced the news to Paul. She smiled at Jan, took a deep breath and said, 'Well. It turns out I'm nice and rich!'

Not long afterwards, Jan had sworn at her phone when she'd noticed the time and hustled out the door, leaving an untouched mandarin negroni on the bench. Caitlin picked at the leftover citrus peel and played the conversation over in her head. Jan had been ungratifyingly practical about the whole thing. In hindsight, Caitlin shouldn't have been surprised — her sister-in-law was a chartered accountant, after all. She had peppered Caitlin with questions about trusts and tax and terms and it was all Caitlin could do but throw the solicitor's email address at her and down the negroni in one.

But it was helpful too. Caitlin felt more prepared for the Great Unveiling to Paul. She debated typing up a list of FAQs for the practical side of things, just to have on hand once they'd stopped crying and hugging each other. It felt right that two years after she and Paul had agreed to finally leave the quest for children behind, they had received this injection of money. Caitlin had abandoned the idea of being a mother, really, some years before. Was it after the second miscarriage, or the third? It didn't matter. She had moved on, it seemed, much more quickly than Paul. And as crass as it sounded, the money would help him to catch up. It was time to get researching.

By the time she'd finished her drink, as well as Jan's, Caitlin had twenty-two tabs open on her laptop. Most were of various 'child-free resorts' along the equator. Some of them were truly expensive, one or two were bordering on obscene. She peered at over-water rooms in the Maldives and felt queasy at the concept of a glass-bottomed bedroom. A resort in Kenya seemed to come with its own coterie of giraffes. Caitlin hoped they were on payroll. And then, a spectacular wooden palace in Ubud. There were frangipani floating in the pool and lush jungle hovered at every open window. This was it. She and Paul would have their own *Eat, Pray, Love* moment in the uphills of Bali, surrounded by rice paddies and flickering paraffin torches. She wondered if the meal she'd serve Paul tomorrow night should be Balinese-themed, and if it was too late to find banana leaves to use as plates. Where would one procure banana leaves in North London?

Caitlin looked around the kitchen, stretching her shoulders and neck out after hunching over her laptop for much longer than she'd realised. She checked the world clock on her phone and saw it was midnight in Dubai. Paul would be heading to the airport as soon as he woke up. She hadn't heard from him since this morning's text, but that wasn't unusual. When Paul was working, he was Working. Unlike Caitlin, who when working was Waiting to Not Work. Caitlin treated her job as a poorly directed stage play she had to perform in order to get paid.

She stopped. For the second time in two days she said out loud to an empty house, 'Holy shit.'

Her job. She didn't have to do it anymore. She and Paul could stay for an irresponsibly long time in the Ubudian palace. It would be totally, completely fine because *she had the money.*

Caitlin was suddenly full of a strange giddiness, a feeling she recognised but couldn't place. She picked up the phone again, because she was about to do something reckless and that meant she had to check in with a grown-up. Which meant, Paul. ('Lie down, it'll pass,' Paul said once when she haltingly suggested they adopt a dog.)

No. That would ruin the surprise and also it would make her feel a little less giddy, and it was a sensation she wanted to maintain, even though it was giving her butterflies. She put the phone down and went back to her laptop instead.

Dear Melanie, she typed, *I hereby inform you of my resignation. I will not be working out my notice.* Caitlin paused. She wasn't sure she'd ever used the word 'hereby' before. She bit at her lip. The butterflies in her belly were multiplying. Yes, she knew this feeling. It came from the knowledge that nothing was going to be the same.

Chapter Three

Butterflies in her belly. She had first felt them in the August of 1997. It was the month the world began mourning Princess Diana, and didn't stop for a very long time. Diana had died on a Sunday. It was the last month of summer and Caitlin was nineteen. The weekend had been grey, drizzly and — as her grandmother referred to any kind of humidity — 'close'.

Caitlin sat in the silence of the empty kitchen poking at some questionable porridge she had just over-microwaved. Her shift at the local pharmacy was beginning in thirty minutes, and she was trying to muster an appetite while looking down the barrel of eight hours on her feet. The grandfather clock in the hall made a hollow *tock* as the minute hand edged forward to 7 am. It wasn't just the time of day — it was always quiet in the house. Bill and Dot were not fans of any music above a barely registered volume. They certainly did not tolerate raised voices. If the wind caused a door to slam, or a pot accidentally dropped in the kitchen, Dot's hands would fly to her chest with an inhalation so sharp you'd have thought she was in physical pain. Caitlin had learnt to move through life quietly.

So, when Caitlin first heard her grandmother wail that morning, she thought it was a cat. Or a car alarm. It only sounded once, but it was so primal, so wounded, Caitlin's mouth immediately dried up. She stood, because something felt wrong, and after clearing her dishes, paused uncertainly at the bottom of the narrow staircase. Her grandfather appeared at the top in his checked slippers.

'It's okay, pet. Your grandmother's had a bit of a shock.' A clearing of the throat. 'The Lady Di's passed on, you see.'

'Oh. How?'

It was gloomy on the stairwell and she could barely see her grandfather's face in the half-light.

'A car accident.' His voice cracked and it wasn't until she was out at the bus stop that she realised he'd been crying.

The day at work had been a strange one, particularly for a nineteen-year-old who found emotional displays uncomfortable. Her boss was Martin — a pharmacist with box-dyed hair who bowed like a priest at confession when old ladies came in to talk about their catarrh. He always left them with a smile and a gentle pat on the hand. He didn't smile that Sunday. He kept his head down and wore a black armband around his white coat sleeve and dabbed his eyes every now and again. Some of the customers came in crying that day too. Caitlin had concentrated on packaging up the medications to be delivered by bicycle after lunch, avoiding eye contact out of embarrassment rather than grief.

When she'd arrived home mid-afternoon, she was surprised to see both grandparents sitting in the TV room. Dot had always said, 'Daytime television is for hospitals and nursing homes.'

The volume was on low, the small screen rolling with footage of red-eyed people with tight mouths laying flowers in London. She'd hesitated in the doorway, not knowing what to say in the face of such public anguish.

'I'm back. I'm going to head upstairs.'

Bill tilted forward from his armchair and patted the empty spot on the sofa beside her grandmother. Dot turned the TV off in the same moment. Everything they did was a quiet choreography. Caitlin assumed that's what being old and married was about.

'Sit down, pet. Your gran and I have something we'd like to talk to you about.'

In the August of 1997 Caitlin wept over a car accident. Of course she'd known her mother had died when Caitlin herself was only five. Her grandparents once told her that it was an aneurysm. A frightening lie delivered with enough gravity to dissuade any further conversation. Until that day. That day, they explained the long Australian highway, the car, the broken gumtree and how their only daughter never returned home.

In the weeks that followed, as news cycles spun from one day to the next, Caitlin watched her grandmother shrink. Dot winced at each word — the broken poetry of *crash, mother, wreckage* and *blood* struck her over and over. Dot, a woman on whose shoulders the whole house had rested, now held her face in a pinch of grief dredged up.

In the August of 1997, while the rest of the world was talking about Princess Di, Caitlin tried to mourn another woman she had never known.

* * *

She hadn't been able to sleep properly after 5 am, when more butterflies had gathered before dawn. Caitlin remembered Jan telling her once that the feeling of a baby first moving inside was 'just like butterflies'. Caitlin wondered if her own baby would have felt like that. Now, it was mid-afternoon and she'd made her way back upstairs after an empty morning of buying groceries and tidying, and lay down again in the pale bedroom. The frosted afternoon light seemed to barely make it through the spindled branches of the silver birch outside. Caitlin counted back — Melanie would have received her resignation email at 9 pm last night, which now she thought about it seemed a little unprofessional. It also felt a bit sad — she suspected people who had just had a significant birthday shouldn't be sitting at home on Saturday nights quitting things. But Caitlin didn't feel embarrassed and she certainly didn't feel regretful. The wonderful consequence to being dispassionate was that while you did miss out on the wild bits of life (fervour, ecstasy) you also had nothing to do with the nonsense (fear, regret, sadness). For years, Caitlin had lived with her own personal flatline. It also meant the unexpectedness of the inheritance wasn't just the money itself, but that she was experiencing a genuine thrill for the first time in, well, ever.

Paul was arriving that evening. Caitlin hauled herself back to the kitchen after a brief doze. She unpacked four cans of coconut milk for the Balinese black rice pudding recipe she had googled last night. There hadn't been black rice or banana leaves at the Waitrose, but the Poundshop next door had a pack of raffia placemats and a two-for-one on microwaveable basmati. So, she'd made do with those. Caitlin turned the hob on to get started on the pudding.

By the time Paul texted from the tarmac — *At LHR now, see you soon* — dinner was almost done. The curry was just passable but the satay was pretty good. The rice pudding tasted like tropical sunscreen. Caitlin was hoping they'd have had enough wine by then not to notice. The house was tidier than she'd ever made it for herself, and now her nervous energy was turning its focus onto the ambient part of the evening. She googled *Playlists to deliver exciting news to*, which hadn't been fruitful. She'd toyed with the idea of creating her own, but given her complete lack of musical knowledge, and Paul's complete lack of musical interest, it was probably a waste of time.

'I don't like to know when one song has finished and the other has started,' he once said to her early in their relationship. So she put on 'Coffee Joint Jazz Blend' (which she'd initially misread as 'Jazz Bland') and that seemed okay.

Right. She'd done the food and the music — time to hit the trifecta and put on a bra.

'He won't know what's hit him,' Caitlin whispered to herself as she climbed the stairs, two at a time like she used to as a kid. In their bedroom she wrestled on a jumper Paul had bought her on his last trip to New York. It was a kind of peachy beige colour, which paired with her pale skin and muddy-blonde hair made her look a little consumptive — but the gesture was there. Her hair had been pulled off her face in a clip and now when she let it out, it fell in wonky curls. Caitlin toyed with the idea of applying lipstick, but that felt icky so she settled for smudging eyeliner into her lashes with her fingers.

There. Caitlin glanced at herself in the mirror and pretended she was Paul, looking at his wife of fifteen years. It was a discomfiting exercise. If she thought about it too hard, she realised, Caitlin didn't actually know how Paul saw her. She shook her head of the idea and cleared her throat. Back to the issue at hand: how was she going to do this?

Paul. I've got some news.

No. That was too cruel. He'd immediately think she was pregnant.

Paul. We're going on an adventure.

It sounded like she'd joined a cult on their behalf.

Hi. Sit down. Guess what.

She should have rehearsed this more.

As the lights of the car lit up the bedroom windows, she heard the boot slam and the driver say, 'Goodnight, mate'. Caitlin hustled downstairs so she could catch Paul's expression when he walked into the kitchen, but he was too fast for her, and they found themselves face to face in the hall. He clearly hadn't expected her to be waiting for him as he came through the door. His expression was grey — tired and dropped and furrowed. It didn't lift on seeing his wife. He just seemed … confused. The house smelt of warmth and food.

'What's going on?'

She laughed. It was good to see him again, with his rain-flecked glasses and sticky-up hair.

'Nothing! Hello! Can't a wife greet her husband after a week away?' She held her hands up like she was wearing a pinafore apron and stilettos, and not jeans and socks.

'Who've you spoken —?' Paul stopped his question when he saw her face looking at him, expectantly, hair brushed and a bit fluffy. His shoulders sunk. 'Sorry. It's been a long day. I'm going to —'

Caitlin interrupted. '— have a shower. I know. It's okay, dinner will keep.'

He always had a shower. Unpacked. Put on his tracksuit pants. Debriefed on the trip.

'No. Let's go into the kitchen.'

Looking back, it was at this point Caitlin knew something was wrong. There were those bloody butterflies again. Caitlin would do anything to avoid the flutters. This is why she didn't ever want a promotion, why she didn't want friends and why now she was focusing on stirring the curry while Paul looked baffled at the raffia placemats.

'What's all this?'

She turned from the stove and picked up the bottle of white.

'Wine?' she asked, both ignoring his question and not waiting for the answer to pour them both a glass.

'No. Caitlin. I don't want a drink.' He squeezed the bridge of his nose beneath his glasses. Closed his eyes. Whispered, 'Shit.'

Caitlin swallowed. Her throat had gone all tight and she felt sticky bile in the back of her mouth. She put the bottle down on the bench between them.

'What's wrong? Are you sick?'

He was in his work-worn shirt that smelt of sweat and aeroplane. He didn't look tired anymore. He looked — he looked at her. He rested his hands on the island bench, arms locked straight and pointing away from him — like he was bracing for impact. Which is exactly what he was doing.

'I am telling you … that I am' — he looked briefly up to the ceiling, then back at her — 'leaving.'

Caitlin became very, very still. Paul was speaking clearly, the words rehearsed.

'I'm sorry I'm telling you this way, straight off a plane. I was going to wait. But it's just —' He sped up as he went off script. 'Jesus, Caitlin, I can't do this anymore. I'm sure you feel it too.'

He sounded almost irritated that she clearly didn't. She couldn't feel a thing, except for the stem of the wineglass pinched hard between her fingers. A drop of condensation slipped down from the rim onto her thumb.

She opened her mouth. 'I …'

He sighed and pushed off from the bench. Now he was pacing about their open living room, hands moving around like he was telling them both a story. She didn't finish her sentence.

'Fifteen years, Caitlin. We had fifteen years, but nothing to show for it, not really. Where's the growth? The exploration?'

'Exploration?' Caitlin repeated, quietly. 'We're not taking a safari.'

He didn't hear her. He sat on the back of the sofa, briefly. Then he was up again. Holding a magazine, throwing it back onto the pile on the coffee table.

'I can't be here anymore. I can't live every day the same as every other. Awake, asleep, every goddamned day, Caitlin. Christ!'

'Why are you so angry, when you're the one leaving me?'

He'd made his way to the back window and was looking out at their, his, tree. Rain fell softly in the beam of the uplights. She realised that she hadn't said that out loud.

She tried again, this time with more volume. 'Why …?'

Paul quickly turned and walked directly at her. She took a step back so she bumped into the stove. Even though there was a bench between them, she wanted to distance herself from the stranger who had taken over her husband's body.

'*Why?* Caitlin. Jesus. Can't you see what a lonely life this is? I'm leaving before we, before *I*, turn to fucking dust.' He was back on script, but she wondered who'd written it. Paul didn't normally swear.

She spoke quietly again, not wanting to spook him any more than he clearly was. 'What are you talking about?' She had to throw him an anchor, a life vest, bring him back to their life. 'You went to Dubai. I had a birthday. Now you're home. What's happened?'

'I'm forty-five. I want a life. I want a partner in life who is truly alive! Alive with music and travel and —' Caitlin's eyes flicked to the raffia placements. She couldn't even consider telling him about the money right now. '— and with goddamn *horses*!'

He said this in a mildly hysterical way, almost laughing. There was a quick burst of warmth in his eyes. She picked it immediately, and he saw that she had. Caitlin steadied herself, lifted her chin a little and took a sip of her wine.

'You've had an affair.'

It wasn't a question. The butterflies had died and her insides were set stone. She clenched her jaw. Paul had the grace to look slightly ashamed. He stuck his tongue into his cheek and stared at the floor.

A beat. The last silence where she thought all of this could be rewound. And then.

'It's not an affair, Caitlin. We're in love. I'm sorry.' He smiled now, with a sadness that was so definite she didn't even consider stopping him, even as he walked out. The front door shut and her wine was still chilled. Her husband had left her in less than five minutes and Caitlin had done the worst thing: nothing.

Chapter Four

It's odd how quietly a life can explode. In the fortnight since she had quit her job and watched Paul leave, Caitlin had not told anyone what had happened. She had taken the bins out. Walked through the sodden winter streets. Brushed her teeth twice a day.

She had spoken to Bill for two Thursdays and reassured him that the money was safe and asked after what pudding he'd had at lunch that day (chocolate mousse; junket). Jan had rung her most days, but with no answer had now taken to dropping off Tupperware containers of bone broth at the front door.

'Just me!' she'd called through the letter box that morning. 'I'll pop by tomorrow to check I can't smell your corpse.'

Caitlin hadn't been completely ignoring her. A few irregularly spaced text replies had prevented the authorities from being summoned.

In all, blowing up your job and your marriage in one weekend created a curious kind of vacuum in which nothing and everything occurred at once. Her life was dead and gone and broken, but at the same time Caitlin managed to sort out her gifted wealth and her separation quite neatly. She'd met with the solicitor her grandad's lawyer had referred — a soupy kind of man called Neil who sniffed a lot. Caitlin felt a bit odd, discussing money that wouldn't have existed if it wasn't for her mother's death. But 'a bit' is where it ended. After Neil said, 'I'm sorry' for the third time after referencing her dead mother, she had to interrupt him. 'It's okay, Neil. You don't need to keep saying that. I was five — I don't remember her.'

This wasn't exactly accurate, but Neil didn't need to know about dirty blonde hair whipping in the breeze, or the smell of earthy skin warm in the morning sheets. Neil had sniffed again and gone back to his keyboard. He'd been a little afraid of Caitlin since their first meeting a week earlier, when she'd asked if he wanted to discuss the 'death money or the divorce money first'.

No. Much like Time, Administration stopped for no woman.

Caitlin had rendered herself unemployed but she hadn't turned off the person that job created. Because the thing with finishing work was that all of one's instincts, bred over fifteen years of customer presentations and sales pitches, had to channel themselves somewhere else. So, she moved Work Caitlin into her home, and because there was an empty space where another human used to be, the new addition fit in easily. Paul had been travelling for so many years that his most recent departure just felt like another business trip, except he had stopped putting kisses at the end of his texts. This one had just arrived: *Caitlin, please call Jan back — she's worried about you.* That Paul himself wasn't worried didn't occur to her until much later. But maybe that was what he had meant when he'd said, 'I'm sure you feel it too.'

Caitlin had played Paul's relatively few words back to herself many times since that Sunday night. Maybe some of what he said was true — maybe all of it was. And that's why she didn't feel hurt by them — like always, she didn't feel much at all.

Paul had been back to the house once, to pack a bag and pick up some things that Caitlin didn't notice had gone until days later. They had avoided each other by a small enough window that she smelt his aftershave in the hallway when she returned home. It was a cologne he normally reserved for dinners in restaurants that didn't have prices on the menu. But it was a Wednesday afternoon, so Caitlin guessed Paul had broadened his definition of a scent-worthy occasion. She didn't know where he was staying. She didn't know who he was in love with. She didn't know why he was suddenly interested in music and cologne and horses. Caitlin wasn't even sure if she missed him.

The whole experience was all at once stunningly raw and oddly familiar: loss, quiet houses and the sense that the only thing to do was to 'Keep going, and keep going quietly'. That was another Dot-ism. Caitlin had been brought up in a world where silence and a stiff upper lip were worshipped next to cleanliness. Godliness sat just below.

* * *

Eighty-one Lavender Road was a brick semi with a pitched roof and a garage, outside which her grandad washed his car once a week. Dot and Bill had bought the house soon after they were married, a deposit saved with grim-faced determination that Caitlin had still felt in the walls, decades later. Dot worked the garden and Bill hung wallpaper, and together they busied themselves with their jobs and their house for the eight long years it took for their daughter Susan to arrive. A third bedroom waited patiently, for more children who never came — until Caitlin arrived, of course. The second, Susan's childhood room, stayed closed and quiet. There was never any question that Caitlin would move in there, even though it was larger than her own. The door stood shut tight, a silent sentry between her room and her grandparents', watching over the small upstairs landing and stairs so narrow you couldn't pass each other up or down.

Caitlin couldn't have been more than eight when Dot found her, hand resting on the doorknob to that middle bedroom. Caitlin had been there for longer than Dot knew, long enough to have opened the door and lain on the neatly made bed and peered around the empty walls to see if her mother had owned toys that she herself would care to play with.

'Not in there, thank you, Caitlin.' Caitlin had kept her hand on the timber knob.

'But I want to see —'

'Caitlin.'

She was too young to recognise the pain in her grandmother's voice.

So she persisted. 'It's —' She couldn't say *Mum*, or even worse, *Mummy*. Instead, she opted, quietly, for 'It's her room.'

Dot was a small woman. Wiry, with bobbed hair that didn't move even when she did. She turned her head to the side, like a bird, closed her eyes — just for a second. 'That's not your mother's room anymore. Please do not go in there again. And we don't raise our voices in this house.' She wasn't angry. Dot was never angry, which was worse.

Caitlin removed her hand and watched Dot descend the stairs, and then she followed. The next week Bill had changed the bedroom into a sewing room when Caitlin was at school. And it was never discussed again. Closed and quiet.

* * *

Caitlin sat at their kitchen bench with her phone in her hand. While she had started sweeping the house more regularly for spare mugs and dust bunnies, the raffia placemats were still set on the table. They brought to mind the parallel universe where she and Paul were dozing on pool loungers in Ubud.

She had eaten the Balinese curry the night he left and it had been pretty good, although she'd vomited it up a few hours later. She wasn't going to blame the curry, or the cook, for that. It was a bad night, filled with the sensation of losing the one thing that made her feel attached to the rest of the world. Caitlin had sat on the floor of the downstairs loo with her knees pulled up to her ribcage and her chin bent down to meet them. That night she found herself completely empty, sapped of all fluids, and — it seemed — emotion.

Two weeks had passed and while she was lonely and increasingly bored, everything else seemed to be going tip-top. Caitlin deposited the still warm container of bone broth into her fridge, and finally called Jan back. It went straight to voicemail. A text pinged to Caitlin almost immediately.

Hello! I'm on a call. Come for dinner tonight? Marigold's out & kids won't be there.

Three dots. Caitlin watched her screen while Jan typed another message.

My brother will also not be there.

Caitlin laughed out loud.

Jan and Marigold's house was a wonderful facsimile of Jan and Paul's family home: the one in which the siblings had been brought up in. That's why Caitlin loved it so much. When Paul had first brought Caitlin to meet his parents, the thing that struck her more than anything was the noise. Even as the new couple approached the stone-clad cottage, Caitlin became aware of a low rumble of voices. Paul had let himself into the house ('He has his own key?' she'd marvelled at the time) and had bellowed out, 'Hello!'

Five — god, it sounded like twenty! — voices hollered in response from the back of the house, 'HELLOOO!'

Caitlin had jumped a little, and then been embarrassed when Paul noticed, and laughed at her.

'Come on, chook, let's throw you to the wolves.'

But the Falstaff family were not wolves. They were bears. Large and warm and loud and cuddly. They ambled around Caitlin, a mere babe at twenty-four years old, and pulled her tightly into their den.

'They built it in the early nineties, but you'd never know,' Paul had said proudly, as he'd placed her duffel bag at the bottom of the stairs. The Wiltshire home was also where she met Jan for the first time, standing in the kitchen peeling carrots. She presented her hand for a slightly damp but firm handshake, which pulled Caitlin into a very tight hug.

'I'm Jan. The Big Sister. We're going to be friends.'

That whole first-weekend experience was one reason Caitlin felt a sense of deep belonging in Jan's own home. They'd actually all discovered the house together — the two Falstaff siblings and their partners. They were playground-hopping through North London's spring-sprinkled streets one April Sunday. It was years ago, when Jan and Marigold's boys were little and most weekends were spent trying to tire them into oblivion. Newly wed Paul and Caitlin stood back rocking the sleeping boys in their pushchairs while Marigold and Jan had swooned at the Georgian terrace awash with wisteria, its yellow door glowing like a lantern through the purple flowers. Jan had dialled the number on the small For Sale sign there and then. Caitlin also loved it at first sight. Since then, the house had become a beacon of light and warmth and family for all of them.

Every room was like a different type of embrace. Worn timber floorboards were softened by a collage of rugs. Plaits of garlic and bunches of thyme swung gently over the kitchen sink. An overstuffed leather couch had held various dogs, the most recent being a completely blind terrier called Bicycle. Marigold was a sculptor and painter, and on one rainy weekend had decorated every doorknob with gold leaf. Remnants of various ball sports played by the boys lay abandoned in the rambling back garden, most now covered with ground ivy. The family painted the front door a different colour each July. This year, it was a pale green. Caitlin banged the brass knocker shaped like a hare and waited for Jan.

The door opened and there was her dear sister-in-law, pulling her in for another tight squeeze. Then holding her firmly by the shoulders and looking her square in the eye.

'Darling. I'm so pleased you're here. Come, let me feed you.' She strode past the coats and skipped down the stairs to the terrace's lower floor, talking as she went. 'Marigold's at a dinner. She didn't want to go, she's sending all her love. Christopher's here somewhere, he's heading out soon. ChristoPHER!' She called her son's name up into the floors above, at a volume much too loud for inside.

There was a galumphing down flights of stairs. A tall man entered the basement kitchen and it took Caitlin a second to realise he was her nephew. She did this every time she saw him now. The giant was fourteen and had a lot of hair.

'Hello, Aunty Caitlin.' Christopher was the younger of Caitlin's two nephews. He walked and talked in a mumble.

Caitlin smiled and didn't try to hug him; he smiled back and appreciated the lack of gesture. Jan planted a kiss on her son's forehead while he bent to collect his bag from the floor, shouting out after him as he escaped back up and out the front door, 'Text me when you get there!' And then to Caitlin, 'He's bloody enormous! They both are. You should see Arthur's feet. I've no idea how we're going to fit somewhere else while they do … all this.'

'All this' was the packing mess scattered between the ground and basement floors of the house. Between the kitchen table and courtyard door, cardboard boxes lay half-filled with life-detritus, seemingly abandoned.

'How long do you have to be out for?'

'God knows. Marigold says three weeks so I'm working on twelve, minimum. Why do we need to paint any walls, I ask, Caitlin? Are my walls not already painted?' She threw her hands up and just for a moment looked like her brother. Caitlin gave her a shrug in solidarity.

It was early, but Jan served dinner straight away and she and Caitlin ate sitting across from each other at the well-worn wooden table, the ancient cross-back chairs protesting quietly. Caitlin hadn't drunk alcohol since the night Paul had walked out, and she appreciated the generous pour of red Jan delivered along with the bolognese.

'I defrosted M's sauce. It's a good one,' Jan said, handing over a block of parmesan and a grater.

Jan cooked as little as Caitlin did, and Paul and Marigold had often gently teased their respective wives over this fact. Caitlin added extra cheese and they ate together companionably; Caitlin's shoulders dropped tension with every bite. When Jan had cleared the empty bowls, they both carried their glasses to the living room, taking up their respective positions on either end of the enormous sofa. Bicycle moved from his spot on the cushion, rotated three times, sat down in the same place he'd begun and sighed loudly. Caitlin scratched behind his ears while she looked around the room. Marigold had added a few more pieces to the already crammed walls, including a disarming photograph of a young woman staring down the barrel of the camera while a cigarette hung from her cupid's bow. Caitlin was about to ask after it when Jan sighed, in a much more sad way than her dog just had. Caitlin prepared herself — it was time.

'I'm so sorry, Caitlin darling. I'm so sorry this has happened, and in this way. It's bloody horrible.'

Caitlin sipped her wine before she spoke. 'Yes. It's surreal. Life feels normal and then my stomach drops and I remember I'm alone —' She stopped at saying *again*. That would have sounded a bit melodramatic, particularly after fifteen years.

'Jan' — Caitlin had been thinking about this question more than most — 'how much did you know?'

Caitlin knew how close Jan and Paul were, and were not. She had been wondering which side of the line the story of Paul's new love had fallen.

Jan raked her hand through her cropped cut and Caitlin saw how much silver was now in her sister-in-law's brown hair. She replied carefully, 'I didn't know he was going to walk out, darling. I'm so terribly sad about that.'

'And the woman? Paul told me he's in love with someone else. Did you know that?'

Jan inched along the sofa, coming close enough that her knees were nearly touching Caitlin's. She said, 'I didn't know he was having an affair. But I did know something was up.'

'How? How'd you know?'

Jan placed her hand over Caitlin's. She spoke quietly. 'Well. He was happy, darling.'

Chapter Five

Caitlin started to cry, softly and without moving much. She hung her head and stared into her wineglass. Jan took it from her hand, placed it atop a pile of books on the coffee table and pulled her in for a cuddle. Unlike other people, this didn't make Caitlin cry more. In fact, the tears dried quickly on her cheeks and she pulled back out of Jan's arms as soon as it was acceptable. Jan had known Caitlin long enough to not take this personally. She'd also known her for long enough to say what she said next.

'I'm sorry he left like he did, darling. It's weak. Terrible. All the life you two have led together. He's an idiot, and I've told him so. But' — she paused and Caitlin braced for impact — 'you two haven't been happy for such a long time. Can you see that?'

'I don't know if I can,' Caitlin said. She brought her wine back to her mouth, and added slightly crossly, 'I don't know what you all mean by "happy".'

Jan put her Accounting face on. Caitlin knew it as the expression she used to wear when she was doing maths homework with the boys.

'Okay. Let's play opposites. Do you know how you felt when your grandmother died?'

Caitlin felt like a teenager learning pronumerals. 'Um, sad?'

'Sad. Yes. Okay. What about your mother? How did you feel when you found out about your mother?'

'… Sad?' Caitlin knew she wasn't getting it right.

Her sister-in-law looked at her patiently. 'What else? Lonely? Angry? Confused?'

Caitlin bit at the skin around her thumb, and shrugged. Jan looked like Paul did when he was getting frustrated. But she shook her head quickly, shaking off the irritation, and gave another big sigh. 'I'm trying to say, darling, "happy" isn't just smiling. It's the opposite feeling from those terrible ones. It's warmth, and laughter, and growth. It's adventure!'

Jan had stood up again and walked to the sideboard that filled most of the opposite wall. The movement took some of the sting out of what she was saying. Not all of it, but some. She returned with a packet of chocolate buttons and sat back down on the couch. 'I'm sorry. I don't want to make you feel more awful. I'm just wondering if you know there are other ways of feeling? And that you're allowed to have them. All of the feelings.'

Caitlin gave a tight-lipped smile and shrugged again. She wanted to tell Jan about Bali, and Melanie, and the raffia placemats. She wanted to talk about the night of August 31st when she lay in her bed and wondered if Lady Di and her mother had known they were about to die. She wanted to discuss her grandmother Dot, paying for her own daughter's travel insurance with cash saved in a Clarks shoe box. Did the policy make it easier for Dot to farewell her only child?

She wanted to talk about all these things. Call the feelings into the rafters. Sing them out into the wind and the winter. Instead, she squeezed Jan's hand and held out her empty glass.

'I'd like to feel drunk. Can we do that please?'

They did not discuss Paul again. After the initial chat, Jan and Caitlin fell into the sangiovese with relief. Jan cackling over Caitlin's imitation of Melanie's office banter, Caitlin sitting with a small smile as Jan wove stories of a golden childhood, for the hundredth time. They talked about Jan's work and the kids and health and all the other chapters that made up a life summarised on a Monday night. They moved in various seated positions around the couch and the floor, and worked their way through wine and chocolate and nuts and cheese and back to more wine.

When Jan received a text from Marigold letting her know she was on her way, Caitlin knew it was her sign to head home too. She loved Jan's wife, but she wasn't strong (or sober) enough to deal with a two-on-one interrogation — which was inevitably what would happen once Marigold arrived.

'Right.' Caitlin rose a little unsteadily to her feet. Swaying forward, she picked up what was left of the enormous bag of pistachios on the table before them. Empty shells were littered at their feet, a confetti of snacking. 'I'll take these. I need them for the — *hic* — trek home.' Caitlin always got the hiccups when she'd drunk too much. Paul used to call her the Hic-Cait. 'Bug — *hic* — ger.'

Jan walked her to the door and squeezed her again. There had been a lot of squeezing that night.

'God, I do love you, darling. You're going to be fine.'

Caitlin's next hiccup was smothered in Jan's bosom.

'Thank you, Jannie.' Her voice was smothered too. She only called Jan 'Jannie' when she was Hic-Cait.

'You're alright to get home?' Jan asked.

Caitlin waved backwards over her head as she zig-zagged down the path. 'Yes! Follow the pistachio shells if I go missing!'

The night was very cold, and sharp because of it. It set her features like a mask, and immediately she felt less drunk. Although the sky was clear, the stars were faint and mostly invisible, thanks to the thrum of London's lights. As she turned onto their road, she remembered something Paul had said to her early in their dating life. They'd been sitting on the worn sofa in his flat and she'd just handed him the small, sad story of her mother's death.

She'd told all the story, which didn't mean much — the difference between all and a little was only a sentence or two. But she really liked Paul, and she wanted to share everything, including the part about the tree by the highway outside of Melbourne. He'd looked suitably solemn. Then he'd said something oddly specific: 'Australia, hm? I saw the most incredible stars of my life in Australia. Gap year. I still remember it. I couldn't believe my eyes. I was under a sky where there was more light than dark.'

They hadn't spoken of her mother much after that, but she'd never forgotten that image that Paul had given her.

Caitlin held her phone torch up to the door and stabbed the key around the lock a few times, vaguely hoping Mrs Maloney wouldn't appear. Inside, she turned the hallway light on and thanked god it was still early enough in the night for the radiators to be running. She shed her boots, jacket and bag in the hall and steadied herself on the banister before making her way into the kitchen.

The danger of a boozy walk home in winter was that you became sober enough to feel like a nightcap, but were not nearly sober enough to need one. Caitlin flung the drinks cabinet open and reached past her negroni-makings to find that dusty medicine bottle, which turned out to be some sloe gin from a few Christmases back. After pouring herself a generous slug, she wobbled over to the couch. Her laptop sat open and while pulling the computer towards her, she took a messy slurp of the ruby drink. A small splash of gin landed on the Google logo. She had to close one eye to get the words in the right boxes.

Fl y tostralia

Persisting, Caitlin took another swig, furrowed her brow and prodded at the keyboard deliberately with a single forefinger.

Flights acomodaton austrlia

She hiccupped, and hit 'enter'.

*

A dry mouth and a text message from Jan woke Caitlin. It was too early for her hangover to have kicked in properly, but when she moved her head from the pillow, she could feel it coming.

'Oh god,' she said into her sheets.

Her words smelt like sloe berries. It turned out hangovers at forty were just as rough as hangovers at thirty-nine. Caitlin made her way slowly down the stairs and methodically worked through water, ibuprofen and hot buttered toast. It was only then that she checked Jan's message.

Darling. We are too old to drink like that.

Caitlin typed her reply slowly.

I know. I am dying. But it was a lovely evening, thank you.

A second ping from Jan? Unusual. Caitlin tried to remember if she'd cried last night.

Can't believe your midnight call! House offer a wonderful gesture — M. delighted. Thanks again. Speak soon love you x

Very slowly, brain catching up to the message she had just received, Caitlin opened the recent calls window on her phone: 12.03 am, FaceTime to Jan. She hit 'Information', and it showed the call had lasted six minutes. Five and a half minutes too long for a pocket-dial.

Caitlin's throat was closing over. She placed the phone carefully beside the toast crumbs and found her laptop, which was resting under a couch cushion. Pulling it open she saw the email sitting, bold and unread, at the top of her inbox:

Booking Confirmed: Your stay at Bluewater Cottage.

No.

Netjet Tax Invoice and Booking Confirmation.

No. NO. It was coming back to her in a slow, gin-soaked wave. The merry back-and-forth on the Live Chat with the very helpful accommodation coordinator. *Have you been to Australia before?* they had typed out. And, later, *What time is it in England?*

The flights. The house. The call to Jan. 'I'll be gone for eight weeks!' Jesus. Had she been slurring? Surely it was illegal to sell a flight to a drunk woman? Then, the thought that made her actually retch: Paul. Caitlin rushed back to the counter and grabbed her phone. She scrambled her fingers to her messages and ... relief. She hadn't texted Paul. Oh, thank god. Because yes — committing to a mini-emigration while under the influence was bad, but it wasn't as bad as sloppily texting your ex when you're full of dairy, nuts and craft gin. All Caitlin wanted was to go back to bed and lie still in a dark room waiting for the drugs to make her brain feel less swollen. But she knew time was against her. She wrapped a blanket around her shoulders and settled in with a grimace at the kitchen table. She needed to get cancelling. The problem was that the people she had sent her money to were now asleep, probably in a hammock between two gumtrees listening to kangaroos snore.

Australia. AUSTRALIA. Why couldn't she have become blackout drunk and spent her money on Barbados? Or even the Hebrides? She still had the posh hotel tabs open on her browser for god's sake!

After firing off two emails that she hoped sounded firm and not at all panicked, Caitlin stood up again and opened the fridge, even though she knew it only contained bone broth and cheese. Good lord, what *had* she been thinking? She knew the answer to that — she had been thinking of nothing at all. Just feeling. Feeling Paul's words when he told her about the stars. Feeling the silence in the house as the heating finally shut down for the night and the windows relinquished themselves to the midnight cold. Feeling the hideous reality of being alone, alone, alone. Feeling with surprise that the gin bottle was empty and she'd just spent a good wedge of her inheritance on BUSINESS. CLASS. FLIGHTS. Caitlin retched again.

There was nothing else she could do until Australia woke up. She had a shower, got into clean trackies and contemplated Mrs Maloney's hedge from her bedroom window. She should go for a walk, breathe in the cold air and tell herself it was all going to be okay. Her phone buzzed.

Hi. Are you home? I need to grab some things.

Paul. She looked down at the grey tracksuit pants, which, technically, were his. Sigh — now she would definitely have to leave the house. He followed with another message.

Can you be there in half an hour? For a chat?

Double sigh — now she'd have to stay home *and* change her trousers.

They hadn't seen each other since the night he'd walked out. There had been the obligatory text messages, and the cologne ghost in the hall. And, of course, there was also the almost constant communication between people they were paying to talk to each other on their behalf. Lawyers. Paul had been adamant that the 'sooner they tidied up the separation, the better'. She hadn't even told him about the inheritance: Neil had said not to. Jan hadn't mentioned it to him either, thankfully. But the big questions remained unanswered, like 'Why?' and 'Did you ever love me?' and 'How is every day different for you, now you've escaped?'

However, they weren't really unanswered, because there was nothing to answer: Caitlin hadn't asked.

'Questions are for spies and gossips,' Dot used to say. Caitlin had spied a little, since Paul's departure. Glanced in his bedside drawer. Half-heartedly run her hands along the pressed shirts still hanging in his wardrobe. But that was dull enough. And so, she just couldn't muster the energy to dig through his rationale for leaving her. She missed him being there, she felt left behind, but she didn't feel betrayed and most definitely didn't feel curious. Which, even she would admit, was odd. The doorbell rang, though he still had a key.

Once inside, Paul followed her into the kitchen and they stood awkwardly on either side of the bench. If Paul noticed the empty sloe gin bottle in the sink, he didn't let on. She offered tea, like he was a visiting plumber. He declined.

'How have you been?' Paul looked concerned, even though she'd had time to brush her teeth and her hair. Maybe he had noticed the gin bottle.

'Fine.' Her arms were crossed.

'My lawyer said you weren't working? What happened?'

'I quit.' *Never explain.*

Paul's reaction showed that he already knew that. Jan must have been updating him, at least about some things, on the side. Caitlin didn't mind, it took the pressure off her. As he raised his eyebrows, his voice went up too.

'Good! They … didn't deserve you.'

Caitlin was uncomfortable in the presence of this small olive branch. She didn't want to understand the new rules of their new relationship. Paul as a supportive pal, but also a bloke shagging another woman? She chewed at her finger and looked at the man she'd been married to for almost ever. He'd grown dark-blond stubble that felt intentional. It made him look much more handsome, but only objectively so. She didn't want to consider that she'd ever actually been attracted to him. Caitlin wondered how long it would take to forget what he looked like naked. He spoke again; his voice back to its normal pitch.

'I … I feel I owe you some explanation, Caitlin. The other night was — it didn't happen the way I wanted it to.'

Caitlin laughed. 'I could say the same.'

Even though her joke made him wince a little, he looked less uncomfortable than earlier. He continued, 'Laura and I are going to be living together. We have known each other for just over a year now. We are' — he cleared his throat pompously and suddenly Caitlin wanted to fly at him with a hundred knives — 'we are in love.'

'You don't need to talk to me like I'm your teenage daughter, Paul. You fucked someone else. Now you love her. I get it.'

Wow. So this was how she was going to feel? Her words had come out before she'd had a chance to vet them. Maybe the hangover had loosened her internal edit switch. Paul, weirdly, looked relieved. She was playing the correct part now — reading from the script he'd rehearsed.

Paul went on. 'I know this must feel completely out of the blue. And you deserve a proper explanation. I'm, we're, we want to make it —'

Oof. That hurt. The 'we'. She felt a bit dizzy about how quickly she'd been kicked off Team We. She swallowed the bile that was rising and couldn't tell if it was gin or shock.

Caitlin spoke evenly, interrupting — but calmly. 'I don't want an explanation, Paul, and I really don't want it from you *and* … "*Laura*".' She put finger quotes around 'Laura'. It didn't make any punctuative sense, but it felt good. The bile dipped away.

'Well,' Paul said, '"Laura" is Laura Conrad. We — erm — work together.'

Half a dozen women flipped through Caitlin's head, like a speed-round of Guess Who. *Laura, Laura.* Brown hair? Pink cheeks? Glasses? Oh. *Laura.*

'Jesus, Paul. You fucked one of the partners?'

'Stop saying "fuck", Caitlin.'

'Stop fucking your boss, Paul!'

He looked exasperated, but self-consciously so. He raked (yes, *raked*) his hand through his hair and — did she catch him eyeing off his reflection in the stove's splashback?

'Caitlin, this isn't helping. I wanted to have a productive conversation. Where we talk about our feelings, and what we want to do with them. But, as always, it's impossible for you.'

He moved his hands like an auctioneer. Her hangover had settled into the base of her neck and was scooping hollows out behind her eyes. Caitlin looked at the man across from her, wearing a T-shirt that was tighter than anything he'd worn this century, and suddenly felt very tired. She needed to go back to sleep.

'Paul. Don't explain. Don't tell me how you fell in love with another person while you, while *we*, were living a life. I don't think I want to hear it. We'll sell the house, we'll split the money, we'll pretend fifteen years didn't happen.'

He shook his head sadly, saying softly, 'Caitlin, stop.' It wasn't a plea, it was pity, and his voice was full of it. 'Being this tough isn't impressive, it's the opposite. When are you ever going to take down that armour?'

She stood up straight and clapped her hands together. Armour — what an excellent idea. Caitlin put on her Work Voice. 'Right. Did you need to pick anything up, because I've got stuff to do.' He wasn't moving. She crossed her arms again. 'Please, Paul, I mean this nicely, but can you go away now?'

Paul stood straighter and looked directly at her. His face had shifted and he looked scared. Caitlin felt those now familiar butterflies swarm back.

'There's one other thing. Caitlin, uh — I don't know how to say this.'

Oh. Shit.

Later, as she lay on the bedroom floor, she thought about what it felt like to hear, 'I don't know how to say this' from the husband who'd already left her. To hear those words and know something much, much worse was coming. And it was.

'Laura's pregnant, Caitlin. We are having a baby.'

Chapter Six

'It's fabulous,' Jan had said to her, when she'd sheepishly admitted to her sister-in-law that she'd bought a Business Class ticket. 'You know you'll be the only one in the cabin who actually paid full fare — everyone else'll be on points and corporate hoo-has. Eat and drink everything. Where do you keep your vacuum cleaner?'

Jan, Marigold, Biscuit, Christopher and Arthur had all moved into Caitlin's (and Paul's) house that morning. Caitlin stood at the doorway to the kitchen and watched another family settle themselves into her home. She wasn't sad to leave it, it had never felt entirely hers anyway. Now it didn't feel like hers at all.

'How long are you away for, Aunty Caitlin?' Christopher walked past her carrying two bin bags of dirty washing, and a football.

'Eight weeks!' She sounded as surprised by this as she felt. She followed him into the laundry. 'It's summertime in Australia —'

'Will you be surfing?' Christopher sounded enthusiastic for the first time in ages. She felt sorry to disappoint him.

'No, but I have rented a beach house. It's practically on the water.'

He turned to her with a softness in his eyes that she hadn't seen since he was a gentle little boy, sitting on her lap. 'I'm sorry about you and Uncle Paul. I'm really sorry.' Caitlin hugged him and he smelt of liquorice and fresh mud. He even hugged her back.

'Champagne, orange juice?'

The flight attendant was leaning over Caitlin while depressed-looking Economy passengers squeezed behind him, continuing their way down the aisle. Caitlin was experiencing self-consciousness and entitlement at the same time. Maybe this was what privilege felt like, she considered, as the bubbles tickled her nose.

Enya played over the hum of the aircraft noise. Caitlin tried to be subtle as she checked out the people settling into the cabin around her. It was more 'Isle of Wight ferry' than 'cocaine on the Concorde'. Families with children already locked on screens, two older ladies with clip-on earrings, and a lot of business shirts. There was one couple at the front of the cabin giggling to each other over their lowered privacy screen. She had a brief image of Paul and Laura quaffing Bloody Marys and selecting matching in-flight movies. She finished her champagne too quickly.

Paul had left their marriage in one evening and she'd shrugged it off like a bad finale to a good television show: it was disappointing, but not unexpected. Yes, she'd been hit with a brutal shock of abandonment, but her overwhelming sense was simply one of … inevitability.

However, the news that her husband would be a parent and she would not was confusing in a quiet, haunted way. Realising Paul was having a baby with someone else was the feeling of seeing someone fall over in public. It was horrible, obviously — but there was also the relief that it wasn't her. No, Caitlin realised, it wasn't the baby that was breaking her heart — it was the betrayal. Every time she thought of Paul walking out of the house for the second time, she felt woozy with psychic pain. Caitlin was left with the realisation that two people were connected to each other in a way she'd never experience. He'd handed that news to her and she couldn't carry it. It was too much.

After he'd left, it was all she could do to get herself up the stairs and into her bedroom. She lay flat on the cream carpet, her cheek against the wool pile. Her mouth gaped like a dying fish, deep rasping breaths fell in and out of her. *That* was the night her marriage ended. That was the night that Caitlin felt something that was deep and cruel and very, very painful.

When she had woken up the next morning, she felt calm in a blessedly numb way. Her sloe gin hangover had been replaced by something much more insidious. It was the hangover of feeling something too deeply. It was a sensation she hadn't had in a long time. She resolved quickly to never experience a night like the last again. That day, Caitlin doubled-down on her trip to Australia. This time, there had been no gin involved at all.

'Never too early, eh?'

The voice came to her more closely than a stranger's should, and it was startling. Her seat-mate had settled beside her, and was smiling over the grey privacy screen between them. Unfortunately this one was not raised either. Caitlin channelled her grandmother whenever strangers spoke to her. Paul used to call it her 'Dot Face'. She gave the man in a pale pink business shirt a tight-lipped smile.

He lifted his champagne glass. 'Only two places I drink before midday — the aeroplane and the golf club!' He had the ruddy, tanned face of someone who had hobbies outside of the house.

Caitlin did the tight-lipped thing again. Smile. Nod. Wait for him to go away.

'So, all the way down under — business or pleasure?'

Didn't he know the number one rule of flying? Plane chat was only allowed in the *final* fifteen minutes of the journey, when everyone had brushed their teeth and was feeling happy about escaping the flatulent air.

'Neither.'

'Okay then! International woman of mystery! I'm off for my sister's wedding. Bit of business on the side so the tax man can help me out with the flights — HA!'

Caitlin jumped for the second time. This man had also just broken the second, and third rules of flying — no sudden movements or explosive sounds. She was going to have to nip this in the bud. She straightened her shoulders and lengthened her neck in a way that Dot would have approved.

'How lovely for you. Enjoy your flight.'

She hadn't finished speaking before she pressed the button to raise the divider up past his face. If this is what being a solo traveller was, she was not excited at all. The partition moved slowly enough for her to see his eyes widen at her impoliteness. As the screen finished its ascent, she nearly waved goodbye, but remembered the twenty-two hours ahead of them. Instead, she distracted herself with her phone, bringing up the rental listing for the house she'd soon be calling home.

Arana Bay Beauty, it read, over the photo of a pale stuccoed unit set back from a long, white beach. It wasn't a house she'd normally choose, but she also wouldn't normally book accommodation 15,000 kilometres away while on the wrong side of half a dozen drinks. Her preference was for unique, characterful buildings. Instead, this was a cookie-cutter house with motivational wall decor and nautical-themed upholstery. There was a piece of driftwood hung on the wall with the words 'Vitamin Sea' painted on it. She suspected somewhere else in the house a cushion read, *Wine Not?* Her drunken self clearly had different aesthetic desires. Thankfully, the manager, Tracey, hadn't been put off by the inebriated email that had arrived from the middle of an English night (thank god for autocorrect). Tracey had replied confirming her 'middle season' reduced rate. Middle season? Caitlin had researched the average temperatures for February in Victoria, Australia. She couldn't believe 30 degrees wasn't high season, but the rental total said otherwise and Caitlin confirmed the booking she'd drunkenly made.

'Arana Bay!?'

Oh god. She flipped her phone face down on her leg and looked up at her seat-neighbour. He was standing over his chair, arms stretched into the overhead locker. This time she didn't bother with a smile, tight-lipped or not. She feigned ignorance.

'Hm?'

Finally, he had the sense to look abashed. 'Couldn't help but notice, on your phone — Arana Bay — is that where you're going? Lovely place.'

She was momentarily distracted from her irritation. 'You know it?'

'Only because I've had a client out that way. It's pretty bloody remote. Like everything in Oz.'

Caitlin had ignored the part where Tracey had told her it was a three-hour drive from Melbourne airport. Maybe she should have looked into a train rather than hired a car called a Kia Mentos. Or a Gesic. Or a Seltzer. Caitlin had a headache. The man was still talking.

'Yah. I remember now. "The Retreat" No. "The House?" Run by another Englishman. You heard of it?' The ruddy man sat down and plonked his finger firmly atop the privacy divider between their two chairs, cheerfully sliding it down like bread into a toaster.

* * *

When Paul was home, and not travelling, was when he and Caitlin did what they did best as a couple: not much. By 7 pm both of them had slipped into various forms of loungewear and were lying on their sofa — stretched out, tail to tail, and gently arguing over what to watch. It didn't matter, really. As soon as the show was on, they'd both be multiscreening. Paul on his laptop (emails) and Caitlin on her phone (memes). Once in a while they'd take it in turns to ask the other, 'Are you actually watching this?' before going back to their glowing devices. The one show that managed to keep them both focused was *Elite Spaces with Skye St Clair*, a series on BBC Two that stickybeaked into architecturally significant buildings around the world. Even though he called the series 'pretentious' and the host 'toothy', Paul liked to critique the rooms.

'Check out the render — it looks like a skin condition!'

Caitlin liked to laugh with Paul, and also secretly dream of working in a building with an 'indoor-outhouse', or sleeping in a bedroom with a 'vertical cloud forest'.

There was an episode they'd watched sometime last year in which the host drove along an Australian highway. Caitlin had thought briefly of her mother, something she was doing more often these days. A wide drone shot opened up the segment, taking in the colours and the waves and the vast, vast sky. But it was the building at the middle of the episode that was unlike anything Caitlin had ever seen. Set in the green scrub of the southern Australian coast, it was a hotel, carved deep into sandy stone. Flowing lines and reflective walls made it difficult to tell where the building ended and the bush began. Inside, black stone and dark timber made for an inky space that Caitlin watched with fascination. Skye St Clair visited in winter, and opened her story next to a fire burning low in a sleek suspended fireplace.

'Here at The Lodge, the guests are ostensibly hosted as a writer's retreat, but they welcome anyone in need of respite.' Skye had smiled as she said this, like she knew a secret the building had told her. Caitlin was captivated. She found the retreat online and bookmarked the page. It was a year later when she drunkenly pulled it up and searched for the nearby town. If someone built something so magical called Arana Lodge, then surely nearby Arana Bay couldn't be that bad?

* * *

'Ah!'

She was becoming used to her seat-mate's exclamations now, so she only jumped a little. Take-off had happened and the seat-belt sign was off and he was still talking. They were on a first-name basis by now. She knew, because he had said, 'We're on first-name basis!'

He was Edward ('Call me Eddie') and she was … Fiona (it just came out, she had never lied about her name before). They were eating tiny salads in tiny bowls and drinking gin and tonics. She was beginning to enjoy herself. Maybe this was what Stockholm syndrome felt like.

'Arana Lodge! That's what it's called! I worked with the owner. Charles. Charlie. Good man. Bit odd. We did some global support for his holding company. Ah — here we are — can't go wrong with a good piece of steak, Fiona! Shall we have the burgundy?'

Charles. So he was the man who commissioned the most beautiful building she'd ever seen. She doubted he'd ever lain on his bedroom floor and cried, and then had to pick bits of carpet wool from his lips. Caitlin tried to butter her bread roll with the semi-frozen spread. Did everyone have thoughts that overlapped like hers were messing around right now? Someone had taken up all the fences in her head and every thought was mingling with every other one. Memories running through paddocks where they didn't belong.

After two films, two miniature bottles of red and two helpings of cheese, Caitlin finally said goodnight to Edward and pressed the magic button that turned her chair into a bed. She was cocooned. Alone. Lying in the grey pod, her feet encased at one end and her head the other. If she'd been claustrophobic this would have been triggering, but instead she felt safer than she'd felt for a long time. The white noise of the engines droned on, her eye-mask cut out the last of Edward's light and the intoxicating privilege of sleeping flat on an aeroplane were all better sleeping aids than any of the drugs Jan had tried to pack in her carry-on.

Caitlin was woken up at some indeterminate time by alarmingly strong turbulence. She wasn't a frightened flier, but the wine and the exhaustion and Edward had worn off and there she was — feeling very small and rather scared. Like a cork being tossed about the ocean, Caitlin suddenly saw a vision of herself from far above the plane — through the clouds and the contrails she could spy herself in her bed. Tiny, lost and very, very alone. She saw Paul's hand coming over from the adjoining seat, warm and steady and safe. She heard her grandmother's voice say 'Oh, Caitlin'. She cried a little, tears beading on the nylon blanket. It wasn't until hours later when the lights of the cabin faded up that Caitlin realised she must have been dreaming it all.

A crackly voice entered the cabin as they bumped onto the tarmac. 'Welcome to Melbourne. The local time is just gone 11 am on Thursday, 25th January.'

Caitlin had never flown anywhere where the date had to be confirmed, as well as the time.

'The outside temperature is a mild 21 degrees Celsius. For your own safety please do not ...'

The back of her skull felt mushy. She couldn't imagine getting into a car and driving anywhere, let alone for three hours. Someone nearby was calling a woman named Fiona.

'Fi! Fiona!'

Oh, yes.

'Yes.'

Now they were back on ground she felt more comfortable engaging with Eddie. He'd scrubbed his face in the bathroom and smelt of liquid soap and aftershave.

'Onwards journeys, eh? Here's my deets.' He handed a dog-eared business card over to her. 'Tell me Fiona, what is it you're doing out here again?'

She looked at the card absently. 'Adventures.'

'Adventures?'

'Adventures and … things. And you can call me Caitlin.'

Chapter Seven

Caitlin was edging into her thirty-fourth hour of travel and the woman on the sat nav with the flat Australian accent was telling her, 'You should arrive in about one hour and ten minutes.' So far Caitlin's impression of Australia was an almost empty airport where the air smelt of rain, and then endless suburbia with spiky names like Cardinia and Wantirna. Now, however, the strip malls and car yards had faded into rural properties with yellow grass and brown hills. Fences and electrical wires seemed to run with her freeway-fast car, undulating and shimmering outside her window. Now she was away from any buildings, the big blue sky was falling open before her, white clouds hanging like water-heavy cotton balls. Caitlin sped through a blur of green dust and the car was filled with the scent of warm straw and fresh grass. In her rearview mirror she glimpsed a ride-on mower. She would have missed the turn if the voice hadn't told her. Which was the point, she ruminated, as she merged onto another long, straight freeway with an only slightly slower speed limit. She was starting to doubt her directionally focused friend when she realised that now the smell of the sea was creeping through the car's air vents. Caitlin wound the window down and was hit with the full force of a buffeting onshore wind. She was nearly there.

*

Scrub. Low, grey-green scrub accompanied her as she rolled into Arana Bay. The freeway had narrowed from four lanes, to two, to one single strip with faded white lines. Sand had been whipped over the road, from the beach she assumed was on the other side of the bushes. It created ocelot-yellow markings on the black bitumen. Caitlin had no idea what time of what day it was. The sun was high, the sky a belting blue. She tried to remember when she'd last drunk any water. The navigation took her on a left turn up a steep hill, where the roofs of houses peeked over yet more pale, foreign foliage.

'You have arrived at your destination.'

As she turned the engine off, Caitlin leant toward the windscreen and tried to see her rental, looking for something that resembled the images she had clicked through back on the sofa in London. There were no trees shielding the home from the street. Because there was no home. Just a block, covered in a freshly poured concrete slab decorated with orange bunting strung between what appeared to be newly embedded steel posts. She couldn't process what she was looking at. There was a knock at her passenger window. Caitlin shrieked.

Standing by her little car was an enormous man carved from wood. At least, that's the only way Caitlin could make any sense of his form. He stepped away at her cry, and she saw that everything about him was a ruddy, mahogany colour — from the calves that ascended like tree trunks out of his steel-capped boots, to his fingers — which, despite being bratwurst sized and shaped, delicately held a lit cigarette between thumb and forefinger.

'G'day.' His voice was low and warm.

'Hi!' Hers was neither of those things. She sounded British and alarmed. Impressive, for one syllable. As she spoke, she made an awkward show of getting out of the car. 'Ah. Hi. Yes. Is this number eleven —' She checked her phone and realised for the twentieth time since landing that she had no internet. It came to her. '— eleven … Neptune Court?'

'Yup.' He sucked on his cigarette so hard she could hear the filter crackle.

'Right … ah … okay. I have rented this house.' She waved in the direction of the Portaloo sitting by the block. 'I mean, I rented a house. At this address.' With every syllable she gesticulated more broadly at the empty block, her palm open. The sun was getting hotter. She was worried she sounded like she was talking to someone who didn't speak English.

Another crackle. This time, it seemed to come from inside the mahogany builder.

'Yeah, nah. We demo-ed last week slab went down yesterday where ya from?'

Shit. Shit shit shit. Had she been scammed*? Jesus. Had she just burnt more of Dot's money? Paul wouldn't have let this happen.*

'You alright, love?' He looked genuinely concerned for her, his face open in an unselfconscious way she didn't recognise.

She was back. Eyebrows up. Smile on.

'Yes. Yes! All fine. Little mix-up, I think. Is there a local —' She paused. She was beginning to realise she had flown thousands of kilometres to a town without a centre to ask after. 'I think I need the internet.'

'Orright head back down the hill chuck a left on the main road and you'll be at the Store in a few k's there's a phone and, er …' He looked her. Wrinkled blue shirt and torn jeans. Eyes bleary with lack of sleep. Gravy stain on her lapel. '… anything else you need. Sorry 'bout the house.'

There was only one car parked outside the General Store, and she pulled in next to it. 'The Store' was a double-fronted timber shop with a corrugated iron awning, painted in wide brown and cream stripes. The bottom half of the windows were covered with yellowing posters advertising newspapers and ice creams and fishing tackle. There was a petrol bowser that looked like it hadn't been used since unleaded was introduced. Clustered around a bench by the door were half a dozen teenage boys, wearing mullets and smirks. Caitlin hadn't seen hair like that since Scott and Charlene's wedding and she forgot until too late that she was staring.

'G'day, gorgeous!' It came out in a pubescent squeak. The boy winked at his mates as they all snuffled into their milkshakes. One of them held a vape uncertainly, as if it might explode.

In the short drive from Neptune Court, Caitlin had recovered herself from the — frankly, pathetic — performance in front of the timbery builder. Dot would have been ashamed to see such a wobbly display of vulnerability. Caitlin was not that person and she certainly didn't intend to begin being that person in this town. She stopped in front of the gaggle and slowly lifted her finger to point at the winker. She held his eyes with hers and spoke in a quiet, deliberate voice. 'No.'

He paled and the rest of them shrunk a bit and suddenly she saw the flash of a nine-year-old boy in his eyes. She felt a little guilty but turned away before he could notice, parting the PVC strips draping the doorway and entering the shop.

Inside, the Store was marvellous. It was cool and big and dark. Round straw baskets were collected on a series of benches, filled with broad beans and garlic and dirt-flecked potatoes. Shelves were crammed full of food with labels she only half-recognised, and a quietly humming fridge in the back glowed with golden dairy.

A stack of newspapers. Sweets. A rotating stand of children's hats and plastic beach buckets. A cardboard box of tennis balls. In the front corner, a table held books piled around a makeshift sign: a paper bag stuck on a chopstick. *WE'RE FREE!*, someone had written in a scratchy marker pen. Everywhere smelt of suncream and sugar and fresh coffee. Caitlin felt a little knot undo itself from her spine.

'Hello.'

Behind the broad timber counter stood a man. He had quite a lot of snow-white hair and almost-as-white teeth against a relaxed tan. Caitlin heard jazz playing on a paint-spattered radio next to the cash register.

'Hi,' Caitlin said. 'I'm in a bit of a bind.'

He smiled and wiped his hands on the tea towel slung over his shoulder. He reminded her of a bartender in a saloon. Or a catalogue model from the nineties. He was handsome in a lantern-jawed way that could sell a thousand cable-knit cardigans.

'Yes, I hear. Neptune Court? Sounds like someone's mucked up somewhere.' He spoke in the rolling way wealthy English people do. Oh god. A *Brit*. How had she managed to fly all the way around the globe to find a member of the Landed Gentry?

'Well, word travels fast.' She tried not to let her lips purse. Caitlin was annoyed he already knew about her predicament. But she realised that she would have to be nice to this posh shop man, as it seemed she'd arrived at the smallest town in the world without somewhere to stay. She also wondered who the winking boy outside belonged to, and whether she'd need to apologise for her pointing.

The man was coming out from behind the counter and Caitlin took a step back. With embarrassment she noticed that he was wearing a crumpled linen shirt, an identical blue to her own. She didn't like being A Type. He held out his hand; he was so tall she had to reach up, like a child.

'Charles.' His accent made it sound like his name was *Czars*. 'Call me Charlie.'

Oh my god. Eddie's brawny voice came back to her: 'I worked with the owner. Good man, bit odd.'

'Hello. I'm Caitlin. I am —'

He finished her sentence for her. 'In a bit of a bind?'

He really did sound like a minor royal, and held himself with the casual ease that privilege afforded people. Charles continued, 'Yes. Scotty said you might need a hand. I don't suppose you've spoken to Tracey yet?'

'Tracey? Yes. I rented the house from her — sorry — are you ...?' She intentionally trailed off, hoping he would follow the conversational rules and fill her silence by telling her why this was any of his business.

Charles smiled again, his face all-knowing and twinkly, 'Am I ...?'

Oh god, was he flirting? *Right. Sod this.* Caitlin began to fold up the wrinkled sleeves of her shirt and smiled, politely — which was the rudest way to smile, when you thought about it. She took a breath.

'My name is Caitlin Falstaff. I've rented a property from Tracey and it seems to have been knocked down. I've just arrived from the UK, I'm a little tired and my phone isn't working.' She closed her eyes. Opened. And said, in a way that was as far removed from flirtation as possible, 'Charles. Would you be able to help me?'

It didn't come across like a question.

Half an hour later, Caitlin was sitting on a stool at the Store's counter with a cup of tea. She was holding Charles's phone in one hand and an old biro in the other. He had retreated to the other side of the counter and was painting epoxy glue on a fishing rod. The radio continued to toot and swing in the background.

The WhatsApp chat with Tracey had been brief, but to the point. Yes, Caitlin was correct: the house had been demolished. Yes, if Caitlin insisted, that was both irritating and probably illegal, given Caitlin had paid a significant deposit upfront. Oddly, Tracey hadn't actually apologised. Instead she had made it seem like this was a challenge that she and Caitlin were going to solve, together. And they had.

Caitlin sipped her tea. Good god, that was a wonderful cuppa. She looked up from the phone to see Charles resting his tall frame on the bench, watching her as he picked glue from his fingers.

'All sorted then?'

She smiled, more genuinely this time. The tea was working.

'Yes. Thank you. It seems Tracey's overseas and — well — I'm not sure I'll ever receive an explanation or …' She stopped herself. From what she already knew of this town, Tracey might very well be Charles's sister.

'You won't get an apology from Tracey. She's finding herself in Bali because she's found herself down here so many times, no-one's that interested in helping her make any more discoveries.' He chuckled in a way that made Caitlin understand he was certainly not related to Tracey.

In the brief time she had spent with Charles, Caitlin had established he was a man who knew almost everything about 'the Bay', as he referred to it. He'd also offered her a room in his 'digs', which sounded as schoolboyish as it did self-effacing, chiefly because Caitlin knew his 'digs' had nineteen rooms and six architecture awards. If Paul was with her, they'd have leapt at the chance to experience The Lodge up close. But Caitlin found herself exhausted at the prospect of more small talk with strangers. She needed solitude.

Charles continued, with a more sympathetic tone than she probably deserved. She was getting the impression she wasn't the first stray who'd wandered through his door. 'That is rotten about the house, Caitlin. You sure Trace's sorting you out, though?'

Caitlin glanced back at the phone, where she'd typed a new address into the search bar. Tracey, owner of the now-dubiously named Arana Bay Chic Rentals had said the replacement property was 'not normally on the market in February'. But going by the map it seemed to be in a well-placed spot, certainly closer to the beach than Neptune Court. Unfortunately, though, Google's Street View cameras hadn't yet made it that far into Arana Bay.

'Yes, she has actually. It's on …' Caitlin checked the address again '… Back Road?'

Charles stood up straight. It was the first time she'd seen his face move in a way that didn't seem rehearsed.

'Bloody hell. She's given you The Cicada House.'

Chapter Eight

Caitlin had never been this far from her own time zone before. Well, not in living memory. She didn't like the sensation of the sun closing the day down, while her body was only just waking again. By the time she pulled up to the woven wire gate, the sky was paling towards evening and the birds were getting noisy. Charles had assured her Tracey was directing her to a real house, that still had walls. And a roof. But now she was here, standing in front of a fence so overgrown she could barely make it out along the unpaved road, she didn't feel so confident. The gate was clearer. It had once been white, but its steel scrolls had faded back to flat metal. The hinges had sunk into the sandy soil, which contained just enough gravel to suggest that once there had been a driveway. Caitlin heaved it up and open, grunting with the effort. For some reason it made her feel teary.

Back in the car, she pulled into the drive and carried slowly along through the tea tree and spotted gums, branches cracking dully beneath her wheels. And then, just around a bend, stood a house.

The Cicada House. It looked as innocuous as the name didn't suggest. Driving from the Store, she'd imagined a golden timber hangar on stilts. Or a speckled mud-brick bunker with porthole windows. Yes, she'd watched too many episodes of *Elite Spaces*.

The house that stood before her wouldn't have made it onto a BBC-funded architectural docuseries. It wouldn't have made it to the window of a local real-estate agency.

Caitlin was looking at a pale green fibro cottage with a low-pitched corrugated iron roof and three stout, square windows. The sills and door were picked out in a faded teal that once may have been closer to cornflower blue. A screen door hung open over a modest concrete porch, the front door closed behind it. It was the house a child might draw. It was the house that someone would come home to from a faraway war. It was not the beach house Caitlin had imagined, all those miles away in England. But then it couldn't have existed anywhere except amid the salt and eucalypt of the southern Australian coast.

The block seemed enormous, and the house felt small, set between two heavy-branched gum trees. Muted greens and greys of ragged scrub finished only a few feet from the front porch, leaving just enough space for what used to be lawn.

She had a bag of groceries Charles had forced into her passenger seat when she, jet-lag woozy, was trying to remember how to start the engine. Caitlin left that and her luggage in the car and picked her way through the leaf litter, up the two porch steps. Tracey had told her the key was under 'the flower pot shaped like a frog', but there was nothing in front of her except a scattering of crunchy leaves and an abalone shell that had once been used as an ashtray. A low decorative railing lined the porch, the rusted iron festooned with spiderwebs.

Caitlin would discover later that this thirties shack with a sixties extension used to be promoted by Tracey as an expensive 'Retro Beach Rental' during the high-summer season. For now she didn't need the internet to tell her that this house had not been occupied for some time.

As the sky turned orange Caitlin continued around the perimeter, trying to ignore the rooms on the other side of the windows, afraid of what she might see. Instead, she focused on her footsteps and searching for places where a frog-shaped flowerpot might sit. Out the back of the house there was a garden that hadn't become completely grown over: a good spread of buffalo grass that held a Hills Hoist and an old swing set. Guarding the lawn was a creaky old lemon tree, and a smaller, squat orange tree. Both had branches pulled low by small, sweet-smelling fruit. Behind them and all around, gnarled tea trees framed the garden and prevented her from seeing where the Cicada House's property lines actually ended.

Leading to the back door was a generous patch of crazy paving, tempting her briefly to think of BBQs and candlelit dinners. But then she saw a timber slatted door that — horrors — hung open just wide enough to reveal an outdoor loo with a hole in its roof. Over the paving hung a corrugated green fibreglass canopy, half of which was covered in winding vines — the combination of which cast everything beneath it in a Midori glow. Caitlin felt a bit nauseous.

Steadying herself on the one plastic chair standing on the paving, she closed her eyes and inhaled jasmine, and citrus, and warm soil. When she opened them again, she was looking at a cracked cement frog returning her gaze from its perch by the back steps.

Returning to the front door with a heavy key, Caitlin opened it a crack and then stopped, frozen, and stared at her feet.

Come on, Caitlin. You can bloody do this.

The Cicada House welcomed her not with a red carpet, but a short hallway laid with grass matting, and an orange pendant light hanging over her head. The house smelt strongly of mothballs and still, dust-filled air. To her right, she could see into a living room with gilt-flocked wallpaper and more crazy paving — this time, around a fireplace. Or, what had been a fireplace. Now it had a piece of chipboard covering the flue with a brown gas heater sitting in front of it. She caught a peek of an orange couch and started to feel ill again. She needed fresh air.

'Adventures and things. Adventures and things,' she whispered to herself as she walked out to collect the groceries and her luggage.

Paul had asked her once, sometime between meeting and marrying, 'Do you always talk to yourself?' She had been surprised he'd noticed. She barely did.

'My grandmother didn't like loud noises. And, well, I didn't have any siblings. I talked to myself because no-one else did.'

Paul had rolled his eyes.

The rest of the cottage was small, mostly clean and had a palette that stayed close to itself, going from brown to cream to orange and back to brown. She was living in an autumnal colour scheme in the middle of summer. A candy-corn palace. A sixties manse of memories. It was now getting dark outside and the lamps she switched on had metal beaded pull-cords that went *clink*. None of the lightbulbs were frosted so the rooms were filled with yellow light that picked up the shimmer on the wallpaper. The bathroom had hand-painted tiles with blue ducks and a mirrored cabinet smaller than her handbag. The bedroom she chose as hers had floor-to-ceiling glossy brown wardrobes with a recessed dressing table in the middle. Small blooms of desilvering decorated the edges of the mirror. Caitlin slowly unpacked the groceries in the U-shaped kitchen, placing tea bags (thank you, Charles) and sugar carefully in the pale green timber cabinets while an old fridge idled like a lorry behind her.

She had no idea what time it was. Her eyeballs were on fire. Where was her phone? Is this what dying felt like? As she spoke to herself, her rounded accent evaporated in the strange Australian air. 'It's jet lag, Caitlin, stop being so melodramatic.'

She pushed the screen door open from the kitchen and sat down on the uneven timber steps that led to the back porch's pavers. Placing her phone and a glass of water down beside her, she listened to the music of a strange garden in a strange land. The birds here were alien with song that was made to arc out over vast and empty distances, rather than burble between gardens. She heard long wails of bell calls, a short shriek from close by, and then a different bird — a foreign carolling from the trees. A brief wind made its way through the trees; Caitlin shivered in the warm air. The breeze had quieted the birds briefly and she tuned into a low rumbling that she realised was the sea. Caitlin pushed herself up and walked barefoot across the rough grass to where the clearing ended and the dense mass of tea trees began. She had missed it before, a narrow path winding away through the scrub. In the dwindling light she could only just make out spiderwebs threading across the way, strung between small purple flowers. She decided to leave exploration for the next day, when she was less likely to be attacked by something wild and poisonous and Australian.

On turning, Caitlin observed the house from the back of the garden. It sat quietly, beneath a sky now streaked with violet clouds. The windows blushed orange. From this angle she saw that the paving extended out to another, smaller patio behind the outdoor loo. Caitlin peered in the gloaming — was that what it looked like? She walked closer and saw — yes — there was a piano underneath the window, leaning between the pavers and grass. Upright, but only just, its yellow paint peeled from both ends. Ivy grew out of the lid and when she pressed a key, the only sound was a small *puh*.

A yellow piano, by an invisible beach, under a big purple sky. She felt light-headed and a bit scared and hurried to the back door. Before her mind could stop her body from being idiotic, she stubbed her toe on the step, and knocked the glass from its perch, which she leapt to grab and in that movement posted her phone neatly down between two slats of timber.

'No!' Caitlin yelled, too loudly. And again. 'No!'

It had felt good, the first bellow. To be angry about the phone that was now irretrievable beneath the deck, but also to be angry about the broken house and the outdoor loo and the fact that she was thousands of kilometres from her home and her husband. She picked up the now-chipped glass and pressed her finger into the sharp edge, the pain centring her back to the present. Under the kitchen's fluorescent strip light Caitlin noticed a fridge magnet on the blue Kelvinator. It was faded and rust-kissed, curling type sitting over blue waves: *Stay the day at Arana Bay.*

Later that evening, Caitlin sat on the back step with the kitchen glowing gently behind her. She swigged a beer, cold and yeasty, and made the twentieth mental note for the day to thank Charles for his groceries, and maybe even apologise for being a bit of a twat today. Today? Had time melted and poured back onto itself? Last week she was weeping into the floor. Last month she was folding Paul's underpants. A lump appeared in her throat. She set the beer down on the pavers and shuddered a little cry.

Where the bird calls had fallen away, the cicada calls began. All at once. How did they know? To each begin their high-pitched thrum that was noisier than anything she had ever heard before. Of course, it wasn't, but right now — as she finished her beer — it was. So loud, those hundreds of cicadas, all doing their very best to drown out her thoughts of regret.

i. Morning

I know when it's morning because the noisy one arrives. I think her name is Betty. In the beginning, when I was still really foggy, she used my name once or twice. At least, I think she did. Hard to remember anything but that voice. Chattering and chittering, so bloody loud: 'Hello, love' or 'Morning, darl'. Her voice is husky, like she gets on the fags at every break time. She doesn't smell like cigarettes though. She smells like lavender and Imperial Leather. I wish I could remember how I knew her name. Or when she first arrived.

This morning I got a whiff of toast, just a vague shadow of breakfast. Wasn't any of ours though. No-one's eating 'round here. None of us are eating or drinking or smoking.

Time passes in a way that doesn't. If that makes sense? I know. Of course it doesn't. Make sense, that is. Not much does in here. Someone's stopped the clock, that's all I can tell you. Same day in and out, and most mornings smell like Betty. A few smell like toast. And a lot smell like the type of decay that would make me retch if I could.

Maybe it's good we're not eating.

It's still early, the light outside hasn't changed too much. I can tell, don't ask me how. The world through my eyelids turns different shades of orange, depending. How can you sleep and wake up when your eyes are taped shut? Don't ask me, but you can.

'Do you think birds close their eyes when they sleep on the wing?'

My mother asked me that once. I was only young; had no idea birds slept while they flew. I spent the next few weeks eyeing them off in the sky, worried one would fall down snoring and clock me on the head.

Huh. Haven't thought of that in years.

It'll do that to you, in here. Thoughts come and go like bubbles — *pop*. Gone. There's always a bunch of them, drifting along, just out of reach. But then a big one lands on your nose and suddenly you're cross-eyed watching the rainbows swirl around the surface until —

Pop.

I wish I knew how I got here. Could work out how long I've been lying down. Maybe it's good I don't know. Thank god no-one's told me what time it is. Or day. Or month.

Or have they? I do forget things, that's for sure. I heard Betty say something the other day, something about my mother. How does she know about my mother? Wonder if I've forgotten Betty before? Sorry, Betty.

Oh, I don't like that. I can live with my broken body but leave me with my mind. No thanks. Don't like that one bit. It's best to think about the lavender and the birds and the bubbles. Best to lie here and listen to Betty say goodbye, until she's back again. In another morning. And until then I lie and I listen and I wait to die.

Chapter Nine

The pounding on the front door must have been going for some time, because Caitlin's brain had managed to integrate the noise into her dream. She was Julia Roberts and Javier Bardem was serenading her with bongos, beating the drum heads in rhythm with the door bangs. She was pretty sure they were both nude.

'Hello? Is it … Caitlin?'

There was a woman in her bedroom, who knew her name. Javier disappeared. Caitlin yelped. Pulling the duvet to her chin, she sat up wonkily and blinked at the blonde in a pair of jeans and clogs, in her doorway. The room was filled with a light brighter than anything she'd experienced before. The morning positively shimmered.

'Oh god, babe, I'm sorry — I was just getting a bit worried when you didn't come to the door.' The woman walked back down the hall, calling over her shoulder, 'I'll put the kettle on while you get yourself sorted.'

When Caitlin exited her bedroom a few minutes later, she could taste perfume and smell Nescafé. The voice carried to her. 'I don't bloody well care when the notice came home, Gary — it's your week and you can sort it.' She smiled at Caitlin over the phone tucked into her shoulder. 'Gaz, I've got to go. … Sorry. It's the ex. He's not a bad bloke, just a bit useless. Have you got any sugar?' She was already opening the kitchen cupboards. A tattoo snaked up and around an impressively defined bicep, her tanned shoulders broad in a tank top. Caitlin was fascinated by her hair. She'd never seen a shade of blonde like it.

'Erm.' Caitlin racked her brain for a Dot-ism that would suit this situation. Nothing was forthcoming. She'd have to resort to an oldie. It wouldn't really work, but — she had nothing else.

She cleared her throat. 'Have we met?'

The woman turned to her, both hands still on the cupboard door handles. 'Ah, no — we haven't met.' She spoke slowly, like Caitlin was ill. 'You feeling okay?'

Shit. Maybe Dot-isms didn't work on Australians.

'Ah! Here we go. No idea how old it is. Shouldn't matter. How many?' She held up the sugar.

Caitlin would have to be more direct. She opened her mouth, wondering what 'direct' sounded like, when the woman handed her a steaming mug of milky instant and said, 'There you are. I think you need three spoonfuls this morning. Let's have a chat, hey?'

The Cicada House's dining table was a polished wooden oval with only a few water stains. It reminded her of the sorts of places the wealthy girls at school sat at for dinner. She looked around for a coaster and when she didn't find one, held the mug awkwardly over her lap. The woman didn't seem to mind about the veneer and plonked her mug straight down, wiping a splash of coffee away with her fingers.

'I'm not sure if Charlie mentioned, I'm the agent round here.' She paused, looking with slight concern at the bleary-eyed Englishwoman sitting across from her. 'Property manager,' she clarified, speaking more slowly again.

She wasn't as young as Caitlin had first thought. The poker-straight blonde hair came from dark roots, and gentle smile-lines sat around her eyes. She was probably Caitlin's age, but she was definitely fitter than Caitlin, who self-consciously crossed her very not-defined arms.

'Anyway. My name's Erin, and Tracey gets me to help out with her rentals over the summer crazy. She takes them back from me after school hols have finished. Tight-arse.' She spoke in a series of up and down questions even though there were no questions. Caitlin liked it: she didn't have to try very hard to get carried along.

Erin continued, peering at the orange sofa. 'Trace hasn't rented The Cicada House out for years now. I used to give her a hand with it, then she took it back over. It's probably a good idea to avoid the online reviews — even Trace found them a bit hard to advertise around, eventually.' Erin took in the room. 'To be honest, I'm surprised it's not in worse shape. But, you know, it's still standing. Not like Neptune Court. Shit, eh? What a stuff-up.'

'Ah, yes. That was not ideal,' said Caitlin. She was surprised to hear how prim she sounded, particularly across the table from this woman who hummed with a quiet confidence. Caitlin cleared her throat and tried again. 'But this seems …' Caitlin moved her hand around the room, not really knowing what to say. She was seeing the house in the morning light for the first time. It was still very brown. But it managed to be light, as well. Somewhere outside another one of those birds warbled and yawned. Caitlin looked over Erin's shoulder and out the window.

Erin didn't even turn around, just sipped from her mug and said, 'Maggies.' Then clarified, 'Magpies. You've got a family of them out here. Spent much time in Australia?'

Caitlin took a big mouthful of the milky sweet drink. She'd never minded instant. It was fine, as long as you didn't expect it to be coffee. 'I was actually born here.'

That was weird. She'd never told a stranger this information. Mostly because the statement opened the door for way too many questions that she was not up to answering.

'Really? You don't sound like an Aussie.'

'No. I left when I was five. I grew up in the UK; my mother was English but she had me — here.'

Erin's eyebrows disappeared into her hairline. 'Arana Bay?' she asked.

'No! No.' *Although*, thought Caitlin, *that would make more sense.* 'I was born in Melbourne. But I don't remember it.'

'Huh.'

Erin seemed happy to receive this information, but just as happy to not pry for more. Caitlin liked her for this. She liked her overall, actually. So much that she didn't even mind about the bedroom invasion. 'What about you? Are you from —?' Caitlin was conscious of using the wrong terminology. She didn't want to feel like more of an outsider than she already did.

Erin helped her. '— the Bay? Yeah, I'm an Arana girl, born and bred. I managed to get out for a few years; I was in Sydney for most of that. But I got pregnant and needed the grandparents around if I was going to manage a kid and a job. Both sets live here — my parents and Gaz's mum.'

Caitlin was only barely keeping up. Erin was sharing more information in half a cup then Caitlin would have shared in a lifetime. 'Gaz?'

'Joshy's dad. Sorry, *Josh*. Not Joshy.' A smile edged into Erin's voice. 'My boy, he's nearly twelve now, he hates me calling him Joshy. You got kid—'

'No.' Caitlin answered before the sentence even curled up in a question. She was very good at answering that question.

Erin didn't seem to mind the abruptness. 'Well, I'm sorry for barging in unannounced this morning. Tracey's not a bad bird, but she's pretty vague and when I heard she'd rented you a building site and then buggered off to Bali — well. I just felt shithouse for you. We're running an open around the corner so thought I'd swing by first and check you were okay.'

Erin's words came out so fast, Caitlin wondered if she had to practise them first. It took her a beat to translate them in her head.

'That's nice. Thanks. It was a bit of a muddled way to arrive but I'll be able to make it work.'

'Well, like I said, I managed this place for a few summers before Trace took charge.' Erin paused, as if she'd just had a thought. 'Actually, do you want the full tour?'

Caitlin's first instinct was to always decline any offer. But she was jet-lagged and alone and suddenly words came out of her mouth: 'Oh, I really would. That's so nice. Thank you.' She had to stop telling this lady how nice she was, it made Caitlin look a bit desperate. She stood up and realised her T-shirt was on inside-out. If Erin had noticed she didn't let on.

Erin stood also and reached her arm out to display the room they were already in. Along with the shiny dining table and orange couch, there were two easy chairs with worn timber arms and seats covered in a green textured boucle. They both faced that radiator that once had been a fireplace. Caitlin wondered who would sit side by side staring at a glowing electric heater. A bookshelf filled the wall behind the chairs, containing two sets of encyclopaedias, an old wooden crucifix, guitar picks and a dusty stack of board games.

'Lounge. Bright aspect onto the front of the property.' Erin pointed at the coppery sunburst clock sitting over the fireplace. 'Retro features. All original.' Her eyes twinkled at Caitlin as she led her out into the hallway. 'Bedrooms are across the hall. You've found the main one, I see. Good storage, excellent mirrors.'

Caitlin was relieved that Erin didn't walk in uninvited for the second time that morning.

'Second bedroom. Carries onto a …' She hesitated. They were both now standing in a smaller room with two single beds. This one was also completely lined with knotted pine, including the ceiling. It gave the space a decidedly alpine feel. A Swiss chalet by the shore. A second door led from that bedroom into a small room Caitlin hadn't noticed before. From where she stood she could see the pine walls of the ante-room had been painted yellow. A small school desk sat in the corner. Erin picked up her train of thought: '… onto an office!'

Caitlin could see a mousetrap in the corner. She closed the door firmly behind them when Erin ventured back into the hall.

'To the left, bathroom — shower *and* bath.'

In her travel-tired haze last night Caitlin had missed the enormous shower head hanging over the blue-tiled bath. That was a relief.

'Excellent water pressure. Potentially cold. We can sort that, don't worry.'

'Ah. About the toilet situation,' Caitlin said.

'Yes,' Erin deadpanned. 'You'll want to watch out for spiders up your clacker.'

'Seriously. It's the only toilet? Outside? I thought maybe I'd missed the inside loo.'

'Sorry, babe, you've gone and rented yourself a true-blue, dinky-di, Aussie outside dunny.' Erin chuckled, a sound that made Caitlin feel like she was in on the joke. 'Something to write home about, eh?'

Caitlin tried not to look horrified as Erin continued back into the kitchen. She ran her hand along the timber benchtop. 'Gotta say, the house is in good nick after not being used for a few years. Maybe Tracey's had some cleaners in …' She drifted off, then interrupted herself. 'There's no dishwasher but … you're staying solo. Suggest you do what I do when Joshy's at his dad's and eat out of the tin, standing over the sink.'

Caitlin looked at Erin closely and saw that twinkle again. She liked this woman, who was now hip-and-shouldering the back door open.

'So this is sticking again.' Erin grunted. 'I know there were always a few issues with the water temp, but this door is rooted. If you need a hand with a tradie I've got a tame bloke I can send over.'

Caitlin was starting to realise she wasn't in Kansas anymore. 'Tame? Tradie?'

Erin laughed. 'A tradesman. Sorry. Forgot about you poms and our lingo.'

The door shot open with Erin's last big push. Sweet air rushed in from the morning-warm garden. There was jasmine again and the lemon blossom. Also, now, the sharp smell of dew drying on grass.

'I know, The Cicada House can seem a funny old place. The owners won't spend a lick of money on it, and Tracey doesn't encourage them. Sometimes I think she's hoping they'll just forget about it, you know, accidentally default her the house. Don't blame her, with the beach path. Have you been down to the water yet?'

'No. I don't think I even knew it was there. It's …' Caitlin was embarrassed to feel a tightness form in her throat. 'It's all been pretty last minute.' Her eyes were getting watery. The cold shower. The mice. The *outdoor cocking loo*. If Paul were here he'd have marched them both out before Erin had even made it to the lack of dishwasher. What the hell was she doing?

If Erin had noticed Caitlin's fear-frozen face, much like the T-shirt, she didn't let on. She was a kind woman. It made Caitlin feel like crying even more. Instead, Erin drained her mug and took Caitlin's, all in one impressive movement. Placing both cups on the back steps, Erin pulled off her clogs and threw them into the corner of the patio with a woody clatter.

'Well then. I need a cigarette. Wanna see your private beach?'

Caitlin followed the barefoot real-estate agent across the grass and down the path. She was watching her own step with alarm as she was also shoe-less and the ground seemed likely to be filled with crawlies hiding in the morning dew. Erin marched quickly ahead, managing to light, hold and smoke a cigarette with one hand while the other swept the spiderwebs out of their path. Caitlin watched Erin's feet glide over the ground, not stopping for sticks or stones, as the soil quickly turned to sand. She also didn't stop talking the entire way, punctuating with exhalations of blue-grey smoke as she went. Caitlin caught 'Joshy' and 'Gaz' flung over Erin's shoulder, but not much else.

Erin was right, the beach was impressively close. With every step the noise of the water grew, a shell to her ear bigger than any she'd held before.

She and Paul had beached together, of course. They had beached in Malta, sun loungers unsteady on hot grey pebbles while tinny radios shot out beats of Euro pop. They had waded in Devon, the water so cold it hurt the marrow in her bones and left her toes blue for the rest of the morning. They had even had a postcard-worthy week on the powdery white beaches of Antigua, where sandflies left a breadcrumb trail of welts around Caitlin's ankles.

But this — this beach — it wasn't like any of those. As the two women crested a small dune, the smell and the noise hit her at once. An explosion of salt and roar and fish and fizz.

'Oh,' Caitlin said softly, unheard behind the waves. 'Oh.'

They were standing on a stretch of yellow sand that banked steeply down to a wide sea. She shielded her eyes from the morning sun with her hand, peering at how the sharp shock of cloudless sky smacked into the distant horizon. Took in how the water went from far-out inky to emerald to an almost transparent-blue in the shallows nearest their toes.

She half-tripped as she followed Erin down the dune towards the water. The breeze was already gracing her cheeks with invisible salt — crystals she'd still taste much later under the shower. The sand was warm under her feet. Soft. Peppered with delicate filaments of pink seaweed and thicker straps of kelp.

It was undoubtably beautiful, but she was uneasy about the wildness of this place. Because while the waves arrived in gentle curls at the shore, she could see them breaking and broiling out in the deep. To their left, larger sand dunes were covered with shifting ripples of long, hay-coloured grass — dry and spiked and foreign. There wasn't another person as far as her eyes reached. Everything about this beach was different to the ones she'd been to before. Raw and wild. They were guests in this place. They existed for it, not it for them.

Erin bent down and put her cigarette out in the sand, carefully placing the extinguished butt in a small canister she'd pulled from a pocket. 'Remember camera film?' she asked, holding the plastic tube up.

'Yes, I do.' Caitlin recalled a sudden memory of Bill bending down to photograph her and Dot at the kitchen table, a carefully iced birthday cake sitting before them.

'Well then, mate, you and I are about the same age.' Erin laughed and squeezed Caitlin on the top of her arm, like being forty was a secret and a pleasure. 'Whaddya think of your big blue backyard?'

Caitlin tried to look less conflicted than she felt. 'It's beautiful. It is. It's just … this has all been pretty last minute.' She hoped Erin didn't notice this repeated statement was not explaining why she was acting so strangely.

Erin nodded, looking out at the foaming waves. 'Okay. It can be a bit wild and woolly out here — but if you get it on the right day, there's no better place in the world to make everything alright.' Erin smiled at her, like she knew just how much Caitlin needed to hear that.

Caitlin smiled back, gratefully.

'Right. I'm off,' said Erin. 'You'll have to come around for a wine soon. I'm getting the feeling you don't know many people around this area?'

'No. I'm alone.' Caitlin didn't mean to sound so melodramatic, but Erin didn't seem to mind.

'Well, now you've got me, and the wild ol' sea!' Erin's arm stretched out along the horizon and Caitlin found herself laughing into the wind, along with the blonde woman whooping beside her.

*

Later that night, Caitlin was asleep again in her bedroom that smelt of pine. The cicadas were silent, and in the stillness that remained, a noise wound its way to her, folding into a dream she didn't know she was having. Piano music, played ever so gently, like the person making it was holding back almost everything. She lifted her head and opened her eyes, but the music remained. It was a melody she'd never heard. Too tired to feel scared, Caitlin buried back into the pillow, and sleep took her away as the music drifted through the creaking tea tree.

Chapter Ten

In the two days since leaving England behind, Caitlin had replayed the break-up conversation with Paul over and over. The subsequent one, about babies, was too painful. She'd done a fair job of locking it away in the same place her other awful memories belonged. But the first, she could stand to re-live. Like poking at a sore tooth with her tongue, she almost couldn't stop. It was a sweet and sour pain.

What had he said? 'I can't live every day the same as every other. Awake, asleep, every goddamned day.'

It seemed like such a lie, that this man with whom she had lived a life, where predictability and repetition was their together-fortress, now wanted to destroy that same arrangement.

Awake and asleep.

'What was that, love?'

Caitlin started, shook herself back to the counter. The bank teller had deep creases around her eyes and a mulberry-red dye job that had bled into her hairline. She looked at Caitlin with concern.

'Oh.' *Caitlin, don't freak out the lady who has access to all of your money.* 'Nothing. Sorry!' She laughed, a little too loudly. The teller went back to sliding neatly stacked folds of cash into an envelope. The thick acrylic window between them muffled their words. This time she spoke up, louder now. 'Is there an internet cafe nearby?'

The teller looked up again, this time with an expression as if Caitlin had asked after the local telegram station. 'An internet cafe? I wouldn't think so, love.' She pointed out over Caitlin's shoulder, towards the street. 'The phone shop's open though.'

Caitlin emerged from the bank, using the envelope to shield her eyes from the nuclear sun. How could it be this hot at 9 am? She had reminded herself approximately a dozen times in twenty-four hours to buy a hat and some sunglasses. Who comes to Australia without a hat or sunglasses? That's what Charles's expression said, if not his words, when she had stopped by the Store just an hour ago.

'I need some money,' Caitlin had said.

'Ah. Good morning, Caitlin.' He had smiled, but there was still a flick of admonishment in his voice.

'Sorry. Good morning. Um, I can't access my phone right now. So, I don't have a map. Could you possibly point me in the direction of the nearest bank?' And then, in an afterthought, 'Please?'

Charles had sketched a few lines on the back of a paper bag which, surprisingly, had managed to direct her to town, twenty minutes away. 'Town' seemed to be a single cream brick strip of shops flanked by a shell grit supplier on one side, and a wholesale seafood outlet on the other.

Standing outside the bank now, she watched seagulls pick half-heartedly at hot chips smooshed into the bitumen at the front of a chicken shop. The smell of fuel from the petrol station next door mixed with the thick scent of donuts from a pink shop manned by uniformed teens. A carwash played nineties pop over the high-pitched whir of water pumps. Caitlin started towards the phone shop, which also seemed to be a lotto outlet and a vape supplier. She thought of Paul, almost saw him there in the periphery of her vision, and of the life she had left back in London that was feeling more distant with each hour.

I can't live every day the same as every other. Awake, asleep … I'm leaving before we both turn to dust.

It wasn't surprising, what Paul had said to her on that horrid night. She *knew* they were dusty. What was remarkable was Paul's sudden inability to live with their commitment to sameness. It was a contract she thought they had both signed — inked in permanent pen and inertia. Caitlin had always lived in dust. Dust of memories uncorroborated, of stories untold. Of silence and curtains and a grandfather clock that went *tock*. And now, to be stranded rather than anchored in this world of powder and ashes was just too painful. Caitlin kept walking, past the phone shop and back to her car. It felt safer to remain unconnected.

Returning to the cool interior of The Cicada House in this sunshine felt criminal. But her visit to town and dealing with the ins and outs of establishing some kind of existence in this unfamiliar place had left her feeling uneasy and cross. Her car had returned to the little green house like it was on rails. Inside, Caitlin rested against the closed door behind her. Her palms sweating, the feeling of isolation cementing itself, which was comforting in a horrible, predictable way. But her breath relaxed into a deep, easy rhythm more quickly than it ever had in her and Paul's soldier-straight terrace. It was as if coming back sans phone, in a state of self-enforced disconnection, pleased the house. And, in return, it graced her with safety.

'We must have tea,' she announced to the empty hall.

Caitlin rested the copper kettle on the stovetop and fiddled with a box of matches, failing to light the guttering gas twice in a row. She was talking to herself again, first in her head, *Awake and asleep. Adventures and things*; then out loud — filling the space, 'Awake and asleep.' She struck the third match, the gas flared to flame. 'Adventures and …' she burnt her finger on the match, and in the rush of pain shouted up the cobwebbed chimney over the stove '… BLOODY THINGS!'

The back screen door opened with a screech.

Caitlin found herself looking at a man, lit from behind by sun coming in from the garden. She continued shouting. This time, at him rather than the flue. 'Jesus Christ!' *Didn't anybody announce themselves in this country?*

He had dark hair that brushed his neck in bends and curls — and shoulders that filled the doorway. His eyes were brown enough to hide his pupils. His cheekbones lifted as he grinned briefly at her. 'Sorry. Needs some oil.'

Caitlin pressed her hand against her sternum and waited for the prickles of adrenaline to recede from under her arms. She was instantly furious at this bearded bloke with the impish smile terrifying her out of a lonely reverie. He was wearing faded jeans and a white T-shirt. His olive skin was tanned. He had a pair of beaten-up old work boots and — *Oh*. Her brain kicked into gear.

'You must be Erin's tradesman?' *Thank god.*

The man didn't reply. Because he'd already turned and crouched down to inspect the hinges of the decrepit screen door. Caitlin's mind decided to bring Dot into the room. *Offer him a cup of tea, Caitlin. It's what we do.*

The kettle started to whistle.

'Would you like a tea?'

A voice, through the grunting of removing the hinge: 'Nah. Hate tea.'

The thing about having a tradie in your house is you must try very hard to stay out of their way, while also having to maintain a presence, should they require you. Caitlin had poured her tea, then spent the next twenty minutes lurking in the lounge as the curly man tinkered with the back door. It was like being a Victorian maid, she decided.

When he suddenly appeared outside a nearby window, Caitlin threw herself at a lamp and pretended to fiddle with the globe.

God, she was an idiot. When she looked up, he was at the sill, watching her through the flywire with a strange look on his face.

'What are you doing?'

'Well. The lamps, I'm just … checking in on them. I've only been here a few days, you see.'

He nodded slowly, but she couldn't read his expression. Her British sensibilities couldn't stand it any longer, so she straightened and walked towards the open window, and him.

'My name's Caitlin. I'm visiting …' For some reason she couldn't complete the sentence. He looked at her with a strange stillness. He had the air of a rock star. Or a Romantic poet. Or the busker in the Finchley Road tube station.

'Caitlin. I'm David.' His Australian accent wasn't one she'd heard before. It was broad, almost rhythmic. It wasn't something she could place. She realised she was blushing a little. Paul tended to manage interactions outside of their immediate circle.

As they stood with the screen between them, the tradie haltingly raised a hand to wave and she did the same. It was awkward. At least, for her.

'Hi, David. Do you think you might do anything about the bathroom tap while you're here?'

David reached his hand behind his head and slowly rubbed his neck. He closed his eyes briefly and Caitlin felt like she was watching someone sleeping. She averted her gaze, pulling away from the intimacy she was sure they could both feel.

Pull yourself together, woman, for god's sake.

He had said something.

'Sorry, what was that?' she asked, flustered.

'I said reckon I could take a look. Toolbox still in the shed?'

Caitlin didn't know there was a shed, let alone a toolbox. She was curious, and as this David man disappeared from the open window she decided to follow, just making it outside in time to see him vanish around the corner. And yes, there was a shed, almost invisible behind a tangled cloud of jasmine. It was a small timber outbuilding leaning at an alarming angle, dropping flakes of peeling green paint like dandruff. She watched as David paused briefly with his hands on his hips, weighing up what he was seeing.

'So you've worked here before?' Caitlin said, a little too loudly.

But he'd already begun attacking the vines with his hands, pulling at the spaghettied knots like a prince in a fairytale. Soon, a door was revealed. David briefly tried the handle but it was rusted shut. He half-turned to her.

'What?'

This man's lack of manners made her teeth itch. Dot's voice needled at her. *'What' is a noise, not a question.*

BANG.

He kicked at the door so hard a small avalanche of dust fell from the roof of the shed, covering his hair and shoulders in grey snow. She said again, practically shouting this time, 'You've worked here before?'

BANG.

He kicked harder, and the door lurched open. All Caitlin could see, past David's head, was dark and shapes and spiderwebs. He turned back to her. When he smiled, the corners of his mouth lifted up in the most disarming way.

'You could say that.'

An hour and some muttering later, David exited the bathroom looking a lot more bothered than when he went in. The dust had mixed in with his sweat and he was filthy. She handed him a tea towel and he took it with a nod, wiping his face and then hands. It didn't make much difference. He looked at her under furrowed brows in a way that Caitlin found oddly irritating.

'Tap's fixed.'

'Great. Thanks so much. Are you sure I can't get you a tea, or a water, or —'

'You got a beer?'

He didn't wait for her answer, instead stepping around her and pulling open the fridge door in a move that was fluid, like a dancer's.

'I don't actually ...' She was using the tone that clearly said, *How dare you sir.*

If he'd heard her, he was pretending he hadn't. David reached in and grabbed two beers (her *last* two beers, thank you very much) and stood holding them both in one hand. Inspecting the labels, he slammed the fridge door with his foot, which caused Caitlin to jump again. With another coordinated move he flipped one of the bottle caps off using his flat palm on the edge of the counter. Beer foamed up and onto the floor. He handed her the wet bottle and opened his the same way.

Caitlin's stood, mouth agape at this performance, while David made for the back porch. She looked down at the two bottle caps on the floor, the dripping bottle in her hand, and the screen door swinging silently closed behind him. He'd fixed the hinges.

When Caitlin followed, David was standing in the middle of the lawn, face to the sky. The sun was high — it was midday now — and the day was pin-drop still. For the second time since meeting him, Caitlin watched this man with his eyes closed against the day around him. She coughed gently but he didn't move. He had clearly missed every lesson in basic human manners. She didn't know what else to do, so she remained a few feet behind him and closed her own eyes, drinking her own beer. Without the wind or the birds, all she could hear were the waves, and the cicadas, and the bubbles quietly lifting in the neck of the beer bottle.

'You're not from 'round here, are you?' His voice cut through the quiet. It was pitched deeper than anyone she'd met before. He was still facing away from her, looking out into the scrub to where the sea was hiding from them.

'Gosh, you're quick. Was it the accent that gave it away?'

She was tired of being polite to this man. He was rude, bordering on offensive, and the only reason she hadn't told him to leave was the roof above the loo was still unpatched. When he turned to her, he was chuckling. 'Fair enough. Not many limeys around these parts.'

'I thought around "these parts", we were "poms"?'

He shrugged again. 'Don't take offence, sweetheart.'

'Wow. Okay.' It was Caitlin's turn to laugh, but not in a good-humoured way.

'Jesus, settle down — I can see your hackles from here.' His hands were up like she was holding him at gunpoint. 'You 'right?'

'No. I don't like being called "sweetheart", to start with. Or having my fridge emptied by strangers. Or being told to "settle my hackles".'

'Oh — come on, darlin', don't get your knickers in a twist. I fixed the door didn't I? And the tap?'

She held her hand out to him, pitching her voice higher and more Dot-like. 'Can I take that for you, David?'

He handed his bottle over slowly, looking at her face properly for the first time that day. She took the beer more quickly than she intended and liquid spilt out onto his boots. 'Thank you, David. And thanks for your work today. I assume payment still needs to be sorted, but — well, not by me.'

Caitlin walked inside with her heart going faster than it had for weeks. She dropped the bottles in the sink and stood in the kitchen with her hands shaking. By the time she looked out of the window, David had gone.

Chapter Eleven

For the second time that day she felt breathless. So far, the Australian trip was not doing great things for her anxiety. But then Caitlin realised, she also hadn't had a proper coffee since she had arrived. She gave up watching out for David, who would have reappeared by now. Instead she squared her shoulders and made for the front porch.

'Fresh air,' she said, her voice sounding quieter now it had had a brief chance to share the space with another. At the front of the house, an old doormat with curling rubber strips had been kicked under the agapanthus bushes that lined some of the concrete. She crouched down and pulled a rusted metal dog bowl from beneath the leaves. Blue-grey slaters scattered, their tiny legs flickering with speed, disappearing into the dirt as quickly as she'd exposed them. Caitlin stood with a grunt and there, in the shadows, was what she didn't know she was looking for. A bike, tucked away behind an old camellia shrub. It seemed to be missing some important bike parts, but the red frame was still solid and the white seat was only slightly cracked. By the time she managed to wobble her way to the General Store without incident, she'd fallen for her rusty steed.

That wasn't to say it was a graceful ride. Caitlin rounded the final corner at speed and only managed to stop by sticking both feet out in front of her and making a noise that almost harmonised with the squealing brakes. Once she'd taken stock of all limbs, she looked up to see the same gaggle of boys who'd greeted her yesterday. Although this time, they were diligently avoiding her eye; which was impressive, as even she understood how ridiculous she looked.

Her long pale limbs stuck out of a creased white T-shirt and an old pair of denim shorts she hadn't worn for years. She knew this because while in the bank queue she'd reached into her back pocket and found a ticket from the Paris metro. She and Paul had last visited in the late noughties, after their first round of IVF had failed to take. They had drunk a lot of white wine and had almost been locked into Versailles after falling asleep behind a large hedge. That was a time when they still had fun together, commiserated with each other; a time before the dust had really set in.

She rested the bike against the bench by the door and caught one of the mullety boys' eyes, greeting him with big smile.

'Hello!'

His head went back down.

'G'day,' he mumbled, and she heard a ripple of giggles run through the group behind her as she entered the store.

Even though it was afternoon, thankfully the store still smelt strongly of coffee. Surveying the room, she noticed for the first time a coffee machine tucked into the back corner, by the fridge. A young woman covered in tendrils of delicate tattoos was working the machine, pulling levers and pumping steam like a laconic railway driver. Caitlin started towards the barista when she heard her name. Charles was back at his post, leaning on the counter — but this time, with a pile of books on his hip.

'Caitlin. Hello again.' He looked at her like they shared a joke, which they didn't.

'Hi' — she paused, tried something on for size — 'Charles.' She thought of the hand-drawn map, and how many of his foodstuffs had kept her going in the past day and a half. The least she could do was demonstrate she'd remembered his name. 'I'm back. I found town, thank you. I — er — I owe you some money.'

'You do? Oh, the groceries. We can sort that out later, no rush. Have a coffee before Sienna finishes up, she's giving us a rare afternoon shift.'

Sienna was patient with Caitlin's stumbling over the Australian currency, which was all rainbow plastic notes and coins with weird animals on them. Caitlin's phone was still lying beneath the Cicada House's back deck, but her cards were safe and after the bank visit she had enough to pay her debt, buy a coffee and use the public phone outside the Store.

Charles joined her as she paused at the Store's entrance, gratefully inhaling the coffee scent.

'She's good, isn't she?' He waved at Sienna as she headed out the back door of the Store, having tucked the machine in under its canvas hood. 'Moved home to the Bay for summer, but thank god she learnt how to make coffee in Melbourne. Before she arrived, I was putting up with the freeze-dried stuff.'

'Mm.' Caitlin closed her eyes and held the cup under her nose. 'I really love coffee.'

When she opened them again, Charles had taken a seat on the outside bench, his long legs crossed and head tipped back to the early afternoon sun. She followed and stood awkwardly by a bollard by one of the two carparks, grateful the mullet gang had departed. A ute drove at speed along the narrow highway, flying past with a quick beep of the horn and an arm outstretched from an open window. Charles lifted his own slowly in reply. He looked at her, eyes squeezed against the sun.

'So. Is now when I ask the mysterious Englishwoman why she's blown in to a one-ute town at the bottom of the world?'

'I'm sure there's more than one ute in this town.' She sipped her coffee and watched wrens dive like fairies through the messy scrub that sat on the other side of the two lanes. The bushes ran alongside the road for miles, hiding the long beach that stretched just as far.

'All — this —' She waved her fingers at the wall of green. 'It's a pity, it means you can't see the beach on the other side,' she said.

'This country has so much coastline, they don't need to cut trees down to enjoy it.' Charles coughed gently. 'I'm not meaning to pry,' he said. Dot would have approved his attempt to return to the subject.

'I think that's exactly what you're meaning.'

He raised his eyebrows sharply in a way that reminded her of Dot, again. Caitlin started a little, self-conscious about being too spiky to a stranger. 'I'm sorry. I'm still a bit jet-lagged. Of course you're not prying. I — erm — just have a little history with Australia. Melbourne, actually. My mother and I …'

Charles was watching her with a calm, knowing expression on his face that irritated her. Nevertheless, she tried to brighten her tone.

'My mother lived in Melbourne a long time ago. I've always wanted to visit, maybe see some of her old haunts.' Now she was just lying. Being a boring Pollyanna. *Stop it, Caitlin. Not now. This will become too much.*

'So I thought Arana Bay might be a nice place to get acclimatised before I hit the big city.' She shrugged. 'Nothing interesting to see here!'

He looked at her for a split-second too long. Held her gaze and — she could tell — weighed up whether to call her on the bullshit story. Instead, Charles gifted her a dazzling smile. 'Well, there's no ulterior motive here either. I'm just a bored old fart working at a general store in a … four … ute town.'

'But you're not really, are you,' she said, a little shyly — relieved to be able to move on from the subject of her mother.

'What's that?'

'You're not just a … shopkeeper.'

'Oh?'

'You run the writer's place.'

At this, Charles sat forward, his hands on his knees. He was still smiling, but looked a little disappointed at the same time. 'Yes, that's right. So you're an author then?' It was a question he'd clearly asked hundreds of times before.

'No, god no. I saw it on TV. The show about —'

'— The Lodge.'

'Yes. I like watching TV shows about buildings. It's a bit weird to say that out loud, isn't it?'

'Not really. I like watching TV shows about politicians. That's more strange. You must come up then, see it in 3D.' He pointed at the building behind him. 'And while there's nothing wrong with being a shopkeeper, you're right. I'm not. Not usually anyway; I'm running a few shifts for a friend.'

'That's kind of you.'

'Oh, I don't mind, gets me off the hill.'

Caitlin blushed, 'No, I mean — it's kind of you to offer about The Lodge.'

'Pah. No worries. We don't have a group for another week, so it's empty and you won't be cornered by someone wanting to talk about plot devices.'

'Thanks, but I think I'll just settle in here for a bit and —' Caitlin stopped, abruptly. She looked at Charles looking at her and at that moment she realised she didn't know what the end of that sentence should be. Her ears started ringing.

'Are you quite alright? Caitlin?'

Caitlin's vision went all black and tunnel-y.

'God, woman, you're white as a sheet. Sit down!' Charles had sprung up and was guiding her to the bench. He took her coffee and rested his other hand on her shoulder.

'I think I'm going to be sick,' she said, immediately surprised she would say that to a stranger.

'No, no, you're okay. Put your head between your knees. There, there.'

* * *

The view of the garden was upside down as she stood bent over, head between her knees, peering through her own chubby little legs.

It must have been summer, as she was outside in just her knickers and the sun was warm through the trees. Trees that were tall with blue-green leaves and bark that mottled pink. There were two women with her in the garden, almost, it seemed, as tall as the trees themselves. This garden was really just a collection of uneven red bricks and stubby bushes and a brownish patch of dirty grass. But it felt happy. The women were clapping and laughing as Caitlin tried to somersault. One of them had long blonde hair that tickled Caitlin's neck as she picked her up.

She said, 'My girl!' and had blown raspberries on Caitlin's belly. She smelt of coffee and milk and sunshine. It was a specific scent that Caitlin hadn't smelt in thirty-five years. And her brain had decided to use it as a switch, a previously hidden switch that, once flipped, produced a precious memory. Yes, this was a real memory, because Dot and Bill had never spoken about her time in Australia. Clearly that's what it was, a shred of her mother that she had uncovered herself, rather than received from someone else.

* * *

'Better?'

'Better. Thanks.' *Never complain.*

'Maybe it was Sienna's coffee. You're not used to Melbourne strength?'

'Maybe — maybe this Englishwoman needs to toughen up?' She hammed an exaggerated shrug.

'Would you like to come up to The Lodge for dinner tonight? I make a very good pizza.' He pronounced 'pizza' like the tower. 'I can show you the corners of the building the old Beeb didn't.'

His light tone belied the slightly nervous look in his eye. Charles was just like those young boys who'd been standing on this very spot, half an hour earlier. That's what Caitlin had always felt about men, men other than Paul — there was always a part of them that still looked nine years old.

'Thank you, but I won't.' *Never explain.*

His face fell, but only a little. Caitlin noticed how pale his blue eyes were. She wondered what colour hair he'd had before it turned snowy. An old phone started ringing inside and Charles was up and heading back into the Store before she could gather herself. She called out after him, 'See you later!' But she wasn't sure he'd heard her. The exchange had been enough — too much, to check. For now, she wanted to be alone. Caitlin got back on her bike and wobbled up the hill to The Cicada House, feeling strangely sad about the whole exchange.

Home, she tried to push the gate open while holding the bike up with her other hand. Her finger jammed between the metal and the timber post and a bolt of pain shot up her arm and spiked into her shoulder. She let out a gasp of shock and suddenly she was furious. The rage and the disappointment and the fear of the last few weeks tingled through her limbs and she threw the bike down on the ground with a yell. She even kicked the wheel, knowing in the moment how ridiculous she looked but, also, how angry she felt.

What the hell was she doing here, a billion miles from home and living in a house with no wi-fi? She was an heiress for god's sake: why couldn't she have had a breakdown in the Maldives? Why did her crisis have to be somewhere without room service? Why wasn't she at home banging her fists on every closed door, demanding her job and her husband and her life back?

The problem with having a tantrum at forty, alone, is there's no-one to see and no-one to help. Holding her throbbing thumb, Caitlin slowly bent down, collected the bike, and herself, and made her way back up the drive to The Cicada House. On the front porch a plastic bag full of small, ripe apricots hung heavy from the door handle. A folded note sat inside.

Drink at mine!? 5ish.
40 Coastal Way
Erin x

Chapter Twelve

Erin's house was one grey box on top of another. It sat in a neat court with a row of other box homes. They all matched but didn't, rather came from the same set. Like collectibles. The front gardens didn't have fences, instead they had smooth black driveways and rock gardens with low-growing succulents. Caitlin hadn't travelled far from The Cicada House, but this estate felt a long way away. It had a name: SilverSea; a lake: SilverLake; and a cafe: Silvers. It felt quiet, and safe, and new — like she imagined her grandparent's home in Lavender Road had felt when they first picked up their keys.

The doorbell carried over six notes, a tune she recognised but couldn't place. She heard it play through twice before Erin greeted her. 'Oh hey, you made it!' She greeted Caitlin with a warmth that felt unwarranted, but welcome. Caitlin handed Erin a bottle of wine, suddenly shy about being a stranger in the doorway.

'Thanks for having me over.'

'Pleasure! Come in — we're a shoes-off house if that's okay.'

For the second time in two days Caitlin walked barefoot behind Erin, but this time they were padding across a tiled floor that looked clean enough to eat from. Dot would have approved. The whole house smelt of vanilla, and was shaded appropriately.

The living room's beige rug lay over a grey carpet which sat under a white couch. Caitlin was glad she wasn't wearing her shoes.

'Pull up a pew.' Erin gestured to a barstool alongside a white marbled island bench. Caitlin wobbled up onto the seat and watched Erin retrieve a tray of cheese biscuits from the oven.

'Joshy!' she yelled into the oven. 'Come say hello to Caitlin!'

A skinny kid appeared from the hallway, gelled hair poking out around a pair of gamer's headphones. Of course it was one of the mullety boys from the General Store. Caitlin smiled and the boy paled, much like he had done when she'd pointed at his friend yesterday.

'Hello, Josh.'

'Hi.'

Josh become the colour of the marble and Caitlin felt a little guilty again. But then he picked his nose and she stopped. Erin handed her son a bunch of steaming biscuits in a serviette and he disappeared back into a room Caitlin could see was glowing with an LED-lit blue.

'Looks just like his dad, little turd.' Erin was smiling affectionately and Caitlin decided she'd never understand the Australian turn of phrase. Erin handed her the plate of warm biscuits, and then picked up two glasses and the bottle. 'Shall we sit outside? It's still so nice.'

The deck led onto a garden that looked like it had been built in a computer game. Carpet-flat lawn and a row of spindly magnolia trees. Caitlin watched the arc of a sprinkler lift and drop away again over the back fence. They settled into a couple of chairs by a glass table. Erin produced some sunglasses (how did Australians manage to have sunglasses with them at all times, Caitlin wondered?) and poured their wine. Somewhere, a lawnmower droned.

'I didn't think you'd come, you know.' Erin was looking at her over her sunnies, maybe in the same way she might weigh up a two-bedroom unit with views onto SilverLake.

'Of course I came. It was very kind of you.' Caitlin nearly said, 'It's nice to meet a friend', but she didn't. She noticed a second tattoo, this one sitting like smudge on the inside of Erin's left wrist. She was wearing another singlet, in bright yellow, and looked like she did Pilates, or yoga. Caitlin made a mental note to pick up some fake tan the next time she was in town.

'How's The Cicada House treating you?'

'I think I like it. It's a little run-down and I am deeply outraged by the loo situation. But … but it's got a really lovely feel to it.'

'I know what you mean, but — oh my god' — Erin cut herself off — 'did you dig up the old reviews yet?'

Caitlin shook her head but Erin was already pulling out her phone, and began reading from the screen. '"A disappointing trip. Tired interior with strange smell. And an outside toilet — archaic!"'

Caitlin smiled tightly. Erin continued scrolling,

'Oh, this one's good: "Do not rent this so-called 'retro hideaway'. Daughter's asthma was triggered by flooring. Plus neighbours making noises all through the night."'

'Dear me,' Caitlin tried, using a Dot-ism that Erin would surely pick up. She did not.

'Oh man,' Erin yelped. '"Only stayed one night. This house made me feel weird."' Erin was really laughing now. 'Tracey shouldn't have given up, just doubled down! Hard to, though, when the owners refuse to play ball. No idea why they won't sell. People go nuts for that kind of retro-beach-shack vibe. Not me though. I'm more of a "spick and span" girl myself,' Erin said, gesturing back to the house. 'As you can see.'

Caitlin said, 'I don't know, maybe coming from the UK I'm used to old houses.' The reviews made her feel more warmly towards The Cicada House, not the opposite. 'Although, it does need —' She stopped herself. *Never complain.*

Erin had a pleasing habit of not following up on unfinished sentences. Maybe she didn't care. She looked at Caitlin. 'Well, the tradies 'round here are pretty good.' Caitlin pictured David, eyes closed and lifted to the sun. 'I can chat to Trace about organising if you like,' Erin added.

Caitlin didn't want to be rude about David, so she was relieved she wasn't expected to arrange his payment. 'That would be great, thanks, Erin.'

'Cheers!' Erin clinked her wineglass firmly against Caitlin's and took a deep sip. 'So!' Here it came. 'What brings you all the way down here?'

'I quit my job and my husband left me for no reason. I saw this town on TV seven years ago and decided to visit.'

Erin nodded, seemingly unphased. 'Fair enough. That'll do it. Cheesy biscuit?'

It felt incredibly freeing to tell someone her sad story — particularly when that someone didn't know any of the other players in the tale. Caitlin hadn't taken this approach before. Of course, the 'long-dead teen mother' was fertile fodder for a woe is me story. But Bill and Dot had instilled such a strong sense of stoicism in her that she never even thought about using her orphaning as a plot point in her sorry tale. Tonight, with Erin, she didn't disrespect her grandparents by digging that far back into the drama. No — Paul and Laura and the house and the job and the IVF — that was all more than enough. As Caitlin rolled out the narrative like she was relating a juicy miniseries, she found she was almost enjoying the story. That she happened to be the slighted heroine only made it more satisfying to tell.

Even better, Erin wasn't shocked by anything Caitlin told her. In fact, it was more like Erin was reading a behavioural report for a thesis she was already two years into writing: no surprises here. Real-estate agents, much like hairdressers, were a nation's unofficial therapists. And Erin was good at it too. She tutted and sighed at all the right times. It was a dynamic Caitlin wasn't used to, the girlfriend to and fro. By the time they'd each finished their first glass she felt captured in the tidal flow of familiarity.

She was also a little overwhelmed: Paul was normally the one who bore the brunt of the conversational load when they spent time with anyone. Apart from Jan, Caitlin hadn't spoken to a person at length, about something that wasn't work, in a long time. Yet she had enough breeding to know that without her husband to take up the slack, it would be rude to not return the conversational serve.

'So, tell me about Arana Bay. You grew up here, didn't you? It must be a wonderful place to be a kid.' As soon as she said it she knew how she sounded – a dumb tourist with no clue. Erin was kinder to her than she was to herself.

'Oh yeah. Joshy loves it — he's got the surf club, his little ratbag mates, pretty much the run of the place. But it's not all sunshine and rainbows. The school's shit. Everyone escapes to Melbourne or Sydney as soon as they turn eighteen and the town is filled with grumpy pensioners whingeing about the one business that's actually bringing any money in.'

'Arana Lodge?'

'Got it in one. When Charlie first rocked up in a pair of boat shoes with a fancy architect in tow, the wanker-meters were dinging all over town. But word is, he's legit. And for some reason, he loves the Bay. Everyone knows that he puts in the time and the effort. In ten years he's done more for the economy than our bloody council has in decades.'

Caitlin felt a little uncomfortable at the cool reception she'd given the floppy-haired man who had been nothing but kind to her. 'He seems like a good man.'

'Pretty sure he is.' Erin looked at her for an extra second, emphasising her point. 'I don't know him well, but from what I hear, he has a tendency to pick up strays, care for them. Not just writers, but others.'

Caitlin bristled slightly at the intimation that she herself was a stray. Thinking about it though: an orphan, miles from home … she shook off the self-pity.

'How does it work? The Lodge, I mean.'

'I think he books five or six retreats in a year. A group of writers rock up, drink wine, take long walks along the beach and … write, I guess? Not for me.' It was Erin's turn to shudder. 'Communal dining is my idea of hell. And I can't spell to save myself. But they spend shitloads, so it must be up someone's alley.'

'Well, it sounds like Charles — *Charlie* — is good at his job. I mean, it seems like he really enjoys what he does.' Caitlin ruminated. 'Which must be nice. Like you. You seem to enjoy real estate. Do you like work?'

Erin looked surprised that anyone would ask her that. She thought for a moment, and then broke into a smile. 'I do, I guess. It's okay here.' She laughed. 'God, I worked for an incredible real-estate agency in Sydney though. I loved it. The scale, the money — it was so shiny. *I* was so shiny!' She chuckled again. 'Jesus. Poor Little Erin. I found out I was pregnant at work. I'd bought a box of pee sticks in between two showings. We'd just closed up after a viewing in an incredible clifftop place in Double Bay. I sat in this ensuite, looking out at a $22-million view and waited for those goddamned lines to appear.'

Caitlin watched Erin as her face settled into something like sad happiness. Or the reverse. Kids tended to do that to their parents, in Caitlin's experience.

'Gaz and I went to high school together. He was in Sydney for the weekend and we went out for drinks — old times' sake, that kind of thing. One night stand, condom broke with the boy-next-door, up the duff and home to Mum and Dad. Such a bloody cliché.' Erin stood up from the table and from the memory.

It was darker now, and the sensor light kept flicking on and off with Erin's gesticulations. She'd offered Caitlin more wine and had gone ahead and poured herself a glass even when Caitlin declined. Caitlin's stomach grumbled as she spied the time on Erin's phone. She wanted to go home and eat dinner and let her face fall from the smiles and eye contact and effort that being with another person — even a nice one — required of her.

'I'm going to have a cigarette. Can you keep watch in case Josh comes out of his bedroom?' And like a ninja, Erin was suddenly standing across the lawn outside the pool of light, a red tip sparked up in the shadows. Caitlin had another one of those feelings, from the plane. Like she was floating far above the scene, looking down. What was she doing? Sitting in the backyard of this person who she barely knew, watching her smoke menthols in the gloaming? Telling stories, asking questions, pretending to be the sort of woman she'd never been?

'Um, actually, I should probably get going. I'm sure you have to feed Josh anyway.'

Caitlin couldn't see Erin's face, but the cigarette smoke curled into the purple sky. She was speaking as she inhaled. 'Stay for dinner! It's okay, I've got a roast chook from the supermarket — I'm just going to tear it up with white rolls and a bag of salad.'

Caitlin felt a bit panicky. Her bare feet were cold on Erin's timber decking. 'It's fine, thanks. I've … I've really got to go.'

She knew she shouldn't be rushing out like this. She knew she shouldn't be letting the cigarette smoke into the kitchen by opening the door so quickly, she knew she should have carried the glasses and bottle and plate back to the sink and rinsed them out. She knew she should have settled in for a night of wine and picking at the roast chicken skin and sharing secrets with a woman who was attempting to strike up some form of attachment. She knew all of these things, because while she could make friends, she wouldn't. And that's why she was a broken person. By the time Caitlin pulled back up outside The Cicada House her heart rate had settled. Leaving in a mess of 'thank-yous' and 'goodbyes' felt unnecessarily dramatic for a quiet Monday night. Erin had looked on bemused while she scarpered out the door and that had made her feel worse. Thank god Josh hadn't been in the kitchen while she made a run for it. Caitlin couldn't understand where all this absurd emotion was coming from. *It must be because of this ridiculous sharing*, she thought to herself. But afterwards, standing in the kitchen eating toast under the hum of the fluorescent light, Caitlin knew she hadn't really shared anything at all. And for the first time since she was a teenager, it felt like something she needed to right.

The next evening, Caitlin was flushed with a shyness she hadn't felt since adolescence. This silly country was rubbing her feelings raw and so other emotions were coming to the surface: insecurity being one of them. She tutted to herself, *Pull yourself together. It's just a bar.* Because along with the companionship, Erin had gifted something else to Caitlin during their catchup — she'd told her about the Arana Bay pub.

'It's not a pub, not really. It started out as the members-only bar at the surf club. It's open to the public now but no-one really knows about it, not unless you've got the inside steer.' Erin had tapped the side of her nose, which made Caitlin feel warm with inclusion.

She climbed the floating timber stairs to find a room the size of a tennis court opened up before her. Deep green carpet was suitably sticky, low lights shone on wood-panelled walls covered in memorial boards, winners' trophies and poorly framed photographs. A pool table filled the end she'd just arrived into, and a bar the opposite. Small tables were scattered around with red baskets of fried things scenting the room. Caitlin liked it very much.

'A lager, thanks.'

A spotty boy with sandy hair who didn't look old enough to serve booze glanced up from his phone. 'Pot or pint?'

'Erm …?' Caitlin hadn't been inducted into this level of drinks detail.

'She'll have a pot.'

Caitlin looked around.

'See you found the place then?' Erin asked. She was standing by a man in a flannel shirt and shorts, whose feet were sandy in his flip-flops. Erin gestured to him. 'Caitlin, meet Gary — Josh's Dad. Gaz, this is Caitlin, she's in The Cicada House.'

Gaz tilted his head like a cowboy just off a horse, rather than a surfer with hair still wet. 'G'day.'

'Hi. Nice to meet you.'

'Likewise. S'cuse me.' He turned away to the other end of the bar and a woman with similarly damp hair.

'That's Gaz's girlfriend Terri. We often use the club to hand over Josh.'

Caitlin hadn't noticed Gaz and Erin's son at the pool table. The bartender handed Caitlin a very small glass of very cold beer. She looked at it, as if surprised. Caitlin steadied herself, took a breath and said words she'd often heard but never spoken: 'Thanks for coming. Can we talk?'

Chapter Thirteen

Erin used her straw to move the slice of lemon around her post-mix cola. 'I've got a shitload of emails to get through tonight,' she said, as if she needed to explain the soft drink. Caitlin set her drink down on a torn coaster. She felt the growing worry of her own inbox, locked away on her absent phone for almost a week now. Pushing the thought back down again, she focused on Erin.

'I was rude to you last night. You made lovely cheese biscuits and said kind things and you even vacuumed before I came.'

Erin looked affronted. 'I did not. Vacuum. For you, I mean.'

'Well, either way, I really appreciated it. It was nice to spend time together, in your home. I'm sorry I left so abruptly.'

Erin shrugged and smiled politely. 'It's all good, doll.'

She could feel that Erin had already closed the door on any potential friendship. Caitlin ignored every instinct to also shut up social-shop and maybe even escape, with her drink untouched. Erin waved as Josh left with Gaz and Terri.

Instead Caitlin went on. 'Of course, I know. It's fine. I just, I don't really have any friends back home. Apart from Paul and his family and' — *Ugh* — 'it's all very odd to be here, so far away and … I've made a few promises to myself about a fresh start.'

She had Erin's attention again. 'A fresh start — like, more fresh than moving to the other side of the world?'

Caitlin imagined how Dot's voice would have sounded if she were still alive, telling her, *'You'll never do one damn good thing until you're over forty.'*

'Yes. More fresh than that.'

'Right, and how's that going to work then?' Erin asked.

'I've been thinking about how I told my story, to you. I mean, it was all true, don't get me wrong. But I don't think I told it fairly.'

'How can you tell your own story unfairly?' Erin asked questions like a news reporter.

Caitlin took a breath. 'I said I didn't know why my husband left me. But I do. I know why Paul left. Because … I just don't think I'm very good at being a human. I mean, I've paid my bills and turned up to the work Christmas party and I've given my husband anniversary gifts and it all feels like —' Caitlin was surprised to feel her throat closing in a choke of a cry. She ignored the small scattering of people at the bar and swallowed the sensation away. 'It feels like I've been ticking the boxes of an application form where I can't see what I'm applying for.'

Erin was still listening, but she didn't respond. It was simultaneously freeing to speak like this, and disconcerting to realise how noteworthy this conversation with a semi-stranger would be, in the grand scheme of all Caitlin's non-conversations.

'I … I cheated on Paul once. We had a work trip to the Lake District and I kissed a man. His name was Ian, he was a sales manager. We were all so drunk, and he flirted with me and I flirted with him and his … oh god, his arm hair poked all *tufty* out of his shirt sleeves.' She wiggled her fingers. Erin raised her eyebrows but Caitlin went on. 'And I never wanted bloody kids. I don't like kids. They smell and they're sticky and they ruin all the bits of life that are good.' She paused and glanced over to where Josh had been rolling billiard balls up and down the pool table. 'Sorry.'

'No, that's fair. Kids do smell.'

'Yes, but what sort of psychopath goes through five years of IVF and doesn't want kids? And not only that, doesn't actually tell their partner? Me! Bloody me!' She was poking her chest, harder than she needed to to make her point. 'I didn't tell my own goddamned husband how I was feeling. It's not like he didn't ask — I. Just.' Every word was punctuated with a poke. 'Never. Said.' Her voice was higher than normal. She'd managed to stop the crying before it kicked in, but hysteria had replaced it. She took a big gulp of her beer, mainly to stop any more words coming out. Erin looked unperturbed and Caitlin wondered what it took to make this particular Australian riled up.

'Why're you saying all this stuff, Caitlin? I mean, it's good to get it off your chest, but why do you care what version of your story I hear?' asked Erin.

Caitlin considered the question. 'I feel like — you were honest with me, so maybe I should be honest with me too.'

Erin reached over and patted her hand. 'Babe, we're good. Promise. I liked hanging out with you. And don't worry — you're not the first woman I've met having a mid-life moment far from home. I'm a real-estate agent, remember? I've seen more marriage breakdowns than Dr Phil.'

Caitlin let out a deep breath; her rising panic disappeared. Erin hadn't removed her hand. 'I think you needed this trip a lot more than you thought.'

Neither Caitlin nor Erin stayed long after that. Caitlin was developing what Paul used to call an 'emotional hangover'. In the rare moments that she let her feelings loose with her husband, the weariness Caitlin would feel afterwards could last for days. She needed to lie down and scroll her phone for a few hours. She needed to sit still and watch some property shows. If she had her phone. If she had a television.

The two women left the surf club together. Outside, invisible clouds of dinner smells were wafting down the road. The clink of cutlery floated out of glowing windows, noises which made their way to the women like wind-chimes on a breeze. Erin beeped her car open with her keys. 'Want a lift home?'

'No that's okay. I've got my ride.'

Her rusted red bike was propped against the gnarled trunk of a tea tree. Erin put a hand on Caitlin's shoulder. 'Caitlin, you seem like a good woman. But I don't know, you might want to think about going a bit easier on yourself? Maybe that's something us locals can teach you while you're down here.'

Leaving the dinner scents behind, Caitlin rode home in the deepening shadows. She slowed down by the General Store; the lights were still on, but she couldn't see anyone inside. She wasn't sure if she was relieved or disappointed. Outside, the lit logo of the payphone hummed orange and Caitlin realised with a heart-thud that she had missed last Thursday's call to her grandad … and the Thursday before that. She patted her pockets and hoped that phone boxes in Australia worked better than they did back home. The call dialled in a strange tone. There was a *clunk*.

'Grandad?'

'Eh-up, Caitlin.'

The relief was immense. He wasn't dead. She exhaled and leant on the glass wall beside her. She felt immediately lighter. Moving to Australia in a drunken fog was bad enough, promptly losing your one form of communication after arriving, *and then failing to replace it*, was pretty irredeemable. Caitlin considered what sort of gap-year backpacker she would have made, given this was her behaviour at forty. Bill interrupted her meanderings.

'How's you, pet?'

She wasn't sure, but Bill sounded quite happy to hear from her. Certainly more than when she'd last spoken to him, which was only two weeks but infinite time zones away. She wondered what he'd think if she'd told him she was in Australia. He said once that it was a country of 'criminals and insects'. She went to tell him, but asked after the pudding of the day, instead.

'A lemon posset. Just lovely.'

'That's good, Grandad. You always liked the citrus puddings.'

'Oh yes. My Dot would make a lovely orange cake. Not too sweet.'

A pause. Breathing. A car whipped by the Store, headlights in rods through the dark night. Caitlin looked down as she scrunched her bare toes on the sandy concrete beneath the payphone. She'd left her flip-flops by the bike.

Her grandad cleared his throat. 'How's that money coming along? You bought yourself something special?'

'I have.' She paused, absorbing the background noise of his television, the squeak of his chair. In this starkly lit call box, the sounds of him were the sounds of home. She gripped the plastic handset, grateful for the steadying sense Bill gave her. 'Grandad, I've gone on a bit of a holiday.'

'Oh yes. That's nice.'

'So I might not be by for a few weeks. I'll keep calling though.'

'Okay then.'

'Grandad?'

'Mm?'

'My holiday is … it's in Australia.' Caitlin bit the skin on her thumb and held her breath. She could hear Bill shifting in his leather recliner. The TV seemed to get louder. He gave another little cough, 'I went to Australia once.'

'I know Grandad. You came here to —'

'Not my cup of tea. Strange country. Too hot. And the flies!'

'Yes. There are quite a lot of flies.'

'Your grandmother didn't like that place. You be careful down there.'

'I will, Grandad.'

There was a voice in the background, the sound of a rattling tray.

'One of the girls are here.'

'Okay. Love you, Grandad.'

'Yes, yes. Love to you, pet.'

Caitlin hung up and stood quietly in the overlapping pools of the street and phonebox lights. She felt so alone that even a few criminals and insects would be welcome. Her grandfather's voice, even though it wavered like a needle over an old record, still managed to ground her. Speaking to him reminded her of who she was — perfunctory, impassive. Or, more accurately, reminded her of who she was, over there. And who she didn't seem to be, here and now.

She turned to see Charles in the doorway of the Store, a mug in his hand. It was completely dark now and he was backlit, so she couldn't make out his expression. She spoke first. 'Hello.'

'Hello there.'

She looked past him into the shop, empty and darker than she'd seen it. He had been shutting lights off.

'Does anyone else work here?' Her tone felt ruder out loud than she meant it.

Charles sipped at his mug placidly. 'That is a good question. Your pal Tracey?'

'House Tracey? She runs the General Store?'

'No. You may recall "House Tracey" is also "Bali Tracey". She's there with her daughter, which means her daughter is not here working. In the store.'

'But — why are you covering?'

He rubbed his fingers along the neat stubble that had only recently appeared on his normally clean-shaven jaw. 'Caitlin, it might surprise you to know but I genuinely like to help people. You could say, I like to "be of service". And now' — he motioned to the phone-box behind her — 'I'm curious. I don't think I've ever seen that being used, unless it's the boys prank-calling the chippie.'

'I've lost my mobile.'

'Ah. You realise there's a phone store in town?'

'I do. But to be honest, it's been nice not to have it with me. A bit of a digital detox.'

Charles nodded. 'Well, yes. But you do need the outside world. Sometimes.' He pulled a folded piece of A4 from his back pocket. 'You have some rather enterprising friends. Today I received an email at The Lodge, asking after you.'

Caitlin held out her hand, instantly feeling nauseous. Thank goodness she'd just spoken to Bill, otherwise she'd be certain the message was of death. Charles was hesitating, holding on to the paper. She felt a little panicky.

He coughed lightly. 'I hope you don't mind, Caitlin, but given it seemed urgent, I …' His voice faltered. He tapped his thumb against the mug.

She looked at him, hand still outstretched. '… You?'

'Well, I dropped them a little reply.'

She tried not to snatch the paper, and partially failed. The page was a print-out of an email, sent to the generic 'reception' address at Arana Lodge:

> *Hello there — we've reason to believe Caitlin Falstaff is staying in or around Arana Bay. If you can ensure she receives this message we'd be ever so grateful. Please tell her to contact Jan or Marigold ASAP. (All is well we just want to be sure she's not tied up in a shed somewhere). Thank you byeeee x*

And then Charles's reply:

> *Hello Jan and Marigold! How clever of you to find your Caitlin all the way down here. My name is Charles Folantau and I've had the pleasure of meeting Caitlin upon her arrival in our little hamlet. I can absolutely assure you …*

The words disappeared into a ghostly nothing where the printer ink faded and expired. She looked up at him. 'How long was your bloody email?'

At least he looked a little ashamed. 'Not very long. I hope you don't mind. They seemed very worried about you, and you clearly don't have access to the internet. I just said that I'd met you, I'd pass the message on, and you were absolutely not tied up in a shed. Oh, and then Jan replied and — well, she's wonderful isn't she? Turns out we grew up in the same county!'

Her mouth stayed slightly open.

'Anyway. They're most certainly reassured. But of course, you should check in with them.'

Caitlin was too confused to be cross. And then a sense of guilt: another new and not-so-welcome emotion that swallowed anything else. She sighed and rubbed her temple. 'Yes. I know. I dropped my phone under the deck at the house and it felt quite liberating and, well, *Eat, Pray, Love* to be disconnected. Now I just feel a bit irresponsible.'

'The offer is there to make use of The Lodge. We have lots of individual writers' spaces set up and I'm sure I can dig out a laptop for you.'

Caitlin must have looked as uncomfortable as she felt. The growing need for her to be more connected to Arana Bay was stronger than the obligation to contact home. She didn't want to be in two places at once, not just yet.

Charles continued, 'I know you're not interested in my pizza.' He held up a hand in a sign of innocence. 'Honestly, Caitlin, I've got no ulterior motive. I just have a desk and a computer and access to the World Wide Web.'

'That's kind of you but —' Caitlin stopped herself just before she declined. Her bare toes pressed into the sandy ground. She breathed in slowly. 'That would be nice, thanks.'

'Good. Come visit us up on the hill anytime. I'll be there more often now, we're prepping for the next retreat.' Charles smiled and tossed the rest of whatever was in his mug into a pot plant. 'Just knock on the door and holler.'

Chapter Fourteen

Cycling home, the folded paper sat thickly in her back pocket and reminded her that she was irresponsible. The night wind graced her face with ocean and eucalypt scents. It was late enough that the cicadas had quieted, and in their stead echoed more peculiar, unidentifiable sounds. Clicks, purrs and an alarmingly close rustle from which Caitlin quickened her pedalling. Where Bill and Jan had busied her brain, now Paul stepped in.

'We're having a baby.'

We. We are. Intruding like a spear — *boing* — vibrating in the centre of her head. She pedalled even faster. She saw images in her mind that she knew couldn't be real. Paul pacing a hospital hallway. Paul holding the hand of a woman that was not her. Paul telling this woman to 'just breathe with me'. Seeing him weep into her shoulder while a squirming baby was placed on this beautiful woman's chest. Did she mention the woman was beautiful? Beautiful and composed and wearing a tiny third piercing on the inner curve of her perfect left ear? Oh, Laura.

* * *

'Caitlin, this is Laura and Felix. Laura's our new VP of sales.'

Paul had been so puffed-up proud that night, an awards do for financial technology advancement. Caitlin had attended her own marketing awards night just the week before. She'd marvelled at how some industries just … made up their own awards. Did everyone do this? 'Best lines painted on an A-road', 'Highest rated barber in the north-east'. How ridiculous they all were.

'Caitlin?'

Paul's voice had cut into her micro-daydream. She smiled placidly and raised her glass. That normally sufficed for a response to a question she hadn't heard.

Felix grinned in response. 'Ha! Well I'm glad someone agrees with me!'

Now, thinking back, of course Caitlin wished she'd spent more time analysing Laura and Paul's interaction. But there hadn't really been any. In their little party circle, Laura had almost spilt teriyaki sauce down her navy jumpsuit, but had just caught it with a paper napkin. Felix had smiled and cracked a few jokes about the bad lighting. Laura's hand had rested on the small of Felix's back while he told the story of their meet-cute at an equestrian event six months earlier. Such banal party happenings, rolling out like a play no-one cared to know the ending to.

And throughout, Paul hadn't seemed to pay any more or less attention than you'd expect someone to relate to their superior. In fact, he and Felix had spent most of the time discussing the superiority of one streaming service over the next. No, Laura was completely normal, and now she was pregnant with Paul's child. It all felt so obscenely pedestrian.

* * *

Caitlin had stopped outside The Cicada House. She'd dropped her feet to the gravel and was resting back on the hard seat of the bike. It was dark, and still, and she missed Paul. *We're. Having. A.*

Baby. It was the kind of night that made her want to fall asleep and stop her brain, but as she willed her legs to move, all she felt capable of was picturing Paul and Laura and berating herself for not noticing a love affair bloom before her eyes. It took longer than it should have to make the final few metres to the house, and even more effort to make it to bed. But when she did, and eventually drifted off, she dreamt of ocean waves and the soft shape of a newborn sleeping beside her.

The next morning was hot. *Hot*, hot. The lack of air conditioning in the house was starting to make itself felt. Caitlin had moved outside in the hope a cool breeze would hold the day's heat off a little longer. She was sitting on the patio's plastic chair, her feet up on the table in front of her. Last night she'd kicked her toe into what ended up being a water-crinkled copy of *Lonesome Dove*, under her bed, and now she was re-reading the same three pages. Caitlin was trying not to think about Jan's email, which sat heavily on the kitchen bench, a piece of origami with the psychic weight of cement. She was also distracted by the loo door hanging open and the sun shining through the gap in the roof, lighting up the funnelled cobweb in the corner. She picked up a broom and gave the concrete floor and walls a good brushing down. She was admiring her handiwork when a 'Yoohoo!' echoed from the front. Erin.

''Round the back!' Caitlin called a reply because it made her feel like she was in a scene from a long-running soap. It didn't feel wrong. Erin appeared in a pair of cotton shorts and a bikini top. She had a balding towel over her shoulder. 'Hello, mate. It's a cracking day and I have a feeling you haven't got your feet wet yet.'

Caitlin and Erin walked down the sandy path to the beach. Caitlin had dug out the only pair of swimmers she'd packed. They were old and definitely a lot more high-cut than she remembered.

She extracted a wedgie while trying to remember when she'd last worn them. A spa day Paul had arranged for her and Jan, after a failed IVF round. The spa's pool was outside and not heated. Their breath had fogged while drizzle settled on their hair. A wet plaster had floated by and stuck itself to the back of her arm. She and Jan hadn't stayed in the water for long.

The beach was a different place compared to the last time Erin and Caitlin had visited. The day wasn't only very hot, but completely still. The water was the colour of the empty blue sky and just as smooth, with only the slightest movements rolling into steady, small waves that appeared on and vanished into the sand. The dunes held the sounds of a thousand invisible cicadas and the swell purred back its own reply.

Being a Friday afternoon, there were people now where there hadn't been earlier. Not many — just a few striped umbrellas dotted along the beach. Caitlin moved from foot to foot, shocked at how quickly the sand scorched her soles. Heat shimmered the ground. In fact, everything was shimmering. Erin dropped her towel and her shorts. 'Come on!'

Caitlin was slower to follow. She was self-conscious about her pale form, and her old bathers with pilled dots on the bum. Erin had already made it to the water's edge.

'Sod it,' Caitlin said to herself, and followed her new friend to the sea.

The heat of the day meant the water felt cold, even though Caitlin knew it wasn't. Erin was already swimming, having run through the waves in a fluid way that appeared very *Baywatch*. Caitlin was slower, moving in deliberate steps through the clear water, concentrating hard on the seabed before her to ensure no accidental run-ins with poisonous creatures. When the water hit her groin she gasped, but it was more from surprise than cold. She kept going. Ribs, breasts, shoulders. She held her breath and squeezed her eyes shut and dropped down under the water. Bubbles foamed past her ears. She pushed back up from the sand to emerge into the sunshine, wet and salty. Erin was swimming back to her. 'Better?'

Caitlin didn't know she'd been worse. But yet, she felt better. 'Yes. Yes!'

'I'm going to head out to the marker and back. Want to come?'

A white buoy rocked slowly from left to right. A long way away. 'No, I'm okay. You go.'

Erin's feet flipped away like fish, and Caitlin was bobbing, alone. Although she wasn't very far from shore, she could no longer hear the children that were scattered along the water's edge. Instead, she only heard the water and her own breathing. The sea was so calm. If she stretched herself to full height, her pointed toes just grazed the sand below, while her upturned chin was kissed by the water. She felt less afraid of the sea than she had earlier that week, even though she was actually floating inside it. Caitlin closed her eyes. A fat, slow current lifted her up and down as she hung suspended, a meditative marionette. Her buoyancy felt ethereal. Consequence and responsibility and obligation all had such *mass*. And yet here, she felt utterly weightless. Unencumbered by all that had come before.

'You're having a baby.' Caitlin said the words clearly, quickly, as she floated beneath the sky. Felt the syllables flit from her chest like moths. She tried again, tried to say the words and muster up the feeling they had given her last night. But they were gone. The four words had flown away.

The two women sat side by side on their towels with the salt drying in prickles on their limbs. Caitlin scratched softly at her shin. Erin poked around her shorts' pocket and pulled out a cigarette. As she lit it, she spoke out of the corner of her mouth, 'Don't judge me.'

'I'm not judging you.'

'Good. Because I am. Filthy habit.'

Caitlin ran her outstretched palms back and forth over the sand, burying her feet in the cool grains below the surface.

'You said your mum was English?' Erin said, through smoke.

'Yeah, like me. Well. More than me. I guess I'm half Australian.'

They were both looking out at the water. It was easier to answer Erin's questions this way.

'You "guess". So you don't know your dad?'

Caitlin shook her head. When Erin smoked and spoke her voice sounded different. Gentler, somehow. It was so long since Paul had asked her these questions, she'd forgotten what it felt like to answer them, particularly when she was doing so honestly.

Erin took another drag. 'Neither do I. Not really, anyway. Mum remarried when I was still in primary school.' She exhaled in a white stream. 'I call Rick "Dad" and Joshy calls him "Pops". As far as I'm concerned he's the one that's earnt those titles. Did your mum remarry?'

'No.'

She died.

She died, she died, on a long Australian highway.

She wrapped herself around a tree.

'She passed away. Died. When I was five.'

Erin's head turned to her, quickly. She stared at Caitlin. 'Oh, mate. That's heavy. I'm sorry.'

'Yes.' Her voice was small against the waves and the kids' shrieks and droning dunes. 'We were living in Australia. In Melbourne, actually, when she died.'

Now Erin was giving Caitlin a look she hadn't seen before. Not from Erin certainly, but — maybe — from anyone else either. Erin watched Caitlin as a mother, rather than a friend. Caitlin swallowed, fixed her eyes back on the horizon. It was excruciating to be beheld in this way.

'Oh, honey. You said you were five. So — you were all alone?' Erin said.

'Yes. I guess I was. For a time.'

'And then, you went back to the UK? Someone came and got you?' Erin asked like she needed a happy answer.

'Yes. Someone came.'

The visit to the beach had made Caitlin's heart feel full and broken all at the same time. She'd declined Erin's offer to join her and Josh for fish and chips, and had settled for picking over sliced ham from the fridge. After, she moved to her back step, ice clinking in a gin and tonic topped with lemon peel from the garden. She'd found matches and mosquito coils under the kitchen sink, and was now watching the glowing tip of the green spiral keep the mozzies at bay. The stillness of the day only increased with the sun's setting. The smoke seemed to pause mid-air, little kinks in the grey column retaining their forms before drifting lazily over her head.

Much later, after the mosquito coil was just silvery dust and she had accidentally finished two more gin and tonics, she pressed the heels of her palms into scrunched-shut eyes and let out a small groan of pain from the back of her throat. She spoke out loud.

'Breathe, Caitlin.'

She was beginning to listen to her own advice.

Chapter Fifteen

Caitlin had only been in Arana Bay for a fortnight, but already her joints felt looser. It wasn't just the swimming that was unfastening her. To Caitlin's great relief, the jet lag had finally washed away, unshackling her from the dizziness of a twisted time zone. But another feeling was creeping into the jet lag's wake. It was a week after telling Erin about her mother, and about the same since she'd spoken to Bill. Jan's email remained folded and untouched on the kitchen bench. It felt like the bruises from all of these emotional exchanges should have faded, but she was still wincing. Hearing her grandad's voice had calmed a klaxon in her head she didn't realise had been sounding. But now with another Thursday that had inexplicably arrived and gone, she still couldn't bring herself to seek him out again. Nor Jan, or even Erin.

Here, in this faraway land of light and salt, Caitlin's lack of obligation was confronting. For years, she was kept from drifting out and away from life's requirements by Paul's sharp tug on her lifeline. Now she was untethered, floating in a suspended reality of exemption. Caitlin was delighted. She was terrified. She was stuck between the two states and so did what she did best: nothing. Instead, Caitlin built a routine that helped each day feel productive even when it wasn't.

Back in the UK, January only existed as a bleak bridge to the rest of the year. Even for those people — like Caitlin — who didn't revel in the festive season, the emptiness of the weeks that followed echoed with the lack of everything that came before. Christmas tree carcasses lay on ever-wet footpaths. Windows hung sadly in the absence of strung lights. The supermarkets pretended soups and salads were sufficient meals when only weeks before they were mere side dishes.

In Arana Bay, January moved into February like the quiet waves of morning. Deliberate, measured and welcome. It was a rhythm that meant her senses also felt more delicate, vibrating more highly than ever before.

Two weeks in The Cicada House and Caitlin was becoming adept at hearing the weather before she saw it, and knowing what it meant for the sea that waited for her at the end of the path. She was increasingly aware of how the waves differed throughout the day. When the gum leaves whisked outside her windows like shuffling cards, she knew she would find the beach dusted with swirls of Neptune's necklace delivered by a night of blustering waves. When the cicadas woke up before the sun was high, the water would be slicked flat all the way into the horizon — so calm she would see fish tails flick beneath the surface.

Whatever the weather, Caitlin would wake up early with the magpies' dappled chorus and be out of the house before the sleep left her eyes. If she lay in bed for too long, thoughts crowded her head and it became harder to get her feet onto the grass matting. She'd established the only way out was to roll off the mattress without thinking, pulling on her old swimmers as she moved through the kitchen and hooking a towel over her shoulder from where it hung on the Hills Hoist — she'd only be properly waking up halfway along the sandy track. And by then the sea-glass sky and the breeze-licked waves were enough to stop any thoughts at all.

An early morning dip had become a delicious ritual and it was the only moment in each day when she felt like a better version of yesterday's self. Caitlin was becoming more confident in the sea with every swim — less focused on what was in the water around her, and more on how that water made her feel. The unease she had sensed about this place on the edge of the world was disappearing. It was yet another miracle in this upside-down world that previously staid January and February had now become months for rebirth.

After every swim, breakfast was fresh fruit eaten on the back step. White peaches and yellow nectarines ripened on the windowsill by the previous afternoon's sun. She picked some up each day from the Store and carried them home in a brown paper bag that sat in her bike's basket alongside the newspaper. Sometimes she added an orange, heavy with sweet juice, pulled from the Valencia tree out the back. Caitlin would cut the fruit slowly, enjoying the way the knife moved easily through the flesh. She'd balance the slices on an old chipped saucer, and greet the ever-lifting sun from her seat on the top step. The ripe fruit, a cup of tea, sand grains dried to her kneecaps and toes — these accompanied Caitlin each morning as she opened the paper. Australian newspapers were thin and devoid of any news beyond their shores, which couldn't be better. It pleased Caitlin greatly: the newsprint on her fingertips allowed her to feel connected, but the absence of actual information between the pages protected her from the world it pretended to reference.

Her feet had become used to the rubber stub of thong (Charles had told her to stop calling them 'flip-flops') that now sat semi-permanently between her big and second toe. Her skin had darkened, only slightly, but enough to leave a pale impression of her bathing suit behind when she stripped naked. After each swim and breakfast, she would stand under the cool shower spray and taste the sea salt that ran down from her hair and into her mouth, which still held the flavour of syrupy juice. One day, in a sudden flash, she was reminded of the salty ham her grandmother used to wrap around sweet melon on Christmas day. It was a memory that was unexpected but, unusually, not unwelcome. As she dried herself with a towel that felt like an emery board, Caitlin realised that she was free to feel anything, remember anything, she wished. This revelation didn't liberate her the way she would have expected. Instead, it reminded her soberly of the world that existed beyond the gum trees.

She was realising that if one were not careful, Arana Bay could easily turn into an emotional Brigadoon: a sun-bleached cycle of swims and peaches and denial and newspaper.

Once she'd washed, Caitlin would swing by the Store to pick up her daily coffee (Charles was trying to convince her of the merits of a 'long black' — a drink which tasted like a punishment) and then she'd sometimes drive, sometimes ride, to explore. Rarely to town, often along small sanded paths between dense scrub that inevitably deposited her back to the sea. Always to the sea.

By Sunday afternoon, something was starting to tug at Caitlin, persistent and petulant. She wasn't sure if it was the repetition of each day or the relentlessly shiny weather or even if she'd just run out of tea bags and was going through withdrawal.

Caitlin had discovered that February in Australia was boorishly hot, and 5 pm was often the peak of the day's heat. Not only did The Cicada House lack air conditioning, but the hot water was tepid and the cold water was also … tepid. She had become almost okay with the outside loo, particularly now she'd resolved to keep it swept clean from anything frightening. But she wasn't game to attack in the same way the papery wasp nest that had appeared in the front yard.

Between the wasps and the heat and the quite frankly desperate need for tea, Caitlin decided it was time to take Charles up on his offer to visit The Lodge. Jan's crumpled email and the overdue phone call to Bill also preyed on her conscience, but if

Caitlin was honest the proverbial straw on her sweaty back was the wasps. They were the size of her thumb. Or at least they looked that way, when she peered at them through the blur of the front door's flywire.

She drove towards where she thought Arana Lodge was, vague and slow in the oven-blast of the afternoon heat. Outside, it was hotter than anything she'd ever experienced and her car's air conditioning was taking a while to do anything meaningful. Caitlin pulled over just past the Store and, for the first time in a week, cursed the absence of her phone. Opening her window, she looked up and down the road, feeling useless. Two sharp toots of a car horn broke into her thoughts and a bashed-up Nissan the colour of old hummus pulled carefully alongside her, the passenger window already down.

'Need a hand?' Sienna looked even younger than she did at the coffee machine. Caitlin went to ask her if she even had her driver's licence, then thought better of it. A hot blast of wind whipped sand across the road and into Caitlin's eyes. She flinched. 'Yes, please. I'm actually heading to The Lodge. But I've forgotten to ask where it is.'

'Yeah, I know — Charlie mentioned. I'm going there too.'

'You are?' There was a silence as they both waited in their cars, looking at each other. 'I don't think my air conditioning is working,' Caitlin said, dumbly.

Sienna looked concerned, like she'd sat down next to a confused old lady on the bus. 'Do you — do you want me to give you a lift?'

Despite the unsettling noise coming from the vents of Sienna's car, the Nissan's air-con was blessedly effective and Caitlin settled into the front seat with relief. The car smelt of patchouli and, faintly, marijuana. Sienna wore a crocheted singlet top and a pair of old 501s that Caitlin suspected were the exact style she herself had worn in 1994. Although this pair had been hacked into shorts in a way that would have killed Dot, dead on the spot, if she'd witnessed Caitlin do such a thing. Sienna's glossy black hair was pulled up in a scrappy bun, revealing a delicate buzz of shaved hair beneath. A filagree of tiny tattooed dots wound from the nape of her neck down her vertebrae. She was probably the coolest person Caitlin had ever been in a car with.

'So what takes you to The Lodge?' Why did she sound like a children's television host every time she asked someone under twenty-five a question?

'I kinda work there. I help set up and pack down from the retreats. Sheets, toiletries, that sort of stuff. I also get to use the space when it's empty.' Sienna looked briefly at Caitlin as she changed gears up the hill. 'Charlie's good like that.'

Caitlin wondered if Charles had put Sienna on the PR trail. 'He did mention that he likes to — what was the phrase? — "be of use"?'

'Be of *service*.' Sienna smiled. 'Don't worry, he's not a whack job. He genuinely likes helping people. It's sweet.'

Caitlin bristled again at the idea of Charles being known for helping charity cases. 'What do you mean, "use the space"?' she asked.

'Use it to … study. Research.' Sienna tapped her nails along the steering wheel. She spoke again, more quickly; as if daring Caitlin to cut her off. 'I'm setting up a food-based community project in Wertham. It's all about sustainability, and seasonality, all in this, like, multicultural, community-led way.'

It was Caitlin's turn to look at Sienna. She was a lot less subtle with her glance, her mouth was slightly agape and she made a noise like, *Oh?*

Sienna laughed nervously, proudly. 'I bet you thought I was going to say I was doing shell art or something, right?'

'Um, yes, actually. I'm sorry. That was really presumptuous of me.'

'Nah, that's okay. I look like a beach rat because I am one. At least, I am when I'm back in the Bay. It's so nice to just *be* here, away from the city. Melbourne's so — ugh — it's not a good place for me at the moment.'

'Oh well, good for you.' Oh, why did she sound like a children's television host every time she asked someone under twenty-five a question, *or* complimented them? 'So are you studying this food project approach?' Caitlin said each word like they didn't connect with the previous one.

'Yeah — unofficially.'

'And officially?'

'My dad's having a coronary.'

Caitlin didn't know whether she was allowed to laugh or not. Sienna had a small smile that permanently played around the edges of her mouth. Young people these days were always so *amused*. When she was around her age it was all she could do not to pass out from the literal panic of becoming an adult. 'Well, I can't think of a better place to unofficially study anything,' Caitlin said, watching the wind tug at a white petal that hung in the small tangle of cobwebs decorating one of the wing mirrors. 'Have you always lived in Arana Bay?'

Sienna changed gears like she worked the coffee machine, slowly, with purpose. 'You're sounding like Charlie with these questions. I don't think I've heard you say this much since you arrived.' There was that little smile, again.

Caitlin bristled, again. 'Well, it doesn't take many words to order a long black.'

'I'm not having a go. It's nice to chat to someone new. We don't get many visitors around here that aren't backpackers or loaded lodgers.'

'Sorry. I'm not usually — it's, it must be this town. Gosh, it does funny things.'

'That's what my dad says.'

'Oh?'

'In a way. I dunno. My nan and pops had a place here, my dad's parents. We used to spend every summer with them before

Mum and Dad split up. Dad even did work here. But since the divorce he's …' She trailed off and Caitlin immediately, clearly, saw the child, the true child, who was driving the car. 'He's not really a fan of the Bay,' Sienna finished quietly.

'He's not?' Caitlin said this incredulously, watching slivers of the blue sea flicker through the trees below as the car took them higher.

'Nope. He's really not. He's not a fan of the Bay, or his daughter or, well, anything at the moment.'

'Oh, I'm sure that's not the case,' Caitlin said, feeling further out of her depth at discussing someone else's parent–child relationship.

'Anyway!' Sienna interrupted herself with a false bravado but a real smile. 'Here we are.' Caitlin bent forward in her seat to gaze up at the climb before them. It was just like in the pictures. Now it was Caitlin's turn to smile.

ii. Lunchtime

The middle of the day smells of soup and farts. Guess that means they're serving cabbage, or broccoli. Another day and another relief that I can't eat anything at all. Me and my knockabout pals, that's us: no eating and no messing around. Must be a laugh a minute in this place. It kind of is, though. There's often laughter from a little while away. Low blokes' voices and lighter ones from the girls. They're doctors and nurses — I've worked that much out — and they're all having a pretty good time. Wish I could hear what's so damn funny. I can't make out a thing over the machines. Christ, they're loud. The ventilator next to me sounds like a sad locomotive, gasping its way around my bed. There's one for each of us, lucky ducks. No-one misses out.

Did I say us? There are three of us. Me, and Fred, and someone else. I know there are three of us because I heard there were originally four. 'We're down to three,' a voice said one day.

I'm jealous of lucky number four. And feeling a little sad that I didn't notice the arrival or departure of a whole other person.

Arrivals and departures. 'Visiting hour', it's called. The ones who can speak are so sad about the ones who can't. Our guests walk around us, stroke our hair and our feet. One smells so familiar I want to cry.

I heard another lady say, 'I don't know how they cope with that noise', and I felt grateful for her, but then she continued, 'although I guess no-one can hear anything anyway'.

I can hear.

I can hear everything including when she whispered to the body in the bed next to me, 'Wake up, Fred. Please. Please my love, wake up.'

She whispered like someone who had broken in two and I wanted to roll away and cover my ears. But I couldn't. None of us can. Poor Fred, having to hear that, right up in his face where he can't ignore it. Hope that one stays away now; haven't heard her in a while. I wonder if she will return to the body called Fred and the machines that wheeze and hum and buzz.

But until then I lie and I listen and I wait to die.

Chapter Sixteen

Arana Lodge declared itself with a large sign carved out of weathered grey timber, set back into the bushes at the bottom of a long, steep driveway. The Nissan complained at the elevation, but Sienna deftly managed the drive with its rises and sharp turns. 'I reckon one of the best things about The Lodge is where it is, tucked away up behind the top of the town — the view's unreal.'

Caitlin wasn't looking at the view. She watched for the building as they turned the last dogleg of road. They both got out of the car and Caitlin stood staring up, like a child on a school excursion. The rhapsodically detailed TV episode hadn't done the scale justice — The Lodge was even bigger than she had realised. A wall emerged from the sandstone face of the hill, appearing to have evolved from the rock itself. The sweeping middle of the building was wrapped in oxidised steel: set back behind trees, a bunker of burnished rust. The top floor was more glass than anything else, smoked so it almost disappeared into the reflections of clouds and gum trees. Sienna was already pushing open the main door, a double-height piece of ironbark pivoting smoothly to reveal a polished floor and a foyer of warm timber, lit by sun piercing from hidden places.

'My mum calls it Blofeld's Lair. I had to google who that was.'

'I guess it's not everyone's cup of tea. But I think it's' — Caitlin was surprised to feel her voice wobbling a little — 'it's just beautiful.' Her voice echoed as she followed Sienna inside and then dropped to silence as she took in the deep, cool space that enveloped them. Caitlin noticed Sienna now held a Birkenstock in each hand. She followed suit, slipping her thongs off. As her bare feet met the floor, she realised that it was not polished concrete but a much softer earthen floor which managed to be cool and warm at the same time. The foyer was irregularly shaped, with the deep red cladding stretching high above, as if the towering gums across the hill were growing inside as well. She saw that it was irregularly spaced skylights that cast beams of light down into the dim room, spotlighting corners of the space.

'It definitely grows on you.' Charles entered from the wide hall that ran into the far side of the foyer, his own bare feet and linen trousers making him look quite like a Bond villain. 'You came together?'

Sienna waved goodbye to Caitlin and disappeared behind another door.

'My map-reading was compromised. Sienna saved me.'

'Excellent. She's a good girl. Bloody clever. Helps me with some of the accounting nonsense. She's going through it right now, I'm happy to help her.'

'Yes, she mentioned something about her father …' Caitlin's voice quietened. She didn't want to be the gossiping tourist. Charles didn't seem to notice.

'Richard? Yes. Tricky business. I'm trying not to get in the middle of it all.' He glanced over to where Sienna had left. 'I'm the last person who should be giving parenting advice. But she is still so young.'

Charles clapped, once — a punctuation for them both. 'Now. Would you like the grand tour, or do you just want to get stuck in?'

Caitlin was full of curiosity, but she had also started to feel acute anxiety about being digitally AWOL for two weeks. Over Charles's shoulder a narrow table stretched between two doors almost hidden in the dark walls. A low vase held sprays of tree branches, beside a fat candle that was filling the space with the gentle scent of citrus and tobacco. It calmed her, a little. 'Maybe just the whistle-stop?'

He nodded, seeing the curtain of worry that had briefly drawn over her eyes. Gesturing back towards the hall, Charles encouraged her. 'Please.'

She followed him through the dim foyer and blinked at the sudden, brilliant sunshine in what was an angled glass walkway. They were floating in the trees, in a bridge between the entrance to The Lodge and the body of it, the glass hall spanning a narrow but deep gully. Far below, Caitlin made out the silverfish flickers of a running stream.

'That makes it all the way down to the sea. It's tame this time of year, but in the winter …' Charles's fingers absentmindedly grazed the timber barre that ran the length of the walkway, steadying himself and making his point.

Caitlin looked at the bunker they had left, trying to get her bearings. 'I didn't realise the building was so big.'

They had made it to the other side of The Lodge. He pointed back to the foyer. 'We started with the entrance, some workspaces and a very underused boardroom when someone thought corporate retreats were a good idea. And here' — he turned to introduce the extraordinary space that Caitlin recalled clearly — 'is our gathering place: the Great Room, or lounge — whatever you want to call it.' Caitlin remembered the TV host had declared it to be 'a cathedral of light'.

The soaring ceilings of the foyer were still there, but here they were lit by a sweep of floor-to-ceiling windows. Nests of tables, couches and chairs filled the room in a way that made Caitlin hear low murmuring and the rustle of pages — even though they were the only two people there. Charles was opening the windows in a concertina of glass that should have taken more effort that the gentle push he was giving with one hand. And with that, Caitlin heard and felt and smelt it all at once. A sea of treetops opened out beyond the silvery deck, the gums rippling with wind and scenting the room with lemon and leaves and creek-damp earth, and beneath it all — the faint smell of salt. Over the trees a thick stroke of blue reminded her that they were floating above the sea. She didn't realise her hand was up to her throat and her eyes were closed, until Charles coughed discreetly.

'Oh,' she said, embarrassed.

He was looking at her with a kind of recognition. 'I know. I still remember when the architect first brought me up here. It was just a shell, but the view: it took my breath.' He turned back to face the panorama. 'I'm not sure I've ever recovered.'

'I only vaguely remember the TV interview, but now I'm here I should look up the episode again.'

'If you do, don't let Sienna know. She's not a fan of our esteemed architect.' Charles smiled, to himself more than her. Before Caitlin could ask him what he meant, he returned to his brisk tour-giving self. 'Now. There's a dining room, and another writing room. A kitchen and, of course, the quarters. But I have a feeling you have some business you need to attend to.'

Caitlin looked longingly at the continuation of the hall, where she could see more doors waiting for her. But her emails were calling more loudly than any floor plan could. 'If it's okay …'

'Of course. I've popped you back here.'

Returning Caitlin through the glass hall and into the almost monastic quiet of the foyer, Charles opened a door, which Caitlin wouldn't have noticed otherwise, blended into the walls around it. Inside, a small room made her gasp. Three of the four walls were glass. The room was a cube jutting out into the bush, surrounded by trees so close she could see their cobwebs and tracery. Inside there was a sofa, a desk, a lamp and a chair.

'It's a bit sparse, isn't it. We've never really found a use for this, which is such a pity because —'

'It's perfect.'

She crossed the room and looked up into the tree canopy through the glass. The light was filtered enough that the room remained cool. Behind her, Charles was tinkering with the laptop on the desk, and muttering. It chimed and he clapped. 'Ah. There we go.' He had his hands on his hips and looked pleased with himself. His wrinkled cotton shirt was unbuttoned to reveal a sprinkling of grey hair against tanned skin. Charles had the face of someone who missed smoking, and the voice of an Oxbridge professor. He may have been growing on her, but if she wasn't mistaken, he seemed a fraction less friendly to her today compared to their earlier meetings. Maybe her initial coolness had made its mark.

'Charles, this is generous of you, thank you. I promise I won't stay long.'

'Don't be silly. *Mi casa et tu casa.* The kitchen is back past the lounge, where you'll find proper English tea.' He smiled tightly. 'Stay as long as you need. I'm heading back to the Store in a couple of hours. I'll knock to see if you'd like a lift.'

After he closed the door behind him, Caitlin unplugged the laptop and carried it with her over to the worn leather couch. Sitting in the corner allowed her to face all three glass panels, and the thousand different shades of green outside. Reluctantly, she moved her eyes from the bush to the screen and reopened the door to her old life.

Jan's email was first, breathless and bringing Caitlin's house with her.

Darling, Charlie told us you're alive and well. So pleased. Isn't he lovely? It would be nice if you would reply to us. Just a little note? House is fine but we've just made this small list …

Caitlin continued through her crammed inbox, deleting messages from recruiters, department stores, a yoga app she'd subscribed to but never opened. Delete, delete, delete, Paul.

Paul.

Caitlin please instruct lawyers to reply in kind I really am very keen to keep things moving thanks Paul.

She was not ready to think about Paul or reply to Paul or even wonder what Paul's lack of punctuation meant. Caitlin's unfastening was allowing her to bend, but this email told her that it was a flex away from Paul and not the other way around.

Delete.

Back to Jan. She pulled the laptop closer and typed out a reply.

Janny & M. I'm sorry. I've been busy swimming. Every day! I dropped my phone down a crevice which was irresponsible of me. I think Divorcee Caitlin swims and doesn't have a phone. Charles is kind. Probably too kind. He's letting me use his computer and his wi-fi and his whole building really. The house I'm in, The Cicada House they call it, is horrific but the strangest thing is happening. I think I love it a little bit.

She hit send without re-reading it. And then followed up, immediately.

Sorry. Paul has a list of all friendly repairs people x

Charles drove her back to her car, talking on his phone throughout the short trip. He'd tapped on the office door just as he'd promised, waving apologies as his Bluetooth headphones blinked from their resting place in his ears.

'Yes, Charles Folantau,' he said, not to her. 'I'm following up the minibus charter that's picking up at Melbourne airport tomorrow morning.' By the time she got out of his car, he — having impressively followed her mimed directions — was shouting at the phone.

'FolanTAU! F-O-L-A-...'

He didn't say goodbye.

Back in her car, Caitlin coasted home with the windows down and the radio up too loud. The connection with Jan, and the check-in email she sent to her grandad's nursing home, had bolstered her mood more than she'd expected. As she slowed to a stop at the Cicada House's gate, she turned the engine off to hear an angry hum and buzz from the banksia. Suddenly, David exploded backwards from the foliage. He was swearing and waving his arms around.

'Bugger off!'

Four large wasps darted around his head, dive bombing his hands as he batted and swiped. Caitlin sat for a beat too long, closing her window and wondering how many stings it was acceptable to allow him to receive before she came to his rescue. When she saw the biggest wasp hit at David's upper arm, she called out through the window.

'David!'

He was frowning and ducking when he looked to her.

'Get in.'

He jogged to the car and she reached over to open the passenger door. He landed heavily in the seat and slammed the door behind him. A couple of angry wasps hit at the window, thwarted and furious.

'I see you found the nest?'

'Bloody bastards.' He was rubbing two painful welts already swelling up on his bicep. Caitlin noticed he was wearing the same T-shirt as last week. Or, maybe the man just owned more than one white T-shirt. He didn't smell bad, that was certain. He smelt pretty good actually, like salt and sun, and a little of freshly mowed grass.

Oh, for god's sake, Caitlin.

She gripped both hands on the steering wheel in an attempt to get a grip on herself. She tried to act professionally distant, even though they were sitting less than a foot from one another. Tried to summon the irritation she'd felt at their last conversation.

'So. You're back?'

He turned to face her in reply, a small smile curving his mouth.

'Looks like it.'

Chapter Seventeen

The fortnight that Caitlin fell for the local tradesman could be stepped out in drinks.

First, there was the beer. That had not been a great start. There was a chip in the laminex counter where David had popped the tops off the bottles during that first day, and Caitlin still bristled when she looked at it. You could say she had a chip somewhere else too. Yes, she'd used the 'sweetheart' moment to be the lightning rod for her anger, but if she were honest it was the way he commanded her home (*her*) so readily. Caitlin had flown around the world to find a place of her own; she didn't want to share it with another man who took up space in a way that was much bigger than his broad shoulders and heavy boots.

Although, she was more primed to be angry than David's behaviour warranted. Because he didn't, really. Take up the space. Not like Paul had. But that's because in Australia, she didn't fold herself away like she had in London. It sounded ridiculous, but being in a sense the 'employer' and David her, well, her tradesman — it helped Caitlin create a different role for herself. Which also meant that when David next called her 'sweetheart', she just … asked him not to. It was that same Friday afternoon, after they'd waited out the wasps. They had both exited the car a little cautiously, braving the walk up the drive. When it was clear the insects had retreated back to the nest David had tried to remove, he spoke.

'Well, thanks for rescuing me, sweetheart.'

'Don't call me that.' She said it calmly, with a note of tiredness.

He pulled a face like the boys on her school bus used to. 'Bloody hell, sorry.'

But then something odd happened. He stopped and looked at her. Really looked at her. The hairs on the back of her neck stood up. He spoke again, voice softer. 'Alright then.'

Caitlin began to unlock the front door. David watched her fiddle with the keys. 'Why'd you lock the door?'

'Why wouldn't I? Who doesn't lock their front door?'

'Everyone 'round here. What are you afraid of?'

Caitlin held the door open and looked at the man standing before her. With his kinked hair and dark eyes, he had a wildness in his face she hadn't come across before. She could have said 'people like you', but she didn't.

'Nothing.' The minute she said it, she meant it. There was a fearlessness in having lost Paul. Her mother. Her life as it had stood. 'I'm not afraid of anything, David.'

He watched her for a second too long, his eyes to hers.

'Yeah, I can see that.'

After that day, there was the next drink. Tea. She'd offered him a cup again and he'd declined, again. She made it for him anyway. David was out on the back porch fixing the pavers that had been lifted and rearranged by thick ropes of kikuyu grass. She'd carried a mug out to him.

'Thanks swee—'

She held on to the mug for a second, so he looked at her, and then smiled down at his feet.

'Thanks, Caitlin. But I'm not really a tea man.'

'Go on, give it a go. It's my national drink.'

He took the mug and sipped at the steaming drink warily. Nodding slowly at her over the rim he said, 'It's … it's terrible.'

'Shut up!' She was laughing.

'It tastes like sad puddle water.' So was he. 'Sorry. I've never liked it. My mum's a big tea drinker but my old man's mad on coffee. Growing up, we always had a pot on the go. I didn't realise how I would miss the smell until I moved out.'

David rested back onto the splintered post. His head tilted up, eyes half-closed in the diffused sun slanting at them through the plastic roofing. Steam buffeted away from his cuppa. He inhaled like he'd missed … everything.

'Did you grow up in Arana Bay?' Caitlin asked. She was getting used to asking questions. They may be for 'spies and gossips', but maybe, Caitlin thought, they were also for lonely people who want to connect with another human.

He opened his eyes, refocusing them on hers, and smiled. It was enough of an invitation for Caitlin to sit down on the back step.

'Nah, not the Bay. Further up the coast. But we moved down here when the factory Dad was at closed. He opened up a fruit and veg store round here.'

'Really? In town? Would I know it?'

David gamely took another sip. 'Don't believe you would.'

In the past, Caitlin would steer away from conversations about family, in case the questions rebounded to her and forced her to talk about Dot, and Bill … and her mother. But David had a steady, knowing calm about him. He made the space between them feel safe, which was something that allowed her to feel okay about filling it with her words for once.

'What about you? Your family back in England?' he asked.

'Well yes, but — I don't really have any family. It's really only me and my grandad. I'm an only child.'

'Righto. But you are a pom?'

'Yes. I'm a "pom". But, not technically. I was born in Melbourne, but I left when I was really little.'

'Ah, I knew why I liked you. You're an Aussie!' Immediately, a faint blush bloomed up his neck. It was almost — but not quite — hidden by his olive skin. It made Caitlin want to laugh. It made her want to keep talking. It also made her want to ask, *You like me?*

Instead, she clarified, 'My mum was English. I don't know much about my father, apart from the fact that, yes, he was Australian.'

'That's all you know about him? I'd call that a little less than "much",' said David.

'You're right. All I know about' — the word 'father' stuck in her throat the second time — 'him, is that he was Australian. My mum left home when she was seventeen and travelled down here with some sort of … band. I think.'

'You think?'

David joined her on the step and she couldn't believe how wobbly she felt to be in close proximity to someone who wasn't Paul. And by 'someone', she meant 'a man'.

This man, who was so different to her husband. Who smelt like a garden in early summer. Whose voice came from the back of his throat like a purr. Paul moved like someone who wanted to be elsewhere, always. David existed in this world like his body was part of the whole ecosystem.

'I don't know why she left home. I never really asked. It was made pretty clear by my grandparents that it was not a topic for discussion.'

He was too close for Caitlin to twist and look at him without feeling self-conscious. But she felt his body bristle and heard his breath get sucked in, fast. 'That's bullshit. Children should always know their parents, whether they're around or not.'

This was the point where, in previous, rare conversations about her family, Caitlin would normally move herself away — often physically. After the first year of their relationship, Paul had learnt not to follow Caitlin into another room when she tried to put steps between her and her past. But on this afternoon she wanted very badly to keep sitting alongside David, to feel the warmth coming from his limbs so close to hers. So she kept talking, to keep them together, plaiting conversation like a rope between the two of them.

'It wasn't easy for my grandparents. Susan — that was my mum — she was their only child. And it sounds like she was pretty wild. I think she gave them a rough time.'

'How do you know, if they didn't talk about it?'

Caitlin had known this man for less than a week and he was asking her questions Paul never had. But it was more than just questions and curiosity. With David, Caitlin was discovering a voice that she hadn't spoken with before. His deep belonging in this place gave her the same sense of security that the house itself had begun providing. It was a powerful combination.

'Go on — how'd you know she was a wild one?'

'Well. I don't. I guess I just picked it up. I heard some stuff about her being "off the rails".' David snorted. Caitlin continued, thinking out loud, 'Although, my grandparents thought unironed jeans were risqué so I'm not quite sure what "off the rails" meant to them.'

'I guess I wouldn't feel great about my daughter flying across the world at seventeen.'

Caitlin's ears buzzed. 'You have a daughter?'

He shook his head and his hair swept his shoulders. It really did smell like freshly cut grass. 'Nope. Just saying, if I did, I wouldn't like it.'

That was the precise moment Caitlin realised she had a little crush. The point when the bearded guy with the olive skin and the faded jeans told her he didn't have kids, and her heart leapt. 'Well, my grandparents certainly didn't like it. Their daughter was seventeen and she left home to tour Australia with *a band*.'

'Groupie.'

'David, don't call my dead mother a groupie!' She was laughing again, because it felt surreal to be joking about someone whose name she hadn't liked to say out loud for most of her childhood.

'Ah, there's nothing wrong with being a groupie. I've hung out with a few in my time.'

'You're a musician?'

'I think you've gotta get paid to be a musician. But yeah, I play a little.' He looked pleased that she'd guessed. 'Like your dad, was he in the band?'

'No. Oh, I don't know. I've only heard this third-hand. The only reason I'm sure she met my dad in Australia was because the band she travelled with were all British. They all came back home for her, for the —' *Oh shit. Here we go.* '— for her funeral.'

* * *

Five years old and on a plane for the first time. Memories this far back were foggy. But some details remained. Bill wore a jacket and tie, both of which clashed with the engine-red upholstery. He sat upright and unmoving for the whole journey from Melbourne to London, while she wriggled and craned to watch the movie projected on the screen at the front of the cabin. Thinking about it now, he mustn't have reclined his seat at any point. A self-flagellation in an already torturous position. A father who had lost his only child. A journey to bring a wide-eyed orphan home, when all he must have wanted was his own little girl back.

* * *

This time, David turned to her, unperturbed by the fact that their legs and arms were pressed up against each other. He pulled his head back a little, as if to take her whole expression in. His voice was already deep, but when he next spoke, it came out almost as a growl. 'Your mum died, when you were a kid.' It was a statement, not a question. His brown eyes had turned black.

She couldn't tell if he was angry or sad. For a quick moment he went very far away.

'Yes.' Her voice was small. It felt surreal to be having this conversation twice in a month after having it twice in two decades. Without taking his eyes off hers, David lifted his hand and lay it over her bare knee. She felt the size, the weight, and the heat.

He said slowly, carefully, 'And look at you, still here, living a life full of wilds and wonder.'

It was so unexpected a reply that she thought maybe she'd blacked out for a second. Her mouth was open as she stared back at his face. He was looking directly into her eyes, with an expression of kindness and wisdom that felt older than both of them. She swallowed. 'Yes. Look at me.'

And finally, there was the whisky. It hadn't come straight after the tea. It could have been two weeks after that first cup. Since then, they'd shared half a dozen mugs of the sad puddle water. Sometimes on the back step. Often with Caitlin trailing David around the property. He had begun to use her as a builder's assistant, giving her instructions while he hammered or pulled or nailed something. Sometimes, they swapped roles and he watched on while she banged the wonky bits of the house back in place.

The falling-down shed was a carpet bag and David was Mary Poppins. Much like the bustling nanny, he came and went with the wind. His scheduling was erratic. At first Caitlin had tried to pin him down, asking after calendars and business cards and suggesting 'set days'. He'd shielded the low afternoon sun from his eyes as he rested against the side fence. 'You like organising stuff, don't you?'

'Well, I guess. I'm just trying to …' She faltered.

'What?'

'I don't know. Make it easier for you … to arrange your day?'

'Don't you mean make it easier for *you*?'

'Sorry. No. I meant —' She was flustered.

'I'm okay, Caitlin. When I'm here, I work on the house.' He grinned quickly. 'Or I teach you how to work on the house. When I'm not, I …' He turned around and inspected a loose fence post. It wasn't a very subtle avoidance tactic, as it wasn't a very loose post. 'I like being here.' He spoke towards the ground.

'Sorry?' She'd heard what he said.

'I like helping out here. If it's okay with you, I'll just come when I can.'

'Sure. Of course, yes. I mean — it's not even my place. I just hope you're charging Tracey what you're owed.'

There was that faraway look in his eyes again, looking over her shoulder at the house. 'What time is it?'

She'd noticed he didn't wear a watch (or a wedding ring — *Shut up, Caitlin*). She looked at her own, a cheap plastic thing she'd bought at the newsagent when she'd decided not to replace her phone.

'It's 5.30.'

He grinned again. It was something she was seeing more often, and it was intoxicating. The edge of his mouth lifted in such a way that she wanted to run away with him. Could a smile do that? And then he was off, striding back across the block, one arm stretched out above him like a flag to be followed. How could one person be so goddamned relaxed?

He called over his shoulder, 'Come on!'

Caitlin found him in the kitchen with a crowbar.

'Where'd you get that?'

She didn't wait for the answer as she knew what it would be, and so they both said in unison, 'Shed.'

He bent down and peeled the lino back, revealing dusty floorboards underneath. The crowbar fitted easily enough under the timber and she heard the cracking of old nails as David lifted it up.

'Bloody hell, David! What are you doing!?'

'Can you hold the board up?' He was motioning for her to take over the levering. She didn't ask why. She was at the point of her crush where she would do almost anything for him, without question. Caitlin bent down and once she had control of the crowbar, David lay flat on the lino, with one arm stretched down into the dark beneath the house, all the way to his shoulder. His cheek lay on the dusty floor beside the hole he'd just created, and he looked up at Caitlin and winked. It was her turn to blush.

There was grunting, muttering and a few swear words. '... Ha!' David pulled his arm back out and Caitlin saw he was gripping a dusty brown bottle. 'Bloody beauty!'

'Can I let go of this now?' Her arms were getting a bit shaky. As he took over the crowbar and put the floor back together, Caitlin examined the bottle. It was whisky, and judging by the label and the amount of dust, it was carrying some age.

'How did you know that was there?'

He was sifting through her cupboards looking for glasses, produced two tumblers and then pulled the stopper out of the bottle with a satisfying *pop*. David poured them both two fingers of Scotch, handed her a glass and raised his. 'What should we toast to?' he asked.

'Erm ... adventures?' Her voice sounded giddy.

'Okay. To adventures.'

Caitlin raised her glass to meet his. 'And things.'

They clinked glasses.

'To adventures, and things.'

It was past nine and Caitlin was washing the dishes. David had hung around for another drink, before heading off. She'd become used to his abrupt arrivals and departures, and found the rhythm had even started to feel natural, like a person adapting to the weather occurring without an accompanying forecast. As she sudsed through the sink, she hummed to herself. They hadn't polished off enough whisky to be drunk, but Caitlin definitely felt lighter. The drink had relaxed them both, and they had talked in a way that felt vivid and easy, ribbing one another about their different accents, and words for things, and Caitlin's obsession with tea. She stood moving the dish brush around and around a now clean plate, and realised she was thinking of the patch of skin she'd seen on David's stomach, when he was on the floor, fossicking for the bottle. It was brown. It was smooth. There was a tiny scar, no bigger than her thumbnail. She shook her head out of her Mills & Boon daydream and looked down to the length of kitchen floor that now sat without any lino.

Caitlin realised David had never answered her question — how had he known about the stash under her floor?

Chapter Eighteen

'So a half is sort of like a pot, and a schooner's a schooner and obviously you know what a pint is. These are jugs. I'm assuming you've heard of a pony?'

Caitlin looked back from the bar to Erin, who was sitting at the closest table with an amused expression on her face.

'I have no idea what you're talking about. Can I just have two beers please? Cold, and served in a glass?'

The young bartender, Jack, was looking dubiously at her, the tanned Englishwoman with wild sea-salt hair. The surf club was quiet again. Two grey-haired women played cards. She could hear the cook watching footy clips in the kitchen. It was less quiet than a night alone in The Cicada House, but only just. She carried the drinks back to Erin.

'Thanks, babe.' Erin pulled on the beer. 'Mm. That's good. I'm sorry I haven't been able to hang out more, work is mental at the moment and Gaz has been away so I've had Josh full-time. This is my first night off in yonks.'

Caitlin carefully opened a bag of Twisties and lay the offering between them. Erin looked around at the nearly empty room. 'You must have *really* wanted to get out of the house. The club's weird on a Monday. I didn't think they opened this early in the week. There's not even any music. How's it all going? You've been here, what, a month now?'

'Yep, almost exactly.'

'Right. No wonder you're bored. Most people would have given up and headed to Melbourne by now.'

Caitlin thought of David's hand sitting on her knee. Her breath fluttered up her chest a little. *Ridiculous.* 'I like it here. It's what I wanted.'

'You wanted an outdoor loo?'

'Maybe not that part. But it's the faraway-ness of it all.'

The way David held the back of his neck when he was thinking to himself.

'And The Cicada House is …'

His eyes creasing with focus as they rehung the bedroom door.

'… it feels like a really safe place.'

The heat of his bare arm against hers as he showed her how to call to the banjo frog.

Erin looked at her, her own eyes narrowed. 'Right.' She sounded suspicious. 'And this "safe space" has nothing to do with a certain rich Englishman living in the hills above town?'

Caitlin couldn't help herself. An involuntary *Ha!* shot out of her, loud enough to cause the two old biddies to pause their card game and look around. Caitlin waved a 'sorry' at them.

'I'm using Charles's internet and his tea-making facilities, both of which are excellent. He's a lovely man. There's nothing going on beyond that.'

'Sure. Whatever you say. But a tall drink of water like that, the blue eyes, the accent, that chest hair …'

Caitlin was still laughing, 'He's old enough to be my dad!'

'Bullshit he is. He's what, fifteen years older than us? And who doesn't love the silver-fox thing he's got going for himself? Women love a man with grey hair. Particularly one that sells them coffee and *The Herald* in the morning.'

'You're bonkers. He's a nice guy and that's that. I am not in the market for a summer romance.'

David's eyes, carefully watching hers, as she told him about the day that Diana died.

Caitlin was relieved to see two men arrive at the top of the stairs, entering the bar in stubbies shorts and work boots. She recognised the bigger fellow as the builder who directed her to the Store on her first ill-fated stop in town, four weeks ago. He stopped at their table while his friend carried on to the bar.

'G'day.'

Erin looked up at him. 'G'day, Scotty.'

He nodded, said, 'Hello, love,' and turned to Caitlin. 'The Cicada House okay?'

Caitlin was reminded that this town was tiny and filled with everyone's stories. 'Hello. The house is great thanks.'

Scotty looked dubious, but before he could reply, his friend brought back a perfectly poured pot, which sat like a thimble in the builder's enormous hands. 'Ladies.' He lifted his drink to Erin and Caitlin and was excused.

'I'm just teasing you about Charlie. He's a good bloke. We're all fans,' she said.

'Yes, I know. You were saying the other night how much The Lodge has helped the town.'

'It's not just that. The people in the Bay love a battler.'

Caitlin laughed. 'A "battler"? Charles has more plums in his mouth than my second-year literature lecturer. And apparently *he* used to shag Princess Margaret.'

'I know Charles is posh. No, it's what he's done. How he's sorted himself out.' Erin sighed, like she didn't want to gossip, but she also really did. 'I don't know him, but I know the story. He turned up at the Bay ten years ago, with a fair few demons. This here' — she tapped the side of her glass with an acrylic nail — 'was not his friend. He lost money, his wife took their kids and went back to the UK. Shit — poor bloke bottomed out in a town where everyone knows what knickers you've been drying on the line. It's no surprise he's kept to himself since then.'

Caitlin inspected her hands. There was still a ridged mark where she'd removed her wedding ring five weeks earlier. She said quietly, 'I didn't even ask.'

'It's okay. You didn't know.'

'No, I mean — I've asked nothing.' She looked up at Erin. 'I've spent so long not telling anyone my story that I've forgotten how to ask after others'.'

Erin rolled her eyes. 'Oh god, here we go. What did I tell you about being easier on yourself?'

'I know. I just —'

'You know what, Caitlin, stop starting sentences with "I". It's not about you. Give yourself a break from the self-pity and try to focus some of that sympathy on someone else for a bit. Pay attention. Ask questions. Listen to the answers!'

Caitlin was taken aback. Her first impulse was to bristle before disappearing into a passive-aggressive fug. That was how she managed all of her irritations with Paul. It was how Dot had managed all of her irritations with, well, everyone. Erin was watching Caitlin's face as she flicked through this thought process. In the end, all Caitlin could manage was blank-faced surprise, then silence, then — and this was new — laughter. Erin joined in and held up her glass.

'Another round?'

Caitlin dipped the sponge back into the bowl of warm water and vinegar. The bathroom tiles were making marks on her knees. David had told her his mother swore by the solution, so she scrubbed harder and ignored her complaining back.

She hadn't stopped thinking about what Erin had said in the days that had passed since their beer at the club. Caitlin had been so disarmed by the laser-like analysis that she hadn't said anything at all. It wasn't just the words Erin had aimed at her, but the laughter they'd shared afterwards. Caitlin had experienced something almost completely foreign: a difficult, honest conversation that didn't end a relationship.

Was she self-pitying? Her (well, Dot's) modus operandi had always been to 'keep going quietly'. Surely that was the opposite of self-flagellation? But then, Caitlin could hear Paul's voice tuning in alongside Erin's: *'When are you ever going to take down that armour?'*

Caitlin sat back heavily, throwing the sponge in the bowl. The weather was cooler than it had been for weeks. She could tell the birds felt it too — the maggies were particularly active today. She smiled, proud of herself for actually knowing when the magpies were up and about. David had spent an afternoon explaining the family's relationships to her, pointing up at the black and white trio perched on the electrical wire by the house.

'That's the dad, you can tell because his feathers are snow white. Mum is a bit greyer, but that's probably because of their teenager. I'd be turning grey too if I had to feed a fat, fluffy one squawking up a storm.'

At the time Caitlin was focused mostly on David's voice, warm and unguarded — a tone she was hearing often as they spent more days together. But, she was surprised to note, she'd obviously been listening to David's nature lessons as well.

Clearly after just a month in Australia, she was changing. Maybe more physically than emotionally. The face that looked back at her in the small, mottled bathroom mirror was different. Freckles she didn't know she had were sprinkled across her nose and cheeks, and spread up to her forehead. Her skin may have darkened, but everything else had become lighter. She didn't know eye colour could change. Hers were now a pale green, brightening from the hazel she had flown over with. Her hair was a lighter blonde too. The sedate bob had grown — in its now almost permanent sea-salt state it was an unfurled mess of coils and half-curls. She may have looked like a local, but she knew she didn't think — or act — like one. And after the psychological dissection from Erin, she was aware that blonder hair and a tan-line weren't the shifts that needed to happen. Caitlin winced, remembering the way she'd let her eyes glide over Charles's face, refusing to really engage him. Taking his office space and the spare key he'd proffered, and even his free groceries, without genuinely thanking him. Maybe it was too late — she remembered his last wave as he dropped her back to her car. It was backwards and vague. It reminded her of Paul. Caitlin knew what she needed to do. She grabbed her keys and headed for The Lodge.

As she punched the numbers into the keypad at the bottom of the hill, Caitlin felt a little thrill that she was allowed private access to a place she'd once gaped at from her sofa in North London. She pulled her car around the back of the estate, behind the recycled water tanks. Another thrill, driving into one of the spots reserved for staff, even though these were just roughly marked spray-painted lines on tanbark and soil. Sienna's Nissan wasn't there, but Charles's banged-up old BMW was; which was good, because he was the person Caitlin wanted to see.

She let herself in through the back entrance and walked the long, central corridor — her bare feet padding on the smooth floor. She came upon the Great Room again, which this time was actually holding a small gaggle of guests spread out across the lounges and tables, some on laptops, some reading. The windows were again folded open in a glass accordion. On the balcony hammocks were dotted around the perimeter, some swinging with middle-aged women, like drowsy possums in culottes. Invisible monks sang from a Bang & Olufsen speaker. Caitlin wondered: what books came from such an environment?

She almost bumped into Charles folded into the shadows of the foyer, looking furtive. Caitlin greeted him, and he shushed her. 'Be quiet! I am *in hiding*.'

'Want to hide in here with me?' She held the door open to 'her' office and gestured him inside. He followed and collapsed onto the couch. 'The latest instalment of guests are' — Charles looked over his shoulder, as if worried they'd followed him into the room — 'rather high maintenance.'

'Yes, Sienna mentioned she was doing extra time on dishes and linen. Aren't they meant to be humble authors, looking for solitude to write the next masterpiece in?'

'You'd think so. This batch are more *Rich Housewives of Sydney*. I think they believed this to be a five-star coastal retreat, with me ghost-writing their memoirs.'

'Sounds like there are worse jobs: a bunch of women telling you their secrets.'

Charles shivered. 'Ugh. Please don't. One of them keeps offering to "align my chakras".'

Caitlin didn't know how to move easily from small talk to real talk. So she didn't. Instead, she sat heavily on the couch next to him.

'Hello!' said Charles, startled by her sudden proximity.

'Charles, I don't think I'm a particularly good person.'

He raised one eyebrow. 'Well, that's a party-starter.'

'You've been so generous in letting me use this beautiful space. I haven't repaid you in kind.'

'Repaid? Don't offend me, Caitlin. I don't need compensation.'

'No. Not money, although, as I keep saying, I would like to pay you some rent. Charles, I haven't repaid you with any friendship.'

'Ah. Friendship?' He looked amused, but there was an angle of knowing that sat hard in his eyes. 'And how would you expect to do that?'

This was too difficult. She didn't like this feeling. Caitlin wanted to shut it, and him, down. But Erin's words hung over her. She persisted; stopped and shook her hands out in front of her to reset. 'I don't know. It's just — I don't think I know how to make friends. I haven't asked you questions about yourself, to start with.'

He was softening. She could see it, in his face, and his shoulders. 'My girl, I am an open book of very few pages. Ask away. But I don't think that's how a friendship is decided.'

'Well, then how is it worked out? Because I've been pondering this and I don't think I've ever made a friend, in all my life.'

Caitlin could sense Charles regarding her, and wondered if he could see how much she'd loosened since that first day at the Store. Surely it was obvious. But maybe not to others. While she was no longer a tightly coiled spring, she still held the energy of an alarm clock that hadn't yet rung.

'How is a friendship decided, Caitlin? In my experience, you ask for help. You are vulnerable. You expose your soft underbelly and hope like hell they don't slice you open.'

Caitlin gulped, losing her nerve in one swallow.

Charles continued, 'Asking questions is one thing. But asking for help is quite another. It's the difference between a companion and a confidant. The bravest thing I ever did was ask for help.'

'Do you think I need help?'

'That's not the right question.'

Caitlin blew out sharply. Irritated. Safe. She'd never felt both at the same time.

'Charles.'

'Caitlin.'

'Would you help me? Please?'

Chapter Nineteen

Charles smiled, with all of himself. Clapped once and shouted, 'Aha!' She jumped a little. 'You know what this means?' he asked. His mood had lifted, in such a way that she saw she'd been right in her earlier assessment. He had been blunted. And now, he wasn't.

Caitlin did not know what 'this' meant.

'It's time for tea, on the roof. Follow me.' He was being conspiratorial again. His voice made her want to tiptoe, so that's what she did, shadowing his long stride as he made his way quickly across the foyer and along the walkway.

'Oh, Charles!' A voice that smelt of Elizabeth Arden. 'Charlie!'

'Be right with you!' he boomed out across the space, and then quietly to Caitlin, 'Stay in the shadows and avoid eye contact — I'll meet you at the bottom of the next stairs.'

He slipped into the kitchen and Caitlin carried on past more closed doors and discreetly lit art. She was watching the sky through high, long windows when Charles arrived with mugs and gestured with his eyebrows, urgently. 'Up!' he hissed.

Climbing past the sign that read *Quarters*, they carried on to the top floor where a slightly larger plaque read *Private*.

'My rooms. Chop chop, keep going.'

Urged on by Charles's flapping, Caitlin found herself on a narrow, steep staircase — not finished to the same exacting standards as the spaces below.

'Why are you still whispering?'

'They have supersonic hearing. Come on, tea's getting cold.'

'God, Charles, your mother … disowned you? Can people even do that these days?'

From where they sat on the roof, they could watch the ocean from over the tree-line, a deep blue smudge with white caps tripping along the horizon. The space had not been finished with lounging in mind. It had a roughly tarred surface that had heated up in the sun and burnt the soles of Caitlin's feet. The edge, unsullied by a railing or balcony, dropped dramatically to the trees. Despite these dangers, it was clearly a favourite spot for somebody. A few oversized cushions had been propped up in the shade where the floor met the back wall, and a couple of bottle caps pointed to a shared sundowner or two. Caitlin wondered briefly if she was the first woman Charles had brought up to the roof.

He shrugged. 'My family's aristocracy. They can do anything they want. No-one served me any papers, if that's what you're wondering. They didn't have to raise the "estrangement flag", although that would be something …'

This was the first time Caitlin had ever heard anything other than affability in Charles's voice. But it was just a little flash of bitterness that disappeared as quickly as it had arrived.

'Caitlin, before I was brave, before I was here — I was a right royal bastard. I lied, I stole and I cheated. I did all of these things so often that they created entirely new pathways in my brain that were very difficult to rewire.'

Caitlin stared. It was hard to reconcile the behaviour he was describing with the person she was getting to know. He looked at her expression and said wryly, 'Oh, I know — "good old Charlie, how could he do such a thing?"'

'Well, yes. You seem very — not like that.'

'Addiction is a beast. It's not an excuse, but it's an explanation. I made many poor choices that delivered me to a point the movies call "rock bottom". I've been sober for nearly a decade, but there were some moments —' He stopped, sighed and continued, 'Caitlin, my ex-wife and my two girls and my mother do not speak to me. They haven't for nearly ten years. Some might think what I did was unforgivable. Others might feel what they have done is just as bad — maybe worse. It has been a source of horrific pain. But I am still here. The sun shines, the waves lift me up, new people come and go through my life.'

'That sounds incredibly well-balanced,' Caitlin said, in a not unsuspicious way.

'Perhaps. Not always. When the girls all left, I was alone and angry and drunk. Which is a terrible combination when you have too much money and nothing else.'

'What happened?'

'I was helped. By this place, and some special people. Therapy was part of it, of course.' Charles caught what she thought had been a subtle roll of her eyes. 'You're not a fan of therapy?'

She flushed. 'I'm sorry. All that talky-psych stuff, I know it's great for many. Just not for me.'

He nodded in the irritating 'That's what they all say' way that people in therapy did, but carried on without pushing her.

'I also attended an outpatient addiction support group for years. Building Arana Lodge was something else. Part of the saving. Of myself. Of course, not many people have a couple of million quid in "go away" money to aid their recovery. I know my privilege.'

Caitlin heard her grandad's voice: *'You have an inheritance'*. She felt guilty for spending some of it on a Business Class flat bed.

'Is that what happened? They gave you money?' She was embarrassed by how shocked she sounded. Shocked, prim and naive.

'Well I should bloody well hope so. I considered opening my own recovery centre, but I needed space to be away from that world. Writers are the perfect antidote to reality.' He was smiling.

Caitlin didn't know what to say. She looked down at her feet on the black bitumen. 'So now? Are you okay?' she asked.

'Yes. Time heals. Except when it doesn't and that's why a support network is crucial. I miss my daughters so much. Mostly, it's an invisible grief. Which can make it harder and easier at the same time.'

He smiled out at the water. Caitlin kept her eyes on his face. In profile, with his heavy stroke of jaw and stridently aquiline nose, he looked like a portrait hanging in a castle. Probably one that his family owned. How could a person be so honest, yet so at peace with their honesty? Charles seemed to sense her incredulity.

'The thing that this whole messy life has taught me, Caitlin, is don't die wondering. I tried to make it better. I still do. I write letters and send them out into the ether. I create scrapbooks and I stick photos into albums and I do it all because one day I know my children are going to come looking for the type of person I became; after I was the person they didn't want to know anymore.'

'I'm sorry, Charles.' She squeezed his hand and it shocked her to feel him squeeze back.

Caitlin's ears were ringing, but this time she wasn't going to faint. No. She was going to ask for something, instead. Something she'd never allowed herself.

'Charles. My mother. She died here, in Australia.'

'I thought that might be the case.'

'Can you help me find more about her?'

He inclined his head, almost like a bow. 'My girl, I would be honoured.'

They started that afternoon. Charles made more tea, and carried in a plate of biscuits Sienna had baked the night before. They returned to the glass study and the leather sofa. Now the laptop was on Caitlin's knee and the biscuits on Charles's.

The cursor blinked patiently in the search box. Caitlin stared at it. Charles ate a biscuit and said to her through crumbs, 'It won't bite.'

'I don't know where to start.'

'Well. Her name? Date of birth?'

Caitlin chewed at her thumbnail and looked back at him. This was harder than she expected. 'I don't think I know her birthday.'

Charles handed her the plate, and in turn gently took the laptop. He lifted both of his forefingers over the keypad, hovering like antennae. 'Okay. Let's start somewhere. What was her name?'

'Susan Kent. She was born in … 1960, in North London. She died in '83, somewhere in Victoria. It was a car accident.'

Charles was typing as she spoke. He paused at her last word.

'She was twenty-three,' he said.

Caitlin nodded. She couldn't speak. He reached over and squeezed her hand, returning the gesture she'd made on the roof. She received it gratefully.

'It feels hard because it is hard,' he said. 'And that's okay. Now, anything else? Your father's name? Do you know where she lived?'

Caitlin thought back to her grandad's desk drawer, the one with the Pledge-scented wood and bronze lock. She used to try it, on the occasions when she was home alone. It was never unlocked and she never worked very hard to find the key. She pictured the small console that sat in the hall by the front door. It held a crystal bud vase with three plastic roses and a framed photograph of Susan, smiling and no more than ten years old — a generic, round-faced portrait.

'No, I'm sorry. I know it sounds odd that I don't have more information. Charles — you have to understand, my grandparents were broken by her death. They may have been old, and a bit dusty, but they were kind to me and loved me to the best of their abilities. But our happiness, our safety as a little trio, was predicated on us never, ever talking about my mother. From an early age I knew that if I asked questions, or spoke her name, they would … well, I think they would have just blown away.'

Charles slowly scrolled the meaningless search results, and spoke to the screen. 'I understand. But we're going to need more than we have.' He turned to her again. 'Did you say you still talk to your grandfather?'

'Yes. He's getting pretty muddled, but he's still answering my calls.'

'Well, you might want to ask him some questions before it's too late.'

Caitlin swept some biscuit crumbs back onto the plate.

'Yes. I guess I might.'

An hour of wading through the internet had left Caitlin with a sore neck and a fuzzy head. So she was grateful for a distraction, even though the interruption was shouting coming from the foyer. She couldn't make out the words, but the up and down of the woman's voice was genuinely furious.

'Sienna,' Charles sighed, rising from the couch. His lack of pace indicated that this was not the first time Sienna's outrage had echoed through the walls of The Lodge.

Caitlin followed Charles out of the room, but was surprised when he turned to cross the glass walkway rather than investigate the source of the one-sided argument. Sienna had quietened by now, and Caitlin stood marooned in the dim foyer wondering what to do. Just then, another door opened and Sienna appeared, wiping the back of her hand across her red, damp eyes. 'Oh. You're here.'

Caitlin was embarrassed. 'Sienna, hi. I — I wasn't eavesdropping. Charles and I were working in there and we heard …' She looked helplessly to where Charles had disappeared. 'Are you okay?'

'Not really.' Sienna sniffed. 'My dad.'

'Ah, I'm sorry. An argument?' Caitlin never had arguments. They seemed to take up so much energy.

'I don't know if you'd call it an argument. More an ambush. You in there?' Sienna pointed in the direction of the study.

'Oh? Would you like to sit down?'

Caitlin followed Sienna back into the small room, wondering where the hell Charles had got to. She was not qualified to discuss parent issues with a twenty-something. Sienna moved the laptop over and folded herself into the sofa. Caitlin perched awkwardly on the side of the desk.

'So.' She felt like a shitty school psychologist, which she guessed was better than a children's television presenter. 'Do you want to talk about it?'

'He's such an arsehole. He's cutting me off. Jesus, the way he talks to me!' The anger was creeping back in.

'Cutting you off, how?'

'We had a deal. As long as I stayed at uni I could live at home, rent-free, and he'd give me an allowance. I know it's pathetic, I'm twenty-two and my dad's still giving me pocket money. But Melbourne is so expensive. I work two jobs and I can barely afford petrol. Now he's kicked me out and cut me off.'

Charles had reappeared with another cup of tea. 'I can't imagine that's the whole story, Sienna. Richard's strict, but he loves you. And you're not pathetic,' he added.

Sienna took the cup. 'Thanks. But he's not being a good dad. He's a stubborn, right-winged arseh—'

Charles cut her off. Caitlin felt like she was watching a game of ping pong. 'Would this have anything to do with your talk of dropping out of university?'

Sienna sipped at the steaming herbal mix and didn't answer.

'I thought you were studying? Food sustainability things?' Caitlin added, feeling incompetent, barely keeping up.

'No. I was doing my Bachelor of Science. I've just formally withdrawn and Dad's lost his mind.'

'Ah,' said Charles.

'Oh,' said Caitlin, at the same time.

'The deal was always that he'd help me while I studied. But I hated uni and I hated the course and I hate Melbourne; and now he's lost his mind. Charles, is it okay if I stay here for the next few weeks? I'll keep the shifts at the Store, and help here of course.'

Charles steepled his hands together. 'My pleasure. Your help is so valued.'

Caitlin turned her head to Charles. 'Erm, shouldn't you check in with — is it Richard?'

'Sienna's an adult, Caitlin, I don't need to check in with her father.'

'Right. But, Sienna, your dad would be worried? It's important to look at it from his perspective. I'm sure he's feeling —'

'Indignant? *Ignorant?*' Sienna's voice was rising again. 'Dad isn't "worried", Caitlin. If he was, he wouldn't have told me "not to come home".'

Charles spoke again. 'Caitlin, it's okay. I've known Richard for a long time. I first met Sienna when she was still in primary school, marching around this building site like she owned the place.'

Sienna and Charles were both looking at Caitlin like she'd missed something obvious.

'Sienna's father is Richard Stockhouse,' Charles said.

'Sienna's father is a dick,' Sienna added.

'Oh shush, Sienna. You're acting like a baby. Richard Stockhouse, Caitlin. Doesn't it ring a bell? You said you'd seen the *Elite Spaces* episode?'

Caitlin was feeling embarrassed again. This was why she hated trivia nights.

Charles added helpfully, 'He was my architect. Sienna's father Richard is responsible for The Lodge.'

She tried to remember what the architect had looked like, from the far-ago episode of *Elite Spaces*. All she could recall was the host Skye St Clair's astonishingly tight leather trousers and oversized knitted scarf. Suddenly, Caitlin was exhausted. She wished she had a phone, so she could have used it to check a pretend message on, permitting herself a break from the conversation. But she didn't have to, because now Sienna and Charles were engrossed with menu chat for the next guest dinner and Caitlin managed to extract herself with little more than a quiet goodbye. She returned to her car marvelling at how much change a single day could hold.

iii. Afternoon

Time has blurry edges in here but I know it's afternoon. It's the quietest time of the day. They shut the blinds to give after-lunch snoozes to the living. For us? My merry band of motionless? No difference in a nap and awake. At least that's what they think.

This goddamned place. The more I work it out, the more I wish I hadn't. Fred's gone, his visitor's not coming back. Mine is though. Every morning she rubs my feet and I know that smell, so bloody familiar. I wish I could remember.

Betty the nurse still comes by, though not as often. When I get a whiff of that lavender I think about the early times, when I couldn't guess what was up and what was down. Not sure what's better: knowing nothing or knowing a bit.

If I could, I'd tear this tape off my eyes. I want to roll over and roll back again. Stretch my arms. Use my voice. Speak to the woman who holds my hand like I might break.

Someone's brought in a radio. It plays low and gentle all afternoon. I don't mind it. Helps to cover up the machines. Classical music, strings and choirs. A piano plays more often than not. Reminds me of my father. Wonder where he is? In here, rememberings arrive like that. There's nothing and then there's something. Haven't thought about him for a while. Dear old Dad.

There's a doc here, his voice is like Dad's: clear, sure of itself.

'Bah!' He laughs outside the door. Probably speaks too loud for a hospital ward. Heard the nurse *tut* after him today. Was good to hear a tut. Made me think of — god, can't remember her name. But someone used to tut at me, I know that much.

Today I got myself all mixed up. Thought I was in a boat. Down in the berth with the waves smacking against the hull. Rocking us all back to sleep. Made sense why I could smell salt. Kelp and sea and salt. Helped me drift off and away to a place where I don't think every moment, of every day, that I am still here.

Lying. Still. Listening. Waiting.

Chapter Twenty

She knew she should have called her grandfather as soon as it was morning in the UK, but after the day at The Lodge, all she wanted to do was dive into the sea. And that is what she did, racing home past the General Store, studiously avoiding the orange beacon of the payphone. It was late afternoon but the sun was still a few hours from setting. Erin had discreetly mentioned the surf shop in town as somewhere she might find 'some new bathers', and Caitlin had shyly tried on her first ever pair of bikinis earlier that week. She was excited to pull them on, and almost ran down the beach path to the water's edge. The wind was strong and it wasn't as warm as she'd have liked, but her near-daily dips had loosened her criteria for what counted as swimmable weather. And she had been doing this for long enough now to understand that swimming in the sea would always be better than not swimming in the sea.

Nevertheless, it was choppier than she expected and the rip was up. Caitlin didn't like the feeling of the undertow edging her knees. She stayed close to the shore and only doggy-paddled long enough to shake the anxiety out of her limbs. Putting her mother's name in the search engine had felt like pumping petrol into a car she didn't know how to drive. It gave her the feeling of a bad dream, its fear stuck at the edges of the day, remaining even when the nightmare faded. Luckily, between her and Charles they had barely managed to scratch the surface of the internet. Her mother had remained firmly entombed.

Caitlin returned to the house, legs chilled by the wind gusting over the dunes. For the first time since she'd arrived she appreciated that this place could exist in a season other than high summer. She jogged and huffed up the last stretch of sand before her feet landed on the grass of the Cicada House's back lawn. David had mown it with a rusty old contraption (*thanks, shed*) the week earlier, and she was grateful for the relative softness underfoot as she towelled off.

'Hello.'

'Jesus!'

She whipped around, the towel not really covering all the bits she'd just stripped the new bikini from. David was leaning on the wooden post holding up the far corner of the porch. He had his hands pushed into the pockets of his jeans.

He laughed, self-consciously. 'Sorry.'

'Stop doing that!' She looked down to check a boob hadn't fallen out, adrenalin still smarting up her arms. 'Fucking hell.'

He kept chuckling. 'You kiss your mother with that mouth?'

She didn't notice how still he became as soon as he'd said it. She was fussing with the towel. But when she looked up to see him staring, wide-eyed and pale at her, his smile had gone. 'God. Sorry, Cait.'

'What?'

'I didn't mean about your mum, I'm sorry.'

She stepped towards him, one hand holding the towel against her, the other her wet bikini. Right now she didn't give two hoots about her mother.

'"Cait"?' she asked, smiling.

'Uh, yeah.' He rubbed his hand behind his neck. 'Sorry.'

'Stop saying sorry. No-one's ever called me Cait before. I like it.'

Now he was blushing. He looked down at his beaten-up boots.

'I didn't mean to make a joke about your mother.'

'Don't worry about it. But you really should stop sneaking up like that. You're going to give me a heart attack. Or get an eyeful, whatever is worse.'

David turned more red than she'd ever seen anyone become, which made her feel brave and funny and a bit sexy. She pointed towards the kitchen. 'Fancy a cup of puddle water?'

It felt strange to be sitting in the lounge room, rather than the back step. The wind had really picked up now and Caitlin had to turn on a few lamps, as muddy grey clouds skidded across the pre-sunset sky. She was wearing the one jumper she'd packed and a pair of pyjama pants. If this weather carried on she'd need to go back to the surf shop. She looked at David, sitting on the other green lounge chair next to hers. He was wearing his uniform of white T-shirt and jeans.

'Aren't you cold?'

'Hm?' David had been staring at the radiator, muted silver rungs against the crazy-paved fireplace. As both chairs faced the same direction, side by side, Caitlin twisted her body to face him, hanging her legs over the arm of the chair.

'Cold. Aren't you cold?'

He shook his head, not in answer to her, but to rid himself of a thought.

'Everything okay? Stuff going on … at home?'

She was emboldened by his earlier blush, by him calling her Cait, by the fact that her bare feet were hanging close enough to his legs that she could touch them if she wanted. David looked at her as if waking up from a dream. 'Home?'

'Yeah. Sorry, I don't mean to be nosy — I just —'

His expression stopped her words. His eyes held a foggy sadness she had never seen before. He looked utterly bereft. She gripped her mug and held her breath. The wind stopped and the clock stopped and her heart stopped.

'David, are you okay?' She asked without thinking, a question she used to loathe Paul handing her. He didn't seem to mind.

'Probably not.'

She wasn't prepared for that. Her silence said as much. He rubbed his hand over his face in an unselfconscious way that made her want to hug him.

'Sorry. I am okay.' He looked at her, tired but present. 'I mean, I'm not. But none of us are, right? Or maybe everyone else is and I'm the only screw-up on earth.'

'David.' When she said his name, her accent sounded particularly strong. 'I travelled 12,000 miles just to *not* think about my mother in a different hemisphere. You're absolutely not the only screw-up on earth. Or, actually, in this room.'

He proffered a little laugh, an act that gave her a bloom of warmth in her chest, which was ironic because now he was saying, 'You look cold. I don't know when that heater last worked — let's try something else. Here. Give me your mug, I'll top us up.'

His face had returned to normal and his shoulders were pulled back and he held his hand out to hers. Caitlin watched him walk away and decided she wasn't going to let thirty seconds of his dark mood ruin four weeks of their growing closeness. As she heard him pop the top off the bottle of floor-whisky, she bent down and tried her hand at the radiator. If he wasn't going to wear a jumper, the least she could do was get some heating on in the room — but he was right, the dial didn't move under her fingers. David returned, handing her back the mug containing a very generous whisky pour.

'I thought you poms were used to cold weather. It's still summertime, what're you doing?'

'I don't know, my blood must have thinned in the past few weeks. It's ridiculous — this is a mild spring day at home!'

She gave up on the heater and returned to her position on the chair. The whisky would have to stand in for the radiator. She raised her mug to David's. 'Cheers.'

He returned the gesture. They sat quietly. She didn't realise she was swinging her feet until she hit his leg with her ankle.

'Oop! Sorry.' It was her turn to blush. In the late afternoon gloom, away from their back step, things felt different.

'I can't believe you've never been called Cait before.'

She shrugged. 'I know. I assume it's the Australian prerogative, nicknaming everyone.'

'Yeah, I used to get Dave a lot, obviously. And "Cats".'

'Cats?' She sounded the word in her head. 'Because you like … cats?'

He was laughing at her again. It was the warmest of sounds, a chuckle from deep in his throat. It sounded like comfort. 'Nah. My surname's Catto.'

Caitlin felt oddly elated, words moving between them, sharing information that felt greater than the sum of its parts. It was like being fifteen again.

'Catto. That's unusual, isn't it?' Her accent was softer on the 't's than his was.

'My family's Italian. Came over after the war.'

'David Catto.' It was her turn to sound husky. She didn't know why her voice had done that, but it had. Become soft and quiet and she realised she was swinging her legs again.

He said her name like a question, 'Caitlin …?'

She didn't want to give him her married name. 'Kent. Caitlin Kent.'

His hands were tanned and beaten up and suddenly seemed too big compared to the rest of him. She lived (and re-lived) the next few seconds in slow motion. David tentatively reached for her leg, but once his skin touched hers there was a deliberate, steady energy. With one hand, he carefully placed his mug on the floor. With the other, he softly circled his fingers around her ankle. She was frozen in syrup. Drowning in air. He looked at her very, very carefully and spoke, 'You smell …'

Her breath and her heart stopped at the way his voice had dropped.

'You smell …' His voice was caught up in the front of his mouth, like hers was. They were suffocating together.

He swallowed, and tried again. 'You smell … good.'

The platitude was nothing compared to the way his eyes were not leaving hers. Words were nothing at all, next to his now tight grip and shortened breath and the fact that every hair on her entire body was standing on end. She laughed. With relief and embarrassment, but really, with utter joy. At being touched with desire. With want. With expectation. Caitlin held out her own fingertips and ran them down his forearm. To touch him turned her insides to mercury and she was absolutely sure she'd never felt so certain of anything as she felt in that second. She leant right over to him and his chair, crossing the space between them.

'I'm going to kiss you,' she said, smiling and still utterly without oxygen. They were drowning. Flying. They kissed like it was their first and last.

It's always shocking — to kiss someone for the first time. The organic intimacy of roiling tongue and warm saliva and, oh my lord, she wanted to climb into his sternum. She wanted nothing more than him, and in that moment, that is exactly what she had.

At the time, she wished they had kissed for longer. But looking back, this kiss — their first kiss — was so intense that she doubted they could have continued without combusting. When they parted, his raw expression was a combination of surprise and desire.

'Hi.' His voice was hoarse.

Caitlin was still awkwardly stretched out towards his chair. She slipped back into her own seat. 'Hello.'

'Well. That was unexpected,' he said.

Caitlin smiled at the man sitting across from her, who seemed less of a stranger than he had a few minutes earlier. 'Was it?'

David bit his lip and looked at the ceiling. 'Yeah. Maybe not.' He reached his hand out to hers, their fingertips lightly grazing. Caitlin felt her stomach flip again. She realised he was touching her ring finger, feeling the indentation where she'd removed her wedding and engagement bands. She waited for him to say something, but he didn't and instead stood up and took her mug. 'Another?'

When he settled back into the chair, she was disappointed. *What were you expecting, Caitlin, a nudie run?* He handed her the topped-up mug. 'Hello? Cait?'

She flushed, shelving the thoughts of a naked David. 'Did you say something? Sorry. I just …'

But his smile stopped her worry or confusion or anything else that had briefly slipped back into the space that the kiss had filled.

'Cait, take a breath. Or a sip, whatever's going to help more.'

'Sorry. Kissing a local wasn't exactly in my itinerary,' she said into her mug.

'Kissing the pommy lodger wasn't on my list either.'

'"Pommy lodger"? Is that all I am?'

David acquiesced, 'You're right. I saw the job you did on the front windowsill. You're my pommy apprentice.'

'You're a good teacher, I'll give you that.'

He looked around the room, the lamps gifting the wallpaper an ethereal glow now the sun had set around them. 'It's not hard. This is a great house. And I can tell you love it as much as …'

'As much as you?' she asked.

'As much as anyone around here. It's a special place.'

'It is. I was terrified when I first arrived. The spiders, the outdoor loo —'

'— the light, and the sea, and the golden sounds.'

'I didn't know you were so poetic.'

'Perspective makes everyone poetic.'

Caitlin's eyes were heavy. With the whisky and her mother and the fire that had ripped through her chest when her and David's mouths had touched. She was vaguely aware of him taking the mug from her hand, of a piano playing. An adagio in G minor. In the borderland of a dream, David was playing the sad piano in the garden, its buckled wood rebuilt and repainted. When she woke up in the chair beneath the moonlight of the early hours, she was under a blanket he had tucked up to her chest, her neck was cricked and he was gone.

Chapter Twenty-One

Caitlin hadn't just forgotten what a first kiss was like. She'd also forgotten the feel of the afterburn: a long tail of comet fire that followed a first physical connection. It carried her centimetres above the ground. It was the way she involuntarily smiled, not just upon waking, but then over and again through each moment of the morning. It was the fizzing sparkle of joy and expectation and nervousness and complete incredulity that at forty just one kiss could shuffle her DNA.

Of course, there was the small voice in the back of her head saying irritating things like, 'It was just one kiss' and, 'He is almost a stranger' and even, 'You're a married woman'. But the comet's flames were so strong that they blew the voice away and Caitlin moved through the morning with helium in her bones.

She was sitting on the bench outside the Store, inhaling the scent of a cup of Sienna's perfect coffee. Caitlin's eyes were half-closed as she re-lived *the* moment for the thousandth time in twelve hours. She saw David's face after she'd pulled her head back. Caitlin had never seen someone so … raw.

Charles interrupted her. 'You look like a cat filled with cream.'

'What? No. The coffee. I'm just enjoying my coffee.'

'Well, that must be a bloody good coffee. What do they say? "I'll have what you're having?"'

Caitlin huffed, 'Charles, I have no idea what you're talking about.' She stood up in a way she hoped was businesslike, all the while the feeling of David's fingers grazing up her arm, making her belly do flips. 'Now. Are we going to continue our search?'

'That depends. Have you spoken to your grandfather yet?'

She sighed, admonished. 'No. But I am *about to.*' She could tell by Charles's expression that he didn't believe her. 'Right.' She counted in her head. 'It's 8 pm over there. Do you think he'll still be awake?'

'I wouldn't know, my dear, but you're welcome to the phone.'

She realised that no-one else was going to do this for her. Caitlin carefully shelved the memory of David's face to return to later. In the small office out the back of the Store, she cleared some newspapers from the chair, and dialled Bill's number. While the phone rang, she rolled a little ball of Blu Tack between her fingers. It rang, and it rang. Then it rang in a different tone and a woman picked up.

'Reception.'

Caitlin's stomach dropped. 'Uh, hello. I'm Caitlin Falstaff. I was calling my grandfather — Bill Kent?' *Please please please be okay.*

'Yes?'

'Uh. He doesn't seem to be picking up his room phone.'

'Hold on please.'

She looked at the roster pinned up above the desk and saw Charles's name alongside various teenagers. She chewed the skin around her fingernail. Hold music played, and then clicked off.

'Mrs Falstaff?' Another voice. Lighter. One who didn't sound like she was delivering the news of a dead grandparent. 'It's Angela, sorry we missed your call. Mr Kent was … indisposed, but he's available now.'

'Oh, okay — is he alright?'

She heard Bill clear his throat in the background. Angela didn't seem at all concerned. Caitlin knew *indisposed* probably meant something coded in nursing home language; a code she didn't want to think about too closely.

Angela was almost shouting now, but not at Caitlin. 'Mr Kent, it's your granddaughter on the telephone.'

Caitlin heard mumbling and then, almost as if he were next to her, 'Eh-up, pet.'

She was relieved to hear his voice, and then scared. She realised she hadn't prepared for this, a conversation of a lifetime. 'Hi, Grandad, you alright?'

'Yes, yes, can't complain.'

'Good movie this afternoon?'

'*Battle of the Bulge*. Ending didn't make sense.'

A voice in the background, 'It was just the first half, Mr Kent.' Bill grunted.

'You still in Australia, pet?' he asked.

'I am, Grandad. It's … quite hot here.' She couldn't think of what else to tell him. 'I've made some friends. I've been swimming in the sea.' She sounded like a nine-year-old on their first school camp. She thought of herself, leaning over that chasm between the two green armchairs.

Sod it.

'Grandad, I'd like to ask you a question about my mother.'

Silence. But she could hear the radio in the background.

'Hello? Are you there?'

'Of course I am, where else would I be?'

Right. Okay. Keep going, Caitlin. She took a deep breath and exhaled the words into the phone: 'Being in Australia, I've been thinking about her — Susan — your daughter.' *I think he knows who his long-dead daughter is, Caitlin, you idiot.* Another big breath. 'If it's okay with you and Gran. I mean, if it's okay with you, I'd like to search for a little more information. About her. Susan. Your daughter.'

'Right then. And what are you searching for?' asked Bill.

Her hands were shaking. She couldn't tell if he was angry or just a bit vague. 'Well, maybe where she — we — lived? Or find someone who knew her?'

'You won't find him. Long gone.'

It gave her pause, realising she hadn't given any thought to the man who was her father. She answered in a rush, relieved to be able to agree with Bill, 'No! No, of course not. I don't want to. It's just Susan. I wanted to —'

'Haven Rift.'

'Sorry?'

'Haven. Rift.' He was breathing more heavily now. 'A band. Musicians. Nonsense name. She left with them.'

Caitlin's whole vision disappeared into a pin-prick and she closed her eyes. She couldn't pass out now, not when she was hearing words she never thought she would.

'What?' *'What' is a noise, not a question.* 'Pardon, Grandad?'

'Birmingham. She'd been away for three weeks. Came home and Dot was so happy, Caitlin. So happy.'

Caitlin had overheard the band story so long ago she often wondered if she'd made it up. Her ears started ringing and she put her head between her knees, phone still pressed against her ear.

'She was just a girl. So young. Dot, oh my Dot, she had a temper. And so did Susie.'

Susie. *Susie.* Caitlin caught a cry before it got out.

'They fought and in the morning a van arrived. It was that group again. They had their name painted on the side — black and yellow, it was — she opened that door and we watched her go.'

Now it was Bill's turn to choke a sob. Caitlin was horrified, she'd never heard her grandfather so much as sniffle, let alone cry.

'Oh, Grandad —'

'We did not see her again.'

She could hear Angela clucking in the background, 'Okay then, Mr Kent.'

But his voice came back over the line, stronger than she'd heard in years, sounding like the man who brought her up.

'Caitlin, you listen to me. You find your mother for me. She sent us three postcards. The George, Georges? She sounds happy.'

The change to present tense hit Caitlin like a mallet. And then he was unsure again. 'I think she sounded happy. You find your mother's story. You go searching, pet. And you tell her that we love her so much.'

Love? Loved?

A fumble.

'Okay, Mrs Falstaff, we'll have to ring off now. It's late and your grandfather is very tired.'

Caitlin didn't hear Angela, or herself, say goodbye. Instead, she sat in the small back office of a general store in the middle of nowhere and cried the tears of someone who hadn't realised how much loss had been had.

Charles must have known something had happened, because when she opened the office door he was standing lofty and awkward holding another coffee. 'I hope it's not too cold.' He was watching her with hope and worry, and, she realised, care.

She took the cup gratefully and blew her cheeks out. 'Phew. That was … intense.'

'Did you get anything?'

'I really did. Holy shit.' She pushed her fingers into her eyes until she could see shapes behind her lids.

'And?'

She shook her head, still in disbelief that there was so much knowledge, just … sitting there … and she'd never asked. She spoke quickly, afraid she'd lose some of the precious information he'd passed to her. 'He told me the name of the band she travelled to Australia with. He told me how she and my grandma had fought. He said she sent postcards, from a place called The George, or something. He …' She started to cry. 'He called her Susie.'

'Oh, Caitlin.' Charles opened his long arms wide and she was enveloped in a hug. Charles was so tall, she spoke into his chest.

'Thank you.' And then: 'But, um, I can't really breathe.'

'Yes, yes. Sorry.' He let her go and awkwardly patted her shoulder. 'This is all a lot to deal with, I can imagine. But it sounds like we have a lot more to go on than we did yesterday.'

Neither of them noticed Sienna, who had cleaned down the coffee machine and was now standing next to the veggie baskets with her arms crossed, watching them. Caitlin caught her eye as she wiped her tears with the backs of her hands. She smiled a little self-consciously, not missing the fact that this was the second time in two days that they'd cried in front of one another.

Sienna tilted her head. 'Is this the "Find My Family" thing you guys are doing?' she asked.

Charles gave her a look and said, sotto voce, 'Sienna!' before turning back to Caitlin, 'Sorry. It — just came up this morning.'

'I don't mind.' Caitlin shrugged. 'Have you got any tips?'

Sienna looked between the two of them, her face a mixture of disapproval and amusement. 'Uh, well if what Charlie told me is anything to go by, you need more than a few "tips". Are you really using Yahoo?'

It was Charles's turn to look disapproving. 'Well, what if I am? The internet is the internet, Sienna!'

His defensiveness immediately made Caitlin realise the internet was not just the internet. 'Sienna?' she asked again.

She sighed, but in a way that showed she was enjoying this. 'Where have you looked? DNA searches? Facebook groups? Subreddits?'

Caitlin screwed up her nose, looking between the two people in front of her. 'Charles, I think we have a new member in the search party.'

Charles put his hands up in defeat. 'Oh, fine. But we should definitely still use the Ya-Hoo.'

Caitlin had biked to the Store that morning, because the wind in her hair felt like the best way to extend the feeling of cloud-sitting that last night had given her. And so now she was sitting in the back of the Nissan while Sienna and Charles gently bickered in the front. It was a much softer sound than Sienna's fury from yesterday. Maybe this project was a distraction the young woman needed. To hear them both equally as invested in the search for Susan was a relief. For the first time in her life Caitlin felt like she'd been granted permission to explore her past, and she had help to do so.

The three of them had settled in the study, Sienna at the desk like a CEO and Charles and Caitlin on the sofa as two underlings. Charles had given them both a pen and notebook, and Caitlin was doodling across her pages, enjoying the ASMR of Sienna tapping at the keyboard. Caitlin had given her all the information Bill had imparted, and now she was waiting.

Sienna sounded like the researcher she was. She rattled off her plan: 'Okay. We're not going to dig anything up in a basic search. "Susan Kent" is a really common name and I'm tipping the Birmingham band never made it to the big time.'

Caitlin nodded. This all felt surreal.

Sienna continued, 'So I'm thinking forums are the way to go. I've drawn up a post we can share everywhere that might have a connection. Messaging boards for music fans in Melbourne and Facebook groups for groupies —'

Caitlin smiled to herself, thinking of her conversation with David.

'— I think "The George" is interesting. If it was on a postcard, what was it — a hotel? A club?'

Charles was nodding, mouth full of biscuit. 'Yes. Yes! This is all excellent.'

Caitlin agreed. 'It is, thanks, Sienna. I feel a bit whiplashed, like I've gone from zero to a hundred in one morning.'

'Well, let's grab five. I've got to call my mum back — she's freaking out about uni too. Charles, I'm tipping you need some tea?'

Charles was already up and heading out the door, Sienna following him. Caitlin stood up too, stretching her arms and looking out of the glass walls to the trees wrapping the building. The whisky was still sitting at the base of her neck in a dull knot. The sky was a pale blue beyond the gums that arched around the glass and her. She let her eyes travel along the ghost-like limbs of one towering eucalypt, the thick trunk reaching into the canopy like a brontosaurus neck. This country felt old in a different way to hers. In the stillness, David's face appeared to her again, a welcome return after the drama of the day. A single dark curl fell over his left eye, and he looked up at her through it. A smile danced in the corners of his mouth. His eyelashes were too long for a man's. That's what her grandmother would have said: 'A waste!'

There was a moment a week ago when she had noticed them for the first time. He had blinked them slowly at her. Gently bit his lip. She had wondered how many times he had played this part, and also what his neck would taste like on her tongue.

Oh god! She almost squeaked to herself. Her belly was fluttering again. She couldn't stop smiling. Caitlin shook her shoulders out, bent over the open laptop and clicked on her email. Her inbox had been a lot healthier since she'd begun clearing it out every few days. So there was only one new message waiting for her.

It was from Paul, and she could see the first line in the preview.

Caitlin — I think I've made a terrible mistake.

Chapter Twenty-Two

Caitlin shut the laptop and sat down heavily on the chair. *Shit.*

She had barely heard from Paul since she'd left. Jan, yes. Paul's lawyers, of course. And her own soupy pal, Solicitor Neil. But barely a sentence from her husband. Her soon-to-be *ex*-husband. She opened the laptop again.

Caitlin — I think I've made a terrible mistake.

I don't know what to say that doesn't sound trite or clichéd or bloody crazy. I should start with sorry. I'm sorry, my darling. I was foolish and confused and there's a lot we need to work on, but there's also so much we already have. What a bloody mess this all is. Jan tells me you're in Oz, which is incredible — but can we talk? WhatsApp? Any time is fine, day or night.

Then he outlined WhatsApp instructions in bullet-points like she'd never used a phone before. Her belly squirmed with broken-winged butterflies. Caitlin heard Charles coming back across the foyer. She closed the laptop and grinned too brightly as he entered the room holding two cups of tea.

'What's wrong?' She turned her smile up even higher. His eyes narrowed. 'What did you do?'

'Nothing! Nothing.' Caitlin settled her hands on the closed laptop. And then in her lap. And then back on the desk.

Charles was looking suspicious for the second time that day. 'First the mooning around and now' — he waved his hand at her face — 'whatever this is.'

'There is nothing going on, Charles. I'm excited and a bit overwhelmed about this whole process. I'm also a little hungover; I drank whisky last night.'

'Ah. A whisky hangover. I do not miss those. Like a carpet vomited in one's mouth.'

'Charles, would it be pressing the friendship to borrow your mobile? I need to make a WhatsApp call.'

'Of course. Although I don't know what that is.'

Sienna appeared just in time. She held out her phone to Caitlin. 'Here, use mine.'

With relief, Caitlin took it and the cup of tea and made her way up to the roof. Her hands were shaking and she felt nauseous. When the phone rang she nearly dropped it.

'Shit.' Caitlin wiped her sweaty palms on her shorts and made sure the phone was okay. A faint, tinny voice was calling out, 'Hello? Sienna?'

Oh god. She'd accidentally picked up a call on Sienna's phone. *DAD*, the screen read. Should she hang up? But that would mean Sienna had hung up on her father and Caitlin couldn't handle any more confrontation.

'Hello?'

'Sie? Who's that?'

Caitlin tried to be open-minded, but the voice did sound kind of arrogant. 'Hi? My name is Caitlin. I've just borrowed Sienna's phone.'

'Oh, alright.' He sounded a bit disappointed. 'Sorry, who are you?' He had a rounded accent that didn't sound as Australian as anyone else in Arana Bay.

'A friend of Charles's.'

She thought she heard a sigh. 'Is my daughter there?'

'She's not right now, I'm afraid. But I can pass a message on?' Caitlin had arrived at the steps to the roof. There was a silence, and she thought about thanking the person who had conjured up this magical place, saying something about the light and how much she loved this building of a hundred different moods.

But instead, Richard shot out two syllables, 'No need,' and ended the call.

She was starting to feel more inclined to take Sienna's side over her father's.

Bringing her focus back to the reason she'd escaped to the roof, Caitlin climbed the rest of the stairs slowly, whisper-counting the time difference equation to herself. 'PM to AM, add one hour and go back a day …'

It was midday in Australia, definitely the worst time to call the UK. It would be 1 am, the very earliest hours of Friday morning. *Sod it, Paul can wake up.* Caitlin settled into the corner's shade, leaning up against the roof's cushion with her bare legs stuck out before her. Her toenails sparkled in the sunshine.

* * *

'Mermaid's treasures.'

'Sorry?'

Paul was bobbing in the sea next to her. It had been their first beach holiday together, less than a year since they'd met. They were in Malta and subsisting on a diet of amaretto, shellfish and sex. The sun was shimmering in long, wobbled rays through aquamarine water. A man on the beach played a ukelele. Caitlin's toes were painted gold and as she kicked them through the waves they glinted in the sun. She had just begun to paint them with glittery polish. Paul's hand grasped her foot in the water.

'Mermaid's treasures. Your toes look like treasures from an underwater cave.'

It was the stage of the relationship where each was intoxicated by how wonderful they thought the other was. She laughed and tried to pull her foot from his grasp, but his hands were too strong. Instead, he slowly lifted her foot out of the water, making her paddle hard to remain horizontal. And then he very gently kissed the inside of her ankle, just a peck, salt water on his lips. It undid her in a way she hadn't felt before and she was so flustered she forgot to swim, slipping beneath the warm waves. Paul was there, of course. In an instant she was wrapping her arms around his suncreamed neck, laughing and sputtering seawater.

This had been the trip that she'd fallen in love with him. He had been so … perfect. His hair had turned white-blonde in the sun; that, teamed with his tan, made him look like a Germanic prince. He'd ordered the drinks, he'd spoken to the manager about the issue with the hotel room's plumbing, he'd called to confirm the transfer back to the hotel. Caitlin was giddy she'd found someone who would shield her from the rest of the world, someone who could relate to it on her behalf. She just didn't realise how much he'd resent her for it years later.

* * *

Holding the phone up to her ear, Caitlin consciously slowed her breathing but stopped when she realised she didn't feel as nervous as she thought she would. Out past the treetops she could see the seagulls wheeling far over the ocean, white lines of wing on the wind. The same gusts were creating their own green waves through the leaves, branches dancing to music they made themselves. Watching this ballet gave Caitlin a strong sense of calm, and she was relieved to feel it remain even as she heard Paul's voice down the phone.

'Hello?' His voice was thick with sleep. Oh, she knew it so well. She knew what he smelt like and how he would be lying, and the way his hair would be sticking up straight like straw in a sunburnt field.

'It's Caitlin.'

A moment of silence to process her voice from across the planet. 'Caitlin. Hi. God, hello. You called.'

He would be sitting up, probably pulling his glasses from somewhere close by, checking the time.

'I did. Sorry it's a bit late.' She wasn't sorry. And it was more than 'a bit'.

'It's fine, it's fine. God. How are you? Are you okay? *Where* are you?' He was nervous, doing that sharp little inhaling thing he did between sentences.

'A little town a few hours outside of Melbourne. By the beach.'

'Wow. An Aussie summer, hey? Incredible. Catching some waves?'

She gave him a short laugh, nothing else. He sounded so foolish.

He carried on: 'Right, yeah. So — god, this is a bit hard, isn't it?'

'Is it?' She said it quietly. It wasn't until now that she realised how angry she was. Paul didn't seem to have realised either.

'Bloody hell, Caitlin, don't make this more difficult than it already is.'

And there it was. Caitlin rested her head onto the wall behind her, looked up at the cloudless expanse and waited for him to tell her how hard it all was. He had shaken the sleep from his voice and now he sounded like the Paul she had lived with for years and years.

'Laura's doing better, you probably want to know. She's been pretty ill, the poor thing. The morning sickness wotsit that Princess Kate had.'

Catherine. 'Oh?'

'Yes, we've been in and out of hospital, on an IV, the works.'

We. 'Right. Well. Sorry?' She didn't know why she was meant to feel sad for this pregnant lady full of her husband's baby.

'Oh, come on, Caitlin. Don't be that way. I know there's a lot to talk through but Laura has been really ill. None of us asked for this, and the baby — our baby. It's healthy. That's all that matters.'

Even for Paul, the 'our' was a bit much. 'Yes. Of course.'

He cleared his throat. 'I have been trying to talk to you. You just bloody disappeared off the face of the earth. It'd be good if you could be a little more present.'

'Sorry about that,' she said.

If he heard her apology he didn't react, continuing instead, 'Caitlin, you have to understand something. There was love there, with Laura and me. There still is. I didn't blow up my whole ruddy life just for a roll in the hay!'

My life.

'But — erm — well, I'm just going to cut to the chase. Laura and I have decided that we can be co-parents better than we can be life partners.' Paul was talking like a publicist's release to *Hello!* magazine. 'I am not proud of how we went about things. Sometimes life can hit you square in the middle of the eyes — but I never sought to hurt you. Not deliberately. And, well, obviously Laura getting pregnant was an added —' He paused. Caitlin wondered if he'd call this unborn child a complication. She remembered the heat from Paul's hand as he gripped hers during that first embryo transfer. She'd looked over at him and been ashamed that he was crying and she wasn't. '— an added ... element to this entire process.'

Caitlin closed her eyes against the big blue overhead. Why did this feel so hard when last night felt so simple? Maybe because she didn't know what David looked like asleep. Or how he sat when he spoke on the phone. Maybe because she'd kissed him one single time, and with Paul, she'd lain alongside him so long that her bones had curved into his.

'Okay. Well. This is a lot to take in,' she said.

'I know. I can't imagine how overwhelming this must be for you. Hiding all the way down there when your life has been blown up. And by me. I'm an arse. I think we should go to therapy when you're back. We both have issues to work through — you know, we need to encourage you to share, and be open to the world and just be a little more … brave!'

And look at you, still here, living a life full of wilds and wonder.

'So you and Laura have split up, but you're still parenting,' Caitlin said.

'Well if you're going to be reductive, yes. There is a lot more nuance to it.'

She picked up a rusted bottle cap and spun it like a top. 'Paul, the reception down here is really patchy and I'm losing you.'

'Okay! Where can I call you?' The reception remained crystal clear. Now he was shouting each word. 'Didn't Jan say you have no phone?' He was talking at her like she didn't speak English. Like she didn't speak Paul.

'I'll email you.' She spoke quietly.

'What? Email? Okay! Okay, my darling! We will get through this!'

Caitlin pressed the red button and placed Sienna's phone carefully beside the mug. She stood up and walked to the edge of the roof, where the lip disappeared to the brush below. The gulls had gone and the wind had died. The steep cliff The Lodge was built into meant the drop-off under Caitlin's golden toes was forty feet to the ground. The treetops rolled away from under her in green clouds. Stretching her arms over her head, she threw her head up to the sky and yelled as loud and for as long as she could.

Caitlin had never made so much noise.

Chapter Twenty-Three

Information Wanted
Susan (Susie) Kent.
Born 1960, Surbiton, UK.
Died 1983, Victoria, Australia.
We believe Susan travelled to Australia with Birmingham-based band Haven Rift (sp?).
May have worked at Georges department store approx. late 1970s and/or early 1980s.

Caitlin stared at the screen. It felt surreal to see all these facts in writing when she had spent so long blinking into a thick fog of silence. Charles's arms were crossed and his head cocked to the side like he was observing a piece of performance art. 'Are you okay? I imagine this is a lot to take in.'

Caitlin had made her way back downstairs with Sienna's phone hot and still like stone in her hand. Re-entering The Lodge was like moving through a cleansing portal. She left her husband's words and her fury on the rooftop. She would deal with them both later.

Sienna cleared her throat. 'I can take it down if you like.' As well as sounding it, Sienna looked worried. She and Charles were both standing on either side of Caitlin while she sat at the chair reading over the five sentences that summed up her mother's life.

'No, no. This is great. I just can't believe it's happening,' Caitlin said.

'From what I can work out, Georges was the only business of that name in Melbourne which was operating around that time, big enough to have its own stationery.'

Caitlin nodded, still muddled by how many life-altering events were occurring all at the same time. Sienna spoke again. 'There's one last thing that may help. Do you have a photograph?'

'No. I mean, not with me.' She felt like a shit daughter, admitting that. She remembered the portrait in the hall. The only other photographs she'd ever seen of Susan were a collection of small frames by her grandmother's side of the bed. Dot and Bill and Caitlin had never discussed them.

'So, what do we do now?' Caitlin looked back down at her hands. The cuticle on her left thumb had been bleeding.

'Wait. Wait for a response, I guess. I've included my email address, so I'll keep an eye on the inbox over the next week or so and hopefully someone pops up,' Sienna said.

Charles added, 'I'm sure they will, Caitlin. I have a good feeling about this.'

With the advert posted in all the forums they could think of, and Charles drawn into the writing group's Edit & Share Circle, there was nothing left for Caitlin to do but return home. Thinking of how she had abruptly ended their call, she did briefly consider emailing Paul, but David's pull was stronger. And even though Susan's story felt closer to her than it had ever been, right now all her mind could do was wander like a teenager's. A teenager with a crush. A teenager with a *requited* crush — and what a confusing, delicious, delightful thing it was.

Sienna drove them back down the hill too quickly, or faster than Caitlin was comfortable with. She tried not to show it.

'All okay with your call?' Sienna asked.

'What? I mean, sorry?'

'You borrowed my phone, I was just checking ...'

'Yes, all fine. Thank you.' *Bugger.* 'Oh gosh. I'm so sorry, Sienna.'

Sienna cut her off. 'Don't say sorry. My dad says, save apologies for death or disaster.'

'Ah, right. Well — about your dad. I just remembered, he called when I borrowed your phone.'

'I didn't see a missed call?'

'I — erm — accidentally picked it up.'

Sienna laughed. 'Oh shit! What did he say?'

'Nothing really. Asked after you. Didn't want to leave a message.'

'Sounds about right.'

Caitlin pursed her lips. 'Have you and your dad always fought?'

'No.' Sienna sounded tougher, like she'd distanced herself from the tears of yesterday. 'Not until recently anyway. His loss.' She shrugged.

The old Nissan pulled up outside the Store. If Caitlin had looked at her driver properly, she would have seen more tears threatening in Sienna's big brown eyes. But the fizzy feelings the kiss with David had given her made it hard to think of anything other than ... well, David. And the sooner she was out of the car, the closer she was to him. She closed the door behind her, forgetting what Erin had told her about asking questions and paying attention and really *listening.*

In the Store, Caitlin picked up a tin of whole peeled tomatoes. It felt pleasingly weighted in her hand. She had been living on handfuls of nuts and mugs of whisky for much longer than was appropriate for a woman her age. Tonight, she would make a proper meal.

She rode home a little unsteadily, as the bicycle's basket was heavy with food. A paper bag contained the tomatoes, glossy black olives, a colourful tin of anchovies and a packet of flour-dusted spaghetti. She knew she had a few bunches of garlic hanging over the sink, and half a bottle of red sitting by the toaster with a cork jammed into the neck. It had been a day filled with overwhelm and Caitlin needed to do something that took her mind off her mother and her husband and the tradie who she had kissed. So she made sure to enjoy the meditation of slicing garlic cloves as thinly as possible. Paul had taught her a knife trick to do that. And she felt proud of herself as she held the first slice up to the window, and saw the golden twilight glow through the garlic's tissue-thin membrane.

The screen door swooshed as David entered.

'Hello,' she said.

'Hello.'

'You're back.'

David nodded. 'I am.'

Caitlin stepped forward and so did David, but it felt weird to greet each other any differently to how they had over the past couple of weeks — which was to barely greet each other at all. He awkwardly put out a hand, and Caitlin held both of hers aloft like a surgeon waiting for their gloves.

'Sorry, garlic fingers.' She wiggled them.

'Righto,' David said, stepping back.

They looked at each other.

'Who are you cooking for?' he asked.

'Just me,' she lied. 'I haven't been cooking much since I got here, figured I needed a proper meal.'

'Do you cook a lot back home?'

Caitlin was feeling bad about lying, which was probably why the truth fell out before she caught it. 'Um, not really. My husba—' *No. No, no.*

There was a silence where Caitlin's half-husband floated between the two of them. She froze, praying David hadn't heard her.

'Husband?'

Shit.

'No. Yes. He …' She screwed up her face. 'We're separated.'

'Sorry to hear that,' David said. He didn't look sorry. He looked confused.

'It's okay. I'm starting to think that we weren't really married anyway. Not like you're meant to be.'

Why had she said that? *Shut up.* Caitlin wanted to stop talking about Paul immediately, and go back to kissing and making jokes about tea. David shifted his weight onto his boot heels and allowed himself to fall the short distance back to the kitchen wall. His broad shoulders hit the timber boards hard enough to make the glasses shudder. He crossed his arms. 'And how's that? How are you "meant" to be married?'

'Oh, I don't know. Like the movies tell you.' She tried to conjure what a movie marriage was like. 'You know, with endless laughter and excitement and lots of —'

David raised his eyebrows in the pause. 'Lots of?'

'— conversation,' Caitlin said. 'Look, sorry this isn't very interesting. Honestly. I was married but we're separated and we're going to get divorced.' *Divorced? That's news, Caitlin.* 'That's it.' She busied her hands under the tap, washing off the sticky garlic. 'Do you want a glass of wine?'

He hadn't moved. 'Alright.' He didn't look like it was alright. But she poured him a glass of red anyway.

'Cait, you can't just walk away from a marriage. Marriage is for life. "'Til death do us part".' David's eyes had gone dark and fogged-over again.

'I didn't "just walk away". David, please. I'd really rather not talk about my ex. I'm here and I'm glad you're here and I've been thinking about you all day.' She smiled, hoping to pull his expression out from whatever cloud it had moved beneath. She took a step forward, quickly. He stood straight and did the same. It was an awkward dance and one she would have felt shy about, if she wasn't so distracted by his mouth. Caitlin put her head down and laughed. 'Sorry. I don't want to make things weird. I just …'

David reached around her waist. They were now so close that she was sure she could feel his heartbeat through his T-shirt. She looked up to his face and suddenly they were kissing again. Oh, thank god, they were kissing again. It was different from the night before, less gentle and more urgent and it took everything Caitlin had in her not to tackle the man to the floor. He had his hand on the small of her back and she was pressing into him in a way she'd never done before … never known *how* to do before. She pulled her head away from his and looked at the curly-haired man whose lips were now slightly swollen and whose breath was heavy in a way that told her he wanted her more than anyone may have wanted her ever. Thank god, thank god this electricity was charged enough to wipe out whatever weirdness she'd created talking about Paul. Silly Paul.

'David.'

'Caitlin.'

'Would you like to stay for dinner?'

His face was relaxing back into its normal softness. 'Righto.'

She took a breath, and Caitlin saw that he too was catching himself. So she moved forward again and kissed him briefly, to make doubly sure he understood her intentions. 'Then maybe you could stay, after dinner …?'

He gave her one of his faraway smiles again and nodded. 'I'll go check on the pavers. You said you'd had a go at levelling the ones in the back, yeah?'

The screen door closed behind him. Caitlin exhaled hard, realised she was grinning and went back to her prep. There was a bubble in behind her ribcage that was excitement about being in the same room with someone she was probably going to have sex with later. She felt relieved and a little smug about redirecting the conversation away from Paul. Silly Paul, drifting around rooms like an angry ghost.

She hesitated over the pile of sliced garlic she was about to chuck into a pan of hot oil, but a good puttanesca required a lot of garlic and Caitlin hoped the excellent meal would balance out the bolshy breath. By the time David re-joined her in the kitchen, it was smelling like a kitchen should. Caitlin wondered for the first time in her life whether she should get a speaker or a radio or something — to bring some music into the house.

'What's that?' His voice was loud and flat and made her turn around even though the garlic was about to get too brown. His face was flat too.

'Puttanesca, it's an Italian —'

'I know what it is.'

They both stood, silenced by the tone in his voice, the oil spitting behind Caitlin. A drop landed on the back of her arm and stung. She had a horribly familiar feeling in her belly. 'Are you okay? What's —'

He interrupted her again. 'I know what it is because it's my wife's favourite sauce. She makes the best goddamned puttanesca I've ever tasted.'

Caitlin's mouth was open. A little shred of breath came out of her, like a life-force leaving. David shook his head and whispered something to himself, so low she didn't hear, before he walked out of the house. She followed him, closely enough that she caught the back door before it closed behind him. But he was gone. He was gone and the kitchen smelt of burnt garlic and falling for a married man.

Caitlin dumped the pan of oil and garlic in the sink, running the tap over the steaming mess with an explosive *hiss*. The car keys dug into her palm as she ran to the dusty rental. Damn the stupid arrogance of not having a phone. What a bloody idiot she was, larking around at the end of the world with no way to contact anyone if she needed. She tried to remember what Erin did on a Thursday night. It had been a week since she'd seen her, Caitlin realised. Damn the stupid arrogance of never paying attention — this was why she didn't make friends, she was terrible at it.

As she drove to SilverSea, Caitlin tried to bring together the few conversation threads that had turned so wrong, so quickly. Was it the mention of her husband, or their kiss? Was it the goddamned bloody puttanesca?

She sat outside Erin's house and turned the engine off. 'Bollocks,' she said to the empty footpath of Coastal Way. The lights were on at Erin's house, but it was 9 pm. What was she doing here? She needed to go home. Her hands were shaking. She wasn't upset, she was embarrassed. She was ashamed. Okay — and she was really upset.

Just then, Erin's garage door began to open, the small electric motor groaning. It was Josh, emerging bent-over through the gap holding a full rubbish bag. Caitlin almost fell out of the car. 'Josh!'

The kid jumped a little, but to his credit didn't run screaming. He stood his distance though, bare feet shifting on the driveway.

'It's Caitlin.' She waved, to make herself seem less menacing as she, an adult, accosted a child in the night. 'Is your mum home?'

'Yeah.' He kept the bins between them. 'I'll get her.'

He closed the garage door behind him and Caitlin was left standing outside the house in the dark. Erin soon opened the front door and peered into the gloom. 'Caitlin?'

'Uh, yeah. Hi, Erin. Sorry for dropping by so late and unannounced.' Dot would have been very disappointed.

'Why are you standing in the dark?' Erin gestured her inside. 'What's up, doll? Are you okay?'

The house smelt of popcorn.

'I'm really sorry for barging in like this. Am I interrupting anything?'

'We were about to start a movie, but don't worry — you've saved Joshy from having to watch *Titanic* with his mum.' She said this last part loudly, rolling her eyes at Josh's room.

'Sorry, Josh!' Caitlin called down the hall.

'Come sit down, what's going on?' Erin guided Caitlin over to the white sofa and offered her the bowl of popcorn.

'I'm an idiot, Erin. I'm such an idiot.'

'What is it?'

Caitlin was barely listening to her. 'I mean, what a grim cliché. First of all my husband leaves me for another woman and now here I am, prancing about like Shirley bloody Valentine and I've fallen for the very first guy who's paid me any attention.'

'Oh, mate.'

'I know. I know. I just thought … well, I didn't think. But it felt really nice, you know? To believe someone wanted to spend time with me? Someone who maybe even liked me?'

Erin nodded and ate some popcorn. She looked sympathetic, but a little confused. 'Caitlin, I thought you didn't like Charles?'

'Charles? What? I like Charles.' Caitlin was still thinking of David's face as he swore at her. There was so much hurt there. She shook her head. 'Hang on. Why are we talking about Charles?'

'I mean, I barely know the guy. But if it felt *nice* and you think maybe he *likes you* …' Erin trailed off. She had Caitlin's full attention now.

'Likes me? Oh god no, not Charles. I told you, we're just friends! No, no, Erin. It's so much worse than that. I've gone and developed an enormous crush on your tradesman. And I've just found out — he's bloody married!' Caitlin picked through the popcorn bowl, tutting to herself. When she looked up Erin was staring at her. 'What?'

'Caitlin.'

'What? Why are you looking at me like that?'

Erin retrieved the bowl of popcorn from her and placed it on the coffee table. She reached over and took Caitlin's hands in hers. 'Babe, there's no tradie. I never sent anyone to your house.'

Chapter Twenty-Four

'What do you mean?'

'I'm really sorry, hon. I know I said I'd arrange someone to come help out with the house. I did call Tim, but he never got back to me and — well — it must've just slipped my mind.'

'I don't understand. He's been coming and going.' Caitlin's legs felt cold and heavy, like they were filling with cement.

Erin spoke slowly in the way she had done on the first morning they met. 'Caitlin. I don't know who has been coming to your house, but it's no-one I know.'

Hairs on the back of Caitlin's neck stood up. His smile, their kiss, the crowbar. His face, just a few hours ago, blank and fogged. His arms tight around her waist. Had she been in danger? Was she still? 'I just … I assumed he was a tradesman. He had work boots on.' It sounded so small and dumb when she said it out loud.

Erin was up and pacing. 'Describe him to me, this guy. Has he been hassling you? Creeping around?'

'He told me I was living a life of wonder.'

Erin stopped and crossed her arms. 'Caitlin. What the hell's been going on?'

'A man turned up, his name is David. He's been coming by for a few weeks now.'

'A *few weeks?* Holy shit, woman! What's he been doing, building a bathroom?'

'Well, no — but he has fixed the back door, and the hot water. The bedroom ceiling. We've been working fence posts. He showed me how to do pavers too …'

Erin held her hands up to stop Caitlin's list. 'Are you telling me you have a stalker who's been teaching you how to do running repairs on The Cicada House?'

'Well, no. Yes. If you want to put it that way.'

'What the hell? What's his plan? Is he preparing the scene of a crime? And then he's going to flip the house? Pretty bloody thorough if you ask me.'

'Don't be silly, Erin. I really don't think he's dangerous. There must have been some crossed wires. Maybe Tracey arranged for him to come?'

'Tracey couldn't arrange herself out of a paper bag. And she's currently in Ubud off her tits on ayahuasca.'

Caitlin's rationale was gathering momentum as she tried to retrofit a story around something unexplainable. Yes, it was sinister to think of what this married stranger could have been working towards. But, really, Caitlin was just disappointed that the connection she had been developing was built on his lies and — worse — her imagination. She could see now what she had thought was an intense bond was rather flimsy. Paul's words from yesterday came back to her: 'There's so much we already have.'

She felt very tired all of a sudden. Tired and ashamed and completely redeemed in her initial instinct that any true pleasure was not worth pursuing.

'Well, I don't know who the hell this Dave bloke is, but I suggest you go straight to the cops in the morning. And stay here tonight.'

Caitlin sighed and chewed on her fingernail. 'I suppose that's wise.'

'Of course it's bloody wise. You've got Bob the Builder–slash–potential murderer over there right now, boiling bunnies or digging foundations or both.' Erin marched off to Josh's bedroom, which was followed by some indistinct whining and then some vicious mum-whispering. They returned, Erin with a bright smile on her face, Josh hanging behind her. 'Caitlin, Josh has kindly said you can sleep in his top bunk. Don't worry, the sheets are clean.' She looked pointedly at her son. 'He's happy to share with me tonight.' Josh slunk off towards the bathroom.

'That's really kind of you both, honestly though, I'm sure it's fine.'

'And I'm sure it's not. Here, have a clean nightie. I found a new toothbrush too.'

'Thanks so much, Erin, really.' Caitlin took the pile from the woman whose Thursday night she had just turned upside-down. 'Um, Erin? There is one more thing. Do you think I could borrow your phone? I've just got a quick WhatsApp call to make.'

'Of course, it's charging on the kitchen bench. Go for your life.'

Caitlin grabbed the phone and unlatched the back door, sliding it open. The garden was still, lawn pumping out the scent of freshly watered grass cooling down after a hot day. She sat down at the table and opened the app.

'Hello?'

'Paul? It's me. I'm sorry. I'm going to come home.'

Caitlin woke staring eye-to-crotch with a sweaty football player. Josh's bedroom was wallpapered with posters of young men and women in short shorts. She rolled over and winced — the bunk may have had clean sheets, but it also had the world's flattest pillow. She sat up and rubbed her twisted neck. A forty-year-old woman couldn't climb down from a top bunk with any grace, but add a sore neck *and* a Christmas nightie with the slogan *Totally on the naughty list*? She was sure she caught Josh smirking at her as she came out from the bedroom holding last night's clothes in a ball.

'Um, morning. Bathroom free?'

'Sure is! Coffee?' Erin called from the kitchen.

'No thanks, I'll be out of your way soon.'

By the time she was dressed, Erin had served up Vegemite toast and a Nespresso, which she had insisted on making. Caitlin sat on a stool at the long white bench and ate alongside Josh, who was busy stacking Weetbix into an enormous bowl.

'Here's the number of the local sergeant.' Erin handed over a Post-it note.

Josh spoke through a mouthful of cereal. 'Who's going down?'

'Oh shush. You're not in a cartel,' Erin admonished.

Caitlin ignored Josh. 'Thank you, Erin. Again. Like I said, I'm sure it's just a misunderstanding. I'll shoot Tracey an email as well, see if she knows anything.'

Erin shrugged. 'Suit yourself. I also spoke to Tim, my actual tradie, again this morning. He's going to come around and have a look at the house.'

Caitlin put her plate into the dishwasher. 'Righto. I'm off. Thanks again, guys.'

'"Righto"? Where'd you pick that up from?'

Caitlin shook her head. 'I'm not sure, one of you Aussies, I guess. Why, what's wrong with "righto"?'

'Nothing,' Erin said, 'it's just a little old-fashioned, that's all.'

There are things that you just know are going to happen, and pulling into the driveway, Caitlin knew David would be back soon. He had no pattern or schedule, so his visits were always a surprise. But this Friday morning, Caitlin readied herself for his arrival. When the back door opened she grabbed a butter knife from the sink. She hadn't planned to, but a spike of adrenaline made her do it. The melamine handle was cracked but the blade seemed sound enough. David stood in the doorway with his brow furrowed. He looked at her, the knife, and back to her face again. 'Cait —'

'You need to leave my house.'

'*Your* house?'

'You know what I mean. I don't know who you are. You're not Erin's tradie.'

'I never said I was "Erin's tradie". Who's Erin?'

She was avoiding his face, and instead focusing on a spot just below his beard. 'Then, why do you keep turning up and … fixing things?' Caitlin spluttered.

David took a step towards her and Caitlin jabbed in his direction with her knife; she immediately felt dreadful about it. She dropped it with a clatter and stepped towards him, realising as soon as she looked at his face that he'd started to cry. And now he was really, properly crying. David was standing before her, in his jeans and T-shirt and boots, his arms loose by his sides and his shoulders slumped. His head, normally high and held with such confidence, hung heavy. His mouth opened and a horrible sound fell out. Raw, guttural sobs came from his chest.

'Oh, David.'

She couldn't stop herself, and she didn't want to. She didn't know who this man was or why he was there, but she did know that she was unable to stand and watch someone in this much pain suffer alone. Caitlin pulled David into her arms, placing her hand onto the back of his head and feeling him drop into the crook of her neck. His crying had taken over his whole body, so now it took over hers too. She stumbled back a little; he was giving so much of himself to her that she struggled to hold him up. But she managed, with the help of the kitchen bench behind her. He cried and he cried. She had wanted to cry this way a number of times in her life, but she'd never managed to let go like this. And while she didn't say anything to him, the way she held and rocked him was just the way she'd always imagined someone who loved her may have soothed her.

Like a thunderstorm coming to an end, the tears came until they didn't, and David pulled his head and body away from Caitlin. His face was flushed, wet with tears and exhaustion.

'You look so tired.'

He gave her the saddest of smiles. 'You have no idea.'

'I may do. Just a little. Do you want a cuppa?'

He smiled again, this time a little more himself. 'What do you think?'

They sat together on the back step with cups of their steaming puddle water. Rather than flinch from this stranger's presence, Caitlin felt closer to him than she had after kissing him. She rested her head on his shoulder. 'You going to tell me who you are then?'

'I don't know where all this cloak and dagger stuff has come from, Cait. I'm exactly who I said I was. I'm David Catto.'

'But you're not a tradie.'

He snorted. 'A tradesman? Not a good one, that's for sure.'

'Then what are you doing around here all time? And' — her voice rose, remembering her outrage — 'more importantly, why are you kissing strange Englishwomen when you're married?'

David sighed so deeply her head lifted and dropped on his shoulder, which she rode like a wave at her beach.

'I'm not married, Cait. Not anymore. My wife died.'

Caitlin sat up and looked at him. 'She died.'

He nodded. 'She did. A few years back.'

'Oh, David, I'm so sorry …' She didn't need to ask the next question, he knew.

'Cancer. It was real fast.' He shook his head. 'It was terrible.'

'What was her name?'

He smiled. 'Giulia.'

'Tell me about her.'

'Nah. It's okay.'

'David, it's a privilege to be able to talk about the dead. Particularly when it's someone you've loved, trust me. Please tell me about your wife.'

'Okay,' he said.

'Okay,' she encouraged.

'She was a marvel.'

'I'm sure she was.'

'No, everyone says that about people who've died. But she really was.'

Caitlin wished she could say that about Susan. David's eyes were still bleary from crying, but the rest of him began to brighten as he described Giulia. 'She sang all the time. Used to give me the shits, but god, her voice was beautiful. She cooked meals with love and flavour, better than my mum, even.' His face was lit from within, and Caitlin saw what she didn't have with Paul.

'Even so, Mum still loved her, and Dad. She was full on — don't get me wrong. But it wasn't anger, it was passion. *Appassionati,* she used to say.' He laughed at the memory, at his bad Italian accent delivered through his broad Australian one. 'She used to get the boys twisting their tongues with their Italian.'

'The boys?' Caitlin held her breath.

David nodded. 'Our boys. My boys. I have two sons.'

'Oh?' In one syllable Caitlin tried to hide that every nerve ending was aflame. She couldn't tell if her world was burning down or building up.

'How … how old are they?'

'George is nine, Nicho's four.'

'I see. And where are they now?'

David put his forehead down into his hand and closed his eyes. Caitlin noticed the fingers of his other hand were dancing up and down his leg, like he was playing an instrument. She began to wonder if this man was entirely well. 'I used to play piano, you know? I was pretty good, they used to say. I played for my boys. I played for Giulia.'

Caitlin opened her mouth, but closed it again. There was the sense of a tidal wave about David today. The water had gone all the way out, she'd seen the empty seabed, and now the wave was coming back — and nothing would stop it. Suddenly, he was up. He stood in the middle of the back porch and steadied himself like a pirate on the prow of a ship. 'Look, Cait. I've got to tell you some stuff. You're going to need to let me talk, alright?'

'Okay.'

'I haven't been a good dad. Since Giulia died, well, I've not been around much. Giules was the best mother. But when she went, it was so fast. And then it was just me, Cait.' He shook his head, still disbelieving. Caitlin watched him.

'Was it recent?'

'Yeah.' His voice was a husk. 'Two years ago.'

'So you had really young boys.'

'I did. Nicho was barely talking. George had just started school. I couldn't —' he said it in a matter-of-fact way, almost daring her to disagree. 'I couldn't do it.'

Caitlin knew it was anything but matter-of-fact. 'So, you left?'

'Nah. I was too gutless to even do that. It was worse. I just turned my volume down.' He shrugged, biting his cheeks as he tried not to cry again. 'I mean — thank god for Mum and Dad. They stepped in. I don't know what I would've done.' He kicked at a few of the pavers with his boot. Caitlin thought that might be all of it, but she sat still in case he had more to say.

'I don't just miss her. I miss the role she played. The matriarch, the nurse, the joker …' He laughed.

… the queen.'

The garden around them was very quiet, like the birds and the wind and the sea had all stopped to listen.

'I don't know how to be me without her around.' David looked at her, dark eyes big with hope that she could help him. It paused her, gave her breath and a feeling of wonderment. The mess and the pain that was broiling around them would have annihilated her in the past. Caitlin would have been shut closed before he'd even stopped crying. Yet now, she felt a steadying purpose of words carried with conviction — and it was something wholly new and powerful.

She spoke. 'I'm not sure what it's like to know someone so intimately, to love them so deeply, and then have them taken from you.' She stood up so they were face to face, and continued, 'But I do know what it feels like to lose the most important person to you. The hole it leaves is bigger than anything you can do to fill it back up.' She thought of her mother's blonde hair tickling her knees. 'I'm sorry your volume is down, and your colour is out. But I'm glad you found your way here. Maybe we found each other, each for the same reason.'

David bit his lip. His voice was low again. 'Just because I miss my wife doesn't mean —'

'I know.' She'd never felt this calm, this confident about anything.

'I'm not a good person,' he whispered, as he pulled her towards him.

'Neither am I,' she replied, as she allowed herself to go.

Chapter Twenty-Five

'Can you hear that?'

'I can't hear anything.' Caitlin's ears were ringing.

'Someone's knocking on the door.'

They were lying on her bed.

'Let them. I can't move, anyway.'

'You smell of pears.'

'It's Erin's shampoo.'

When you've just had sex with a kind-of stranger, every word is imbued with meaning and drama. Right now, Caitlin figured, they could be reading from Dot's *Reader's Digest* and it would still feel erotic. The knocking got louder.

'Bugger off!' called David. Caitlin hit him with a pillow.

'Stop it — you'll let them know we're here.'

He ran his finger along the dip between her rib cage and her hips. 'I like this bit.'

Her insides went all squirmy.

A man's voice: 'Hello? Caitlin, is it?'

'Damn.' Caitlin rolled out of bed and started to pull clothes on. 'What time is it?'

David didn't move, just lay back with his arms above his head, gazing at the ceiling with his eyes half-closed. She tried not to stare at his dark chest hair against deep olive skin. So different to Paul. Caitlin couldn't believe the past hour, day, month had happened.

The voice came again, 'It's Tim — Erin sent me.'

She looked at her watch, it was after lunch. 'Coming!'

As she left the bedroom she closed the door behind her. 'Stay here,' she whispered. David's eyes were closed, but he lifted his arm and gave her a thumbs-up. She opened the front door with what she hoped was a bright enough smile, to distract from the obvious post-shag hair she was wearing. 'Hello!'

As she looked at the man standing on the welcome mat, she realised how ridiculous it was that she'd ever mistaken David for a tradesman. Because this man here, *he* was a tradesman. He wore a pair of faded blue utility shorts and a yellow hi-vis hoodie. His hair was cropped-short and his fingernails were white with plaster dust. He even had a carpenter pencil in his top pocket.

'Caitlin?'

'Hi, so sorry about the delay there. I was …' she pointed behind her; Tim looked over her shoulder '… having lunch.'

He hesitated; she could see him wondering why she'd lie about something so dull. 'Erin said you had some jobs needed doing?'

'Ah, yes. Gosh — you're prompt!?' She was stalling for time, holding the door open but blocking Tim from entering. She watched her bedroom door from the corner of her eye, and was pleased to see it remain firmly shut.

'Not really. I owe Erin a favour.' He didn't look happy to be there, on a warm Friday.

'Wow, well — that's so kind of you. Tim. But please, don't ruin your sunny afternoon on my account. The house is fine, we've — I've — managed to clear up a few of the issues.'

Tim looked dubiously at the freckled Englishwoman standing in front of him in a sleep-crumpled T-shirt. Suddenly, she had a thought. 'There is one thing actually. I've dropped my phone under the back step, through the slats — would you be able to help me get it?'

She watched Tim trudge around the back of the house to investigate how to pull up the step without too much mess. Certain she was alone for a moment, Caitlin darted back down the hall and opened her bedroom door a little way. She slipped through the gap while explaining, 'I think he was here to do more of a welfare check, but I've thought up a job for hi—'

Caitlin stopped. Her bed was empty, the white sheets rolled and twisted in shadows of what had happened this morning. She looked around the room. 'David?'

Four walls, two wardrobes and one door. She circled the bed, and felt stupid checking the wardrobes, but did it anyway. He wasn't there. She reached forward and placed her hand on the pillow where his head had been. It was still warm.

'Well this is ridiculous,' she said, to no-one. He couldn't have left through the door, she was standing outside it the whole time. Caitlin walked over to the window. It hadn't been opened any further than a crack.

'David?' calling a little louder now. Then she heard the back door close and felt more relief than she should have. She hurried to the kitchen, ready to admonish him for his disappearing act, but pulled up quickly when she saw Tim standing in the doorway. He was holding up her phone. 'This it?'

Tim admitted Erin had asked him to confirm Caitlin was okay. He also passed over a SIM card, explaining, 'She said to give you this.'

Caitlin took it, impressed by her friend's forethought. Tim handed Caitlin his business card with Erin's number written on the back. Caitlin then waved him off distractedly, still bewildered by David's sudden disappearance. 'I really am fine, thanks again. Tell Erin I'll give her a call as soon as my phone's charged,' she said.

David was never one for goodbyes, but this latest departure was both oddly timed and, also, just odd. She plugged her phone into the charger, the charger into the adaptor, and the adaptor into the wall. It felt strange to have tech in The Cicada House — like it didn't belong there. While she waited for the black screen to come to life, she thought about everything David had shared with her.

He was right, he'd never lied to her — never told her he was anyone except himself. So putting the pieces of the David puzzle together couldn't be that difficult, surely. He was a man who knew the toolbox was in the shed, and the whisky was under the floorboards. Yet it was hard to push past the louder, more intense thoughts — namely, those of him and her and what it felt like to wrap her legs around someone that wasn't Paul. Her stomach flipped. *No, Caitlin.* She had to think about things rationally. He was a widower with two kids and parents who ran a fruit shop. Didn't he say something about playing music? He certainly knew how to repair stuff. Yes, this much she knew.

But no. She knew more.

She knew that he smelt of freshly cut grass. That his hands had callouses on them and had lifted her up by her waist and carried her to the bedroom. That he kissed her like he was hungry.

Bugger. Stop it, Caitlin. Get a grip.

Ping!

Her phone lit up — she was back. Caitlin pushed the SIM into her phone and wondered if Erin was just a real-estate agent, or if maybe she was some kind of psychic super sleuth as well. After logging in, the alerts started pouring through and she felt dizzy with the barrage of communications. All her emails loaded simultaneously — the ones she'd been fielding at The Lodge, but also new emails too. Mainly from Paul, subject lines mirroring his train of thought after the call she'd made from Erin's.

11.22 pm – Return flights to UK
1.18 am – Did you buy travel insurance??
4.01 am – Custody discussion w Laura
6.45 am – Zoom invitation >> lawyers

She didn't open any of them. Instead, she rang Erin. 'Thanks for the SIM card.'

'Oh, thank god. I thought Tim might help you out. Are you okay? Any more stalker action?'

'Kind of, not really. Are you around? Want to go for a swim?'

'I've got to drop Joshy off at a mate's. I can be at yours in an hour.'

An hour and five minutes later, the two women were drifting in the water together. It was a hot afternoon and the beach was heaving. Early weekend journeyers and locals alike covered the sand with umbrellas and cabanas and teepees. Erin and Caitlin observed the scene from the sea, treading water where the sand dropped just out of reach of their toes. Caitlin felt tension leach from her joints. In a short time, the beach had gone from being a monster hiding behind the scrub to an ever-ready source of comfort. Or had she herself become a little wilder?

'Why do Australians go to the beach and then sit in the shade?'

Erin was matter-of-fact. 'Because the sun can kill you.'

Caitlin felt the sting of the heat along the part-line in her hair. 'I guess so. That's sad, though — to come to the beach and stay covered up.'

'What do they say about "mad dogs and Englishmen"? You don't want to muck around with Aussie UV, mate. We don't have much of an ozone layer down these parts.'

Caitlin closed her eyes and wondered which of her freckles was going to kill her later.

'Thanks again for last night. I felt a bit silly, driving home this morning. I think we both overreacted a little.'

'Speak for yourself — not sure I'd be happy with a stranger hanging around my house for weeks without knowing who he was.'

'But I do, I know a lot. More after this morning, actually.'

'You saw him again? Jesus! You're a sucker for punishment.' Erin dunked beneath the water and shot up again, slicking her long hair back. 'Go on then, tell me everything — you know what Arana Bay's like, I probably do Pilates with his wife.'

'Erin, no. His wife's … she died.'

'Oh, honey.' Erin looked like she'd heard the next plot-point on *Days of Our Lives*. 'A stalker *and* a widow.'

'Widower.'

'Whatever. His wife's dead and he's sniffing around you for what? Does he need someone else to look after the kids? You need to be careful, doll.'

'Erin. Stop it, it's not like that.'

Caitlin cupped her hands, pushing them like rudders through the water. She was regretting calling Erin, who was irritating her today. Her Australian brashness and crassness wasn't sitting well against Caitlin's mood. Which was, admittedly, confused. But it was too hard to make sense of how she was feeling against the noise of Erin's outspokenness. Caitlin wanted to tell her how she was enjoying feeling small under a fiery Australian sky. How making love to a grieving stranger after telling her husband she was returning to him wasn't even the most important thing happening to her at the moment.

'Caitlin!'

'Sorry?'

'Babe, pay attention — I said, I've got to head back. You coming?'

'I might stay here for a bit.'

'Okay, see ya.' Erin dove off, feet splashing in Caitlin's face. Caitlin dipped beneath the surface, the sun filtered green and golden between her and the sand below. There was one more thing she should have told Erin today: that this country was helping her grow a voice, and maybe a heart too.

Early that morning she had been certain that David would be waiting for her. This evening, as she walked back along the path with skin smarting from sunburn, she knew he would most certainly not be there. The Cicada House had been empty since she left and with no-one home to switch any welcome lights on, it was dark. For the first time since she'd arrived in Arana Bay, the house took on a vaguely menacing appearance. Her mind went back to the reviews Erin had read out to her, that didn't seem so funny now. The black windows could hold anyone, looking out at her, and she wouldn't know. Something walked over Caitlin's grave. But now was not the time to let her imagination run away to the scary parts of her brain. She pushed through the back door, switching on every light that she passed: a one-woman Blackpool Illumination. Her phone lay on the counter. Caitlin picked it up as she went by. Paul's emails remained unread, but there was another, newer message that stood out.

> *From: Sienna Stockhouse*
> *Hey Caitlin — not sure if you'll get this before I see you, but wanted to forward asap. I've had a response to our post, the one on the Facebook forum for ex-employees. It's pretty amazing! Have a read below and see what you think. Sienna x*

Caitlin put the phone down and took a deep breath. Her inhalation sounded as shaky as she felt. It was probably nothing. It was probably a coincidence, or a scammer, or a confused old man lonely for something or someone ... she picked up the phone again and scrolled down the email.

> *hi there my name is maggie doble and a friend sent me your post and I think I can help. I'd be happy to talk to you if I can be of help. I've included my phone number and address. I knew susie. We lived together from 1977 until she passed.*

She read the note so fast that she skipped every second word and landed on just one. Susie. Someone out there knew her mother, knew her well enough to call her Susie, and in a rush, a rope had been thrown and Susan was pulling at the other end. She slid down the counter and landed on the kitchen floor. Caitlin looked at her feet, still sandy from the beach. The room glowed purple from the sunset outside. The cicada chorus swelled. She had found her mother.

Chapter Twenty-Six

Caitlin threaded her fingers through the metal grate on the side of the phone box. She pushed the sand on the concrete around with her toes, forming miniature ant hills. She knew Charles would be out soon.

'Hello there.'

'Morning.'

Charles looked down at the sand city. 'Something on your mind?'

'About a million things, yes.'

'Sienna told me about the email. Caitlin, it's pretty extraordinary.'

'Yeah. I guess. I just didn't think it would happen so quickly — or at all.'

'What are you going to do?'

'Run screaming for the hills?'

Charles put his head to the side and, not for the first time in her life, Caitlin imagined what it might be like to have a brother.

'What can I do to help?'

Erase any memory of my dead mother?

Track down my mysterious disappearing not-tradie?

Tell my husband I'm not coming home after all?

She shrugged at Charles and kicked all of the sand back towards the nature strip. 'Can you put me on the first plane back to England and pretend none of this ever happened?'

'I'm afraid that's a little outside of my remit.'

'Okay. Probably not, then.'

Charles patted Caitlin's forearm. 'You must allow yourself to feel apprehensive, I certainly would be.'

Caitlin gave him a tight smile. She was getting a bit sick of people telling her how she should *feel* about things, and what she *needed* to do. But it wasn't Charles's fault. She'd biked down here just to see him, hadn't she?

'Thanks, Charles. I think I just need to give this Maggie woman a call.'

'Well. He banged the side of the phone box like a father sending off a taxi cab. 'Sienna tells me you won't be needing this anymore. Good news about your phone!'

Caitlin instinctively patted her back pocket. She was ashamed at how safe it felt to be carrying it around again — a big lozenge, holding all that she needed in the world. Or was it? 'Erin sorted me out with a local SIM card so I'm pretty much back online.'

'You two have developed a nice friendship, haven't you?'

'I think so. Like I've said, I'm not very good at making friends.'

'Rubbish, Caitlin. You're just telling yourself that — maybe it's convenient for you to feel like it's impossible to be nice to people.'

'I didn't say that.'

'Yes, but that's what you meant.'

Caitlin didn't like the uncomfortable feeling this discussion was giving her — she wasn't used to it, and maybe that's what Charles was getting at. He obviously sensed it too, as if he thought he'd pushed her just enough.

'Okay, Caitlin, I'll get back to the Saturday hordes and you go work out what you're going to do next. Swing by The Lodge later and tell me how you went.'

*

Even with the weight of a phone in her pocket, Caitlin forgot that she could make calls on the move. It wasn't until she was slowly cycling along the back road home that she realised she could call Maggie, call her *now,* if she wanted. Without thinking she turned her handlebars left rather than right and found herself on a steep path cresting the sand dunes. At the top, a weathered wooden bench looked out over the ocean, surrounded by low scrub growing sideways with the wind. Caitlin sat down, being careful to avoid splinters in the backs of her thighs. She pulled up Maggie's email again and held her thumb over the number.

Sod it.

'Hello?' A voice answered, sounding like a call was unexpected.

'Maggie Doble?'

'Yes?'

'I …' She didn't want to say any of the words she needed to: *Susan, mother, car accident.* Caitlin had to stop picking up the phone and making life-changing calls without a rehearsal or a script.

'Hello?' The voice sounded old, and worried.

'Oh, sorry. It's Caitlin.' She was flustered.

'Caitlin?'

'You, er, wrote an email. I think you knew my —'

Maggie cut her off. '— Susie.'

'Yes, Susie.'

Silence. *Well, this was going terribly.*

'I'm sorry, love, my hearing is buggered and the kettle's boiling. Hold on.'

Caitlin listened to fossicking noises. She heard Maggie sit down with a grunt. 'That's better. You there?'

'Yes! Yes. I just wanted to —' *What the hell do you actually want, Caitlin?* '— I'm trying to find out a little more about my mother. And I think you knew her.'

'Knew her? Oh, love, we practically lived on top of each other for a good few years. I've always wondered if you'd be back. Now, are you going to come see me?'

Caitlin baulked. 'Oh, that's — er — no. That's not necessary, thank you. Maybe I could just email a few questions?'

'Email? Questions?'

Caitlin felt at a loss. The sun was getting higher in the sky. Small black flies irritated the back of her neck.

Maggie continued, 'I've got class in half an hour, love. Life drawing. Sam's modelling today. Come visit me. We need to have a chat. A proper one. Okay? Bye then, bye —' Maggie hung up while she was still talking. Caitlin held the phone in her hand for a good few minutes, staring at the darkened screen, the wisps of her hair reflected in the glass. She wasn't quite sure what had just happened, but in that instant she resolved that she would not be visiting this vague old lady to hear what fuzzy memories she may have invented about her mother. Who knew if she was even legit, the woman could have googled … well, something. And now she could be out to scam her! Yes, that was probably it.

There. It felt good to close the door on the silly mother-goose chase. Caitlin hoisted herself back on the bike and rolled slowly down the hill, but as she did, David's words returned to her: *'Children should always know their parents, whether they're around or not.'*

There was a woman standing on the porch of The Cicada House when Caitlin pedalled up the drive. Her long grey hair sat in a statement-sized chignon atop her head. A fuchsia silk scarf curled around her neck and fell down over a similarly toned tunic. She looked like a menopausal musk stick. When she waved at Caitlin, bangles stacked halfway up her forearm jangled and shook. 'Helloo!'

Caitlin pulled to a slow stop but remained astride the bicycle. She didn't think she could deal with two crazy old ladies in one morning. Just then, Erin appeared from around the back — she wasn't wearing thongs, which Caitlin realised meant that she was in work attire. She even had her Arana Real Estate name-tag pinned to a crisp T-shirt, which was tucked into black jeans.

'Mate! I've got a visitor for you,' Erin said, striding through the summer-dried leaves in her wood platforms, kicking up eucalyptus scent as she approached. 'This is Tracey.'

'Caitlin. We finally meet.' Tracey held her fingers out like a royal greeting well-wishers at a garden party.

Caitlin clambered off the bike and shook hands, all in one tumbling move. 'Hi, yes. You're back?'

Tracey turned to face the front door, ignoring Caitlin's question. 'Shall we?' she asked.

Caitlin looked at Erin confusedly. 'Uh, sorry — did I miss something?'

'It's all good, babe. Tracey's home early and just popping by for a quick chat and hello. I mentioned there's been a bit of work done to the house while she's been in Bali.'

Caitlin noticed a key in Tracey's hand. She was certain a visit like this required 48-hours' notice. She was also sure that Erin hadn't told Tracey that the work had been done by a doe-eyed Englishwoman and a mysterious stranger — neither of whom were registered tradespeople.

'Yes! Erin told me, someone's been busy?' Tracey raised her pencil-thin eyebrows at Caitlin, and threw in a wink too.

Caitlin opened her mouth, but Erin gave her a small shake of the head, and Caitlin closed it again. Whatever story she'd told Tracey, Caitlin's version was not welcome.

'Um, well I'm afraid the house is a little untidy — I wasn't expecting an inspection.' She glared at Erin with the last word, but if the agent had noticed she didn't let on.

'Don't be silly! This is just a little pop-in to say hello. Nothing official, don't worry,' said Tracey as she unlocked the door, her words carrying with her as she disappeared towards the bathroom. Caitlin heard her voice echoing around the tiles. 'Goodness! Lovely job!'

Caitlin turned to Erin, ready to get a whispered update from her. Erin shrugged. 'Sorry. I may have mentioned you'd sorted some of the un-sortables and she got a bit excited.' Before Caitlin could respond, Erin followed Tracey into the house calling out — 'And come see the paving, Trace, completely done!'

Caitlin rested on the front doorframe, waiting for the women to finish. She could hear Tracey exclaiming over the work David had finished on the side fence. The landlady had a voice like tyres on carpark concrete. It didn't feel right to have Tracey and Erin poking around this house, particularly without notice. She noticed the vaguest hint of woodsmoke on the air. It reminded her of autumn and Bonfire Night and England and her life, the one she had told Paul she was coming home to. Erin appeared from around the back of the house.

'Are you doing circuits now?' Caitlin asked, a little archly.

'Trace is hilarious, isn't she?' replied Erin, ignoring the tone. Dot would have been disappointed in her granddaughter: Caitlin was losing her touch. 'I told her a mate of Tim's did all the work — thought you'd appreciate me keeping your mystery man out of the picture. I'm tipping neither of you are insured.'

'Oh.' Caitlin got the impression that she should say thank you. 'Thanks?'

'No worries, babe. Trace is stoked — maybe I'll see if we can get a little reduction in rent for you?' Just then, Tracey floated out from the house, catching the last of Erin's sentence.

'Oh, Erin Clay! Always working an angle!' She jangled a finger at Caitlin. 'Now don't you get any ideas. There is the small matter of the lifted lino in the kitchen, but I'll look past it and we can call it even, yes? I hear you've been adding a bit of your own elbow grease as well? I had no idea the little shack could scrub up so nicely. Busy little bee you've been! But seriously, thank you, pet.'

Caitlin frowned. She was unsettled by how invasive she found this visit, while also knowing she held no rational claim over such a hostile reaction. She realised Erin's breeziness was just a reflection of an intimacy their friendship should have achieved. Instead, Caitlin just wanted them both to leave. Neither of them noticed.

Tracey was still talking. '… alrighty then. Erin, you still okay to drop me off in town?'

Erin followed Tracey up the drive, calling out over her shoulder, 'Thanks, babe, chat soon yeah?'

When the last glimpse of fuchsia disappeared around the bend, Caitlin entered the house. It smelt of Tracey's patchouli and Erin's cigarettes. She walked into her bedroom and cranked open the awning window, airing out the room — although from the women's scents or the memory of David, she wasn't sure.

David. David Catto. Where have you disappeared to? 'Mystery man', Erin had called him. Caitlin didn't appreciate the creeping idea that she had been lied to, and David collecting this nickname made her feel like the story of their relationship was heading in a direction she neither liked, nor could she control.

She looked over the bedroom. One bed, a built-in wardrobe, a dresser and a chair. Looking at her rumpled white sheets, half-dazed with the memory of David's lips on her belly, she turned her phone around and around in her hand. Where had he gone? *How* had he gone? His hands on her hips, his mouth to hers. Around and around the phone went, flipping like a dealer cutting cards. Around and around and — Caitlin stopped. She looked at her phone like she was seeing it for the first time. Very slowly, she pulled up her browser and typed, steadily:

David Catto Arana Bay

It took 0.3 seconds for Caitlin to discover that David was lying to her. David, her David, did not exist.

She scrolled through blue words tagging men with nothing in common but their name. Even the closest David Catto geographically was decades away from her. Had he made the name up? Had he stolen an identity? It didn't matter really. At this shiny moment in time, when the world could be carried in a pocket, everyone existed somewhere online. Except her David. Or, this version of her David.

What was it that made her call Erin, despite her irritation that was still fresh? Fear? Curiosity? If she were honest, it was probably hope. Hope that she was wrong and David was living in a house down the road from her. Erin picked up quickly. 'I'm about to do an open, what's up? Did Trace leave something behind?'

'No, sorry — just a quick one. Have you ever heard of a David Catto?' Saying his name aloud to someone else made him real. Or, at least, she hoped it did. Erin was distracted. Caitlin heard voices in the background.

'Is this the stalker? Name rings a bell actually.' Caitlin's mouth dried up and at that sentence she realised how much she wanted him to be real and honest and — 'Sorry, hang on, Caitlin. Yeah, can you open the back doors and turn on the patio lights? Okay. Right. I'm here. David …'

'Catto,' Caitlin said, in a small voice, tight with hope.

'Yeah I do, I reckon my old man used to surf with a bloke called Dave Catto. Want me to ask him?'

It turned out that the sound of hope breaking was the same as a phone hanging up: quick and quiet and followed by silence.

Chapter Twenty-Seven

The weekend Paul had proposed, they had been camping. It was early enough in the relationship that she was still pretending to like things. He'd pitched the tent in a Hampshire field and Caitlin was impressed by how quickly he'd had the fire going.

That first morning she had woken early with condensation dripping on her face from the tent plastic that had sagged to just two inches above her nose. Paul was irritated at such an obvious demonstration of his failings and spent the next hour fussing over the pegs. Caitlin didn't help, but instead lay on the slowly deflating mattress and chewed every one of her fingernails down. She couldn't remember feeling unhappy, not at all.

But the tent had been fixed, the autumn sun had come out and the steam from their enamel mugs curled in a wholesome, picturesque way that made them both feel smug. After breakfast they had gone for a walk in the nearby national park. Paul had marked out the route on a map and they'd brought a rucksack that they had filled with doorstop-thick cheese and onion sandwiches. In the golden wood, sunlight drifted through the dying leaves and Caitlin watched her new hiking boots get pleasingly muddy. More than once, she ran her hands reverentially over oak trees knotted with age. It all felt so pure. Bill and Dot were not for family holidays, and so even though she was as British as the next, trips like this made her feel like a tourist in an ancient land. This sensation only doubled with what happened next.

Caitlin and Paul both laughed with delight as the path they were walking rounded into a clearing and they came upon a family of enormous, grunting pigs. They had hoped to find them, after spotting home-printed signs taped to a fence that had warned them to keep their distance: *Forest pigs can AND WILL bite!!!*

But they were so cute. Even with their filthy trotters and prickled arses, their pink ears flapped adorably over their eyes. Caitlin smiled as they snuffled acorns from the undergrowth. Paul turned to her, his eyes shining. He wobbled a little as he knelt down.

'Marry me!' He was unsteady on one knee as a large pig came alarmingly close. Later, Caitlin couldn't remember what she'd said first, 'Yes', or 'Watch out!' Either way, they were both laughing as they half-ran, half-stumbled back towards the campsite.

That night, Paul had served up an incredible potato hash cooked crispy on a frypan followed by a campfire apple crumble that she savoured with eyes closed. The orange flames had reflected in her diamond ring and the whole thing felt inevitable, and not in a bad way.

It wasn't until a year later that Jan, shrieking with glee during a Sunday dinner together, revealed Marigold had pre-prepared the whole weekend's worth of food. 'Call it the greasing of the wheels. We thought you were fabulous, darling — M and I were just as intent on proposing to you as Paul was!'

Paul went quiet like he always did when he was cross and embarrassed at the same time. And while it was part of her own proposal tale, Caitlin had immediately stopped laughing at the story. She thought it a funny and lovely detail, but she had changed the subject to make Paul feel comfortable again. Because even before she'd worn a ring, Caitlin had learnt to do that without thinking.

* * *

Caitlin had left her engagement and wedding rings back in London, but as Paul moved his phone around she caught a glimpse of his own gold band, still snug on his finger, like nothing had happened. She and Paul were FaceTiming. She couldn't bear to trawl through the now twelve emails from her husband, sent with ever-increasing administrative fervour. So instead, she was sitting on the front porch in the early morning sunshine waiting for Paul to finish listing the agenda items for the call he'd scheduled with their lawyers later in the week. If she didn't nod every few seconds he stopped, and his nostrils came close to the screen.

'Caitlin? Darling? Are you there?'

'Yes.' *Here I am on the other side of the world watching as my life shrinks back to the way it was.* 'Yes, I'm here.'

'Now I've shifted roles I'm going to be home a lot more, Caitlin. I think it's worth discussing a renovation. This spring might be the time to put in a conservatory.'

Paul had explained that he was transferring departments at work: 'I've told Laura it's for the best. We all need a little space.'

For the first time, Caitlin considered this woman who was pregnant and probably alone. Considered her as a person as opposed to the foil to her husband's fidelity. It made Caitlin feel selfish, to not have viewed the situation from this perspective earlier. She waited for the familiar feeling of shame. But like many things since arriving in Australia, her emotional patterns had changed. Instead Caitlin forgave herself, just a little bit, for not thinking in a wholly detached way.

There were voices and a familiar shriek from the back garden of The Cicada House. Paul saw Caitlin's head turn.

'What is it? Caitlin? Darling? Are you there?'

'Yes, I am — I just — hang on.' Caitlin stood up from the front step and carried the phone along the hallway.

Paul's nostrils spoke, 'Bloody hell is that flocked wallpaper? Oh, Caitlin.'

Tracey was standing in the back garden, wearing fluorescent bike shorts and a Bintang T-shirt. There were two similarly hued women standing behind her.

'Yoohoo!' Tracey waved and her wrists rattled.

'Sorry, Paul. My landlady has just turned up.' She glanced back at the phone. 'Should I call you back?'

'No, darling, we really need to keep working through this. If you'd just replied to my emails,' he tutted. 'Can't you tell her to come back later?'

Tracey was talking to her friends, her arms waving in wide circles.

'I don't think so,' Caitlin said.

Tracey noticed her. 'Caitlin! We were just completing our walking meditation and I thought I'd show the girls here the amazing work you've overseen at the house. This is Nicola, and Lindy.'

Caitlin wasn't sure which was which. One had a cloud of red curls around her head, the other a tight silvery pixie cut. They both wore as much jewellery as Tracey did.

Nicola (or Lindy) looked around the garden with confusion in her eyes. And Caitlin had to admit, it didn't exactly seem like there had been much 'amazing work' going on. Long weeds sprouted around the base of the Hills Hoist. The outdoor loo door hung crookedly on its hinges. Lindy (or Nicola) walked over to the sunken piano and pressed on some keys.

'Don't touch that!' Caitlin had shouted before she knew she was doing it. All four people — the three women and Paul, looked at her. In the silence that followed she was certain she could hear a single, perfect note ringing across the garden.

'Caitlin?' Paul seemed surprised to hear a tone in his wife's voice that was … fervent. 'Caitlin? Who else is there? What is going on?'

Caitlin felt the intensity in herself too. These three women, walking around on her block, had an energy that Caitlin didn't feel good about.

'Who's that?' Tracey pointed at the nostrils on the screen.

Caitlin shook the phone like a sad maraca. 'It's my husband. In England. We're in the middle of a call and —'

Tracey interrupted her, speaking to her friends. 'I know it doesn't look like much, but honestly, the improvements have made a huge difference. It's been listed at three-five-five, but they think if we get the tail-end of the summer weather it might crack four hundred.'

'Surely that's just for the land, though?' asked Nicola/Lindy. 'No-one's actually paying that for this house?'

'Tracey, what are you talking about?' Caitlin asked.

'The house, gorg. It's just been listed for sale.' Tracey smiled and jangled.

'What?' Caitlin felt panic prickle across the front of her chest, and followed with a whisper, 'You can't do that.' She'd forgotten Paul was in her hand.

'It's okay, darl, I've told the owners that we'll honour your rental terms,' Tracey said.

'But you said they'd never sell?'

Tracey continued, undeterred, 'You may just have to put up with an open for inspection once or twice. You're only here two more weeks, right?'

Caitlin flinched, like she'd been slapped. She smelt the sea salt and the gum trees and the scent of fresh, green grass. 'I'll buy it.'

'What?' Tracey asked.

'What?' Paul called.

'I'll buy it. I will.' She felt desperate. She wasn't ready to let go. She needed David and this house and the feeling it all gave her. 'Whatever you ask, I can pay it. Don't sell it, you can't. It's not yours to sell.'

'Caitlin, you bloody idiot. Listen to me right now.' Paul's voice was tinny but held weight. The four women in the garden each slowed, stilled in the face of his rage. As women, they had all been spoken to before in a way that expected that very reaction.

Caitlin held the phone up to her face, which was suddenly flushed with fear and upset. 'Paul, I — I'm sorry. I —'

'Take me off speaker.'

'It's FaceTime,' she said quietly. Caitlin felt ashamed how quickly the pleading, placating tone had come back into her voice.

'Alright then. If you want your friends to hear what you need to hear, let them. Because I've been very patient with this whole Eat-Pray-Love bollocks, but this is ridiculous. I don't know how things work down there, but I'm guessing that even in Erinsborough Bay you can't buy a house on a verbal offer and a tantrum.'

Caitlin turned her back to the three other women standing in mute witness to this man who, like most men, was used to being heard. She hunched her shoulders to try to stop his voice from polluting the air around her, but it continued to cut across the garden. 'In case you've forgotten, *you* told *me* you were coming home. *You said.*' His voice was pitching higher, and he was sounding more like a child. 'Come back to where you belong, where we belong. And hold the bloody phone up so I can see your face.'

An angry, scared child. She saw his face, and a flash of something behind him. A window? Where was he? It was the first time she'd wondered where he was staying, if he was no longer with Laura.

'Caitlin? Oh please, pay attention! Caitlin — do you need me physically beside you to make sure you don't do anything else so bloody stupid? I knew you were confused, but I didn't know you were unwell. I will get on a plane if I have to, if it's come to —'

Silence.

Suddenly Tracey was holding the phone with one hand, and Caitlin's wrist with the other. Caitlin looked from the phone to her hand to Tracey and back to the phone. Paul was gone: Tracey had hung up on him. Caitlin felt a bit dizzy.

'I think we can all agree,' Tracey said, nodding to her girlfriends, 'that no-one needs to talk to anybody in that way. And a shouty man, speaking with that tone, never deserves to be heard.' She placed Caitlin's phone back in her palm, gently letting her wrist go. 'Now, Caitlin, I can see that you're really *feeling* the energy of the house, and I understand that. I'm sorry. I've been disrespectful of you and this place. Nicola, Lindy, let's hold some space for Caitlin here.'

Caitlin gaped like a fish. She had no idea what had happened in the last few minutes. The three women joined their hands around her.

'Erm,' Caitlin looked nervously at their clasped fingers, 'I probably shouldn't have said I'd buy the house.'

'Shush, darl, all is well.'

Tracey closed her eyes, Lindy and Nicola followed. They all breathed slowly, deeply and in unison. Did they rehearse this stuff? Caitlin couldn't help but measure her breathing along with theirs. The shouting and the fear and the shame of the last five minutes was replaced by slow breathing and ocean waves. In the aftermath of the yelling, Caitlin was curious to observe a familiar feeling missing: emptiness. Can one notice the absence of nothingness? Normally she would be busy ridding herself of any emotions about such a brutal encounter. Ignoring shock at Paul, shame at herself, even anger at Tracey. Tracey — who had radically overstepped Caitlin's English boundaries by hanging up her own phone call. No, instead, her head was awash with thoughts and feelings and — oh, this was new — sympathy. For herself and also for the women around her who were unified against what had been erupting from the phone, and what it stood for. Their breathing continued, in and out like the sea, and

Caitlin found hers had regulated as well. She didn't know what to do with her hands, so she wrapped them around herself in a hug, and closed her eyes.

If this is what happened when you spoke up, then maybe keeping quiet wasn't always the only way. As Caitlin stood surrounded by three quiet women wearing noisy jewellery and brash clothes, she felt another knot undo itself inside of her.

Chapter Twenty-Eight

Sienna picked up the reception line at The Lodge, her voice sounding different. 'Arana Lodge, how may I —'

Caitlin interrupted her spiel. 'It's Caitlin.'

Sienna returned to normal. 'Ugh. Thank you. Dad sometimes calls the main number just to laugh at my phone voice. He's so annoying. How are you? You have a phone! I haven't spoken to you since Maggie's email — holy shit!'

'Holy shit indeed. I called her.'

'What? Oh my god. Charlie will die. He's been flapping around like an old chook all weekend. We've got this retreat's farewell dinner tomorrow.'

'Oh?'

Caitlin's heart sagged. She was hoping for some company. The three women had left her with hugs and the promise of a property contract ('Just in case', Tracey had winked). And while she understood Erin had nothing to do with the sale itself, she felt an uneasiness about spending time with her right now. Caitlin missed Jan. She missed her house. She even, and she knew this was insane, missed top-and-tailing with Paul on their sofa with a takeaway lamb saag and BBC Two.

'Actually ...' Sienna continued, 'you should come do Monday dinner! Charlie will be so pleased to have someone else around who isn't a guest. He's sick of this bunch. And I think he misses you.'

'That's very kind but I couldn't. I mean, they don't want an interloper joining them at their last supper.'

Sienna paused, a little embarrassedly, 'Um. I was actually thinking you could help me *do* dinner. Like, serve it and stuff.'

'Oh.'

The Caitlin of a month ago would have been mortified at her faux pas. Instead, she laughed.

'Well, I'm an absolutely terrible waitress but I wash dishes like a machine. Let's do it.'

Which is how Caitlin came to be standing at the large sink in The Lodge's commercial-grade kitchen scrubbing at a roasting pan. Sienna unpacked clean glasses from the dishwasher. The dinner had been easier to prepare than she'd expected, but the dishes were just as tedious.

'Thanks again for your help,' Sienna said.

'It's not a problem. This would have been a big undertaking on your own.'

'You get used to it. But, yeah, I'm not really feeling it this month. Everything seems a little bit harder right now.'

Caitlin propped her hip against the steel counter as she dried her hands on the tea towel.

'Your dad?'

'My dad.'

'I'm really the worst person to talk to about parenting, or daughtering for that matter. But, I am —'

Sienna cut her off, words tumbling. 'He's still not talking to me. I mean, unless I say what he wants to hear. He's so, so … pugnacious!'

Caitlin raised her eyebrows. 'Are you sure you're not switching to an English degree?'

'It's Mum's word. She uses it all the time to describe Dad.'

'You said they split up, right?'

'Yeah, divorced. Just after he finished this place, actually. When I want to tease Charlie I tell him The Lodge is a monument to my parent's lost love.'

'Oh, that's mean.'

Sienna chuckled. 'He knows I'm joking.'

'You said the other day that the two of you didn't used to fight. Before you dropped out of uni, did you and your dad actually get along?'

'Sort of. We're probably a bit too similar. And we've definitely spent too much time together. When I finished year twelve, Mum went back to Thailand to help out my uncle, so I moved in with Dad. Mum now goes between Melbourne and Bangkok; and Dad and I want to murder each other.'

'I know I'm a repressed Englishwoman, Sienna, but you do use pretty severe language to talk about your own parent.' Sienna opened her mouth to interrupt again, but Caitlin held up her hand. 'I know you're angry at your dad, but I'm sure he just wants what's best.'

Sienna crossed her arms. 'Dad's shit scared. In his life, there's a "right" way to do things: there's only one school, one uni, one car, one type of locally sourced, super expensive hardwood. You use the right one, and Dad's happy. And if you don't?' She slammed the dish drawer shut with a bang, answering her own rhetorical question. 'C'mon, let's go check on Charlie,' Sienna finished.

Caitlin watched on as she bounced from the kitchen. She was impressed, and a little concerned. Sienna clearly believed in her own destiny so strongly that she was willing to stand and fight her own father. This young woman was full of confidence, buzzing with an indignation and passion that Caitlin had never come close to manifesting. It felt like standing near starlight.

Caitlin sat with Charles and Sienna at the end of the vast table in The Lodge's dining space. It was a sumptuous room. Different to the rest of what she'd seen in The Lodge, its walls had a deep, muddied crimson wallpaper that, combined with low brass lights and a faded silk rug, made the long room feel intimate, clubby even. All of the guests had drifted off to sit in small groups on the terrace, lipsticked glasses of wine in hand, deep in conversation. Sienna and Caitlin picked at a cheese board, as they'd missed out on eating the dinner they'd served Charles and the guests.

He topped up both of their wineglasses and said, 'The lamb was outstanding. I love it when the caterers do that thing with samphire.'

'I love it when they don't. I hate using those tiny tongs,' said Sienna.

Caitlin poked at some brie. 'I wish I had caterers do my dinners. I'd be very happy to take the delivery, tweezer the samphire and heat up jus in the microwave. The dishes, not so much.'

'Yes. The cooking is much easier this way. For the first few years I was trying to cook, serve and provide witty repartee. The guests got restless and hungry, which also meant they got very drunk. So thank you again, both of you. It was a wonderful success and I couldn't have done it without you.'

Caitlin popped some red grapes in her mouth. 'I'd much rather be back-of-house than sitting here. I don't know how you do it, retreat after retreat. There's just so much *chat*.'

Charles laughed. 'Yes, I suppose. Endless country weekends with extended family were good training grounds. These are easier, actually. I'd much rather discuss fanciful plot twists than actual family skeletons.'

'I agree with Caitlin. It seems like a lot of work, hosting the groups. Just the bits of conversation I overhear — ergh,' Sienna shuddered.

Charles raised his glass of kombucha. 'Well, that's your last for the season, so no more dishes and no more small talk. Well done, Sienna. You're a marvel.'

'Where are you off to?' Caitlin asked, as they all clinked glasses.

'Nowhere, she can stay here as long as she wants,' Charles said firmly.

Sienna held her chin up. 'And now February's done, I want to double-down on Wertham. I *need* to make it work.'

Charles raised his glass again, this time to the window and the silhouetted trees in the moonlight. 'So goodnight to our last summer retreat.'

Caitlin panicked. 'Hang on — summer is over?'

'Don't fret, my dear. Dates don't mean much anymore — last year I seem to recollect we managed a top of 38 degrees on the 1st of March.' He shook his head. 'Terrible business, this end of the world palaver. Still!' He brightened. 'At least it means your final few weeks down under will likely be filled with sun, sand and surf.'

But it wasn't the weather. Caitlin wasn't thinking about swimming and suntans. The end of summer meant the end of her trip, which meant the end of cicadas and mosquito coils and … oh, she missed him. Again, the stuck-record of David repeated in her head and she wondered what his real name was and why he had lied to her. Caitlin picked up the wire from the top of a champagne bottle, twisting it hard against her fingers so it hurt. She needed to distract herself.

'I spoke to Maggie,' she said.

'Oh god, yes! Let's talk about that. How thrilling. I told you we'd find her,' said Charles.

Sienna raised her eyebrows at him, '"We"?'

Charles waved her away. 'Pah. What did she say, Caitlin?'

'Not much, really. She was pretty insistent I meet her in person. She's in Melbourne.'

'Yeah, she shared her address. She lives in St Kilda,' said Sienna.

'Well you must go! You must!'

'No, you two. Come on. She's probably some scam artist. Not worth it. Right?'

Sienna and Charles both looked at her patiently. Caitlin sighed. She was getting tired and this wasn't the response she wanted.

Charles prodded. 'Why do you assume that? Why would she lie about who she is?'

Caitlin thought of David in her bed.

'Hey, Charles, didn't you say you were heading into Melbourne this week?' Sienna asked.

'Yes. Why?'

She looked to the heavens. 'Honestly, Charlie. You and Caitlin can go to Melbourne. *Together.*'

'Oh no.' Caitlin laughed. 'Absolutely not.'

Charles looked hurt. 'Whyever not?'

'Go on, Caitlin, you can't come over from the UK and spend all your time in Arana Bay. Have a day in the city. I know I said Melbourne sucked, but it's not that bad, really,' Sienna said.

The idea of going on a road trip with Charles made her feel a little shy, but a lot less shy than she'd feel about visiting Maggie on her own.

'Okay. I'll come for the drive,' Caitlin said. 'But I'm not promising I'll actually visit this Maggie woman. I don't know how helpful she'll be. She seems a little strange.'

'Wonderful!' Charles clapped his hands together. 'I love a good eccentric!'

Caitlin swallowed a yawn, and Charles looked at his watch. 'It is very late. You've had wine. Are you sure you don't want to sleep here?'

Sienna nodded. 'I'm shattered. Caitlin, you can bunk in with me if you want — top room, twin beds, and I don't snore.'

Caitlin thought of The Cicada House. Over the last few nights it had felt tighter, colder and darker. She nodded, and found she was feeling tearful, which was embarrassing. 'Yes, that would be great, I appreciate it.'

'Excellent. Well, I'll say goodnight. Thank you both again.' Charles bowed his head to both women.

Sienna stood up too, and stretched. 'Leave the rest.' She motioned to the cheese and wine. 'We can clear it up tomorrow. I'm too tired to do it now. Are you coming up?'

'Yes, I'll just finish this,' Caitlin said, circling the wine in the bottom of her glass.

When she was alone, Caitlin carried her glass and what remained of the bottle to the front of The Lodge, back to her little space. She'd never been there at night, and was worried the glass and trees would feel spooky. But like everything else in The Lodge, it felt grounded and safe. She placed the wine on the floor by the couch and pulled the laptop into her lap. She hadn't planned what she was about to do, but it all came suddenly. David's name was at her fingertips. They flew over the keyboard. Why had she never sought information on her mother like this? Maybe it was the wine, or the fact that an Australian autumn was on its way. Or maybe it was because what she needed to know about Susan wasn't online. For David, it was the opposite. She knew what the warm patch of his neck smelt like when he came in from the sun. She felt how his fingers lightly grazed the inside of her wrist. She saw the lightness in his eyes when he spoke the poetry of the trees, words like *acacia*, *banksia* and *moonah*.

But she didn't know where he lived, or what he did, and why he was invisible. Caitlin dove online again. This time, she was determined to find her David.

iv. Evening

The radio this evening has me reeling. An adagio in G minor. Guess I must have played a little, up in the world. Or wanted to. Memories keep swooping in just over my head, landing like maggies on the wire. Watching me with beady eyes and wondering when I'll catch up.

Time doesn't help, because it doesn't exist. I hear a lot of things from my horizontal post, but the tick of a clock isn't one. Instead, marker points help me anchor the day. And now it's evening, with its noise and movement. Dinner trays rattle. A telephone rings. Kids visit. Running steps, heavy footfalls that land unselfconsciously. Just more noise to distract from the dreams. These crazy dreams I've been having. Of golden light and someone who smells brand new but feels like home.

Who?

That's something: I've started a new habit. Now, I ask myself questions:

Why am I here?

Am I dead?

And when can I dream again?

And already, one answer's arrived. The woman who rubs my feet — she's Mum. With her hard-soft hands and voice that chides the doctors. It feels good to know there's a mother here, my mother. She brushes my hair, says a prayer over my chest. Breaks my heart when she's crying, though. Wish she wouldn't do that. Save it for outside, Mum.

But where is outside?

And who's there?

So I've added an extra arrow to my waiting-bow. Now I can spend my days lying, listening, waiting and asking.

And if I ask enough, then maybe someone will answer.

Chapter Twenty-Nine

It looks like there aren't many great matches to your search.

'No shit. What's the definition of insanity, again?' Caitlin said aloud to the small room. She read the disappointingly short page of results again, the same names she'd scrolled past before. A Boston-based academic, a fundraising page set up by a teacher in Rome, and the old bloke who probably surfed with Erin's dad. Caitlin hovered her cursor over each result and wondered what else she should search for.

Tradie + musician + Arana Bay?

Black hair + good listener + looks good in a pair of jeans?

Maybe she should enlist Sienna in the hunt, seeing as her track record had been rather impressive. Just as Caitlin was about to close the laptop and put the search off until she could bug Sienna in the morning, she had a thought. The David Catto of Arana Bay may actually be her David's father ('her' … *get a grip, Caitlin*).

She hit the result and was taken to the homepage of Arana Primary School, the one Erin's Josh attended. A brightly coloured digital newsletter filled the screen, with the smiling faces of students in broad-brimmed sunhats and green and gold uniforms. For just a moment, Caitlin imagined what it would have been like to attend a school like this herself. Where the ovals were dusty and the sun shone more often than it didn't.

Where her mother would pick her up from the front gate with an Aus-English accent and an ice cream for the walk home.

Pull yourself together, Caitlin.

Last year, the APS grade six class had completed a 'History of Arana Bay' community project, which involved digitising the family notice pages from the now defunct local paper, *The Arana Star.* Births, deaths and twenty-first birthday celebrations had been scanned in and diligently catalogued by earnest eleven-year-olds learning about the 'olden days', before the internet.

And there, in slightly blurred newsprint, Caitlin read:

> *1968*
> *CATTO — Giuliana Anna (Cherisi) on March 22, after a short illness. Giulia, loved wife of David Catto, dear mother to George and Nicholas. Only child of Isabella and Alfredo (dec). Daughter-in-law to Marco and Nina. Age 28. At rest.*

And there it was. *Huh.* She felt a bit sick, with betrayal, but mostly disappointment. The giddy adrenaline that had carried her through the last few weeks — dealing with Paul, searching for any information on her mother and finding Maggie — all flooded away. She felt it leave through her fingertips and her toes. And she was left, deflated on a couch in a cold room, lit by the lonely blue of a computer screen after midnight.

Caitlin's holiday fling was a con man who had lifted someone else's identity. He hadn't even tried very hard, Caitlin realised grimly. He was probably just an uncle reading a nephew's school newsletter, or, even worse, a father scanning his own child's. Her nausea mounted.

She wondered, why her? But that was the simplest question to answer. She was an easy mark: a pommy girl with a broken heart alone in an empty house. Was he playing for the fun of it, or would he be hitting her up for money soon? Closing the laptop felt like a deflated ending to a barely begun new beginning.

*

The next morning Caitlin woke up craving The Cicada House with a strength that surprised her.

Charles walked her to her car, and as she started the engine, he bent down and said through the passenger door window, 'I'm aiming to be on the road to Melbourne tomorrow by nine. I'll pick you up with coffee?'

No, I don't want that at all.

'Yes, thanks, Charles.'

'Good you are.' He closed the door and tapped the roof of her car.

When she arrived at the house, another fruit-gift hung from the door handle. This time, figs weighed down the plastic bag. There was no note, but it didn't need one. Caitlin detected Erin's attempt at an appeasement, in light of the decision to sell. She felt irritated.

Caitlin carried the bag into the house, quietly pleased to be back. In the still warmth of the morning, with a handful of dust particles drifting through a beam of sunlight cast through the lounge window, it felt like hers again. Caitlin was drawn to the front room, with its smell of old books. She sat down on one of the green chairs and rested her feet on the other, carefully selecting a fig from the bag in her lap. Pinching the end of the fruit and splitting it open, Caitlin unfolded the purple skin to reveal a languid eruption of flesh and seeds.

'Perfectly ripe.'

Caitlin shrieked. The two halves flew out of her hands and hit the ceiling, raining down in a small pink fig-shower. David laughed from the perch he'd taken up, against the far wall.

While there was a part of her brain that definitely wanted to run at him and wrap her arms around his, the louder part of her mind was angry and, yes, a little scared. She jumped up from the chair and took as many steps back as the room allowed, bumping into the windowsill.

Her heart was racing, not just from him creeping up on her, but also from the knowledge that she was in a room with someone she'd slept with only a few days earlier, without even knowing his real name. 'David's' arms were crossed against his T-shirt and he looked at her, partly amused, partly confused. As he opened his mouth to say something, somebody knocked loudly on the front door.

Caitlin would observe later that when something monumental occurred, the first thought was often, 'This is actually happening.' An incredulity. A disbelief and a refusal and yet a complete certainty.

And, at that moment, that was what Caitlin thought: 'Oh, this is actually happening.' Because as she looked at David, and David looked towards the front door, and as they both heard it being opened by a *yoohoo*ing Tracey, Caitlin saw David disappear.

He disappeared like she'd never seen a human disappear before. Which may sound obvious, but was not. Because people disappeared all the time — in movies, and TV shows, and sometimes even on stage at expensive Las Vegas magic shows that your husband had booked. Your husband, who then spent the whole time whispering, 'I know how they're doing it.'

So Caitlin had seen people disappear. But not like this.

Caitlin's peripheral vision dissolved first, a twisting, narrowing tunnel. But not of black — of colours. Technicolour shards and shapes spiralling into each other, much like the cardboard kaleidoscope Father Christmas had left in her stocking one eighties Christmas. In the remaining small cylinder of sight, Caitlin could make out David, and then couldn't. He was there, and then he was not.

'Caitlin?' Tracey stood in the doorway of the lounge and surveyed Caitlin, panting in the corner, covered in fig. 'You look like you've seen a ghost! God, don't tell anyone — the house won't sell.' Tracey laughed, then focused. 'Actually, have you? Do I need to organise a sage ceremony?'

Caitlin's mouth was open but she couldn't say anything. Tracey had already turned and walked away back down the hall. 'I was just popping my head in to let you know the boys are out the front putting the for sale sign up. Don't mind them, won't be long. I have to run but I'll send you the inspection schedule!'

And the door closed. Caitlin bent over, her hands on her knees, her head close to the floor.

Breathe. Breathe. Breathe.

'Sorry.'

He spoke again, and he was there, again. This time standing right beside her. Caitlin thought she might wee her pants. She moved like a confused puppy, all spaghetti-limbed, trying to distance herself from whatever he — this — was. His body was whole again, she couldn't see rainbows anymore. Keeping her eyes on his face, Caitlin groped through the bookshelf beside her. Some *Reader's Digests*, a porcelain horse, her hands landed on something heavyish … the crucifix. A little cry came out from her, was it relief? Amusement at the cliché? She held the cross towards him like she'd seen people in the movies do.

'It's upside down.'

He had that bloody look on his face, like the day they first met. The corners of his mouth lifting ever so slightly.

'Oh, for god's sake!' She righted the cross but by that time he was laughing. Some of his hair had fallen down over his face, and his eyes were creased and twinkling and she really didn't think this man was a ghost.

'Are you *flirting*?' she asked, in disbelief.

'No,' he said, still smiling. 'I'm sorry, I guess that was pretty frightening.' It set him off again.

'Stop bloody laughing! What the hell, David!'

He pushed his hair back from his face and exhaled sharply, as if trying to shoo the laughs from his chest. 'I really am sorry, Cait. I'm just relieved, honestly. I didn't know if you seeing me … like that … meant I wouldn't make it back again.'

'Back? Back from' — Caitlin swallowed, her eyes round as dinner plates — 'from *heaven*?'

This time it wasn't a chuckle and he didn't even try to hold it back. David tipped his head to the ceiling and laughed, open-throated and with joy.

Caitlin put the crucifix back on the shelf and placed her hands on her hips. 'This might be all supernatural and stuff, but you're still being extremely annoying.'

'Sorry. Sorry.' He was laughing still, but now softer, deeper in his chest. 'Come here.'

He reached out and hooked one finger into the waistband of her shorts. Caitlin tipped away from him, her hands still on her waist.

'I'm sorry,' he said, his arm holding her whole weight.

She took one step towards him. 'Are you dead?'

'No.'

She took another. 'Did you just disappear in front of my eyes?'

'What do you think?'

He gave a gentle pull and Caitlin filled the last space between them, so her nose was almost touching his.

'Are you lying to me? Are you out to trick me and take everything I have?'

When he spoke, his lips brushed hers, 'I have never lied to you.'

Caitlin kissed David and he was three-dimensional. At that exact point of time, she decided that was all she required.

Common scams in Australia
Can ghosts have sex?
Sex with ghost mental illness
Hallucination common cause
Waking sex dreams

Caitlin put her phone down. This was probably something she should have turned incognito mode on for. It was 5 am and she was awake, alone, and wondering how she had come to a point in her life where she knew the definition of the word *spectrophilia*.

It was still dark and Tracey's mention of a sage ceremony should have spooked her. But, instead, she was feeling grateful to be alone in the house again. After spending so much time with others, the walls breathed and folded in around her. She thought she'd be frightened, but she was relieved.

Caitlin had slept with David again. This time, on the lounge floor. She hadn't had sex on a floor since she was in her twenties, and she definitely didn't feel as crooked then as she did now. It was much nicer to be back in bed — albeit alone — with a faint bruise on her coccyx and a google search history she didn't want anyone to see.

They had shagged on the floor in the urgent kind of way that people do when they can't bear anything other than being with the other. They had shagged just under the window where outside they could hear the mallet pounding wooden sign-supports into sandy soil. By the time she sat up and pushed her hair out of her face, Caitlin could make out the sharp lines of the property board through the trees. She hoped David wouldn't disappear in front of her again, and he didn't. But he didn't stay either. She went for water and when she came back he was gone.

Caitlin had a theory. Of course she did. She had hallucinated the disappearance, in a micro-seizure likely brought on by the stress of her impending meeting with Maggie. David probably *was* a scam artist, who had lifted his fake story from the death notices in the school newsletter. She hadn't pressured him on this because she was lonely and in denial and traumatised about her mother and — *Oh, be honest with yourself, Caitlin* — she just really liked spending time with him.

And lying beside him.

And running her lips along his collarbone.

And listening to him whisper in a way that distracted from her mother or husband or even herself.

She rolled onto her back and threw her hands over her eyes. If that was the price to pay for being lied to, then Caitlin was coming around to the idea. It had been a surprisingly solid night's sleep, but now she was awake too early and confusing herself on Google, mostly because it was a good distraction from the journey she'd promised Charles they'd take today. And her subconscious was being extremely noisy about David and micro-seizures and the fact that *this entire thing did not add up at all.* But before she could continue down that path of thought, her phone lit up with a message. Paul.

I'm sorry. I'm so sorry. I miss you. I love you and I am just so scared I'm going to lose you. I know I need to work on my anger and myself. Please can we talk?

Caitlin pushed the phone deep beneath the duvet and tucked the pillow under her neck. She could get a couple more hours of sleep in before Charles picked her up, and that was preferable to weighing up the shady Australian that she barely knew, and her husband who was trying to make everything better. Caitlin closed her eyes against both men as the up-and-down warble of magpies sent her back to sleep.

Chapter Thirty

They had been in the car since 8 am. Charles had worked through most of The Eagles' and Fleetwood Mac's back catalogues. When she glanced at her chauffeur, she saw a man whose silver-white hair brushed the roof of the car, who wore a pair of banged-up Wayfarers that were so scratched Caitlin worried he couldn't actually see, and who drove with his index finger and thumb barely holding the wheel. Charles's left hand sat on his leg, tapping to the music. She'd also seen the briefest glimpse of what he had tucked into the underside of his car visor. A folded photograph of two little girls, blunt-fringed and big-eyed. The two daughters reminded her of another daughter, angry and wild.

'How is Sienna doing? Really?'

'She's going to be fine. The work she's doing in Wertham is genuinely brilliant. I know a councillor out that way and they're very impressed. I think Sienna and the team might even get a grant this year.'

'That's wonderful.' Caitlin was surprised at how truly happy this news made her. 'But what about her dad?'

'It's so frustrating.' Charles smacked his free hand on his knee. 'I see them butting heads, it's getting worse, and no-one's going to win. Richard's a genius. Certifiably. But with that degree of focus and drive comes … oh, I don't know. There's not much empathy there.'

'But Charles, from what little I've seen, Sienna is not an easy daughter. I mean, god, she doesn't pull her punches.'

'That may be true. But the fact remains, he is the parent, and he has a duty to love unconditionally.'

Charles gently put his sun visor up, thumb resting on the dog-eared photograph. Caitlin tried not to watch his face too obviously. But she knew this was a moment to be quiet and let *Rumours* fill the silence.

'So. Where is this Saint Kilda?' she asked.

'St Kilda,' Charles corrected. 'And don't let anyone hear you calling it Saint, that's like pronouncing the 'y' in Marylebone.'

Caitlin chewed at her finger and scrolled over Maggie's message again. She had toyed with the idea of writing down questions, either to share or just to refer to as notes. But Caitlin decided she'd let the meeting roll with fate. She didn't hope for much, just a glimpse of the woman who was, for a brief moment, her mother.

'My appointment's in Toorak. I can drop you off first.'

'You're not coming with me?'

Charles looked at her over his sunglasses. 'You don't need me to come with you, Caitlin.' And then, when he saw her face: 'Do you?'

'Well, no. I think I was just hoping you would. And anyway, you said you wanted to meet an eccentric.'

'This Maggie person might be a little more open about things if it's just the two of you. What are you worried about?'

'Nothing. Nothing!' Caitlin wondered why she felt so defensive.

'I think it might be tricky to fit in Maggie and still make it to my meeting in time. I'm sorry, I didn't think you'd seriously want me to come.'

'It's fine,' she said with a mouth terse and tight. She knew she was being passive-aggressive. *I can see your hackles from here.* She took a breath. 'I mean, I understand. Sorry — I'm being a cow. I'm just really …' Caitlin shook her hands out in front of her and made a noise in her throat.

'Self-awareness is next to godliness, in my book. But please don't call yourself a cow. You're nervous. It's understandable.' Charles smiled and changed lanes in front of a semi-trailer, turning Chicago up to drown out the noise of the truck's air horn.

Soon, the city of Melbourne emerged from the haze along the horizon. A shimmering grey Oz of towers the same colour as the silver sky. The skyscrapers didn't seem to move or grow for a long time, until at the very last minute, when Caitlin was alarmed to see they were almost on top of them.

Caitlin pressed the intercom at the entrance to an Art Deco block of flats. Its white walls shone behind sprinklers lit by the late morning sun. Behind her, fat old palm trees paraded along the Esplanade like dusty dames.

'Hello?' The voice was expectant, and already pleased.

'It's Cait—' The front door buzzed before she could finish, and Caitlin heard another door open from above.

'Hello!' Maggie was waving demonstratively from the interior balcony like there was a football pitch between them, not one short flight of stairs. She kept waving as Caitlin climbed, keeping her eye on the curtain of hair hanging over the railing. And then, before Caitlin could avoid it, Maggie had her. It was a marshmallow of a hug, pressing arms and bosom all scented with an odd mix of citrus and turpentine. Maggie pushed Caitlin away from her and, Caitlin was alarmed to see, regarded her through tears.

'Caity-girl.' She said the name with relief.

Caitlin felt uncomfortable hugging strangers, and receiving nicknames she'd never heard before, but her trip to Australia had taught her that sometimes discomfort was necessary. She tried a smile through her nerves. 'Hello — Maggie, I'm assuming. Thank you for having me.'

Maggie wore makeup, which, after a month of speaking to sand- and salt-dusted faces, made Caitlin feel a little displaced. Two parallel lines of red lipstick announced Maggie's mouth, an equals sign in her face. Her hair was the colour of slate and very long, fringe swinging heavy like a beaded curtain over damp eyes. She looked nothing like Caitlin had imagined, which was unsurprising as, now she thought about it, Caitlin had pictured a chain-smoking nineteen-year-old with a mullet.

'Look at you. You haven't changed. Much, anyway. Please, come, sit.'

Maggie bustled her into the apartment, which meant one step through the flat's dark entrance hall and then into a warm room where sunlight ricocheted between the parquet floor and the intricate white plasterwork on the ceiling. But it was the walls that made Caitlin exclaim, forgetting her awkwardness. Blue brushstrokes covered the white surface, painted lines bending and wandering into shapes that were sometimes fish, then flowers and finally a naively rendered woman's face taking up most of the far corner. Around the windowsills blue-painted grapevines twisted over each other, with little azure bees scattering up towards the ceiling.

Caitlin turned to Maggie, who — she realised — had eyes the colour of her murals. 'Did you do these?'

'I did! I do lots of these, and a little of that. Sit, sit.' Maggie gestured at the sofa that faced a clinker-brick fireplace. The coffee table held two piles of *National Geographic*s and a bowl filled with — from what Caitlin could make out — a collection of old keys, shining buttons and blushing shells.

Caitlin chewed at her fingernail as her eyes settled into the bright space. Maggie was busying herself in the little kitchen that fed off the open room, so Caitlin let her gaze move from the walls and out Maggie's large front window. Across the tram tracks and beyond the palms, Caitlin saw the sea, flat as a puddle. Joggers ran along the promenade with the sun reflecting from their expensive trainers. It felt like a bland second-cousin to the untamed beach of Arana Bay.

Maggie returned with cups of chai.

'Caity-girl, I can't believe it. I'm looking at your face. Again. Goodness gracious me.'

'Yes, it's — I don't know where to start, really. Oh!'

Maggie had come to sit down — not in the chair across from Caitlin, but directly next to her on the small sofa. They were squashed into each other, Maggie's trousers against Caitlin's jeans. Suddenly, Caitlin's hands were in Maggie's, who was gripping them with some force. Maggie moved even closer and half-whispered, 'I *loved* your mother.'

With every shred of her energy, Caitlin remained still, when all she wanted to do was rear back, jump up and run away as fast as she could. Instead, she smiled, gently extracted her hands and picked up the mug closest to her, using it as an excuse to lean away from the smiling woman.

'That's nice to hear. I — I would love to know what you can share about her. I've travelled from England, to —'

'Yes. *Yes.*' Maggie was nodding emphatically, her hair shifting around her. 'England. Of course. How are your dear grandparents?'

'Oh. I'm afraid my grandmother passed away. Some time ago.'

'Well. I never met her.'

Caitlin nodded slowly, not sure how these two statements related. 'And my grandad Bill is in a home now. But he's well.'

More nodding. 'Mm, mm. Yes, good,' Maggie said with eyes closed, inhaling the steam from her own chai.

Caitlin was unsure if this woman was eccentric or heavily medicated or both. The apartment pointed to neither, it was neat and clean and apart from the winding murals throughout, it looked more Conran Shop than Camden Market. But Maggie's manner threw her. Her conversation patter flowed as if someone had shuffled the cards in her punctuation pack too well. Caitlin decided to take command of the conversation. She tried on her Work Voice, rusty after being unused for so long. 'So, Maggie, thanks for having me around. I had some questions if that's okay.'

'Of course, love. That's why you're here.'

'Well, yes. How did you and Susan meet?'

'Have you been past the old building? Georges. We started on the same day. Salesgirls in haberdashery. Susan and I shared shifts on the second floor. Maybe third? Seersucker and lace.'

Talking to Maggie was like failing a *Choose Your Own Adventure* game. Caitlin had no idea what to ask next. There was too much to know. If Maggie was confused that Caitlin didn't have a tumble of questions, she didn't show it. Instead she continued, her light voice filling the space in a to-and-fro cadence like a poetry class in high school.

'We were both new to Melbourne. I'd come down from my parents' property. She'd not long arrived from England. The country girl and the London girl. We just fell into each other. Both new to the city. Two girls. Wild and free.' She smiled at Caitlin. The lipstick made her thin lips look smaller. But her eyes remained big and blue. Caitlin began to relax into the stop-start rhythm of the conversation.

'So you were close?'

'Close? Oh yes. Susie and me. Like sisters, they used to say. I was the older one. Three years older. Back then that really felt like something. I drove! We moved in together the first month we met. Maybe the second.'

'You lived together?'

Maggie put her tea down. 'Caity. I lived with you! We all lived together, while Susan was pregnant. As you grew. I was there for all of it — right up until she left us.'

Caitlin swallowed. *Oh boy.* Maggie reached out and patted Caitlin's knee.

'It's okay. Not sad. We lived in a big house in Prahran. Not too far from here. Huge old Victorian. Still had the old servants' laundry out the back. Lots of bedrooms and lots of cats. We had parties. Dancing. Music!' Maggie punctuated each word with a twist of her head that made her hair swing. 'Such *fun*. We had a big dinner each Sunday. We'd come together and cook. And play. So much music! We didn't have money of course. Lots of lentils — Susie was vegetarian. I think. Or was I? It was perfect. Exactly what I imagined when I left the farm.'

Caitlin got the feeling that she was receiving more longing than fact. 'It sounds idyllic,' she said.

'Hardly!' Maggie shouted and Caitlin caught a splash of chai in her palm before it landed on the couch. 'You tell me. Stank of damp carpet. No heating and no cooling. Boyfriends skipping out without paying rent. Those days. So many silly boys.'

Caitlin blinked twice, quickly.

Maggie pursed her lips. 'Susan had been living there with her boyfriend, yes. But he wasn't your dad, love. She was going around with Ken, the pommy drummer with the band. Bit surly. Smoked a pipe. But he'd left. Some of the band headed home to England but she'd stayed on. Said she liked Melbourne. Not sure why.'

Caitlin was trying to keep the timeline straight. 'So she got pregnant after the pipe guy?'

'Ken. Yes, she did. I can't tell you much about your dad. I'm sorry. I only met him once. He didn't hang around long —'

Caitlin cut her off. 'It's okay, you don't need to. My grandad has all that information.'

For the first time, Maggie looked surprised. 'You don't want to hear more about your dad? I'm sure it was Peter. Or Mark.'

Caitlin coloured, realising she'd exposed some of the strange inner-workings of what she could and couldn't manage to think about. She tasted her tea, tried not to grimace at the sweetness. 'It's fine. I'd rather we talk about her, Susan, if that's okay.'

'Well that's a relief. Because I only met him once. I think.'

My mother my mother. Tell me about my mother.

'So you were already living together when she fell pregnant?'

'Yes. She was scared. Then she was angry. I helped her. My older sister had been through a similar thing back in Edenhope. But Susie was only eighteen. And so far from home.' Maggie gave a short laugh. 'Stubborn! Gosh, she was stubborn. She refused to go home. I even offered to drive her back to the farm for a few months.'

'She had the baby in Melbourne?'

'Yes, love. But she didn't have "the baby".' Maggie smiled, pulling in closer, widening her big blue eyes. 'Caitlin, she had *you*.'

Chapter Thirty-One

Once Caitlin had entered the timeline, Maggie seemed to become more natural in her storytelling.

'Susie had a bed by the window at the Royal Women's. Blue skies on your birthday. Such a busy ward. There was some chat about adoption. She knocked that on the head. Quick smart. We all said we'd help out.' Maggie shook her head. 'We thought we had it sorted, us in that Prahran pile. Well. Susie definitely did. Have it sorted. Oh, she was a tough one.'

Caitlin was trying so hard to remember every word she was hearing about Susan. Taking them and holding them tightly to her chest. 'Tough in a good way?' she asked, hopefully. Sounding like a five-year-old who wanted to hear a fairytale. Now who was longing?

'Well yes, of course tough in a good way! Is there anything else? Things weren't like they are now. We were more free. Life was simple. The house was full of special folk. Some are still dear friends. Although, most are gone now.' Caitlin noticed Maggie briefly touch the small cross hanging on a delicate chain around her neck. She continued, 'It was a lovely time. You, my girl, were always being held. Safe and warm. Lots of cuddles. I was the one who started calling you Caity-girl.'

Maggie smiled at Caitlin, continuing to ladle out dollops of the golden syrup tale. 'Such a beautiful little baby. We all loved you. I can still see you — that white-blonde hair, running around with no pants on most of the time. Suze and I would make sure our shifts didn't clash so you always had someone you knew at home with you. We'd take you to the park. Or down to the beach on the tram — not far from here!'

Maggie stood and held onto her lower back, wincing a little. She carried her mug to the window, looked out at the tattered palm fronds against the sky. Caitlin felt a growing sense of frustration. She wasn't sure what she had been expecting, but it wasn't this tale of patchouli-drenched Camelot. 'Why did you do all that? Help her with me?'

Maggie turned, this time without a smile. Her brow creased. It made her look older, and more serious. 'I told you, Caitlin. Susie was dear to me. And it's what you do.'

Caitlin felt like she was in trouble. 'I don't mean to be rude. It's lovely, that you did that for her. Thank you,' Caitlin said.

'Don't thank me, love. Suze would have done the same. More?'

Maggie returned to the kitchen to top up her mug. Caitlin had barely had any of her perfumed milk drink. She scratched at an ambiguous stain on her jeans. Sienna and Charles's faces bobbed around in her head. She couldn't leave Maggie, holding only a fabled story of a ramshackle house and a blonde baby. She felt an important chance slipping away.

'I'm sorry, Maggie. I don't think I was very well prepared for this conversation. I thought writing down some questions would be foolish, but now it feels like not writing them was stupider.'

'Hush.' Maggie hadn't sat down, but stood by her. Her hand almost absentmindedly stroked Caitlin's hair. 'You're talking like this is our one chance. But I can tell that this is just the beginning. Of us. Our next chapter. Oh, but I do wish I could find those photographs. Did I tell you I had photographs?'

Caitlin didn't answer. It felt agony to admit it, even to herself, but the sun-spotted hand patting her head was making her heart happy.

'And now, we should take a turn on the roof. Whatcha say, Caity-girl?' As Maggie stood over her, her blue eyes held Caitlin's for a long, suspended thread of time. Caitlin realised her own were achingly wide, her hands on her knees as she stared up at Maggie.

'Oh my god.'

Maggie smiled, relieved. 'I didn't think you'd remember.'

'I don't. I didn't.' Caitlin's voice faded off into a whisper as she repeated, 'Whatcha say …'

'"Whatcha say, Caity-girl?" We all used to say it, not just to you. To everyone. But you started it, little thing. That small voice of yours. "Whatcha say, Maggie?" "Whatcha say, Mama?" Oh gosh.' Maggie was crying; sad, small tears this time. She pressed her fingertips gently to the soft pouches under her eyes.

'Maggie, I'm sorry. I —' Caitlin stood and awkwardly placed her hands on Maggie's arms. 'I'm sorry, turning up like this, asking you to remember things that must have been so hard. And sad. I didn't think. I never think.'

She said these last words to herself, closing her own eyes at how even after so much time she was still thoughtless. When she opened them, Maggie was smiling again. Sad, damp, but smiling. 'Come on, Caity, we can do this together.'

From the landing, she took Caitlin up more stairs and through a heavy door onto the roof. Terracotta tiles shone. A little wind-worn table was set wonkily by a parapet that was lined with fat pots of blood-red geraniums, leaves latticed by snails. The two women sat together and looked out across the muddled waves of Port Phillip Bay.

After a silence Caitlin gauged was long enough, she asked, 'Can you tell me anything at all about how she died?'

'Oh, love. There's not much to tell.'

'Please.'

Maggie pressed her lips together again. The lipstick had faded with the chai, Caitlin noticed.

'Suze was away for a weekend. Maybe a bit longer. She had a new boyfriend. Another drummer, I think. His band was touring around country towns. She was alone in a car — she had her licence by then. Driving ahead to the next pub. The band were following.'

In the pause, Caitlin gave a little smile, imploring her.

'It was morning. Wet, apparently. They said she lost control. The car hit a tree.'

Maggie reached out for Caitlin's hand again. This time, she let her have it.

'Where was I, when it happened?'

'Home. With me. The police came that night. Just horrible.' She looked at Caitlin. 'I'm sorry, my love. Maybe it's a terrible thing to say … but … I'm glad you were too young to remember. You …' Maggie looked pained.

'Say it, it's okay.'

'You cried for her for three days straight.'

Maggie's voice cracked and she turned away from Caitlin. It was Caitlin's turn to squeeze the woman's hand. She had memories of the flight home with her grandfather, but nothing before then. Only shreds and whisps caught in the corner of an eye. It was as if her mother dying had reset any consciousness she had been growing.

'I was the one who called your grandad. He always included his number when he sent notes and postcards, the ones with the wire details.'

'Wire?'

'The money he sent to Susie every month.'

'Money? I don't think so. Grandad wouldn't have —'

This time Maggie interrupted her. 'Bill sent money. Every month from when you were born. He never missed. I don't believe your nan knew about it. She and Susie had fallen out. Badly, I think.'

Caitlin heard her grandmother's wail at the news of Princess Diana's death. Saw Dot's pain-closed eyes on the landing outside Susan's bedroom.

'Susie told her parents about you, but said she wouldn't come home. So, money came here.'

It wasn't a car around the tree, or police knocking at the door. It wasn't even the weeping blue-eyed woman missing a ghost. That day, the moment that broke Caitlin was the image of Bill walking to the bureau de change every month, to send money to his lost daughter, and to his invisible grandchild. It took everything in her not to fall to her knees.

Caitlin left the flat with an envelope. It contained a postcard Susan had sent Maggie during a week away in Sydney, before Caitlin was born. As she sat on the steps leading from the apartment block to the street, Caitlin looked down at the card's washed-out sky behind the yellowing Opera House. Susan's writing was deliberate and curved, a rounded script that conjured up images of a schoolgirl, and not a mother.

Charles's message pinged on her phone: he was a few minutes away. Caitlin stood up and dusted dirt from her bum.

'Caitlin.'

She turned to see Maggie leaning out of her front window. She had to raise her voice to be heard from above.

'I couldn't find those photographs. I will send some. But, please, you must come back, soon. I'm sorry I couldn't tell you more today.'

Leaving Maggie's flat had broken the maternal spell Caitlin found had begun to take hold. She knew that even from the ground, her body language revealed how frustrated she was. Maggie continued, calling down to Caitlin: 'Susie was so young. We all were. But she was just a child. Nothing had really happened to her yet.'

Caitlin squinted up at the woman. 'But, me. *I* happened.'

Even from where she sat on the ground-floor steps, she saw

Maggie flinch. But then she smiled, bigger than anything before. 'You and me. We'll get there. Whatcha say, Caity-girl?'

Charles didn't speak until the palm trees were small in the rear-view mirror. 'Do you want to stop and get something to eat?'

'No, thank you.' She had been running the edges of the envelope through her fingers and it was already fraying.

'Caitlin,' he said hesitantly. 'Do you want to …'

'Talk about it?'

'Well, yes.'

Caitlin sighed, tired. 'I don't know what I expected, but it wasn't that. She was lovely, very kind. It just hurts, to know that … well, there's not much to know.'

'Surely that's not right. You were there over an hour.'

'It's not that.' The Doobie Brothers played gently in the background. Caitlin stared out the window, factories flashed past in a grey blur. She flipped the visor down to shield her eyes from the afternoon sun, and turned up the music.

'It's time I stop using my dead mother as an excuse, Charles. Now, let's go home.'

It was dark when they pulled up outside The Cicada House. Charles twisted his stiff neck to either side.

'It's such a lot of driving for one day. Thank you,' Caitlin said.

'It's no worry. I'm glad I could help and I was very glad for the company.'

'And now look at both of us, single and sad and heading home to dark empty houses,' Caitlin said glumly, thinking of David.

'Speak for yourself,' Charles replied.

Caitlin jerked her head around. 'Excuse me? Oh, Charles! Is there a lucky lady?'

'I wouldn't know. But the lucky gentleman is Brian and we've been together for two years,' Charles said. He was smiling at her, amused.

'Oh. Right.' Caitlin wanted the passenger seat to swallow her up. She rushed some questions out to try to shield her embarrassment. 'Where does he live? Can I meet him?'

'He's in Sydney at the moment, he's the director in residence for the summer at the Elmswood Theatre.'

'Wow. Cool.' Caitlin couldn't sound or feel more like an idiot if she tried.

She was grateful to Charles for making an effort to ease her discomfort by asking, 'When are you leaving the Bay?'

'My flight is booked for the twentieth.'

'Ah. You'll miss Brian. He's back the week after.'

'I really am sorry, Charles. I'm an idiot.'

'Caitlin, my darling, you need to stop swinging between self-pity and nihilism.'

'Have you been speaking to Erin?'

Charles laughed. 'No. Are you receiving life advice in stereo?' Looking at the house windows staring back at her, Caitlin recalled his earlier words, *You expose your soft underbelly* …

'Yes. Kind of. I guess. There's been some other stuff going on too. Come in for a bit?'

Charles glanced at his watch. 'Well, I definitely need to use the facilities, but yes — a cup of tea would be good too.'

They sat at the dining table. It was one of the few corners in the house that she'd not spent time with David. She handed Charles a mug while he looked around at the lamp-lit wallpaper.

'Heavens. I haven't seen fixtures like this since my Aunt Gladys's pied-à-terre in Chelsea.'

There was more of the companionable silence they'd enjoyed on the drive home. Charles blew on his tea. Caitlin tapped her fingers against her lips. And then, before she knew what she was doing, the words came: 'Charles, I've met someone.'

Chapter Thirty-Two

'*Met someone*, met someone?'

'I have, yes. Here.'

'In the Bay?'

'Well, actually, I mean *here*. In the house.'

Charles looked worried.

Caitlin continued, 'There was a little case of mistaken identity. I thought David — that's his name, David — I thought he was the tradie Erin sent around.'

'I've not heard of a tradesman around here called David.'

'Yes, I know that now. But I didn't before, and, well, we've spent quite a lot of time together.'

'Well, if he's not a tradesman then who is he?'

Caitlin bit her lip. This was sounding even stranger than she expected it to. 'Well, that's the thing. I don't know. Or, I didn't. But then I found him online. But I don't think it's him. I mean, I think he's maybe taken someone else's identity.'

Charles put his mug down, a little too firmly. 'Caitlin, this does not sound right at all. Are you safe? Is this …'

'David.'

'Is this David fellow, is he still coming and going?'

Caitlin pictured David, disappearing in a pinpricked

kaleidoscope. 'Yes, he is. But not in a bad way. I like having him around. But, well, sometimes he just disappears on me.'

Charles's eyebrows were almost up to his hairline now. Caitlin could see how he'd misinterpreted what she was trying — poorly — to explain.

'Oh good lord.' Charles stood up, his long frame unfolding from the chair. He began to walk around the room.

'It's not like that, Charles. It's just, more confusing than anything.' Her mouth wasn't doing what she wanted it to. Caitlin knew she should be more explicit, and share what she believed was forming between her and David. But disclosing this would weaken what they had already begun to build. Or could it mean that Charles would raise alarm bells with the others? With a bone-deep comprehension, Caitlin understood that she could not tell anyone, even Charles, what was actually happening.

He was still pacing. 'Of course you're bloody confused, Caitlin, you're going through a series of extraordinarily traumatic events — all at the same goddamned time. Your husband, your mother and now you've got a man who's not who he says he is. It's all very *Talented Mr Ripley*!'

'Christ, why does everyone think he's a scam artist?'

'I don't think men lie about their lives and have sex with women on holiday just for shits and giggles.'

'How do you know we've had sex?'

He raised his eyebrows again, this time at her. 'Please. That morning at the Store? You positively reeked of it.'

'Not then. But, oh.' She sighed, and rubbed her eyes. 'What a mess.'

'Caitlin, you're vulnerable right now. Physically so, being alone here. But also emotionally. You need to look after yourself.' He sat down again and placed his hand over hers. The touch stilled her, reminding her of Maggie's hand on her head.

'My conversation with Maggie was so — odd. I just expected more. It turns out that my mother didn't hold the secrets to the universe,' Caitlin said.

'Did you ever think she did?'

'Well, no. But I thought maybe she held the secret to my unhappiness.'

'Are you unhappy? I mean, have you always been?'

'Maybe not unhappy, but I've never felt special, or excellent, or wonderful.' Caitlin grimaced, she wasn't articulating herself in the way she needed to. She tried again: 'Do you know when it's so dark that you can't tell if your eyes are open or closed?'

Charles nodded.

'Well, that's how my life has always felt. It's dark enough that there's no point in opening my eyes — because there's nothing to see anyway. So I've just … kept them shut.'

'And you thought you felt that way because your mother died.'

'Yes. I've blamed her for it, I guess. For feeling so blank. For not knowing who I am.'

'And now what do you think?'

'Well, it's worse. Because now I can't blame anyone. It wasn't Susan, or Paul. It wasn't even my grandparents' fault.'

Charles nodded, more soberly this time. 'And so maybe that's why you thought it was a good idea to shack up with a stranger?'

He's not a stranger. He's made me feel me. He's turned the lights on.

Caitlin had already told Charles so much, but she couldn't bring herself to voice what she thought. What she felt for David. Charles took her silence for agreement.

'Caitlin, I think you need to extract yourself from this man immediately. No good can come from deception like this. I can help you if you need, in any way. But it's vital you give yourself the space to process what you're learning about your mother. She may not be the source of all your problems, but she's still a monumental part of your life.'

Whatever she was feeling about David, Caitlin knew Charles was right about something. She needed to clear the fog, and make space for what was to come.

As she farewelled her friend and shut the screen door behind him, watching his long legs take him away through the shadows and noises of her garden, Caitlin put her hand up to her breastbone and breathed in the evening. She had three phone calls to make, and the first one was going to be the hardest.

'Hello, Grandad, it's Caitlin.'

'Hello, pet.'

No. She couldn't do this. Her throat was closing over and she'd only said four words. Caitlin settled into the back step, the waves sending foamy noise through the twilight.

'Have you had a nice morning?'

'Mm?'

'A nice —' She was shouting. She stopped. *Breathe.* Caitlin hung her head to her chest. Took a deeper breath. Her grandfather was taking his own into the phone from his recliner in South London.

She spoke louder, but without yelling. 'Grandad, I met someone today. Her name is Maggie. She lived with my mother.'

'Maggie.' Bill didn't say the name with any recognition.

'Yes, she lived with Susan. She was caring for me in Melbourne when you came. Came to get me.'

'Right you are.'

There was a phone ringing in the background. Voices and the clatter of dishes. And more breathing, laboured from Bill. *Come on, Caitlin.*

'Maggie told me you gave Susan — Mum — you gave us money.'

Silence.

'Grandad?'

'Yes?'

Caitlin did not give up. She persevered, slowly, clearly. 'You sent us money in Australia. You cared for us.'

'Not me.'

The tightness in Caitlin's throat returned *No, please. Not more confusion. No more mystery.*

Bill cleared his throat. 'Not just me. Us. Me and my Dot.'

'Gran?'

'We had an agreement. We'd look out for our girls, no matter what. No matter where. Even in that bloody stupid country.'

'Oh, Grandad.'

More silence. He was never a man to fill a silence. Then a voice from his room carried its way to her, 'Book trolley, Mr Kent!'

Caitlin gabbled, suddenly desperate to say the words. 'Thank you, Grandad. And thanks to Gran. You both looked after me. After us.'

She ended the first call and sat quietly in the dark, watching the spotted gum that reached over the back garden. Silhouettes of possums paraded along its limbs before the purpling of the night. Caitlin thought of Bill and Dot, and of all the years she believed that they couldn't do for her what her mother would have. She owed so much to her grandparents, and she'd never said thank you. Until tonight. Thanking a deaf man and a dead woman. It didn't seem a fair trade.

She sighed, stood up and shut the back door against the mosquitoes. After washing the mugs and eating a handful of peanuts and a mandarin, Caitlin found Jan's name on her phone. The sky had turned velvety. The noises had changed; sharp sounds were now muted under the falling night.

'Darling!'

'Hello, Jan.' It was so good to hear her voice.

'I thought my latest email would shake the tree a little. M and I have been terribly worried about whether to send it or not, like I said —'

'It's okay. I'm okay. Are you alright? The boys?'

'We're all fine. I think I've killed most of your plants though. And blimey your neighbour can talk. But tish-tosh, that's not why you're calling.'

'No. It's not.'

'Yes. But before we get there, are you having a lovely time, darling girl? Have you become very Australian?'

'Maybe a little.' Caitlin sat heavily at the kitchen table. She was so tired. The weight of the day was collapsing onto her shoulders. 'Jan, your note was vague.'

'Of course. You want me to explain.'

The email had arrived on Caitlin's phone as Charles's car had crossed back over the Westgate Bridge, the jagged skyline of Melbourne in their wake. She'd read Jan's words quickly, absorbing the facts before re-reading it to gather the tone. The note was kind, practical and matter-of-fact: just like her sister-in-law. Caitlin hadn't said anything about it to Charles, mostly out of relief that there was now — finally — nothing left to say. But tonight, before she spoke to her husband, Caitlin knew she had to speak to his sister.

Jan exhaled once, hard, and got on with it. 'We asked Paul, my darling brother, to tell you straight. But he's really got himself into a pickle and just will not listen to sense — or threats, come to think of it. And you know how scared he is of M.'

Caitlin smiled, and it felt good. 'Yes, I do know.'

'Paul told me that you two had discussed some form of reconciliation. I can't say I wasn't relieved. And I didn't want to get involved, any more than we already are. But then …'

'Then?'

'Well. This city — it's too bloody small. It turns out M's working on a commission from a woman who lives next door to, well, I don't know what to call her. Paul's paramour?'

'You could try, "the mother of his child". Or just Laura.'

'God.' Jan said the word with a groan. 'Anyway, the source doesn't matter. I can confirm its veracity and I'm so sorry to say,

Caitlin, but Paul did not leave Laura. She kicked him out. And he's been fired. They both have! Although I think they called it a voluntary redundancy.'

Jan's words numbed her through the phone. 'Right.'

'I don't know if any of this matters, darling. If you're delighted to run back to my brother's arms then I am just as happy. But any relationship worth its weight needs to have honesty at its core.'

'That's right. You're right.'

'M and I agreed we would give Paul the chance to tell you the truth. And he hasn't. Gosh, Caitlin. I'm not sure my brother will forgive me, but I'm certain I couldn't forgive myself.'

'Oh, Janny. Don't worry. I think I already knew. Thank you.'

The confirmation that Paul had truly exited her life was an almost overwhelming comfort to her. It wasn't because he was a bad man, it was because now it meant she couldn't escape back to him. This fact brought something else home to her — that is what Paul had always been: a calm, safe, suffocating escape hatch.

She rubbed her hands over her face. Caitlin needed to turn a light on. The kitchen was gloomy and muted. Instead, she picked up her phone for the last time that night. It was hot, scorched by words from another hemisphere. It was time to call her husband.

'Caitlin — hello? Hello?' Paul picked up every call from Australia like she was on the dark side of the moon. 'Did you get my text? Hello?'

'I did, you apologised.'

'Yes.' Paul sounded annoyed that she'd remembered that part. 'Can you just come home so we can talk properly?'

Caitlin put him on loudspeaker as she wandered the darkening rooms of The Cicada House. In the lounge she slowly turned each lamp on, a distinct metallic *clink* that one by one lit up her walls like soft glowworms. She spoke quietly, taking on the mood of the space around her. 'Don't you want to talk about the house?'

'The one you said you'd buy? With the wallpaper?' He sighed. 'I get it. I've been inattentive to your needs — if you want to put in a conservatory at home then that's fine, Caitlin. Like I said, I'm going to be around more now. I know we need to make this home more "you".'

'I never said I wanted a conservatory.'

'What?' Paul sounded confused, and then bothered at his own confusion. 'Well, whatever redecorating you need. Just — just ...' She could hear him taking a breath, calming himself before he got worked up. When he spoke again his voice was a lot smaller, and a little afraid. 'Just, please come home.'

It was time. Caitlin placed the phone onto the dining table and sat down, her hands flat, bordering the device like guards. She spoke with a calmness that had come over her since Charles, and Bill, and Jan. 'Why did you decide to co-parent with Laura, rather than stay together?'

'What?' There was that irritation again.

She continued, 'Paul, I know you haven't "shifted roles" at work.'

The silence echoed across four oceans. Caitlin bent down to speak slowly and clearly into her phone. 'I am coming home, Paul. But I'm not coming home to you. Because I know. I know everything. I know you were both asked to take a "voluntary redundancy" at work' — she couldn't help herself. 'I did say you shouldn't bonk the boss.'

She swallowed, gathered herself and continued, 'I know *Laura* left *you*. And I don't think you had any intention of telling me the truth, ever.'

More silence. She could almost hear his brain working, waiting for his mouth to catch up and fix everything. And then, he scoffed, 'Well —'

Caitlin decided she didn't care about what he had to say. 'I'm happy you're going to be a father, Paul. I know how much you wanted that. But I also know that I don't love you, certainly not enough to help you raise another person's child. I probably would have apologised for that, a while back. You were right, you know, we were turning to dust. In fact, I don't think I've ever been made of anything but. Yet this place' — she looked around the room, her eyes resting on the two green chairs — 'this place has made me feel flesh and blood. Now. That's enough. As my gran used to say, "Never complain, never explain".'

'Caitlin, for Chrissakes —'

'Enjoy the conservatory, Paul.'

Chapter Thirty-Three

Caitlin's hands were shaking as she hung up the call. As brave as she'd felt standing up to Paul, her knees felt too wobbly to leave the chair. In his wake she sat in the room, ears ringing in the sudden hush. But she wasn't alone. Caitlin's mother, Maggie, Bill, Jan and Paul all jostled at her elbows and shoulders. The silence of The Cicada House seemed to invite them in. And, of course, David stood at centre stage, his black hair glinting in the spotlight. The familiar feeling of emotional exhaustion was slinking in, its cold fingers snatching at her temples. She could feel the beginnings of a headache that she knew wouldn't leave for hours. Caitlin didn't have time to give over a night to an emotional vestige: she needed to distract herself, to mindlessly scroll something inane. She stared blankly at the corner of the room where a television might have sat, until she was struck by an idea.

the lodge + richard + elite spaces

As the soaring theme tune rang out from her phone, Caitlin's Pavlovian response kicked obediently into gear and she actually put her head back in relief. She carried her phone over to one of the chairs, and settled with her legs tucked up beneath her. It had been almost eight weeks since she'd watched anything on any screen, and to self-soothe with her favourite comfort show was almost too much. Caitlin may have even slipped into a coma, if it wasn't for the fact she was holding her breath in anticipation of seeing Arana Lodge on screen again. Because now, she felt part of the building.

Skye St Clair's breathless voice-over drifted over the drone shot. Seeing Arana Bay, the Store, the sandy stone of cliffs from above — everything felt upside down now Caitlin understood how they were connected in reality. She scrubbed her finger past the beginnings of the episode to where Skye and the architect were strolling through the Great Room. Skye followed his gaze as he pointed out over the treetops, explaining something beneath the soundtrack. Caitlin held the phone close to her face, unselfconsciously nosy about Sienna's father.

Richard was fine-boned like his daughter, with angled brows and eyes. But she was surprised to see how fair he was — the sandy hair that he'd neatly combed in a side-part showed a slight copper in the light.

Now the episode cut to Richard and Skye sitting in one of the Lodge's smaller lounges, a lit fireplace behind them. His white shirt was crisply ironed and he looked like he'd be more comfortable in a tie than with the top button he'd undone. Observing this, Caitlin wondered how well Charles and Richard had actually got along.

'Richard Stockhouse, Arana Lodge must surely be your crowning glory.' Skye exhaled her words over her subject. Was it Caitlin's imagination, or did Richard try to suppress a smile?

'I wouldn't say that, Skye. I always hope my next venture is my best. But yes — this project has been a pleasure.' When he spoke, it was the voice Caitlin recognised from the call. A rounded accent that sounded of money, a side of Australia that she realised she knew nothing about.

As Skye continued talking, she sat forward and touched her fingertips briefly to the architect's knee. He lifted an eyebrow and let his eyes rest for a split-second too long on the spot where she had touched him. The host of *Elite Spaces* didn't notice, but Caitlin did. This was a man used to things being a certain way. She felt a pang of worry for Sienna.

As the clip cut to a commercial, Caitlin broke out of her property trance. It was just before 9 pm. Caitlin pulled on her jumper — the nights were getting cooler now — and left the invisible crowd of The Cicada House behind her.

As she drove up to the surf club, she noted banks of cars along the grassy verges, more than she'd ever seen before. Caitlin climbed the stairs with some trepidation and as the loud music hit her chest she realised with a sinking feeling that it was Trivia Tuesday — something she'd heard Charles and Sienna whisper like an expletive. As she was about to turn around and head out again, someone called her name over the crowded floor. Looking across the tables filled with people, Caitlin saw an arm waving from near the bar. It was Tracey, resplendent in a shimmering kaftan. Caitlin recognised Nicola and Lindy, in matching sparkles. The three women bustled around their table like rainbow lorikeets at a bowl of seed.

'Caitlin! Didn't know you were a trivia buff? Are you here to join the Multiple Scoregasms?'

Caitlin walked closer to be sure she'd heard Tracey correctly. 'Excuse me?'

'The Arana trivia night. Gary hosts once a month, there's a meat tray on offer and the Multiple Scoregasms are the reigning champions!'

Caitlin had just wanted a quiet counter meal somewhere warm, that wasn't The Cicada House. Now she was in the middle of the proverbial village square. Her shoulders dropped.

'I'll grab you a shandy, yes?'

As Tracey stood up she squeezed Caitlin's arm, leaving her hand resting there as the other banged on the bar. She declared, loudly enough that all the tables in that half of the room looked up, 'Yoohoo! Caitlin here may well be the newest member of the Arana Bay community!'

Tracey winked like a pantomime dame as Caitlin looked at her, mortified, and extracted her arm. A loud man with fat stripes on his shirt called out from two tables away, 'Ah, so I see Erin's finally got her claws into the house, Trace?'

'Shuddup, Nev, she wishes — they've been thinking of selling for years!' Tracey passed Caitlin a drink, spilling some of it on both their feet in the process. Caitlin couldn't work out why everyone had to shout this particular conversation.

Nev wiped beer foam from his goatee. 'Bullshit. I heard it wasn't until Erin got some city tradie to clear out most of the old place that you even thought about putting a board up.'

Caitlin was completely motionless, looking down into the slowly ascending bubbles of her drink. The voices around her surged up like the waves off her beach.

'Well, the house sure does look a lot better than it did a few weeks ago — isn't that right, Caitlin?' Tracey called.

Caitlin's brain was Polyfilla, expanding and hardening at the same time. Tracey didn't wait for her response, pointing at the still-standing Caitlin. 'And now this one wants to buy it! Seems like Erin's white whale has landed!'

Finally Caitlin found her voice, even if it was decibels quieter than everyone else's. 'White whale?'

Tracey drank her pink wine. 'It's a literary reference, dear.'

Nev was approaching now, making his way through the tables. It was difficult, given the size of his stomach. He gripped a handful of peanuts, eating them out of his fist like he was feeding himself in a zoo.

'She knows what it means, Trace. She's English, aren't you, sweetheart? They love their books over there.'

Caitlin put her drink down on the table, ignored Nev, and focused on Tracey. 'What do you mean, "Erin's white whale"?'

'I'm just being silly, duck. But, Erin has had a thing for The Cicada House ever since she moved back to the Bay. She's a bit obsessed. Always banging on about how it's the "only house with direct access to the beach". Which is right, I guess. But it's a bloody dump — until you find an out-of-towner ready to pay stupid money for it as is, backyard dunny and all!'

Tracey put her hand over her mouth as Nev snorted.

'Whoops, darl! Sorry — didn't meant to offend.'

Caitlin didn't smile, she was furrowed and focused on what Tracey was saying. It was like fiddling with a pair of binoculars. Caitlin wasn't quite able to get things in focus. 'So, Erin has always wanted to sell The Cicada House?' Caitlin asked.

'Yes, love!' Tracey was losing interest; Gaz had turned on the microphone and was tapping it loudly.

'And when you saw the house and its improvements, you told Erin to sell it?'

'Yes! No. What?' Now Tracey was distracted by another drink being handed to her from Lindy. It had a yellow paper umbrella in it.

Caitlin persisted over the voices and the music and the smell of frying. 'Tracey — you called her up and said you wanted to sell it?'

Tracey centred back on Caitlin, looking a little exasperated. 'No, dear. No. I'm just the landlady. She called me. In Bali, she called me and said we *had* to sell the house. The owners weren't sure, but *she* convinced *me* to convince *them*. Said an English tourist had shagged her way through some home improvements!' Nev snorted and Tracey put her hand over her mouth again, with eyes on Nev. 'Oh, I am a naughty one, aren't I?'

Gaz was playing the *Sale of the Century* theme tune from his phone down the mic. Caitlin stepped back and bumped into the table behind her, spilling more sticky drink.

'Y'right, darl?'

'Come join the Scoregasms, Caitlin!'

'Well that's the first pom I've ever seen that can't hold her drink.'

Leering faces and sweaty brows looked up at her. Caitlin put her hands to her hot cheeks and felt her own palms had gone clammy. The squeal of microphone feedback cut through the crowd like vinegar through chip fat and the conversation faded in her wake as she ran out of the club, tripping down the stairs two at a time. Panting, head down, she rested against her car for a good five minutes. The noise of the trivia night floated down from the windows and mixed with the sound of the high tide waves crashing into the shore past the dunes. Caitlin drove home crying angry tears. This is why she didn't have friends, particularly female ones. They could be sneaky, and mean. They were the type of people who smiled with their mouths and not their eyes. Who invited you to parties but didn't care if you came.

Caitlin pulled up to the house and turned off the car. She banged the steering wheel with her open palms, and kept banging until it felt like she'd been hit across her upturned hands with a strap. A wretched noise came from inside her. A keening volume of grief and missing. Of believing she had found a friend. Of falling in love with a mystery. Of giving herself over to the loss of a mother and what that loss had meant. Anyone standing nearby would have seen a small pocket of light in the nighttime. A lit-up car interior spotlighting a rocking, yelling woman with broken blonde curls and a throat full of pain. But there was no-one. No-one looking at her or looking out for her. Caitlin was all alone with nothing but the realisation that this was grief, and it was awful.

v. Night

The night nurse is my favourite because she doesn't call me love or darling or even by my name. I know she's the night nurse because she says 'Good night' when she leaves and the light through my eyes disappears down to a inky dark. Sometimes, just for a moment, she rests her hand on my arm. Other times, like tonight, I'll feel her there a long while. She'll sigh and pat me before she leaves. She feels sad. Hope it's not my fault.

Fault and guilt. They're not welcome but they're here anyway. Partners in crime, side by side, walking like brothers in arms. Brothers — ah, shit. Here comes the guilt, that follows the fault. Because there are children, I know that now. Mum told me. She tells me every day, when she visits. And that's when I wish she would just bugger off.

When your eyes are closed it's the sounds and the smells you get the most. They're the signposts that take you through the day. Taste — that's gone. Touch — barely there. And then night comes and the buzzing and wheezing continue but they seem to carry less through the night air. Or maybe I'm just asleep. I can still sleep, thank god. Sleep and dream — what a bliss, what a goddamned wonder. To be able to fall asleep and go away from this horrific place, just for a little while.

And so I lie and I wonder
and I listen
and I
wait
to
go.

Chapter Thirty-Four

Yet again, she had fallen asleep in one of the green chairs. Caitlin winced as she sat up, her whole back ached and pain shot down both arms. Her eyes were still half-closed, and given the amount of wine she drank last night, should probably stay that way. She needed sea water. She needed drinking water too — but a swim was what would fix this broken feeling.

She stood up and stretched her arms out and that's when she noticed the other Caitlin staring back at her. A little noise escaped her mouth as she realised she was looking into a large mirror that was hanging on the wall above the lounge's electric heater. Her tanned face brought out her green eyes in a way she'd never see in the UK, which added to the surrealness of the whole scene. Maybe Tracey had installed the mirror for the open for inspections? How drunk had she *been* last night? She remembered coming in from the car, wiping tears away as she cracked the seal on a bottle of red. As her mind shuffled through rational explanations, Caitlin noticed the electric heater was gone. The crazy-paved stone fireplace now surrounded, well, an actual fireplace. Fresh logs lay in a firebox while a pile of kindling sat on the hearth.

'Huh,' Caitlin said out loud, and looked around for her phone. She should probably call Tracey and alert her to some interior decorating intruders. Not seeing the phone on the chair, or the floor, Caitlin patted herself down. Then — *ah*. She had a foggy recollection of leaning on the fridge after midnight, shaving parmesan off with a knife and eating the slices straight from the blade. She walked into the kitchen; her phone wasn't there. Something wasn't right — it was the smell. Caitlin turned to see an enormous stockpot sitting on the stove, simmering strongly enough to vibrate the lid. A small chimney of steam had erupted from the corner, filling the kitchen with the smell of chicken, and carrots, and buttery onions.

'Hello? David?' Caitlin called out, the cogs in her brain gummed up by hangover and the absence of logic.

She stepped outside to get some fresh air, because the thick scent of chicken broth was making her headache worse. The pavers of the back porch shone especially brightly. The garden was different. The lawn was a flatter, neater space — almost like a putting green. The bushes surrounding it were smaller and more spread-out. Caitlin could almost see the sand dunes from the back step. She walked forward carefully, her hand unconsciously moving up to her collarbone and holding it there, like armour. She turned left past the outdoor loo and saw the shed standing, freshly painted and without drifts of jasmine surrounding it. She rotated slowly to see a collection of potted herbs where the dilapidated piano had been. These changes were far more than David, than anyone, could have undertaken in a day.

'This isn't funny.'

She said it quietly, like she didn't think anything was funny. She didn't know if there was anyone there to talk to, but there was a crawling feeling up her neck, the slow realisation there was a stranger in The Cicada House.

Noises. A woman's voice calling something she couldn't catch. It was coming from the beach path. Caitlin didn't want to meet whoever that was. She hurried back past the porch and around the perimeter of the house, craning her neck to see who might be around the next corner. Her hand remained up to her chest.

The front garden had changed in the same way: it was neater, younger and much less overgrown. On the front porch, a deep green motorbike sat lifted on two planks of wood atop sheets of chipboard. Oil had dripped underneath and dried in marks like tiger stripes. The front door was sitting open, but Caitlin could still see that it was a bright, freshly painted blue. She looked for somewhere to sit because she thought she might fall over. A collapsed tea tree trunk lay alongside the driveway, its twisted limbs presenting themselves to her. She half-sat, half-crumbled onto the make-do bench and tried hard to breathe deeply. But there were stars in her peripheral vision and ringing in her ears and a strange taste of metal in her mouth. She closed her eyes, tightly, and counted her breaths the way the NHS nurse had taught her when she'd once had a panic attack inside the fertility clinic waiting area. The nurse's name had been Josefine, with an 'f'.

'Breathe in one, two, three, four. Hold one, two three, four. Breathe out —'

Her attempt at calm was broken with the sound of a horn coming from around the bend of the driveway. Caitlin was now thinking that the only way this experience could be occurring was via a dream. The most lucid dream she'd ever had. Because not only could she still smell the aroma coming from the kitchen stove, and feel the sun hitting her on the shoulders, she could also hear wheels crunching up the drive. A delivery truck pulled up outside the house. A noisy old thing, with curved fenders, rounded headlamps and dented hubcaps. But it was clearly loved, the deep blue duco had been carefully polished and the side mirrors shone in the sunlight. The tray behind the cabin was stacked high with wooden pallets and boxes and Caitlin could see leafy greens, red apples, pears and dusty beetroot through the slats. She was a little hidden, sitting off the drive behind the tea tree — but she was still wary of being spotted. She crouched down on her perch so the driver wouldn't see her when they got out.

'Nonno! Nonno!'

Children's voices came from behind her and Caitlin properly ducked this time, knees hitting the dirt and her chin getting close to the ground. Two kids burst through the bushes to her right and ran past her, so close that she could have touched them, if she wasn't trembling in the leaf litter.

The Dodge's door swung open and Caitlin saw the driver's legs first. Beat-up boots, a pair of dark blue jeans and lapels that were as wide as his sideburns. He was short, with slicked-back grey hair and a tanned, lined face that made him look even older than he probably was.

'Ah, my boys!' His arms were out wide and he bent down only to be almost pushed over by the two children who had launched themselves at him.

'Easy! Easy on your nonno's knees!' He was laughing, helping himself up against the truck seat behind him. 'Where's your nonna?'

'She's wetting her feet,' the taller boy answered. He was wearing a singlet and shorts but no shoes.

'I see. And are you being good for her today?'

'Yes, Nonno,' the two children chorused in unison. The man let them both go and turned to close the cab's door.

'Come now, let's see how strong your arms are getting then, yes?' He had an accent, but Caitlin couldn't pick it. She watched as the boys ran to the back of the truck, out of her sight. Their grandfather slammed the heavy truck door and carried on after them. Caitlin's eyes settled on the hand-painted lettering that he had just revealed. Across the door read *MNC GROCERS*. And then, in smaller letters, *ARANA BAY AND SURROUNDS*.

'What. Is. Going. On,' Caitlin whispered to herself, as she chewed on her little fingernail. 'This is ridiculous. Stand up, Caitlin. Walk inside. This is a dream.' She bit down as hard as she could on her finger. It hurt like a bastard. 'Wake up. Come on.'

She half-stood and, realising that the man and two boys couldn't see her, ran in a bent-crouch to the front door. Once she was inside, panting with her back against the wall, Caitlin pressed the heels of her hands over her eyes.

'Wake up wake up wake up.'

She opened them again to see the Cicada House's hallway, which she'd left only ten minutes earlier. But she could still hear the boys' laughter tinkling among their grandfather's. A creeping fear was turning into a full-blown panic. She needed to lie down and fall asleep, and that way she could wake up properly — any hangover was better than this nightmare.

Caitlin opened the door to her bedroom and whimpered. It was transformed. The bed had been made with bright yellow sheets. Shiny blue bedside tables held red plastic lamps. Hand-sewn curtains with yellow and blue pop-art flowers were pulled-closed, casting the whole room in an underwater glow. She closed the door as quickly as she could without making a noise. Caitlin had gone from being one of the three bears to Goldilocks herself. The next room, surely the next room would do. Caitlin prayed that the house remained empty while she tried to return from this dreamscape she was trapped in.

The next room had been closed off for all the time she'd been staying in The Cicada House. The two single beds had remained untouched since Erin had showed her the room a month earlier. But now, the door stood open and the beds were different. Tightly made with matching navy chenille bedspreads, the one closest to Caitlin had three toy cars and a comic resting on its foot.

'Boys?'

A woman's voice, strong and clear, came from the back door of the kitchen. Caitlin thought she'd be sick from the adrenaline now pulsing across her chest. She looked around the room — the beds were flush to the floor and the wardrobe was much smaller than hers. Where was she going to hide? And how did she know she had to hide, in this house — her house?

'Are you inside, boys?'

The voice was coming closer. Caitlin was about to throw herself under a bedspread when she noticed the small door leading from the bedroom. During Erin's original tour this anteroom had contained a mousetrap, but she was willing to risk a whole rat colony at this moment. She opened the door and slipped inside, closing herself in.

Before Caitlin collapsed, she saw things. Things that she shouldn't have seen. That she'd never forget.

She saw the garden-piano was now standing in the little room, still yellow but freshly painted and glossy. It was proudly upright, all straight lines, with its white keys gleaming and ready to be played.

On top of the piano was a collection of votive candles, burning low in their red glass holders. A curled posy of nasturtiums in a small crystal vase. A toy motorbike. A guitar pick. And all of them surrounding a large silver frame with a rosary hanging from one corner. In the middle of the frame, in the middle of this little shrine, was a black and white photograph of a man. A man with rippled hair, a jet beard close to his jaw and eyes that burnt through the glass.

David gazed out at her. Caitlin fainted back.

Chapter Thirty-Five

Caitlin woke up on her bed. *Her* bed, with its white sheets and phone charger plugged in beside the table and no psychedelic curtains filtering the light. She only just made it to the bathroom before she vomited, knees on the tiles, the blue ducks staring impassively at each other over her head. Her hands shook as she sat back on the cold floor. The shock and fear had gone, but she still felt overwhelmed at the prospect of leaving the bathroom and seeing what version of the house awaited her. She moved slowly, head throbbing in a strange way that felt much deeper than a hangover.

The kitchen stood empty, bare and clean and softly lit by the morning sun. Her phone lay on the counter, where she had left it the night before. The knife she'd used for her cheese snack was in the sink, next to the empty wine bottle and a glass. Her pulse slowly returning to normal, Caitlin walked back down the hall and turned into the lounge. No mirror, no fireplace. She took a deep breath because she knew there was one more room to check. Entering, she passed the two beds lonely in the absence of colour and comics, and steeled herself to open the door to the ante-room.

Nothing. Buttery paint peeling in the shadows, a small desk, a mousetrap. Caitlin exhaled. Maybe the 'don't eat cheese before bedtime' adage had more truth to it than she'd thought.

'Caitlin?'

Erin.

The anger that Caitlin had tried to drink away last night washed over her.

'Coming.'

Erin's figure stood blurred through the frosted window of the front door. This was the first time she had not just wandered, uninvited, into the house and it put Caitlin on edge. She opened the door without a smile.

'Hi.'

'Hello.' Erin was tapping something into her phone and didn't lift her head immediately. Then, when she did, she responded to Caitlin's expression. 'What?'

'That's a noise, not a question,' said Caitlin.

'What? What are you talking about?' Erin shifted her weight between her wedges. She was impatient.

'Can I help you, Erin?'

The snippiness that had entered her voice felt wrong, but she didn't correct herself. Hearing Erin's voice had brought back Tracey's words at the pub, and the feeling that they had given her. Erin raised her eyebrows and crossed her arms.

'Okay, well, while you sort out whatever bug crawled up your arse this morning, I'd like to come in and get some measurements.'

Caitlin was taken aback. She'd gone to the door with animosity but didn't expect Erin to return serve so easily. The agent took one step into the hall.

'Excuse me!' Caitlin blocked Erin's path even though she knew she was being ridiculous. Erin looked at her with irritation and — even worse — pity.

She sighed and spoke with resignation. 'Caitlin. The owner of this property has requested I enter to prepare for sale.'

Erin was looking at her the way she looked at Josh when she asked him to put his plate in the dishwasher. Admonished,

Caitlin stepped back and let her pass. As Erin clopped her way to the kitchen, Caitlin exited from the same door, taking the long way around the outside of the house. She felt defeated, with bile still smarting down her throat. She needed space: where air lifted sea spray into the sky and cleansed her in a breezy blessing. She needed her beach. Caitlin snuck down the path — a broken woman wearing the Christmas nightie she'd stolen from the woman she was hiding from. She relaxed a little once she emerged from the other side of the scrub, greeted by burly grey waves that reflected her mood. Caitlin plonked herself on the soft sand and looked out into the glare.

There was a voice in her head that told her it hadn't been a dream. That whispered, fiercely and persistently, that David's disappearing act was not a migraine, or a vision — and that she was most definitely not losing her mind. Between her headache and dry mouth, she reviewed the pieces of information she had, shuffling facts around like Scrabble tiles.

There was a David Catto who lived in Arana Bay, and had been born in 1935.

This David's wife, Giulia, had died in 1968.

Her David, whose hands felt like home, was surely around her age. So he would have been born around 1978.

Those were the facts. Then there were the … other things. His face looking back at her in a dream with a distinctly sixties feel. The brief spell when she had imagined him disappearing before her eyes.

The waves crashed, the gulls wheeled and Caitlin tried hard to keep the facts and her experiences as far away from each other as possible. It felt like trying to keep two magnets apart.

'Caitlin?'

Erin's voice called again, this time from the direction of the house. And then Caitlin had one more thought. She quickly made her way back with the sand still damp on the back of her nightie. Erin was standing on the lawn with a sheaf of papers under her arm and her long nails clacking rhythmically on the back of her phone.

'You still in a strop?'

Yes. But you can wait.

'Erin. You mentioned your dad used to surf with a man called David Catto?'

Erin stopped tapping. She was confused by Caitlin's swift change of tactic. 'Yeah. Why?'

'Do you think I could speak to your dad? About back then?'

Erin was now baffled enough to forget she was being combative. 'What?'

Caitlin shook her head, shook off Erin's confusion. 'It, it doesn't matter. Erin, please. Can I talk to him?'

'Well, no. Not right now anyway. He and Mum are caravanning around the Top End and they won't have reception for another few days. What's going on?'

Caitlin's head dropped and she kicked at the kikuyu with bare feet. She wondered when David was going to come back. The grass was getting long.

Erin sighed, relenting. 'So what did I tell you? Dad used to surf with a bunch of local blokes? Yeah, that's right. Years ago. He was young but the group went right up to salty sea dogs. If you want a history lesson you can always go back to the surf club. It's full of dusty relics … and the memorabilia.'

Caitlin looked up to see Erin smiling at the attempt at a joke. She didn't respond in kind. 'Thanks. Let's talk about the other stuff later, okay?'

Erin's smile dropped and she looked blankly at her for an extra beat, then turned on her heel. As she walked away, Erin tossed words like sand over her shoulder. 'Sure. Your lease wraps in two weeks. And keep the nightie. It suits you.'

Caitlin was becoming adept at segmenting the dramas in her life. She wondered, as she pulled jeans on under Erin's nightie, was this how other people lived all of their lives? A gaggle of family and friends, ghosts and wishes, hustling for attention and resolution and goddamned enrichment? Is this why Paul always looked so tired, because he was spinning a whole crockery cupboard of emotional plates while she just … well, banged on a pot with a wooden spoon?

Regardless, she was not practised in plate-spinning and so she added Erin to the back burner her family, and Charles, Sienna and Maggie sat on, and drove to the surf club with one single thought in her head: *Find David.*

The surf club was closed.

Caitlin stood on tiptoe and peered through the window in the pine door before stepping back to assess the building. A bronze plaque muddled with burnished green read, *Opened in 1962 by Sir Samuel Bayles.* A thousand (or more?) hands had pushed open these doors over the years, turning the pale timber an oily brown. A row of windows had been wound open on the first floor. A bank of surfboards filled a U-Haul by a timber electricity pole. She heard the clanging of metal on metal, and followed the sound to the side of the club where a wooden gate had been wedged open with an old paint bucket. It was Jack, the young bartender, rubbing down the underside of a surfboard with wax. He squinted into the midday sun when he saw Caitlin coming through the gate.

'Hi, Jack.'

'Hey.'

'How are you?' Keep those plates spinning.

'Fine.' He kept scrubbing.

She'd forgotten how monosyllabic men under twenty were. 'Great!' She was being Pollyanna-ish, again, in front of this young human. 'Um, do you think I could get access to the club? The first floor?'

He stopped and stood tall, eyeing her somewhat suspiciously.

She held his eye, and smiled while the white noise of the surf smudged between them.

'Yeah … nah,' Jack said, in an affirmative-negative way that only Australians could. 'Beryl isn't here. She normally runs ins and outs.'

Caitlin persisted, feeling a little bad about coercing an innocent. 'I'm doing some research on the town. Before I go back to England. Just names and dates, things like that. I won't be long.'

Jack gave up his interference even faster than she'd expected. 'The back door's open,' he said, and went back to his board.

The bar was quiet during the day, daylight filtering through the salt-encrusted windows, while ceiling fans rotated lazily overhead. Somehow the room felt older in the day, with light showing up corners the night covered. Caitlin looked over at the mahogany wall plaques filled with names old enough that they were new again. There was a sagging armchair with brass studs and a metal plate hammered into the leather arm inscribed *Jock's Throne.* Long timber oars were nailed in a cross and hung close to the rafters. Faded pennant flags wafted in the fan's breeze — once vibrant, they were now the colour of parchment

She made her way to the display cabinets and inspected the silver plates and crystal goblets and dusty wooden paddles.

ANZAC Memorial Swim, 1934 — E. Vincent

Senior Belt Race, 1953 — J. Curtis

Invitational Women's Surf Boat Race, 1968 — National Title

Nothing showed David's name.

After completing a circuit of the room, her hands clasped behind her back like an art critic at a gallery, she found herself where she'd begun. Caitlin didn't know what she'd expected, but felt more defeated than she'd prepared for. Defeated, and tired.

Then, there was a noise from the stairs. Caitlin watched a woman slowly climb into view. She moved in the underwater way that older people do, when each step requires effort. Short grey hair peeked out from under an Arana Bay SLSC bucket cap. She had a pair of enormous fit-over sunglasses covering half of her face. Caitlin was worried she'd frighten her into falling down the stairs, so she cleared her throat as gently as she could.

'Who's there?' The woman spoke towards the windows.

Oh bloody hell. She's blind.

'My name's Caitlin,' she said, using the voice she kept for her grandfather.

Don't throw Jack under the bus, Caitlin.

'Jack said I could come in.'

'Where are you?' The woman turned her head from side to side, then said, more quietly to herself, 'Bloody glasses.' She unclipped the black sunnies from her normal ones beneath. 'That's better. Forgot I had them on. Who are you?'

'Caitlin,' Caitlin said, loudly.

'Jesus F. Christ, you don't need to shout. I hear you. Caitlin is it? I'm Beryl.' When she spoke, air whistled through her impressive dentures. Caitlin didn't quite know what to do with this sweary Australian lady.

'Sorry. Um, I'm staying in town and I am doing a little bit of research into …' She paused. Here she was again, blundering into important conversations without preparation. She heard Jack hammering out in the yard like David at the fence and, suddenly, it came to her all at once: David's ease as he cracked open the fridge. His knowledge of the carpet-bag shed. The confidence as he dug under the boards for the floor-whisky. His face as he talked about his dear, beloved wife who … *oh god.* His wife, who died in 1968. Caitlin's throat closed over and a cry started in the top of her chest. She said, very quietly, because it was all that she could manage, 'Oh.'

Beryl walked towards her, a slight limp in her orthopaedic shoes, saggy knees drooping into socks pulled up high. Her hands were covered in the liver spots of a woman who had lived through decades of sun damage when it was called 'colour'. 'What is it, dear?'

Caitlin found her voice and the lie at the same time. 'I'm doing research into the family of a house I have been staying in. I believe a previous owner was a member of the club. He surfed here in the …' She had to persist through this bit, her throat was choking again. 'He surfed here in the late sixties. His name is — was — David Catto.'

Beryl observed Caitlin like a currawong watches from a tree, alert and curious. 'Well. That was a time ago. I was here, of course.' She spoke with pride. 'The new club house had just opened. My husband was one of the founding members. I had young kids back then, little rugrats. But I helped Barry with fundraising for this building.'

Beryl gestured at the timber room around them, like it wasn't covered in forty years of dust. Caitlin noticed how contorted her arthritic fingers were. She tried to do the maths on Beryl's age and realised with a flush she'd been caught staring.

'I'm eighty-five, love.' She tapped the side of her head. 'But I've still got it. Which means I know that you are talking about The Cicada House.'

Caitlin swallowed. 'I am.' And then, very quietly, not knowing if she wanted the answer, said, 'So you knew him? David?'

Beryl mustn't have heard her. 'Do you know why it's called The Cicada House, dear?' she asked Caitlin.

'Erm.' Caitlin wanted to hear about the man, not the house.

Beryl cupped her wrinkled palm before her, empty except for papery skin. 'You ever held a cicada shell?'

Caitlin looked back and forth from the empty hand to the old lady's eyes. 'I can't say I have.'

Beryl didn't seem to be listening to Caitlin. She placed one finger into her other palm, slowly circling. 'Brown and sharp, a bit spiky. But you have to look out for what left those shells behind.' Now she fixed Caitlin with a stare, surprisingly powerful, coming from watery eyes. 'Green emeralds flying under magical wings. Make a sound louder than a steam train. Beautiful things, once you understand them. And that house has always been surrounded by them.'

The slow beat of the ceiling fans punctuated ellipses between the two women.

When she felt it was okay to speak, Caitlin asked again, 'You knew David?'

'I did. Not well, but the Bay was so small back then, everyone knew everyone else. He surfed, of course. Helped out with the club. I think he and his old man were on the team that built the original deck. What do you want to know?'

Beryl was on the move, shuffling towards the back of the room where the bar and kitchen were. Caitlin followed her.

'Well, anything really.' Her mind was working fast but her words came out haltingly. 'His involvement with the club, or anything about his family?'

They had stopped at a cabinet with shuttered doors beneath.

'You'll want to open those. I can't get down, with my knees.'

Caitlin crouched and pulled open the cabinet; the smell of mothballs fanned out into the room.

'There should be a box or something all about the construction. The young folks here did a special exhibit on it, for the thirtieth anniversary, not too long ago.'

Caitlin realised she was looking for a box from the late nineties. But she figured once you're as old as Beryl, decades meshed into one.

'Don't be afraid, get up in there, deary. I'll go make us a cuppa.'

Beryl moved into the kitchen and Caitlin sat on the dusty floor, pulling out scrapbooks and folders and stacks of newspapers. It didn't take long — the box file wasn't hidden, someone had even labelled it *30 Anni*.

Inside, plastic sheet protectors were slippery against each other and Caitlin's fingers. There were yellowing builder's plans and newspaper cuttings. One had a dot-print copy of a blurry photograph. Caitlin could barely make out a smiling dignitary standing by the plaque she had passed by the front door. In the back of the folder, a final plastic pocket was thick with a collection of loose photos. Her heart rate picked up as she slid a handful out. They were small, some were black and white, but she was surprised to see colour photos too. Photos of smiling men shirtless in the sun, holding up hammers and saws as a building grew behind them. Hazy shots of children running over yellowed grass, through a small sprinkler that opened like the leaves of a palm. Two girls pulled faces at the camera, each with bobs of glossy caramel hair touching their brown shoulders. Every photograph was surrounded by a white border with small, black text recording the month and year. Caitlin flicked through them; most read *JAN 68*.

'Find what you needed?'

Caitlin got to her feet crookedly, embarrassed to be stiff in the presence of this sprightly octogenarian. Beryl saw the photos. 'That'll be the working bee. We had a few over the spring.'

Caitlin kept sifting through the stack of snaps. Smiles, sun, cigarettes for days. And then, there he was. She stopped and stared at the little coloured print in her hands: a photograph that ended the world as she knew it.

Beryl leant over. She smelt of talc and tea. 'There he is. David. With his dad.'

David was smiling, his arm slung over the shoulders of an older version of himself. Caitlin couldn't believe she hadn't seen it earlier. The similarities in the eyes, their jaw line. Here was the man she'd watched get out of the truck outside The Cicada House. In the photo his sideburns were shorter and his hair a little less silver, but it was unmistakably 'Nonno'. She took in every detail of both of these men. Before she could ask what she needed to, Beryl continued, with a sigh. 'So sad. This was taken only a little while before the accident.'

'Accident?'

'Yes. Poor young man, had a terrible car accident. Although some thought, with the grief of his wife dying, that maybe it wasn't an accident after all.' She shook her head. 'Awful business.' Beryl paused, a crooked hand on Caitlin's. 'Is that what you needed, dear?'

Caitlin had no idea how to answer her question.

Chapter Thirty-Six

It had been over a week since Caitlin had stood in the memory-bound clubhouse and looked at a fifty-year-old photo of her current lover. In the days that followed, some of her last in Australia, she entered into a sort of slow reverie that reflected the changing of the season around her. March brought cooler nights and mornings crisp with dew, the sun rising through a veil of smoke-tinged air.

The cicadas no longer sounded in the mornings. Instead they'd been replaced with power tools as the summer rentals turned themselves back to owners, accompanied by lists of repairs. But what surprised Caitlin the most was the light. The new month was unfolding beneath a special kind of golden glow she hadn't seen before. Syrup-thick sunbeams filtered through the turning leaves and made everything feel like a memory.

She had slowly been closing her life down in Australia. Gathering the ribbon ends of her mother's story and placing them quietly away on the dusty top shelf of memories that she might access, one day, when she needed to. Her more recent calls to Bill had not touched on Susan or Maggie again. The shameful upside of Bill slowly fading away was each conversation now began with a completely clean slate, so she was in control of what to discuss.

Caitlin had also been pottering around The Lodge, helping Charles and Sienna prepare for the next coterie of guests. Sensing a growing restlessness in Caitlin, Charles had even suggested she take a couple of shifts at the General Store. The army of summer-jobbers had returned to school and there were a few slots going free. But Caitlin refused. She preferred the anonymity of changing linen and restocking toiletries.

On a Friday morning, Caitlin and Sienna were both out on the Lodge's broad deck, sweeping brown pellets of possum poo from the railings. Sienna flicked an old towel, Caitlin brandished a broom.

'They look like chocolate raisins,' Caitlin said.

'Taste like them too.'

She looked sideways at Sienna. 'I've been here two months now, I'm not that gullible.'

'Tell that to the drop bears.' Sienna laughed.

Sienna was in a good mood. Over coffee that morning she'd told Caitlin and Charles about submitting the grant application to Greater Wertham Council. Her words had tumbled out in a disarming mix of enthusiasm and ideological resolve.

'… and we're aligning with the native plant nursery in Beechford, and we're going to start running monthly Indigenous cooking workshops, and some of the primary schools might share space for additional community gardens if we can include our classes in their syllabus …'

It was only clearing possum shit that had quieted Sienna's stream of excitement.

Caitlin took advantage of the brief silence. 'Have you spoken to your dad recently?'

'Why are you bringing my mood down?' Sienna asked.

'I've been thinking about what I said a few weeks back, about your father.'

'Yeah I know, I should respect his wishes and be a better daughter and he wants what's best —'

'No.' Caitlin banged the broom clean on the deck, making sure she had Sienna's attention. 'I don't think that. Not anymore. Your life is your own, and you're doing really extraordinary, wonderful things with it. It's important —' There was a catch in Caitlin's voice that stilled Sienna, who was now watching her closely. 'Sienna, it's important you untie yourself from whatever your father's going through.'

'Shit. Where's this come from? Am I witnessing a midlife crisis?'

Caitlin did wonder if this new attitude was another 'damn good thing' about being over forty.

'Maybe. It doesn't matter. Just — don't frame what you're doing now through the single lens of your dad. Don't let his story become central to yours. I mean it — from one daughter to another.'

Sienna's cheeks reddened, she kicked some leaves off the edge of the deck. 'You think I should go nuclear? Blow it all up with him?'

'Sienna I think you should take up as much space as you can. And if that means exploding, you bloody well go for it.'

Caitlin remained sweeping at the deck long after Sienna and all the possum scat had gone. Her arms ached but her shoulders felt a little lighter after the exchange. It had been a while since Caitlin had spoken to anyone except Charles and Sienna. Hiding — because that's what she was doing, hiding — away in The Lodge for her final week in Australia meant there was less chance of running into Erin, or Tracey, or any other person that reminded her that Things Had Not Happened the way she wanted them to. It was also the reason she hadn't visited the surf club again. Caitlin had firmly left the photograph and the reality of what she thought had occurred in the stale timber cabinet guarded by a profane senior citizen. She did not give any more thought to whatever overlapping of reality and dreaming had mixed her version of Australia up.

*

But what a lie.

What a lie that was.

Because every moment of every day since David had looked back at her from that small photograph had been an echo. A repetition of a memory and a smell and a taste of what he and she had done and where he may have come from, and perhaps even where she may have gone. Caitlin was never going to rid herself of the wonder of David, or the disbelief in how they had come about. She knew that. Which is how she could afford to lie to herself about leaving him behind.

It was also why, when David walked back into the kitchen that March evening, there were no histrionics. No noises of fear or shock or even joy. Why, instead, Caitlin simply looked at the man standing before her, in the same jeans, boots and white T-shirt he'd been wearing since they'd first met. And when they embraced with an exhaustion she recognised in him but now felt herself, he simply inhaled her.

Together, they moved quietly to their back step, and sat, their bodies pressed into each other. Caitlin felt the warmth from his self against hers and wondered why she couldn't muster anything other than relief that they had been returned to each other.

David put his chin up, as if to say something, and then let it fall again. Caitlin took up the mantle.

'Tell me about your wife.'

'I've told you.' Today, there was gravel in his voice.

'Tell me more. Tell me about Giulia.'

His face settled into relief, the relief of someone who was beginning to feel understood. 'Alright.'

He took a hold of her hand, his fingers through hers. 'We met in Melbourne. She'd arrived at Station Pier and was learning English at night in the city. She was living in Carlton, working in a restaurant. I was playing piano at the pub around the corner. We fell for each other.'

He squeezed her fingers so hard they hurt. He was encouraging himself to talk, as much as he was needing her to understand.

'Go on.'

'She was this windstorm, Cait. All care and efficiency and love and song, and she looked after the three of us so well. Giulia loved like a dragon, fierce and full of fire. My whole family was … drunk on her. Almost as much as I was. But' — he blew through his lips — 'she raged from the rooftops when she was angry. Which was a lot of the time. Especially after she got sick.'

'How long was she ill for?'

'Not long. Less than a year. She died in hospital, only two days after leaving here.' His thumb hooked over his shoulder at the house behind them.

Caitlin caught her breath. It was the first time either of them had voiced the magic that was insisting on making itself known. She couldn't think of what to say, about the cosmos that was mixing in a cloud above their heads. So she decided to focus on the very human story just in front of her.

'I'm sorry.'

David shrugged. 'Life breaks sometimes.'

'Yes. But knowing that doesn't mean it can't hurt.'

David fully turned to her, his lashes heavy. 'Cait. Do you know what's happening here?'

'Not really, no. Do you?'

He pushed his hair off his forehead with one hand, while he held on to hers with the other. She could see the muscles clenching and unclenching in his jaw. How could brown eyes be so dark, but so bright? 'The thing is, I'm —' He stopped, his mouth open and then shut.

She smiled at him, in the way a person does when they are absolutely certain of something. 'Oh, I am too.'

The relief on his face was so beautiful. 'I want to tell you all the reasons why.'

She laughed. 'Me too.'

'There are a lot of reasons.'

Caitlin was nodding, smiling, and feeling a helium inside herself that she hadn't experienced for a long time. But she was forty now and life was rolling in a different way and sense often sang in harmony with something more wild, illogical.

'David. We can do all of that. But there's … some other stuff we should discuss first. Don't you think?'

He nodded, sorry and serious. 'You're right. I need to come clean. Goddamn it.'

She laughed. 'Goddamn what?'

'I can't … I know I'm going to sound like I've lost it, but I have to … I have to say it.'

She pulled herself as tall as she could go, while still hunching on a step holding the hand of a handsome man.

'It's okay. You don't have to. I know.'

'Know what?'

Here we go. Behind them, the home stilled. Not a creak of wall, not a flicker of dust. The Cicada House held its breath waiting for the two of them to shed their skins.

Caitlin began, 'I know you lived here fifty years ago. I know your dad drove a fruit and veg truck. I know you helped build the surf club. I think you rode a motorbike. And I know you had red bedside lamps.'

She wasn't sure what the revelation would bring from him but she hadn't expected affront.

'It's not just a bloody "motorbike", Caitlin, it's a Bullet.'

'Really? God, okay. Sorry. You rode a Bullet.' He nodded, reassured. So she continued, 'David. I've asked you this before but I need you to be honest with me. Are you — I can't believe I'm saying this — are you … dead?'

He didn't waver. 'I told you, I've never lied to you. I'm not dead. At least, I'm pretty sure I'm not.'

'But what about the car accident?'

'Jesus. You do know a lot.'

'Beryl told me.'

'Beryl …' He furrowed his brow, then didn't. 'Bez? Barry Peterson's wife. She makes a good chicken sandwich.'

'David. Please tell me what you know.'

He closed his eyes. She braced herself.

'I was driving along the Princes Highway. In my Fairlane. I hit a pothole, the radio died and, well, I think I was trying to fix it. The tree came up to me, real fast.' He shuddered in a way that he didn't seem to be able to control. 'I can still see the windscreen buckling, it was like ice.'

Caitlin felt a little woozy.

'You know my mother died in a car accident? She hit a tree?'

He nodded. 'I've been thinking about that a lot. I thought that's maybe why I turned up back here.'

Caitlin paused to let this latest wave of serendipity and sorcery wash past her.

'But you say you didn't die?'

'I don't think so. There's a hospital bed and nurses and a bloody noisy machine. My mother comes most days. She rubs my feet.'

'There *is*?'

'Yeah. Right now.'

Caitlin's eyebrows were beetled like she was looking at her A-level maths exam.

'So you're in hospital. Right now. In nineteen …'

'1970. I think. That's when the crash happened, anyway.'

She looked at him, in the analytical way Beryl had looked at her.

'Do you know what year it is, here?'

'I've tried not to think about that. Makes me feel a bit wrong in the guts, to be honest. But I know it's not close to 1970.

I mean, I know you're a pom but that can't explain all of …' he waved his hand over her '… this.'

'"This"?'

'I don't know, Cait. You're just so sharp.' He clicked his fingers. 'Fast. I haven't seen much. But what I have, and what I can sense, life here seems really sped up.'

She came out with it. 'It's the twenty-first century.'

His head went back like he'd been hit. 'Holy hell. Jesus Christ.'

She paused to let him take it in. But she couldn't wait too long. She wasn't that selfless. Curiosity clawed at her heels. 'So you're in hospital but you're also here?'

'Yeah — I'm number eight.'

'Eight?'

'Bed eight, Western General Hospital. I'm in a coma. That's what the doctor said to my mother.' He snorted. 'She gave 'em hell after that. Said they were talking *cazzate* and I needed olive oil massages and some hot wine.' He looked at her drily. 'It didn't work. I'm still pissing into a tube.'

Caitlin scratched along her jaw, and then chewed on her thumb.

'You shouldn't do that,' he said.

'What?'

'Chew on your fingers. You do it all the time.'

'My grandmother used to say the same thing. Said "no-one wants to see those things in your mouth". But my grandad told me once that my mother had the same habit. I think that's why I never tried very hard to stop.'

'Well, you should.'

'Why?'

'Because it looks like it hurts. Because it looks like you don't care.'

And there it was again. In the midst of this ridiculous, nonsensical maelstrom of fantasy, David said something that floored her. It felt like song was mainlining her veins, to be seen so clearly. She couldn't acknowledge it though. Not when reality was teetering around them.

So instead, she huffed. 'I'm not taking analysis from Australia's Marty McFly. And you don't need to get all cerebral on me. Just say it: you think it's ugly.'

She hid her eyes from him as her words fell out. What shame her terrible self-esteem brought upon her. David had just told her he was a time-travelling coma patient and all she could vocalise was a response to the criticism he'd made about her scabbed cuticles. Without the armour of apathy, the exposed self-hatred was raw and disgusting — a snail without a shell. Caitlin wanted to crawl away. Instead, she dared herself to raise her eyes and meet his.

One of the things that made Caitlin want to devour this man was the way he watched her when she was feeling her most vulnerable. His gaze gave her strength. And he knew it.

'I want to make you feel beautiful.'

'Oh, piss off.' She was smiling, but her voice was hard. 'Take your hippie shit and shove it.'

'No, Cait. I want you to see how beautiful you are. You're a beautiful ocean. I want to swim into your skin.'

'How many times have you used that line?'

David's brows meshed down into his muddy eyes. 'I'm dying. Why would I use "a line"?'

He brought her wounded fingers up to his lips and met them with the most barely there of a kiss. She closed her eyes and breathed in, deeply, right to the well of her lungs. The cicadas had started up and it was only then that Caitlin realised what time it was.

'Do you get hungry?' she asked.

'Nope. They've got me hooked up to drips and stuff. But I like tasting food. And whisky. And other stuff.' He gave her a small smile.

Caitlin stood up and held her hand to him. 'Come inside and you can taste some cheese sandwiches. I'm starving.'

Chapter Thirty-Seven

She'd kept the ugly fluorescent kitchen light off, so they both stood in the dim flicker of a stubbed candle melted to the bottom of an old Vegemite jar.

'I'm glad it's dark, you don't want to see how much butter I'm putting on these things,' she said, too loudly. The kitchen felt smaller after they'd shared a lifetime of moments on a small step under a few early stars.

David was leaning on the bench, slowly running the tip of his thumb over his lips, seemingly lost in thought. Was it her latest knowledge combined with her imagination, or did he look more ghostly tonight? The flickering candlelight meant his brows cast deepening shadows down across his angled cheekbones. A brooding, Byronic ghost. Caitlin dropped a hunk of butter into the hot frypan, and the sharp sizzle seemed to shake him clear of whatever was drawing him away. He didn't say anything, but she could tell by the way his shoulders and arms and hips shifted, that he was now present and focused on her, and only her. The bread smelt sweet as it became golden in the pan. She had goosebumps down her arms. Every part of her was alive to the electricity in the room.

'You okay?' he asked.

In three long syllables knitted into each other, she noticed how his vowels took over most of his words. His accent, or his very self, Caitlin couldn't tell what it was that made his voice sound like a purr or a growl or something else primal that hit her belly. He reached to her and she held her breath, but his arm passed hers and took a pinch of melted cheese.

'Good,' he said, eyes briefly closed. She breathed again.

They ate cheese sandwiches — Caitlin hungrily, David with a meditative pace. She'd poured two glasses of white, and was also fishing sweet and sour pickles from a jar.

David licked his finger to gently collect crumbs from the edge of his plate.

'What is it like? To lose a parent?' he asked.

'I don't know. I was five.'

'No. Bullshit. Answer again.'

She looked at him, and understood. 'You're asking because of your boys.'

'Yeah.' He was quiet. She pictured the two children running with bare feet down the Cicada House's drive. He deserved her honesty.

'Losing a parent when I was that young felt like I'd lost a treasure before I knew its value. Imagine if everyone else enjoyed one specific piece of music, but you couldn't hear it. And every day of your life you saw people dancing around you, dancing to the best music they've ever heard, while you're in complete silence.'

He nodded, like he understood, even though she was talking nonsense.

'And after this summer? After you've found out everything you have about your mother?'

'After this summer I've realised that treasure and song mean bugger all.' She looked at him over her drink. 'You know I walked through this house? Saw it how you saw it?'

'Shit. That's how you knew about the red bedroom lamps?'

'Well, yes. Among other things. I also saw your boys.'

'You did?' His expression lifted. There it was again, like Erin had shown her — the sad happiness of being a parent.

He nodded. 'Yeah. Makes sense. Mum talks to me, in hospital. Even though they're not sure I can hear anything. Told me she and Dad have moved into The Cicada House. It's not as hard on Georgie and Nicho.'

'So this was your house?'

'Is. Was. Yes.'

'There's an altar, David. I saw it — with your face. That's why I thought you were dead.' She'd blurted it out. He blinked slowly.

'That'd be right. Mum had one for Giulia too.' He shook his head, put his forehead into his hands, and said quietly, 'God, I'm such an arsehole.'

There was that despair again. She had to pull him out of the fog that was taking him, or they wouldn't get any more answers tonight. Caitlin reached across the table and shuffled his shoulder, to wake him up from a dream. 'Come on, there has to be some sense to this.'

'Cait, none of this makes sense. It's crazy. When it turns to night in the hospital, when the sounds die down and the nurses move around less often, suddenly I'm here. I can walk and talk and, thank god, take a piss. And for a few hours I can forget that I'm dying and my wife is dead and my two boys are …'

Oh. Sweet lord, there it was again. That look of dispossession, the face of a man who had lost it all. But now, Caitlin understood where it came from. His eyes moistened and he swallowed hard. Caitlin knew she was selfish to drag him away from the magnetic pole all of his emotions were taking him to. But she also knew that there was no time. She knew the house was going, and she was going, and David was probably going too. She persisted. 'So, you fall asleep. Is it possible to fall asleep when you're already in a coma?'

He sighed back at her over the empty plates and the candlelight. 'I guess so. I fall asleep and then suddenly I'm walking into my house that doesn't look like my house, and you're here, with your freckles and your green eyes. Then after an hour or two or seven, I wake up back in bed and I can't fucking move.'

She'd pushed him too hard. 'I'm sorry.'

'It's okay. Don't apologise. This' — he moved his hand between both of them — 'this makes no sense, which means there is no right or wrong or sorry or not sorry.'

'Have you tried to … stay?'

'Here? Shit yeah.' He laughed. 'I've tried everything. Staying awake. Sleeping on the beach. Sleeping in the shed. I just can't make it past midnight.'

'You slept in the shed?'

'Tried to.' He shrugged. 'Like I said, it doesn't make any sense.'

'None of this makes sense,' she said.

'Yeah. You're right. Of course it doesn't make sense. None of this is real. It can't be — you, me, this house. It's all a fever dream while I die.'

'And in the meantime?' She dropped her voice, lower and quieter — how could she move from devastation to desire in such a short time?

But he got it immediately: the confusion of their state meant emotions were as tangled as timelines. He spoke the next words slowly, with deference. 'In the meantime I want to bury my face into you and make your scent my oxygen.'

Caitlin bit on her lip because she didn't want to bite on her finger. He reached for her across the table.

'Stop trying to make parts of yourself hurt.'

Caitlin took his finger gently into her mouth as the candle guttered and died.

Chapter Thirty-Eight

His breath was warm and ragged on her neck. They held each other for long enough afterwards that the kitchen table started to press into the back of her thighs. She shifted and he stepped back and all of a sudden they were both awkward teenagers. They looked at each other, blushed and flushed and a little bit shy.

'I'm sorry we had sex after talking about your … being in a coma and everything.'

'It's okay. It's not the first time.'

Caitlin's eyes widened as an entirely new prospect opened up before her.

'Oh my god. Are you — are you travelling through other times as well?'

David had turned away from her, but she could tell he was laughing as he filled the kettle. 'Well, there is a convict called Nellie …'

She watched his shoulders shift beneath the cotton of his T-shirt as he chuckled.

'You're a jerk.'

He turned back. 'That, I thought, was already well established.'

Caitlin looked at the kettle. 'Excuse me. But are you actually making some puddle water? Of your *own volition*?'

David looked almost as astonished as she did. He glanced

down at his hands and flexed his fingers, as if he was surprised to see them there. 'Jeez. I suppose I am.'

She shook her head slowly. 'Huh. You think you know someone, but then it turns out they're a time-travelling coma patient from fifty years ago who actually does like tea.'

He laughed. She loved when he laughed. He was all curls and teeth and twinkles and a husky cough just at the end. Something occurred to Caitlin. 'Are you a smoker?'

'Isn't everyone?'

'Not here. I mean. Not — now.' She crossed her arms. 'A lot's changed.'

He shrugged. 'My parents don't smoke.'

Didn't, thought Caitlin. She didn't want to go down that path of thought.

'I don't think I want tea. And I've drunk all the whisky,' she admitted.

'Christ. All of it?'

'You had some too!'

They looked at each other. The kettle whistled.

'Shall we go down to the beach?'

The moon had arrived early and hung low and full as they walked down the path. David walked behind her, his boots heavy on the sand. It was brisk, but she tried not to think why he didn't need a jumper. The tide was out and the wet, hard sand on the shoreline reflected the night sky like a dirty mirror. Caitlin slipped off her thongs and felt the cold grapple at her toes. David stepped from behind and wrapped his heavy arms around her. Beryl's words came back to Caitlin.

'David, how did you crash?'

'I told you, I was mucking around with the radio. I hit dirt and then … I hit a tree.'

Caitlin looked up at him, the moonlight was playing at the edges of his hair. She ran her finger along his brow. 'Was it an accident?'

His nostrils flared briefly, his mouth twitched. 'What are you saying? That I'd leave my kids?' His voice was low.

Caitlin was calm as she witnessed his pain. She had seen worse. No, she had felt worse. 'Maybe. There's no shame in a grief that feels unending.'

He scratched at his cheek. Caitlin pondered if there was a nurse somewhere, trimming a motionless patient's beard.

'Cait, after Giulia died I was living in agony. A pain that only stopped with music, or the sound of the wind going past my side mirrors. Even in hospital, even with all the legal dope they've hooked me up to, there's pain. I think now … it's even worse. But I didn't — I'd never run from any of it. Not intentionally.' He let go of her and crouched down to shift his fingers through the broken shells and curled seaweed at their feet.

'I know you don't want my sympathy,' she said.

'That's bloody right,' he agreed, inspecting a piece of sea glass.

'But you have my empathy. I know what it's like to live with the kind of permanent pain that ends up as part of your bones. David, the past weeks have made me realise something. Escaping to Australia hasn't helped that go away — it's meeting you that has.'

He spoke to the flotsam and tangle of the high tide mark, but his words carried her to the sky. 'I know. It only feels better when we're together.'

'And then the times when we're not together, it seems to be getting worse. Whether it's by absence or comparison or whatever.'

'I think about you all the time. I can't stop it.' He stood up. 'I don't know what sort of shit bloke I am, but I'm pretty goddamned low. I lie in a hospital while my parents look after my half-orphaned kids, and all I can think about is getting back to you.'

'I don't think you're a shit bloke, David. I think you're broken.'

'"Nineteen places", the doctor said.'

Caitlin winced. 'Not in that way. God, nineteen? Your poor mother.'

'Don't. Don't make this harder than it is.'

'Sorry. No, what I meant is, like you said, you've been living broken with the pain of loss. I can't imagine what it feels like to lose the love of your life.'

'Yes you can. You've lost your husband. You told me — he left you.'

They had both started walking now. In step with one another, the waves sounding oddly quiet for nighttime, as if they'd hushed to better hear how these two were going to proceed.

'Paul wasn't the love of my life. My wedding manicure hadn't even chipped when I realised I'd made a mistake.' Caitlin stopped and shook her head. 'God. That's utter bullshit, sorry. The reality is, well, I never realised. I never thought anything other than "This is who I am and this is what my life is". It never occurred to me that those statements could become questions. "Who am I?" "Do I want my life to be this?"'

'Okay. So. Who are you?'

'I'm Caitlin.'

But David gave her that look he did, the one with kindness but also a touch of challenge.

So she tried again.

'I'm Caitlin and …' But she faltered. She was too scared to answer in case he wasn't really, genuinely, asking.

David was patient. 'Your life, do you want it to be like this?' he asked.

She shook her head. 'No. I know that for certain. I can't live like this anymore. My whole life has been a platitude. I've existed in a bubble …' She looked up at the stars. 'A bubble of tedium and blame.'

He stopped. They'd gone far enough along the beach now that the dunes had turned into limestone cliffs. The sand was loose and dipped and becoming hard to walk on. They were both a little out of breath.

'Cait, I'm not asking if you can live like you have been living. I'm asking if you can live like this, now, here.'

This is a proposal, Caitlin thought. *This is what a proposal is meant to feel like.*

'A life of … wilds and wonder,' she said quietly.

'Yeah.' He smiled. 'And adventures, and things.'

'Together.'

'Here.'

'And now?' She was surprised to feel she was crying.

'Yes,' he said. 'Together, here and now.'

By the time they made it back to The Cicada House, the moon was high and small but still casting everything in silver. David quietly washed the plates in the sink while Caitlin rinsed the sand off her feet under the bath's tap. Her toes were cold enough that the hot water stung.

She went to the bedroom and slowly undressed, getting under the sheets nude. Tonight seemed a good time to stop wearing Paul's T-shirt, or Erin's nightie. She sat, leaning on the pine boards behind her, and pulled the sheet up to her chest. David appeared in the doorway.

'I just realised, this was — is — your bedroom. With Giulia. I'm sorry, that must be really odd,' she said.

'It's not.' He was getting undressed as well. It felt incredibly normal and utterly extraordinary. 'This was our bedroom, but everything is so different. The trees, the smell, even the birds call different. It's only the cicadas that sound the same.'

He sat on the edge of the bed and pulled his boots off. Caitlin couldn't help but notice that her phone showed 12.16. Midnight had passed. She flipped it quietly onto its face so she couldn't think about what the numbers might mean, and instead focused on David's bare back, tanned and smooth but for a few freckles scattered over the tops of his shoulders.

'You don't have any scars. From the accident, I mean.'

'Nope.' He ran his fingers along his forearm, and touched his elbow gently. Then gingerly felt his left cheekbone. 'Pretty sure I don't look like this in 1970, I can tell you that for free.'

He turned and crawled towards Caitlin, rolling under the blankets next to her. She watched as he burrowed his face into the pillow. He looked like a little boy. He looked like one of his little boys.

'David. You staying here, with me. If it — if it works …?'

'Mm?'

His eyes were closed, his breath was already slowed with sleep, his brow unfurrowed. He'd thrown his arm over her. It lay heavy, smooth and unbroken. When she eventually slept (and oh, it took some time), she slept terribly. She dreamt of hospitals with running feet in white shoes and a beeping that went long and loud and then stopped.

Caitlin woke up the next morning with David's fingers still gripping her waist. They weren't, though. She felt them nevertheless, her flesh pressed in like a Bernini sculpture. She rolled over, trying not to cry. But already there was a heavy lump in her throat and her eyes were stinging. She'd been so, so certain that the strength of whatever they'd discovered between them would be enough to keep him here. The disappointment tasted awful.

'What's Candy Crush?'

He stood in the doorway holding her phone. His hair had become, if it was possible, even wilder overnight. It surrounded his sleep-folded face like a mane.

A whimper came from Caitlin. She rubbed the heel of her hand across her damp eyes.

'What's wrong?' he asked.

'I thought you'd — I didn't realise —'

He dropped his hand. 'I know. I'm here. It's the next day.'

She nodded. 'It is. It's the next day.'

Caitlin climbed out of bed quickly lest he disappear before her and followed him into the kitchen. It was raining, velvet pellets hit the corrugated iron roof. But the kitchen was light and the floor was warm. They were both quiet about what this morning meant for bed number eight at Western General. As she moved between the kettle and tea bags, David tossed her phone from one hand to the other.

'Be careful with that,' she said.

He stopped, holding it up like a piece of offcut. 'It's a telephone, isn't it?'

'Yes. And other things.'

'Candy Crush? Sounds like a stripper.'

'It's a video game,' she said.

He looked at her blankly.

'An arcade game?'

'Pinball?' He sounded dubious.

'Not really. Erm, do you know what a computer is?'

Caitlin was embarrassed at her ignorance around the timeline of discovery. She tried to remember watching episodes of *Tomorrow's World* with Bill, but he'd tutted at any television that wasn't the news or a police procedural.

'Yes, I know what a computer is. Cait, I'm from 1970, not 1870.'

'Righto, Stephen Hawking,' she said, holding out her hand. 'Give it here.'

He tossed it at her and she nearly dropped it. She glared, and he grinned back. Caitlin turned so he could see the screen, and let her fingers fly through her apps. In her head, she looked a bit like Tom Cruise in *Minority Report*.

'This is a phone. But it's also a camera. A mailbox. It's a photo album. It plays music. It searches the internet —'

'What's the internet?'

'Um, we'll get back to that. It's a TV, a cinema, a games arcade and, and …' Caitlin faltered, her finger over the screen. He was irritatingly unimpressed. 'A calculator!' she finished, triumphantly.

'A calculator, you say. Well screw me sideways,' he said drily.

'How are you not more amazed by this? *I'm* amazed by this!'

He shrugged, 'Dunno. My dad and I watched a lot of *Star Trek* with the boys. And there's the Armstrong bloke on the moon. I've had a lot of time to lie around and think about this stuff, Cait. I knew it would be different.'

David's ability to remain utterly calm in this vortex of voodoo was astounding. It made her feel safe. And maybe, looking back, that sense of safety made her a little complacent.

And so commenced a condensed chapter of time-stood-still magic for two people seemingly breaking all known laws of relativity. During that time The Cicada House was tender and dreamy, and it felt all the more so given they were aware of how soon they'd have to vacate for good. They didn't do much. Played music to each other, walked along the beach at dusk, rolled around in cotton sheets. And they both continued to work on the house, even though Caitlin repeatedly stated there was no point.

'Aren't you sad about it being sold?' she'd asked him, as they patched the hole in the toilet roof.

'Why would I be? It's just a house.'

It was like a honeymoon on death row, if death row smelt of freshly mown grass and sea spray, and felt like falling in love every day over and over.

vi. Awake

The only running in the hospital is the visiting kids being shushed along the corridors. Until this morning. It's very early. The milk-grey light is barely seeping through my lids, the coolness of the air lifting the hairs on my arms.

I'm here, just the same as every day for however long this has been. But all around me is different. Running: doctors and nurses running. Rubber soles slapping lino floors. Buzzing: static and squeals from the radio that should be sending out Brahms or Albinoni. Shouting: that old doctor, sounding more like my dad every bloody day.

'David.'

They're calling David.

'David, can you hear me?'

A torch light in my eyes, someone's pinching my earlobes. A cuff tightens against my bicep.

'David, wake up.'

Is that Giulia? Or my mother? What did she say?

'You're awake.' Or,

'Wake up?'

And is there a difference? And,

do I want there to be?

Chapter Thirty-Nine

'Do you mind if I pop to the Store this morning?' Caitlin asked.

David stood resting against the back fence, listening to the waves thump into the shallows. 'Sure.' He didn't turn around, just sipped at his mug. His bare feet were wet in the dew. The morning was mild and still.

'Sure' is concession not consent, she thought. That was a Paul phrase, not a Dot one. She was surprised at her own suggestion, but the house was becoming a little heavy with practicalities and theoretical physics. She did have to leave sometimes — to get more supplies and remind herself that the world existed out of the time-bent whirlpool she and David were circling in.

He reached to her. 'Kiss me before you leave.'

'I'll only be gone twenty minutes.'

'Kiss me twice, then.'

In the car outside the Store, she opened up her phone. The calculator was still on the screen. She smiled and flicked it away, keen to get to her emails. She found using her phone in front of David created more questions that were becoming more difficult to answer. Caitlin also didn't want to talk to Bill while David was in earshot. She wasn't ready for those two parts of her life to overlap. But before she could call her grandad, her notifications began to ping. Paul hadn't messaged again, but the lawyers had, picking up from when they had gone silent. If they were confused by the brief white flags of reconciliation between the divorcing parties, they didn't show it. The decree nisi would be lodged on her return to the UK, and, some months after that, a divorce would follow.

Another email loaded and her heart sank. The plate-spinning she'd been working at had neatly shelved Maggie's sad blue eyes away in the place where her mother also was. But now, Maggie had come back into the room.

Caitlin, sienna gave your E-mail address I hope that is okay.

I wished you'd stayed longer I'm sorry I didn't give you what you needed.

Like I said I wasn't expecting you to ask questions like you did, which was silly of me I guess. I found the photos. If you give me your address I'll post them to you. susie would have wanted you to have them.

Here's the thing love — your mother didn't have a life of stories because she hadn't had the chance. She wasn't fully formed. Im not insulting her, Susie was just too young to be rounded out. All of us were.

She hadn't got there yet, caitlin. You need to understand. I'm sure she would have — had she the chance. Like I'm sure you already are, caitygirl.

Maggiex

Caitlin ran her finger across the screen, touched her mother's name.

'Whatcha say, Mama?'

Caitlin pulled up Bill's number. Caitlin told him about the changing weather, and how she was coming home soon. He was watching Chelsea–Spurs and it was tied one all. The TV burbled in the background. He wasn't very talkative today.

'Did you hear me, Grandad?'

'Pet?'

'I know I said thank you for looking after Mum and me, in Australia. But I also want to say thank you for everything after. To you and Gran — you took care of me all those years.'

'That was offside by a mile.'

'Yes, Grandad.'

'Yes indeed.' A cheer rang out from the TV. 'I'll ring off now, pet, it's too dear, this calling long-distance.'

They'd only been on the phone for a few minutes.

'Okay, Grandad. I love you.'

She could hear Martin Tyler's voice pitching high over the crowd. But then Bill spoke again. 'You are a light in our lives, pet. You shone through the darkest of days.' He spoke louder over the volume of the football. 'Susan was our child, but you were our future. You deserve all the best.'

Caitlin made a small noise that didn't reflect the utter enormity of what she felt, in response to those words. For the first time in two months, she felt lost being away from the UK, because at that sentence she would have run to him. Just to touch him, hold his hand, confirm that he was real and so were his words.

'What's that, pet?'

'Thank you, Grandad. Thank you.'

'Yes, yes. Get it up you, Spurs!'

* * *

The day Caitlin realised she wasn't a very good person was also the day she heard her husband cry for the first time. *Really* cry; not just sniff through a Pixar film. The noise that came out of him sounded organic. The night they lost the second pregnancy, Paul was a wounded animal.

'Lost' a pregnancy, like coins down the back of the couch. As they limped through the IVF process, Caitlin often wondered why the baby business came with such foolish euphemisms. Why did a process that was so primal, filled with fluids and pain, attract such a collection of trite words and phrases like 'expecting' and 'trying' and 'being late'? It was a gentle tea-party of pretence to cover a massacre of biology. That's how she'd felt, anyway. Paul was more optimistic and open to the Hallmark phrasebook of procreation.

They'd been married for five years when Paul and Caitlin began IVF, which was four years after he'd announced to his family that they were 'officially trying'. Paul had taken to fertility treatment like he took to everything else — with an administrative fervour that carried Caitlin along like a wave. It was her uterus, her cervix and her stomach that was prodded and pricked. Yet it was Paul's hopes that were dashed when, round after round, a baby failed to materialise through the miasma of money and medicine. Caitlin had never actually voiced her reticence to him. She didn't feel she should, or could. So, like everything else in her life, she stayed quiet and hated it with a silence that came across like indifference.

The first 'loss' was small, just as tiny as the pregnancy itself had been.

A gentle call from the IVF nurse had provided the encouraging news of positive numbers in her blood test. 'It's very early days, but we believe you are currently pregnant.'

Her period had arrived a few days later and she'd stared at the bloody toilet paper with a sinking feeling, knowing she'd have to tell Paul. He'd given her a perfunctory squeeze, and kissed the top of her head.

'We'll be fine, it's a good thing. It shows everything is working the way it should.'

His optimism took him too high. She'd known it at the time, seeing him soar over her gripping a helium balloon of hope.

Caitlin knew she should bring him down, or at least hold on to his ankle for a while. But she didn't — instead, she kept on taking the pills and injecting the needles and when she was pregnant again it was as if he'd added a hundred balloons to his fist.

Caitlin had been pregnant for such a long time. Fifteen weeks, apparently. Long enough for family celebrations to occur over champagne (them) and orange (her). Long enough to feel queasy at the sight of catered sushi carried into a meeting room on plastic trays. Long enough to lie awake all night and wonder how she was going to be a mother when she hated the very word.

But not long enough to feel the grief her husband did when the doctor sent them home from hospital with a sad nod and a piece of paper that said, *D&E*. She'd gone to bed because that's what she'd been told to do, and it was then that she'd heard Paul's cries. Deep and bruised — slow like a tape deck running out of batteries. She heard every piece of love and pain come from her husband's voice, and that was when she knew she was a bad person.

Paul had loved Caitlin so much. He'd chosen to love her, because it was all he'd ever known from his own family. Indeed, she chose to be loved because it was all she'd experienced from Dot and Bill. So she sat still and, through the death of her mother and the death of their baby and all of the other tiny deaths her life accumulated, she just took the love and held it and gave nothing back.

* * *

After the call with her grandad, Caitlin couldn't help but pull up her notes app and tap out the words Bill had spoken to her. She'd received one of the most special gifts and it had been delivered over the soundtrack of Sunday night football. It felt self-indulgent to write down a compliment, but Caitlin already knew she'd treasure those typed phrases more than any blurred photographs from a share house in the late seventies. She put the phone down and looked at her ignition. The Cicada House could feel small when her future was walking around inside, whistling the soundtrack to Candy Crush. Instead of returning straight away, she took the keys and left the car in its spot. The walk through the brush across from the Store was less than a minute and she found herself on a deep stretch of beach looking out to the wide, wide ocean.

'Hello.' It was Charles.

'Christ, don't do that!' The noise of the waves had smothered his steps and she hadn't heard him until he was right behind her.

'You're looking rather ominous here.'

'What do you mean?'

'Oh, I don't know. There's something about the silhouette of a person staring out to sea. It looks as if they're plotting a murder. Or about to scatter some ashes.' He looked around Caitlin's feet. 'Anything you want to tell me?'

Caitlin ignored his joke. 'How are you, Charlie?'

'Oh god, there *is* something you need to tell me.'

'What do you mean?'

'You've never called me Charlie.'

'I don't know what you're talking about.'

'You've very intentionally called me *Charles* since the day we met. So now I'm Charlie, and I'm suspicious.' He kicked a piece of driftwood away from their feet and sat down on the sand, patting the space next to him.

'Join me? Sounds like I should know what's going on.'

Caitlin settled next to him and pulled her knees up to her chest. 'After you left the other night, I called Paul and told him I wasn't coming home to him.'

'Okay. Well that's not an enormous revelation. I didn't know you were even considering a reconciliation in the first place.'

'I wasn't. And then I was, briefly. But I think that was just fear talking. So I told him it's over.'

Charles nodded. 'Very well. I'm glad you've made that clear to him, and yourself.'

Caitlin chewed at her finger, then stopped. 'And then there's Susan.'

'Your mother, you mean.'

'Yes. My mother. Susie. Susan — whatever I'd have called her. I've realised I need to let her go. To let her off the hook, you could say.'

Charles was silent, regarding the ruler-straight line of the horizon.

She continued, 'My own mother was just a girl. For so long my life has been dictated by the absence of someone who was just … a girl. And that's been no-one's fault but my own. It's not my grandparents', or my mother's, or Maggie's. It's not even Paul's fault.'

He nodded. 'That all makes sense. It also sounds like you're more open to that — what did you call it — "talky-psych-stuff" than you care to admit.'

Caitlin glanced at him. 'Point made.'

'Self-awareness is somewhat of a superpower, Caitlin.'

'Yes, you've said. I can see now. I've always allowed myself to be swept along in the wake of other people's decisions. I've just been floating between apathy and' — she paused, trying to find the right words — 'and self-pity.'

'Oh dear. That's a little rough, Caitlin.'

'I don't think it is. I think it's honest. And now I feel like I've travelled to the other side, to this life where I can see how powerful responsibility and resolve can be. Look at me now.' She smiled sadly. '*I* made my way here. *I* sought Maggie out. I …'

Caitlin's eyes inadvertently flicked back up in the direction of her car, and beyond. Charles's followed and then quickly settled back on her face.

'You …?'

'I feel like I understand now what love can be, what it *should* be. It's messy and broken. It comes with failure, and it comes with sacrifice.'

'Yes. All of this is true,' Charles said sadly.

Caitlin thought of the small photograph of Charles's daughters pinned to the underside of his car's sun visor.

'So. You've discovered that your mother was simply human,' he said.

'Yes. She wasn't dastardly or heroic or tragic. She was just a girl who ran away from home and became pregnant at the other end of the world. And I've spent all my life putting her "sacrifice" up on a pedestal. And giving that so-called sacrifice too much power.'

'Nothing good can come from being on a pedestal. I can attest to that.'

'Exactly. Now I understand the power that I felt came from those who actually did surrender things, on her behalf. Susan's power wasn't in herself, it was in the people around her and how they held her up. And when they couldn't hold her anymore, they held me.'

Charles looped his long fingers through each other, slowly twisting the delicate signet ring on his little finger. 'That's very profound.'

'I don't know about that. But it helps. It helps to know how much love can be found in sacrifice.'

Charles looked at her, studying her face and how it had become set with decision. 'Caitlin, are you still talking about your mother?'

But she was already gathering herself, standing and dusting the sand from her legs. 'Does it matter?'

As Charles stood up beside her, he looked as worried as he had the night he'd left her alone in The Cicada House. 'Your man.'

'My man.'

'David.'

'Yes.'

He crossed his arms, ready to admonish her. But then a film of sadness washed over Caitlin's eyes, and instead he opened up a hug. For the first time in her life, Caitlin accepted it. She wasn't expecting to, but she began to cry. The sound of buried sobs she'd heard in others, but not herself.

After some time, Charles gently held her out by the shoulders, and studied her face. 'I don't think I've never seen anyone so full of loss and love at the same time,' he said.

She shrugged. 'I guess that's a sign I'm finally alive, then.'

Caitlin asked Charles to leave her, and told him she'd be just behind. But instead she walked to the water and stood with her feet in the waves.

Oh, this big brown country with its thousands of years in the soil. It was tearing her apart. It was building her up. She couldn't stand it anymore. For the first time in her life, she cried without reservation.

Chapter Forty

As Caitlin returned to The Cicada House, she held on to a small but strong feeling in her gut. It was like a very simple morse code, repeated in her pulse with a definitive beat of knowing. By the time she'd arrived at the front door, she had also reached her decision. And what a painful one it was. Caitlin considered turning around and sprinting back down the drive.

David was sitting in one of the green chairs, staring at the heater where his fireplace used to be. A book lay open on the floor beside him, its spine cracked. Later, much later, Caitlin would try to remember what book it had been.

'Where did you go?' he asked.

'I stopped down by the front beach. I bumped into a friend.'

David nodded, but he didn't look at her. He was flipping something over in his fingers.

'What've you got there?'

He held it up. Caitlin saw a single earbud from her phone.

'I found it down the side of the chair. I'm assuming it's a mind control thing.'

She knew he was joking. But there was a bleakness to his voice.

'That's right. I've been manipulating your brain this whole time.'

David nodded, playing along. 'Which is why I just can't leave the hinges on the back door alone.'

There was a silence where they both should have laughed but didn't. Caitlin thought of what was happening and felt sick.

'Want to go for a swim?' she asked.

'Um, no? Have you seen the sky?'

'Come on, don't be a wuss.'

David grunted as he sat up properly in the chair. 'I'm not a wuss. I'm the bravest bloody bloke going around.'

'Is that right?'

'I'm surviving a coma, aren't I?'

'Maybe. So how about you come survive a swim?'

She was breathless with an almost-hysteria, but not because something exciting was happening. The very opposite. She ran down the back path fast enough that the sand kicked up and hit her calves like a crop. She could hear David complaining from the rear. The beach was broken and mushed in the heavy air. The late afternoon sun was muted behind layers of woolly cloud. The water was going in all the wrong directions. She just about heard David's voice on the wind as she ran into the water. *Jesus, it's cold.* Waves batted at her thighs and hips and chest and she kept going because she was so furious that her love for him had made her feel this vulnerable. She was also proud enough of her summer swims, that she wanted to show her surf-smarts off to the Australian watching from the beach. In her head, as she tried to dive through sideways waves, she imagined him looking dubious. Judgemental, even. If she'd actually turned back, she'd have seen how singularly scared he was as he watched the woman he wanted to protect throw herself into the wash cycle of a king tide.

Being dunked would be humiliating if it didn't hurt so much. Sand scraped along Caitlin's shoulder, then cheek. Her lungs fried. She reached out her arms and was shocked to discover the world outside the sea had ceased to exist. Now, everything was in brine and she was going to die. Then suddenly, but also after forever, she was a fish and a hook had caught her under one armpit — which hurt almost as much as her screaming lungs did.

David. David was standing in the chest-deep, dragging foam in his jeans and T-shirt and holding onto her tighter than she had ever held onto anything.

'You bloody idiot!'

It wasn't what he said, it was the fear that he said it with. He stood over her while she coughed salt and water onto the sand. She could see out of the corner of her eye how much he was shaking. She should have been contrite, or relieved.

'You bloody, stupid idiot, Cait.' David was crying now. 'Never do that again.'

She heaved. She understood. He loved her. She needed to let him go.

Caitlin sat on the lounge floor, at his feet, with the blankets from one of the single beds around her. They'd finally worked out how to turn the heater on. It was filling the room with the antique scent of hot dust. It was the smell of long ago. Of changing seasons. Of a dying man saving you from drowning.

'Are you sure you don't need to call a doctor?'

'I'm fine. I'm cold and my arm hurts where you saved me. I don't need a doctor.'

His clothes had somehow dried in the walk back to the house. She pressed at the fresh graze on her knee.

'David?'

'Mm?'

'Thank you.'

'You're welcome.' He grabbed at her wrist, a little too hard. 'Promise me you will never do anything that fucking stupid again.'

Caitlin held her hand up, daring him to continue to grip her like a bravery trophy, her eyes sparking. He let go. Caitlin acquiesced. 'I promise.'

She adjusted the blanket and walked to the bedroom. Why did this brief week of love hurt more than anything she and Paul ever had?

Over the next two days, they didn't mention the event at all. Caitlin didn't want to admit it, but her lungs still ached and her head throbbed on and off. Though it seemed David attributed her subdued manner to her near-death experience, she knew it wasn't the cause. She rebuffed his attempts to fuss over her, and he gave up fretting, which wasn't something he was good at anyway. They tried to return to the tender, floating rhythm of their earlier days. But the deadline to vacate the house was imminent, and real life felt impossible to resist for much longer. The weather didn't help, either. A last wheeze of summer had rolled in the morning after Caitlin nearly drowned — but this felt different to the preceding weeks of clean, sparkling sun. These days were smoky and still, with heavy clouds and no breeze and a temperature that made sleeping difficult. Maybe this was why David seemed more subdued as well. He was working less on the house and had turned his attention to the piano.

'Do you think it's salvageable?' she asked. Caitlin stood on the grass watching him pull weeds out of the pedals.

'Nah. It's more rooted than when I drove it here in the back of Dad's truck.'

She thought of the yellow paint she'd seen in the bedroom. 'This is the one you played in Melbourne?'

'Yeah — it was nearly a pile of hammers and strings back then, but I wanted it here. I was going to use it to teach the boys.'

For the hundredth time since her conversation with Charles, Caitlin pictured those two young children, running like foals around a house empty of a mother or a father. She looked up at the clouds that hung, pregnant and slow, over the garden and went back inside.

Caitlin wasn't sure how much time had passed. She must have dozed off in the lounge chair, but the scent woke her. She followed it to the open window and leant on the sill, inhaling with what she realised was reverence. Rain was falling, hard enough that the drops kicked earth up as they hit the ground. They were releasing an aroma that was so biological it grabbed a hold of her at a cellular level. It puffed up from the ground and circled around her, unhooking a deep memory. *Petrichor.* The word sounded like the ending of a spell. The light through the storm clouds was the most unearthly blush of pink and orange, filtering the scene in an apricot haze. The sound of the deluge seemed to have a colour too. Everything was golden.

And there was David. And he was dancing. In the steaming storm, his shirt was off and his arms were up and Caitlin couldn't look away. His eyes were closed and rain fell from the tendrils of his hair like the end of a baptism. She wasn't sure if it was rain or tears falling down his face, but his head was to the sky and there was a small smile on his face as he moved to music she couldn't hear. In that moment, Caitlin felt a love she hadn't known was possible. It was time.

'You asked me a little while ago what it was like to lose a parent,' she said.

Now it was his turn to sit with a blanket around his shoulders. They were back on their step, the cloud had rolled away, taking the rain with it, and the only drops falling were those from the leaves of the trees. The petrichor had given over to a fresh swipe of eucalypt — the garden shimmered with it.

'I did. And you told me it was like losing a treasure, or not hearing some music. Which, I've got to admit, wasn't the answer I expected,' he said.

'Yes, okay. But there's so much else I didn't tell you. I didn't talk about the pain of longing, of wondering "what if". The over-and-again trauma of dreaming a life where someone had saved my mum, and then waking up and realising they hadn't.'

'Wow — pain, trauma — who didn't eat their eggs this morning?' His voice was light but his face was pinched, like she was hurting him. Which she was. Caitlin steadied herself, because she knew she had to continue.

'The biggest thing was how I let my mother's death take over my whole personality. Like a parasite getting fat on grief. Maybe if I'd been stronger, or older ...'

'You're one of the strongest people I've ever known.'

She smiled. 'That is absolutely not true. Or, at least, it hasn't been. Until today.'

David now refocused entirely on her. He pitched forward, his elbows on his knees, and held his hands out like he was saying a prayer. He looked scared, and tired. 'Cait ...'

She touched his fingertips. 'David, I have a power — no, *we* have a power — that no-one around us has ever had. We have the chance to intervene. To change things. Because I can't stop seeing them, running along that dusted drive with their bare feet.'

He was crying.

'We can reach out for those two little people.'

Without a sound, tears melted down into his beard.

'You know,' she said.

There was a long silence. 'I know.'

'You have to go back. I have to let you go back. Be a father to your beautiful boys.'

The worst bit about doing the 'Right Thing' is when the person across from you, the person you want to run away and hide with, agrees. It hurt desperately to hear David say nothing in response. There was such a big part of her that wanted him to gnash his teeth and stomp his feet and rail against the world around them.

But he didn't. He just let the tears keep rolling while he held her hands like she might disappear.

Caitlin didn't cry until much later. That evening, she only watched as he dried his tears and his hair with the blanket. He stood from the step, pulling her up with him as he went.

His hand was big and firm and brought her whole body into his in a single movement that made her insides turn to liquid. Then those hands made their way to the back of her head, holding her like she was something valuable while they moved through the doorway and into the kitchen in a single entanglement, bumping into corners and rattling the crockery. The fridge complained as the two of them made contact with it, David with his back flat against the door.

Caitlin wondered if anything would ever feel this right again. She considered how she would drown in a thousand waves just to feel his heartbeat against hers for one more day. But then she thought she might cry, so she closed her eyes instead and let him kiss down her neck like he'd been gifted something that was about to be taken away.

Later that night they held each other and wept and farewelled those they had both lost, and farewelled each other too. Caitlin fell asleep before David, and only stirred once in the deep of the night, to the sound of a piano playing and David singing along to that adagio, his deep voice melodious and sad, sounding words she couldn't make out but understood deeply with everything in her.

When she woke just after sunrise, he was gone.

Chapter Forty-One

'Here, hold this.'

Jan presented Caitlin with two more paintbrushes, seemingly surplus to the rollers she already had in her hands.

'How many brushes do you need to paint one door?'

'Darling, if Marigold sees but one streak or patch — well, there won't be any dinner, that's for sure.'

Jan had bubblegum-pink paint specks across the backs of her hands, and cheeks. She looked like a very pretty pox victim. Caitlin put the brushes down and waved a giant bee away from her face.

'Your wisteria is incredible this year. The house looks like the cover of a National Trust calendar.'

'I know, the purple does look fantastic against the door. That's how M convinced me to paint it early — if we waited until July, the flowers would all be gone.'

As if on cue, three teenagers paused across the road and snapped pictures of Marigold and Jan's house, giggling as they took turns posing and pouting.

Caitlin watched them, her nose wrinkled. 'Jesus. Maybe I should paint my front door pink. I could definitely do with the publicity.'

'Oh, don't be silly. You and Paul are going to sell that place in a heartbeat. It's spring, and the air is full of blossom and scent and … minted couples in the market for a renovated North London terrace.'

The mention of Paul's name niggled, but only mildly. Caitlin wondered how long it would take for 'Paul' to become just a name, rather than the identifier of marriage and divorce and loss and socks.

'Caitlin?'

'Mm?'

'Where were you then?' Jan looked at her suspiciously. In the two months since she'd returned from Australia, Caitlin's vacant spells had become more frequent.

'Oh, nowhere. Just considering the semiotics of ex-husbands.'

Christopher appeared, leaning out of the sash window with his phone in his hand. 'Mum says to tell you that Uncle Paul is on his way over.'

'Shit,' Caitlin said, immediately. She glared at Jan, embarrassed to be flustered in front of her nephew.

Christopher stayed at the window, clearly curious about what would happen next. Jan was having none of it.

'Of course. Lovely. Christopher, thank you.' Her eyebrows said *bugger off.* Christopher did as he was told, his tall frame disappearing back into the house. 'Have you seen Paul since you got back?' Jan asked with a false lightness.

'No, Jan. You know very well that I haven't seen him. It's all lawyers and estate agents and weird text conversations about "styling the house for sale".'

'Yes. I know, sorry.' She put her rollers down and brushed her hands off on her jeans, checking her phone as she did. 'Well, he did try to call me first. That's something.'

'Phone on silent?'

Jan nodded.

'Paul will hate that. I used to accidentally leave my phone on silent all the time. He'd get so *irritated.*'

'Caitlin, Paul and I have had our differences — particularly after the last six months. He's behaved poorly, and you know how M and I decided to manage that. I'm not sure if going behind his back was the right thing to do —'

'It bloody was,' Caitlin interrupted.

'Well, yes it was. But what I mean is, I'm not sure acting like Paul was always a villain is the right thing to do. I'm not just saying this as his sister. He royally stuffed up. But —'

'"But"? You're going to give me a "but" about my philandering husband who fathered a child with another woman?'

The Caitlin who had arrived back from Australia was more punchy; she spoke with less pause and more cause. Jan had openly admitted to Caitlin that, though she didn't dislike it, she would need some time to get used to it. Jan sighed, trying again. 'Yes Caitlin. I was going to give you a "but". Because Paul is not a bad person. He is, actually, a good one. He is emotionally faulty, and he has control issues. *But* we're all broken in some way and he is trying jolly hard to get better. As I think you are.'

Jan stopped, but Caitlin gestured for her to continue, if only a little facetiously.

'I'm not suggesting a romantic reunion amongst the bee-blown wisteria, but I am asking, please … for some form of peaceable understanding.'

And then, just like that, Paul arrived. He paused outside the gate and looked at his paint-spattered sister and unsmiling ex.

'Evening.' He held up a bottle of champagne and a large bag of pistachios. 'I brought supplies.'

Caitlin walked down the path, reaching for the pistachios. 'I'll have these, thank you. Hello.'

'Hello.' He looked past Caitlin to Jan, who was smiling at her brother. 'Hello, you.'

'I'll be back in a sec.' Jan was already disappearing down the side of the house, calling over her shoulder, 'Don't touch the door, it's still wet!'

Paul and Caitlin stood in an awkward single file on the path. She sat heavily on the raised wall of the garden bed, tore open the bag of nuts and poured herself a handful.

'Come on then, let's get this over and done with.' Caitlin tapped the stone next to her.

Paul joined her, accepting the bag to take his own handful. 'You're very tanned,' he said.

'I shouldn't be. I got back ages ago.'

'I'm sorry to hear about Bill. Was it sudden?'

Caitlin threw the first of the pistachio shells over the fence and into the gutter. 'Yes. I saw him on the Sunday and they called me Monday afternoon to say he'd died. It was a stroke, apparently. But I don't think they investigate that thoroughly when the person is eighty-nine years old.'

'Well, I am sorry. He was a good man,' Paul said.

'He was.' Caitlin's voice wavered a little. 'Better than I knew, actually. It's funny, it took me going all the way to Australia to get close to my grandad.'

Paul looked a little bewildered at Caitlin's near-tears. It was the main impression he'd given since she'd returned from Arana Bay. Bewilderment and a gentle contrition that Caitlin didn't want to admit she enjoyed.

'I'm glad you were able to spend time together. After you got back,' Paul added.

'Yes, I guess. He was pretty doddery towards the end. But we'd said everything we needed to say. Finally.' She smiled.

'So, you talked about your mum?'

Caitlin made a non-committal *Mm* sound and pushed her hair behind her ear. It was getting long again. She didn't care to tell Paul any of the lessons she'd learnt or wounds she'd opened, and then closed, about Susan.

'How's Laura?' she asked, changing the subject.

'Pretty big now. Due in August.'

'But all is well?'

'It is. I'm going to move in for the first few months, just to properly share the nights and feeding and stuff.' He looked at her sideways. 'I'll be in the spare room.'

'Paul, I mean this without anger, honestly. But I don't care what you do with Laura, or in what bedroom you do it in.'

'I know, I know. It's still important for me to tell you that though.'

'Okay.'

There was a silence as they both cracked pistachios and licked the salt from their fingers. Paul looked at the wet paint, and cleared his throat.

'I'm bricking myself,' he said quietly.

'I'm not surprised. I would be too.'

'Great, thanks.'

'Just being honest. It's the lack of sleep that would scare me most. What lunatics willingly put themselves through that sort of torture?'

'Erm, us? Or, at least, we tried to.'

'That we did. We gave a lot of things a go.' Caitlin looked down at the bottle at Paul's feet. 'That champagne's cold. Pop it open.'

'We haven't got any glasses.'

'We've shared enough fluids, Paul. Come on, let's have a toast.'

He picked up the bottle and unwrapped the foil, then twisted the wire cage. Caitlin noticed the hand-painted label.

'Christ. Who are you trying to impress? Not me I hope.'

'No. Not you …' The cork was stiff and he had to work hard to prise it from the neck. 'Marigold,' he said, grimacing with effort.

'Ah. Yes. Still pissed off?'

'Jan had to forgive me, she's my sister. M's taken a little longer. But we're doing okay. She invited me tonight, which I'm taking as progress.'

The cork shot out of the bottle and sailed over to next door's garden. Champagne fizzed out across their toes.

Caitlin burst into laughter, the type she'd discovered in Australia.

Paul stuck the bottle into his mouth and drank the foam.

'Oi. Hold on,' Caitlin said, taking it from him. 'What about me? *I* haven't forgiven you.'

Paul wiped the champagne dripping from his chin. 'You don't *need* to forgive me, so I don't need to impress you. I fucked up, Caitlin. Everything that's come after means less than that.'

'Maybe.' Caitlin felt uncomfortable, but she was learning to live with that sensation. Learning not only to complain, but to explain, as well. 'I wasn't perfect either. Far from it.'

'Imperfection isn't what we're talking about here. I did something worse. I know I've said sorry but I'm not truly sure I meant it until recently. I hadn't been able to work out why I did such a grim thing … and then tantrummed all the way through your trip to Australia.'

'And now you have? You've worked out why?'

'Yes,' he said. They were passing the bottle between them: a private communion. 'I was angry. At you.'

Caitlin nodded, even though she didn't really understand. Paul answered her un-asked question. 'I know, how could anyone be angry with someone like you? Who was just so … blank?'

'Oh wow, Paul, thank you.'

'I'm not making excuses. But Caitlin, you were so quietly sad. It bloomed everywhere you went, like algae. And you just … accepted it. And I did too. Until I didn't.'

Caitlin tossed the rest of her spent pistachio shells in the garden. 'I know. I know I was.' She took the bottle from Paul. 'I'm sorry, too. Let's have a toast.'

'To what?'

'To Bill. To us. To the house.' She took a swig and handed it back over. As he drank, she added, 'A Funeral, A Divorce and An Auction. It's like a shit Richard Curtis film.'

He snorted, expensive champagne going down the wrong way. Caitlin laughed as she clapped him on the back.

'Come on, you can't choke to death just when we've started talking properly again. We've got a house to sell, and I've got an emigration to complete.'

Paul shook his head, still coughing as he spoke. 'I can't quite believe you're leaving us all, Caitlin.'

'Can you not?'

He regarded her, his face softened with a feeling she also now recognised: the wistfulness for a love that was once there, but was no longer.

Paul answered her, 'You're right, actually. I can believe it. Caitlin, I think you leaving here might be the realest thing you've ever done.'

Chapter Forty-Two

The morning of Caitlin's forty-first birthday began with coffee. Thick coffee with a swirl of tawny crema. She stood and inhaled its scent, appreciating the silence of Arana Lodge's kitchen before the guests began making their way into the lounge.

Sienna entered and lifted her head to Caitlin, neither of them awake enough to talk yet. She started to pull bowls off the shelf and Tupperware containers of fruit from the fridge. It wasn't until she passed Caitlin on the way to the pantry that Sienna spoke, inspecting the coffee as she did. 'Nailed it. Well done.'

'I've had a good teacher,' Caitlin said. 'Want one?'

'Thanks.'

The hissing of the coffee machine softened Charles's entry into the kitchen. More of a morning person, his need for silence was not as compelling. He sniffed loudly, like a cartoon character with a bunch of flowers. 'Oh yes. Smells wonderful. One for me too, please. Although shouldn't we be making you coffee, Caitlin?'

'Why?' asked Sienna.

'It's Caitlin's birthday today.'

'Oh my god, Cait. Why didn't you say?'

Caitlin didn't move from the coffee machine. 'Because I didn't. Charles, how do you know it's my birthday?'

'Oh, don't be so suspicious.' He looked sheepish, as if Caitlin had every reason to be suspicious. 'I may have noticed it on your employee file.'

'Charles! That's a breach of privacy!' Sienna was young enough that her outrage still sounded valid, no matter what it was directed at.

'Don't be silly. Privacy doesn't count when it's one's birthday.'

Caitlin handed Charles his latte. 'I think I burnt the milk a bit. Which you deserve.' She directed her attention to the makings of the continental breakfast Sienna was collecting on a serving trolley, and started to stack plates alongside the bowls of berries and yoghurt. 'Yes, it's my birthday and there's not much to celebrate. I'm forty-one, I'm divorced, I have no family or friends, and I work for an old man who has no respect for my privacy.'

'You forgot the bit about being homeless,' Charles said.

'You're right. I'm living in the eaves of a hotel, like a ...'

'... a Dickensian scullery maid!'

'Thank you, Sienna.'

'You're welcome. Although I'm a bit hurt about the "no friends" part,' Sienna replied.

'And I'm more than a bit hurt about the "old man" jibe.'

Caitlin ignored Charles and held the swinging kitchen door open with her hip while Sienna followed her through with the trolley. 'We can't be friends, Sienna, you're young enough to be my daughter.'

'No-one has babies at eighteen anymore.' Sienna looked quickly at Caitlin. 'Sorry.'

'Don't say sorry. You're right, thank god. Forty-one years ago today my mother was probably terrified. Eighteen isn't the ideal age to become a parent.'

They were standing in the hall outside the lounge. The morning sun was galloping through the towering glass windows, lighting up motes drifting lazily through the air. It reminded Caitlin of another room, not so far away. She shook it off.

'Although,' she continued, 'today is the first day I've marked a birthday in the hemisphere in which I was born. I guess I haven't had an accurately timed birthday since I was five.'

'Well, as my gift to you, Cait, I'll finish setup. I'm sure you've got other stuff to get on with anyway,' said Sienna.

She was pushing the rattling trolley into the lounge as Caitlin heard the first of the guests descending the main stairwell. She didn't stay to argue. Making conversation with Sienna and Charles was hard enough early in the morning, but small-talking with a gaggle of enthusiastic authors was a trial she didn't care for on any morning, let alone today.

She took her coffee along the walkway and through the foyer, which sat dark and quiet this early. Her door was still as hidden as it had been the first day Charles had opened it for her. But the room on the other side had changed. Now it was her permanent office, Caitlin had filled it with the ephemera she didn't realise was her own unique style until Charles had commented on it. 'It's rather eclectic,' he'd mused. 'Like Eames meets the Magic Faraway Tree. By way of Vegas.'

Caitlin had never before had a room filled with only *her* belongings. Now she had a bookshelf groaning with things that were mostly books but included a jar of curved sea glass, a bunch of paper carnations and five wax pears. She had framed photographs of her mother and grandparents on the wall and a rug the colour of the sky after a summer storm. A lamp that glowed low and orange, and a beaten-up old chair she'd found in a garage sale. Charles had told her it would have been extremely expensive if it hadn't been stored next to salted surfboards for the past forty years.

Caitlin sunk into the office chair, rotating slowly until she faced out into the bush. She couldn't remember having a happier birthday beginning, ever. There was a hesitant knock on the door.

'Hello, Charles.'

His arm entered first. It was holding a plate containing a small pain au chocolat, a lit candle stuck crookedly into the top. 'It's a birthday pastry and a white flag.' His voice was muffled behind the door.

'Come in, you big idiot.'

He followed the wavering candle. 'I'm sorry, I shouldn't have blurted that it was your birthday. That was a terribly intrusive thing to do. And very unprofessional.'

'Charlie, just because you've employed me doesn't mean anything about this is professional.' She waved her hand around the office. 'You're not even charging me board, and I've been staying in your house.'

'It's a lodge and no, I'm not charging you rent. But you're not charging me for the extra work you're doing, so we're even. Here. Eat your gift.'

She blew the candle out and pastry flakes cartwheeled across the desk. Charles settled into his now favourite spot on the couch and crossed one long leg over the other. Caitlin tore the still-warm pastry in half and glossy chocolate dripped out onto the plate. She licked her finger. 'That's delicious. Thank you.'

'Do you have any plans? Birthday-wise?'

'No. And I don't mean that in a self-pitying way. I'm absolutely delighted to be here and turning forty-one and not have any plans. Honestly.'

'Brian is back from Sydney this afternoon. Should we go for a counter meal at the surf club? They'll have parmas on.'

'That sounds splendid, thank you. But Brian's been gone for a week — surely you two want some alone time?'

'I believe we can keep our hands to ourselves for an evening,' Charles said. 'Or at least until the meal is finished.' He smiled at her.

'Well, in that case, I'd love to. Seven pm?'

'Seven pm. And please don't work all Saturday. On your birthday. In the middle of summer.'

Caitlin was already opening up her laptop. 'Yes, Charles.'

As soon as he shut the door behind him, Caitlin saw the email. The pitch she'd submitted to *Luxury Nomad* magazine on behalf of The Lodge had been picked up. Caitlin whispered a 'Get in' to herself. The next email Caitlin opened was a digital invitation with animated cartoon doves. They held pink ribbons in their beaks and pulled a banner onto the screen that read, *Join us for Ava's christening.*

Underneath, Paul's message read:

Caitlin. Obviously you're miles away but wanted to make sure you knew you were very welcome. Laura said so too. Sorry about the invite. It's bloody ugly (Laura didn't say that bit). Hope all's well down under. I'm so tired I put a pair of my socks in the letter box and didn't notice for three days. But it's great, it really is. Paul.

He hadn't remembered her birthday. And that was better than any text message from Dubai. Caitlin closed the laptop and checked her watch. It was 10 am, the perfect time for a swim.

Bumping into someone rarely happens like it does in the movies, with suddenness and noise and stunt-perfect props. But that morning, on her way to a birthday dip, Caitlin literally bumped into Richard Stockhouse.

'Holy shit!' she called as the last inch of espresso left her cup in an impressive arc, sweeping across Richard's white shirt.

His hair was combed in the slick, smooth way she remembered from *Elite Spaces* all those lifetimes ago. His pale eyes narrowed as she flapped around him, inadvertently splashing more coffee.

'Fuck. Shit! Sorry. God —' Caitlin was rotating like a top. 'Let me get a tea towel or something.'

'No need.' His voice was cold, echoing around the dim foyer. In direct contrast to Caitlin, Richard had barely moved.

Caitlin stilled then, brows knitted. 'We haven't met —'

'We haven't needed to,' he cut in. The coffee had dried instantly in a Pollock-esque spray across the crisp cotton, but he still managed to look immaculate.

Caitlin sighed, pennies dropping. Since she'd returned, Sienna had danced around the updates of her and her father's relationship, but Charles had been more indiscreet. 'You didn't so much put the cat among the pigeons, Caitlin, as unleash a rabid tiger in the midst of a very well-maintained dovecote,' Charles had said, gleefully.

'Well — hello then, Richard. I'm Cait—'

'I know who you are. You're the unhinged English orphan who decided to have a mid-life crisis all over my daughter's future.'

Caitlin let out a little exhalation of shock. She raised her eyebrows as high as they could go, a bit dazed at the sucker-punch Richard had just delivered. 'I beg your pardon?'

'I'm glad we've finally met. It means I can tell you this directly.' He pulled his shoulders back and lifted his chin. His sharp cheekbones angled over a mouth set in anger. 'It has taken me nearly a year to recover even a semblance of relationship with my daughter. And I have you to thank for that. Not to mention her lost degree and the ongoing absurdity of her apparent "lifestyle choice".'

'Oh please.' Caitlin motioned with her coffee cup, her surprise fading quickly. She was gratified to see him take a small step back. If Richard — if anyone — had come at her like this a year ago, the adrenaline rush she was experiencing would have been caused by fear of conflict. Today, she was surprised to observe herself relishing the sensation. 'You should be proud of your daughter.' Her voice was firm, and loud. 'What she's done in less than a year with the local schools, and partnering with multiple councils in the region, people twice her age would kill for momentum like that.'

Words shot between them like fiery ping-pong balls. Caitlin noted how odd it was that they'd literally just met. Richard didn't seem to be troubled by that detail. Her skin was tingling with confrontation and indignation.

'My daughter is twenty-*two*. You getting involved when you did was incredibly irresponsible. Thanks to you, she has no money, no degree and no prospects.' His voice was also getting louder, his clipped vowels bouncing around the foyer's ceiling.

'She doesn't want a banker, she wants a father.'

He didn't flinch, even though Caitlin felt that was a low blow.

'Sienna has a father. A father who loves her, but —' He stopped, exasperated.

Caitlin could hear her heartbeat in her ears. Richard went to answer, then huffed loudly instead and waved her off, turning on a brown leather boot. Caitlin followed him across the foyer.

'You love her, *but?* Why does there have to be a but?'

He stopped at the Lodge's glorious door, hand on the timber that he had designed, and looked back at Caitlin. She noticed a flush coming up from the neck of his shirt, smudging across the freckles that covered his fair skin.

'Why do you care?' he asked, the faintest tone of pleading in his voice.

She was breathless from combat, looking at his neatly combed hair, the vulnerability of his neck. Caitlin shook off the edging feeling of pity. He was breathing heavily too. Eyes full of anger. They stood staring at each other for longer than was comfortable.

Caitlin smiled, big and bold, in a way Dot would have approved of. 'Well. It was … extraordinary … meeting you Richard. Now, it's my birthday and I'm going for swim.'

This was her second summer in Arana Bay, but Caitlin knew she was still a blow-in tourist as far as the townspeople were concerned. Regardless, she had been to the beach enough times to put her towel down at the locals' end — away from the rip and the screaming kids and the bastard rocks that were exactly the same colour of the sand. The water was cold, which was always a sign of a hot day to come: the air was heating up already. She ducked fast under the surface, letting the last shred of the tense exchange with Richard disappear beneath the bubbles and blue. As she moved out deep enough for her toes to spring up and down from the soft sand below, she saw two familiar figures. Erin and Josh were walking along the waterline, Erin talking, Josh not. Caitlin was embarrassed to feel so nervous of Erin sighting her. Since she'd returned she'd managed to avoid any run-ins, which was impressive in a town the size of the Bay. Caitlin lowered herself so the sea was playing at her mouth and nostrils, and held her breath.

The mother and son duo walked straight past her towel. Caitlin came up for air and felt like an idiot. No-one was looking at her. No-one was looking out for her. She dunked her head back under the water and listened to the echoing of the sea.

After drying off, Caitlin found herself lingering. She should have been hustling out of there — a busy beach wasn't her idea of a good time. Instead, she walked back into the dunes and towards the path. She'd been in the Bay for a month but she hadn't seen it. Not yet.

The path had grown over again and Caitlin was happy about that. No-one had been walking in their steps, since they'd left.

'Me not Us; My not Our,' she chanted.

Those six words had become something of a mantra in the past twelve months. Sometimes, to remind herself that she and Paul were genuinely no longer. But often it was about him, not Paul. Him and his absence and the reason the space by her side was aching, where he should have been.

The overgrowth meant the tea tree had also thickened up and she didn't see the house until she was almost upon it. It remained.

Standing for her. Maybe it had sagged a little deeper into the sandy ground, and the grass was long enough that it had created its own ecosystem — but the cicadas hummed a welcome that sounded like home. Caitlin managed to smile through tears that tasted like the sea she had just left.

Chapter Forty-Three

'Chips or salad?'

Brian held the menu at arm's length and peered down his nose. 'I can't read that. Can you read that, Charles? I think I need glasses.'

'If you can still read screenplays then you don't need glasses. I'll order you the chips,' said Charles.

'Don't order me the chips. I don't need the chips.'

'Well you can't order the salad and then eat all my chips. I'm ordering you the chips. Caitlin, chips or salad?'

'Chips. I'm not a monster.'

'Parma and chips times three, coming up. Shandy, Brian?'

Caitlin was building a card house from folded drink coasters. The surf club had had a bit of marketing help itself in the time she'd been away, and now branded cardboard coasters were scattered across the bar, to go with the new sign out the front. It felt a bit too shiny for her liking. Brian and Charles's patter back and forth over Caitlin's head was just like being in the ocean, a gentle to and fro. Her card tower collapsed.

'Has it been a good birthday, Caitlin?' Brian asked.

He bore a passing resemblance to Sigmund Freud and Caitlin felt mildly disconcerted every time Brian asked her a question.

'Yes, it has. I've never swum in the sea on my birthday, so that's been special.'

'I've just heard some sad news.' Charles set the drinks on the table. 'Beryl died.'

'Bez Patterson?' Brian sounded surprised. 'I thought she'd died years ago. She must've been one hundred.'

'She was eighty-five,' said Caitlin.

'Eighty-six, but how did you know?' Charles asked.

Caitlin looked over at the sideboard that likely still contained a photograph of her love. 'I met her once. Here. She was a nice lady.'

'Well she died last week, in her sleep. Jack says they're going to rename the bar after her. Bez's Bar.'

Caitlin raised her glass. 'To Bez and to birthdays. May we all have at least eighty-six of them.'

Every chip was gone from each of the three plates. The tables around them were emptying and Brian only just managed to stifle a yawn.

'You both call it a night, I'm going to have another drink here,' Caitlin said.

Charles looked around the fluorescent-lit room, which had taken on a vaguely nuclear glow after sunset. 'Are you sure? Why don't you come back with us, have a birthday cuppa?'

He hadn't noticed the person Caitlin had. Erin was at the bar, typing on her phone.

'It's fine, honestly. You two head home. Thank you for a perfect birthday dinner.'

Caitlin wouldn't have welcomed a drink on her own a year ago, and certainly not when the room contained a person she'd been avoiding for nearly twelve months. But forty-one-year-old Caitlin was brave and calm and didn't want to hide behind the waves anymore. She tapped Erin on the shoulder. 'Hello.'

'Hello,' Erin said. She didn't look at all surprised to see Caitlin, which made her realise Erin had also spotted her earlier.

'Were you waiting for me?' asked Caitlin.

'Why would I be waiting for you?' Erin paused, put her phone on the bar. 'Sorry, that was rude. Want to sit down?'

'Thanks. Can I buy you a drink?'

'Nah, I'm good.'

They both looked at each other a little blankly. But, Caitlin was relieved to see, Erin didn't have the combative gleam in her eye that she'd held at the end of last summer.

'So,' Erin said, 'you're back from Blighty. And I hear you're working with old Charlie?'

'Yes. I'm doing some marketing for The Lodge. I'm staying there too, just for the month. I was worried it would all be a bit much but it seems to be going okay.'

Jack placed a beer down on the bar. 'It's on the house,' he said. 'Charlie told me it's your birthday.'

Erin checked out the now empty room. 'Well, you sure picked the right place to celebrate. Saturday night and the place is heaving.' She raised her half-empty glass. 'Cheers, to the birthday girl.'

Caitlin smiled stiffly.

'When did you get back in?' Erin asked.

'I left London just after Christmas.'

Erin nodded. The overhead lights buzzed. A car tooted outside, twice. Caitlin twisted around in her stool. 'How's Josh?'

'He's really great. Gaz has taken him up to Queensland for the rest of the school hols. I miss him but it's good actually: he'd be bored shitless here and I'm working my bum off. I got a promotion.'

'Great. Good for you.'

Don't say it. Don't say it, Caitlin.

'Sold any houses recently?'

Don't be a bitch. It was too late. She'd used the Dot voice and Erin didn't like it. She put her wineglass down and leant ever-so-slightly towards Caitlin. 'Is there something you'd like to get off your chest?'

Caitlin swallowed hard. She was trying not to be intimidated. Or passive-aggressive. 'There is actually, Erin.' She took a breath. 'I was hurt by how you managed The Cicada House: putting it on the market, contacting Tracey in Bali, making comments about me and … it was very …' They both looked at each other. '… deceitful,' Caitlin finished.

'Deceitful.'

'Yes.'

'Cait, you don't get it. It had nothing to do with you, doll. It's business. My business. My life.'

'It's my life too!' Caitlin was embarrassed to hear how shrill she sounded. This was not going the way she wanted it.

Annoyingly, Erin wasn't shrill at all. She was steady, her voice was level. 'It's "your life"? No, babe. It was your *holiday*. You and Charles and Sienna and the rest of your privileged little posse, sitting high up on the hill, playing pretend. There are some of us who have to work for our money. Who don't have anything to fall back on. Any. Thing. It's just us.'

Erin's voice was so hard, it came at her in angles. But Caitlin listened. It's what she needed to do.

'The Cicada House is nothing. Did you hear about the Kenning's farm? And the huge place in Wertham? You wouldn't have. Well, I closed the two biggest sales in the district. And do you know what that meant? Bugger all. I could pay off a bit more of my mortgage and put a bit more in savings for Josh. And I got a promotion that pays just a Little. Bit. More. I work so bloody hard, Caitlin.'

'I know that.'

'You might *know*, yeah, but you don't feel it. You don't know what the fear feels like, to not ever feel safe or comfortable or just … relaxed about it all. The assumptions.' Erin was shaking her head. 'Blowing in here with your woe-is-me divorce and Little Orphan Annie story and thinking that you were the most important storyline of everyone's summer.'

'Wow,' Caitlin said loudly. 'Okay.'

'Okay.'

The two women sat side by side, staring at their empty glasses.

'Happy birthday, Caitlin,' said Erin.

Caitlin couldn't help herself, she started to laugh. Erin did too.

'Sorry, that got a bit intense at the end there,' said Erin.

'Yes, it did. You certainly made your point though.'

'Two more please,' Erin called out to Jack, who'd disappeared into the kitchen. 'I've had a really rough week, Cait. A sale fell through. Again. I'm sorry, I didn't mean to get personal. And I didn't say that stuff about you shagging the handyman,' she added. 'That was Tracey being a pissed idiot. I am really sorry I didn't tell you the house was going on the market. I didn't know it meant as much to you as it clearly did.'

'It's okay. It's just — it was a great house.'

'It *is* a great house: it's not gone. That damn place — it's like it's waiting for someone. Three sales, all fell through, *poof*.' Erin flicked her fingers in emphasis. 'But it wasn't just the house, was it?'

'No. It wasn't just the house.' Caitlin didn't want to cry on her birthday.

'Have you seen him again?'

'No, we … we decided to go different ways.'

'So he was a bit of an idiot?' Erin was trying to be kind, Caitlin could see. But she didn't want to call him something he wasn't.

'It just wasn't meant to be.'

'Fair enough. I get it. Summer romances, hey? There's something about 'em. Even now I watch tanned boys wearing mullets smoking a cigarette out the window of a P-plated ute and you know what I feel? Nostalgic. Nostalgic! For a guy who is probably carrying a pants-load of thrush and confusion around.'

Caitlin was laughing again, was happy to leave him and The Cicada House aside, along with the feeling that she might cry.

'God, Erin, there's an image.'

'Come on, babe, Jack's forgotten us. I'll give you a lift back up the hill.'

Caitlin tiptoed past the Great Room and along the hall, climbing the narrow steps as quietly as she could. Sienna wasn't staying in The Lodge this summer, but Brian and Charles's room wasn't far away. Despite the little rooftop ceremony she'd intended, Caitlin didn't want to be the sort of houseguest who made noisy nocturnal trips — no matter the reason.

The wind was up tonight, hot and blustered like a cheeky kid pulling at their mother's nightie. It was going through the trees making noise like surf, while the real surf was arguing with the beach beyond. The whole Bay felt wired. Caitlin could taste electricity on her tongue.

Forty-one years ago today. How did the years melt down like that? Caitlin wasn't sure what time she'd been born. That was something else she could ask Maggie. It seemed ridiculous to her now that she'd been so close to someone who knew her mother, and she had not spent more time asking questions. But twelve months ago was a different time, and back then, Caitlin's heart could only cope with so many people tugging it in so many different directions. Now, with her love unmoored, the past seemed like a less scary place to revisit. She sipped her drink, looked out into the night and considered how many people she'd let go in the past twelve months.

Paul. Well that was the obvious one. Besides the christening invitation and the final legal paperwork, it was shocking how little communication they needed to have. And while she still felt winded by how he had done it, she didn't regret that he had left. In fact, there were even moments when she envied him the audacity of being the one to blow everything up.

And what was the opposite of an explosion? *Oh, Grandad. Lovely Grandad.* All of her life, he had been an ever-present shadow of pickled onions and Old Spice; the most steady line of order that ran through their lives. And now he was gone. One of the greatest gifts she had received over the past year was getting to know Bill over a distance that brought them closer than ever before. The months of phone calls, wheezes and 'pets' down the line had gifted the knowledge that her grandparents had loved her, as deeply as any parent would have.

Then, of course, Susan. Who was there the day she was born under this Australian sky. The one who left first, but also, the one who left over and over for all of Caitlin's life. And finally, after so many moments — a lifetime of them — of haunting every breath Caitlin had taken, she was gone. Whoosh. Just like that. A year later, Caitlin still savoured the absence of hurt that now represented her mother.

Finally, inevitably, David.

She had tried to say his name aloud a handful of times in the past year, but the word, or David himself, had remained stuck fast. Caitlin had wondered repeatedly if he'd actually existed, if their love had been real. But the loudest question that recurred was, had she really done something to help? Had they gifted those two little boys a future without more loss?

Tonight, Caitlin put her head back and made an effort to speak instead of question. To leave the wondering behind. Tonight, she added another name to her list.

'Goodbye, David.'

This time she hoped she meant it.

Chapter Forty-Four

Charles appeared at the Lodge's new coffee machine with two empty cups.

'Table four needs another flat white please.'

Sienna hefted the plastic milk jug out from the bar fridge while Caitlin followed Charles to the Lodge's kitchen.

'This is a good crowd for a Tuesday,' she said.

'It is. And I know why.' He pulled his phone from his back pocket. 'Brian sent me this from the plane. Look.'

The blurry photo of a magazine page had Brian's thumb and reading glasses covering half the frame. But behind them she could just make out a small image under the headline, *Arana Lodge Opens Up.*

'You're a genius,' he said.

'It's only an in-flight magazine, Charles.'

'Well look out there!' He pointed to the Great Room they'd just left. 'Something's working!'

Caitlin counted the customer's heads through the kitchen's pass window. 'I'm just surprised so many people want to trek up the hill for coffee and cake.'

'For Arana Lodge's marketing director, you're quite cynical about … Arana Lodge.'

Caitlin smiled. 'Marketing is my job. Cynicism is my career.'

'Well, whichever is which, we're clearing more profit after one month than our forecast had us at three.'

'That's brilliant, Charles. Keep it simple though, okay? I overheard you and Sienna talking about opening for dinner …'

'I know, just "cake, coffee and conversation". You can stop banging on about it. Now the Wertham project is humming, it's tempting to let Sienna run wild on this place. But our core will always be the retreats. That's where the big money is.'

'Now who's cynical?'

Sienna swung open the kitchen door. 'Can I get some help, Charlie? We've just had the bridge club rock in for scones and cream.'

* * *

Marketing a writer's retreat was, surprisingly, a lot easier than marketing fizzy drink. Maybe it had something to do with her personal interest levels. Or maybe the product was infinitely superior. Whatever it was, Caitlin was delighted in her new role as Arana Lodge's marketing director. Not long after she arrived back in the Bay, she and Charles had hashed out a rough job description over a cheese platter. Charles's first flutter of PR (including the piece Caitlin had seen on *Elite Spaces* all those years ago) had been organic, unprompted and therefore short-lived. But this year Charles and Brian were keen to do more travel, which meant Charles needed to increase profit and invest in some staff to run the retreats in his absence. And that was where Caitlin came in.

'Fewer retreats, higher income, happier Charlie,' he'd scrawled on the bottom of her job description in pencil.

'I'm not sure that's a KPI, Charles,' she said.

'Well, you get what I mean. Can we make it work?'

'I think so. You'll need to give more if you're going to charge more. Keynote speakers, bring in some guest lecturers. It might be worth hiring an in-house chef too.'

'Yes, yes. Marvellous.' Charles had raised a glass of mineral water to her rosé and they shook hands over the brie. Caitlin felt happier than she had in years and years.

* * *

Caitlin moved through the lounge straightening pillows and pulling dead leaves from the indoor plants. They had only added a couple of tables and chairs, along with the coffee machine, and removed some of the more stealable books. The rest of the space remained the same. Caitlin couldn't believe Charles hadn't thought of it earlier. Using areas of The Lodge every day rather than once every six weeks made sense — particularly now they were considering autumn and beyond in their marketing calendar. She had already planned some winter-themed Sunday afternoon events with live music and a fire pit. And she'd also instructed Soupy Neil to invest some of Dot's inheritance in Arana Lodge. She already felt emotionally invested in this special space above the trees, maybe it was time to put her money where her heart was.

Erin's name lit up Caitlin's phone screen.

'Hey,' Caitlin answered.

'How's it hanging, babe?'

Caitlin may have formally emigrated to Australia, but it wasn't because of its inhabitants' delicate turn of phrase. She tucked her phone into the crook of her shoulder and picked up two more empty cups.

'I'm not sure. Low? High?'

She could hear Erin out walking, and make out the white-noise of waves in the background.

Erin laughed. 'Well, I guess I asked. Joshy's at Gaz's tonight — you up for a pizza at mine? We can find some reality television to cry at.'

Recently, Caitlin and Erin had discovered a shared love of docutainment series where people wept on screen, and Caitlin and Erin wept at the people weeping. Ambulances, adoptions, births and deaths. They couldn't get enough. 'Sounds good. I'll bring the pistachios.'

Caitlin wandered to the far corner of the lounge where no guests were. The sky was turning the colour of mould.

'Excellent, babe. And I'll sort the wine. We can swill riesling and howl at the moon.'

'Um, Erin — are you outside? The clouds look like they're about to detonate.' In good timing, a crack of lightning feathered across the horizon, and a drum of thunder followed. Somehow, a storm appearing in the sudden gloom of the afternoon was much more eerie than in the middle of the night.

Caitlin heard Erin yelping as she broke into a run. 'It's not pouring, it's bloody hailing — I'll call you back!'

The bridge club ladies were flustered at the sudden weather event. Their chatter rose through the lounge like birds from the trees. Charles hurried outside to the deck with his head pulled down into his shoulders, grabbing at throw cushions as the raindrops fell like dive-weights. Caitlin shoved her phone in her back pocket and joined him.

'Thank you, Caitlin. Now where did this come from?' He had to shout over the noise of the weather. 'Can you grab that pile of newspapers please?'

The rain was falling even harder now, drops slipping cold and fast down the back of her neck. Caitlin stacked the armful of water-studded papers into the recycling bucket. The overhang of the roof was protecting her from the worst of the downpour, and so even after Charles escaped inside, Caitlin remained — watching the weather front move across the water. Gusts of eucalyptus and soil scents blew up the hill to her and she closed her eyes. It was fresh and cool and crisp, but she missed the petrichor that recalled last year's summer storm and what it contained.

A tap at the window brought her back, and Caitlin opened her eyes to see Sienna through the fogged glass. Her voice was muted from inside, but Caitlin caught what she said. 'Can you cover coffee? I've got to take a call.'

Sienna walked away and in the space she left there was a figure, standing across the room with his shoulders silhouetted against the light of the hall.

Oh, this is actually happening.

David.

Caitlin re-entered the busy lounge, but the thunder and the chatter and the coffee machine arced away like a distorted yawn. Silence. And then, the fuzzy noise of a thousand cicadas in her head.

He had come back.

Her ears rang louder and she felt as though she was about to faint. She was vaguely aware of her hair dripping rainwater down her cheek. He hadn't moved, he stood fixed in place while she continued into the lounge. He stepped forward out of the doorway's shadow and, even before his mouth opened, her heart dropped as she saw that it was not David. His nose was smaller, more fine. His hair gently waved rather than wildly kinked. She was a fool and her mind was a bitch, playing these cruel tricks on her. How could it be?

'Yes?' she asked.

He smiled. His teeth had the order of 21st-century dentistry. How could it be?

'Hi, ah — are you guys still serving food?'

His accent was American. *American*. How could it be?

Caitlin's breath shuddered out like her lungs were made of corrugated iron. The disappointment and the embarrassment slipped around themselves, coming up her gullet and out of her mouth like anger. 'Excuse me?'

He spoke up, louder but also smaller at the same time. 'I'm sorry — a lady at the Store said this was where you could get something to eat?'

'We don't serve meals.' Caitlin plunged her hands into her pockets to hide how much they were shaking. He was different but still so much like David. She wanted to throw something at him to make sure he was solid.

'Okay. Well, how about coffee, to go?'

'To go? You mean takeaway?'

Caitlin's words came with a sting and there was a shadow of confusion across his face. She turned around and said, over her shoulder in case she cried, 'What would you like?'

'Cappuccino please.'

Now she was half-hidden by the coffee machine she could look at this Not-David properly, and work out what was happening. He was wearing a black T-shirt with a small logo on the chest. She should have guessed he was American by his jeans. There was something specific, and wrong, about the way some American men wore their jeans. Tight where they shouldn't be and loose in the rest of the places. His hair was the same colour as David's, but he didn't have a beard. He was watching her too.

'Is … is a cappuccino okay?'

She had been staring. And not making a coffee. 'Yes. Yes it is.'

Go on, Caitlin.

'You're visiting Arana Bay?'

'Yeah. Just got into town.' He smiled, but showed no recognition of the English barista who was looking at him with wild eyes. She knew she was gawking but she couldn't help it. He took in the Great Room behind him.

'This is an impressive space. It's huge.'

Don't say it, don't say it.

'David?'

Thankfully, another thunderclap blanketed her voice.

'I didn't catch that?' His accent bent over the counter.

Shit. 'Um. Yes — double. The ceiling's double height.' She cupped the milk jug under the steam spout.

It was his turn to look at her properly now. Caitlin could see in this man's face everything that was different and the same as David. She wondered if she was having some sort of episode. She cast around for Charles, or Sienna, or anyone.

'What a building. You would have no idea it was here.' She realised it wasn't an American accent. It was Canadian. The milk jug sat hot in her hand. She needed to say something innocuous or she was going to say something insane.

'So, you're here for a holiday?'

'Kinda.'

She handed him the cup. 'Lids and stirrers are on the shelf there.'

'Thanks. What do I owe you?'

An explanation? 'It's on the house.'

'Really? Oh, wow. Thank you so much.' He smiled again and she couldn't let him leave, not like this.

'Just be careful on the driveway in the wet. It's not great going down.'

'Oh, okay. Thank you.' He looked out at the rain. 'Boy, it's really heavy isn't it?'

This was interminable. 'The Australian weather does have a tendency to be a tad melodramatic.'

Talk of the weather is for the bored and the boring, Dot tutted in Caitlin's ear.

'I'm Marcus.' He smiled again. And there it was. His eyes crinkling, just like his eyes had crinkled.

'Caitlin,' she said, a little too softly.

Then another voice, tanned arms twisting around his waist, 'Hey, hon. Can I add my order?'

'Sure. Melissa, this is — shoot, I'm sorry, I didn't catch your name.'

Caitlin's mouth was dry. She tried to smile. 'I'm Caitlin. Hi.'

Marcus and his, *quick check — yep,* wife were standing, arms wrapped around each other like an ornament in a gift shop. Both looking at her in a pleasantly open, unselfconscious way. He was much taller than David. And he had an energy that was more boyish, even though he looked no younger than she was. Than David had been.

She couldn't say it. She had to say it.

'Are you …' she was speaking quietly, afraid Charles would walk back in and interrupt at that very moment '… are you related to a David Catto?'

'David Catto?' Marcus repeated in his accent that made the name sound even further away than it already was.

Another rumble and the lights of The Lodge flickered. Melissa gasped and the bridge crew tittered and she could hear Charles bellowing something in the kitchen.

'David Catto was my grandfather!' exclaimed Marcus.

Oh, David. We did it.

Marcus was immediately excited. 'Do you know the family?'

'Not really.' Caitlin's heart was racing, and her mind had to catch up. The next part came out in a tumble, 'The surf club has lots of memorabilia on display. I've seen photos. Arana Bay's a small town.'

'Right. Wow. What a coincidence.' He turned to his wife, who was warily watching the wind whip the trees outside. 'Lissa! Did you hear?' Then back to Caitlin. 'The surf club, you say? We should check it out. We're actually here to —' Marcus was interrupted by a clap of thunder that seemed to sit on top of the roof itself. It rang long and low and followed with the backwards moan of all the electricity in The Lodge disappearing. The lounge was dipped in the deep gloom of a stormy late afternoon. Charles bustled in towards the old ladies who were packing up through a mess of raincoats and pashminas.

'Sorry. It's always a bit mad here,' said Caitlin. She didn't want the power-cut to get in the way of what she needed this man to explain to her. She rested both of her hands on the bench, aware she was looking at him in a very intense way. 'What are you here for?'

'Well, I've actually come back to see where my grandfather brought his two boys up: my dad and my uncle.' Marcus shrugged apologetically, self-conscious of his cliché. 'You see, my grandpa, David, he always talked about this town. Arana Bay. It's a bit of a family legend.'

Caitlin stepped back. Marcus took his wife's hand. The lights came on.

'He did?'

Her heart was suddenly so full, it was all she could do not to laugh, or to cry.

'Yeah, he did,' Marcus smiled. 'He always said this was a place full of "wilds and wonder, and adventures and things".'

Chapter Forty-Five

Caitlin leant on the fence and gazed back into the steaming garden. An evening shower had passed quickly, leaving the sun to set slowly through a tawny-filtered gauze. Hunks of golden twilight clung across the treescape, like butter flicked from a knife. She breathed deeply, inhaling the sky-damp leaves and coastal tang.

'It smells like possum piss down there.' He emerged from the tea tree and myrtle leaf with raindrops decorating his shoulders. He was rolling down his sleeves. 'And the mosquitos are everywhere.'

Caitlin watched him dust off his hands and shoulders with a towel pulled from the Hills Hoist.

'For a local, you're not exactly at ease in these surroundings,' she said.

Richard settled into one of the timber chairs she'd installed on the Cicada House's new deck.

'I'm not a local, I was born here. And I left.'

'And then you returned.'

'As I've said before, I am merely visiting.'

She smiled at him, and he smiled back, and they both became a little shy. Moments like this were still so new and delicate, just as fragile as the rain-hung spiderwebs around them.

'How does it feel?' he asked.

'How does what feel?'

Richard gestured to her hands, where she was moving the old key back and forth, the brass warm between her fingers.

'Not as strange as you'd think. It's felt like home for a long time now. This just makes it official.'

Richard nodded but remained quiet. They had spent enough time together in the past month that she was as comfortable with his silences as she was becoming with his words.

He cleared his throat. 'So I've walked the whole boundary, you've definitely got enough room for a guest house. Foundations won't be an issue, there's good drainage.'

Caitlin shoved the key to The Cicada House in her back pocket.

'I'm not sure I can afford your advice. What was it? Award-winning Richard Stockhouse, "genius mind" behind Arana Lodge and recently appointed lead architect to the "revitalisation project of Melbourne's Northbank theatre complex",' she quoted, using her best English RP.

He shook his head, slowly. 'I wish Charles would keep his news clippings to himself.'

'It was your daughter, actually. Sienna's proud of you. She sent the link around the Lodge's WhatsApp.'

He made a *humph* sound, which she was beginning to recognise as acquiescence. 'Well, my advice is free and I'm happy to help. This is a good site.'

'That's kind, but having you oversee a small renovation on The Cicada House is a little like bringing a bazooka to a knife fight.'

'How many times do I have to say it? Architects used to be blue-collar workers. We were the original tradesmen.' He cocked his chin high with pride and a little smile.

Caitlin looked at the man she was beginning to know. His loose Henley shirt was faded but pressed, and he had bare feet sticking out of a pair of cotton trousers. But with his fair hair always pushed back, and high cheekbones dusted with a patina of freckles, Richard still managed to look … elevated. Like someone who walked in quietly expensive shoes, across the floor of a beautifully appointed office.

'I've had enough tradies to last me a lifetime,' Caitlin said, 'and, I'm more handy than you know.'

Richard said, his eyes twinkling, 'Caitlin, that I do not doubt.'

* * *

It had been the week after her birthday. Charles and Brian and Sienna conspired against the two of them. It took until much later for the trio of cupids to confess that there wasn't just one Arana Lodge WhatsApp group, but two. *R+C Sitting in a Tree* had been started as a joke by Sienna. She set it up the day she heard her father and Caitlin painting the serene foyer of The Lodge with their fury and fireworks.

Despite Richard's indignant assertion that Caitlin had 'turned his daughter against him', Sienna and Richard had actually been getting along well. In the months that Caitlin had spent back in London, Richard had begun visiting Arana Bay more regularly. Encouraged by Sienna's mother, Richard offered up two things he was willing to give in lieu of money: his time and his old Land Rover. As involved as she was with her burgeoning sustainability project, Sienna's Nissan was not up to the long distances between suppliers. So Richard and Sienna spent every second weekend throughout the winter ferrying irrigation piping, packing materials and food parcels across the district. Bumping along in the mud and rain, the two spent more time together in those months than they had in years.

Richard was still deeply frustrated about Sienna's rejection of the career path that he felt was his responsibility to lay out for her. He had also been genuinely furious at the disregard he felt Sienna had shown, particularly after the English outsider encouraged his daughter to blow things up. And, as he'd once railed, 'relegated her to a lifetime of poverty and compost'. But as time went on,

Sienna's project became more tangible and the light got brighter in her eyes, and Richard softened.

Or maybe softened wasn't the right word.

'You must be bloody joking,' he'd said, when Sienna suggested he ask Caitlin for a coffee. 'That woman is completely unhinged. And she owes me an apology.'

In the end, it was Caitlin who came to Richard. She'd had a free afternoon on a pleasantly mild late February day. The Lodge was filling with retreat guests, and she'd slipped up the stairs with a solo roof escape in mind. She'd stepped out onto the bitumen before she saw Richard. He was sitting in the shade, eyes shut and head back with the breeze bringing the sea to him across the trees.

'Shit, sorry. I didn't know anyone —' She was embarrassed.

He held up his hand to block the sun as he looked at her. Eyes with creases in the corners, and a brow that was lined. The ruggedness of his age balanced out what would have been almost too pretty a face, back in the day. He looked at her as if for the first time.

Richard placed one hand flat on the bitumen beside him.

'Don't say sorry. Would you —' He hesitated, a little shy. 'Would you like to join me?'

* * *

Later that evening, after Richard had left and she had been for a swim, Caitlin did something for the first time in over a year. She sat on the back step of The Cicada House. Leaning her shoulder and head into the door jamb like it was someone she loved, she swirled a glass tumbler of wine before her. Lifting her drink to the pitch-navy sky, Caitlin spoke, 'Here's to you, Gran. And Grandad. Here's to you all —' She smiled to the glistering stars. 'Here's to doing all the damn good things once you're over forty.'

Caitlin's voice was strong and clear and so was she.

Acknowledgments

Thank you to my publisher, Catherine Milne. A glorious person who continues to be a beacon of encouragement, creativity and sparkle. Every time I see Catherine's name in my inbox, I get excited. That's weird but true (and says a lot, I think). This book would not exist without her.

The rest of the HarperCollins team are, as always, a group I'm delighted work with. Rachel Dennis is the project editor a new novelist can only dream of: helpful and calm, creative and supportive. Working with Meaghan Amor's copyedits felt like brainstorming at a table with a friend. I am grateful for proofreader Suzanne O'Sullivan's fortitude, particularly in the face of my consistently incorrect punctuation. Thank you, Hannah Jermyn, for the passionate work you do on the audiobook. And how good is the cover design by Christa Moffitt? It brings a juicy punch to the story that I just love. Thank you all.

I'm very grateful to the HarperCollins sales, PR and marketing team including Kate Butler, Luiza Grinstein and Tina Szanto. I work in advertising so I am a nightmare client. Thank you for pretending I'm not.

My agent, Pippa Masson at Curtis Brown, is patience personified in the face of my constant … everything-ness. Thank you, Pippa, Caitlan Cooper-Trent and the rest of the Curtis Brown team.

I greatly appreciate the input from Dr Godfrey Williamson. I feel very lucky to have been connected with someone whose experience of working in the ICU at The Alfred Hospital many years ago so perfectly matched what I needed.

Endless gratitude/hero worship to creatives (and people I like to whinge to) Jessica Dettmann, Esther Walker and Rowan Mangan. Further examples of strong women who pull others up with them include Madeleine Spencer, Martha Beck, Georgie Abay, Lise Carlaw and Sarah Wills. THANK YOU for your generosity and support.

And to the rest of my ladies, women whom I would love to win the lottery and run away with: thank you.

Thank you, Tom, for doing every single other thing while I lock myself in a room with noise-cancelling headphones. You and our girl patiently listen and say 'keep going' and really mean it. This book couldn't have been written without your support.

Finally, thanks to my mother, Kate, who is the most creative and encouraging person I know (and who told me what share houses in the seventies really smelt like).